Bermuda Grass

Bibliography

The Alan Saxon Mysteries
Bullet Hole, 1986
Double Eagle, 1987
Green Murder, 1990
Flagstick, 1991

The Merlin Richards Series
Murder in Perspective, 1997
Saint's Rest, 1999

The Nicholas Bracewell Novels (as Edward Marston)
The Queen's Head, 1988
The Merry Devils, 1989
The Trip to Jerusalem, 1990
The Nine Giants, 1991
The Mad Courtesan, 1992
The Silent Woman, 1994
The Roaring Boy, 1995
The Laughing Hangman, 1996
The Fair Maid of Bohemia, 1997
The Wanton Angel, 1999
The Devil's Apprentice, 2001
The Bawdy Basket, 2002

The Domesday Books (as Edward Marston)
The Wolves of Savernake, 1993
The Ravens of Blackwater, 1994
The Dragons of Archenfield, 1995
The Lions of the North, 1996
The Serpents of Harbledown, 1996
The Stallions of Woodstock, 1998
The Hawks of Delamere, 1998
The Wildcats of Exeter, 1998
The Foxes of Warwick, 1999
The Owls of Gloucester, 1999
The Elephants of Norwich, 2000

The Christopher Redmayne Series (as Edward Marston)
The King's Evil, 1999
The Amorous Nightingale, 2000
The Repentant Rake, 2001

The George Porter Dillman Series (as Conrad Allen)
Murder on the Lusitania, 1999
Murder on the Mauretania, 2000
Murder on the Minnesota, 2002

As Martin Inigo
Stone Dead, 1991
Touch Play, 1991

Bermuda Grass

Keith Miles

Poisoned Pen Press

Poisoned Pen Press
6962 E. First Ave. Ste. 103
Scottsdale, AZ 85251
www.poisonedpenpress.com
info@poisonedpenpress.com

Printed in the United States of America

To Robert Rosenwald and Barbara Peters,
with thanks for giving me the chance
to swing my golf club again.

"Golf is a lot of walking,
broken up by disappointment and bad arithmetic."

—Mark Twain

Chapter One

Marriage is a murder weapon. At least, it was in the hands of Rosemary, my ex-wife. She was, of course, far too ladylike to wield it like a blunt instrument in order to dash out the brains of her victim. That would have put me out of my misery too quickly. Rosemary preferred a more subtle form of destruction. Venomous poison was administered in tiny doses over a long period so that my death could be drawn out almost indefinitely. Circumstances favored her. Motive, means and opportunity are there on a regular basis for a truly dedicated marital assassin. Rosemary, as always, reveled in her work.

Some men actually like their former wives. Others manage a brisk civility, as if dealing with a lawyer or a bank manager. A few even contrive to be on amicable terms with their old spouses, prompted by regret, remembering the good times, subject to upsurges of affection and able to learn the bland new language in which they have to communicate. I belong to none of these groups. Life with Rosemary disqualified me. After years of punishing me for the crime of marrying her, she pronounced my death sentence in the form of a divorce. From that point on, it seemed, the only conversations I had with her were posthumous, conducted in morse code as I tapped on the underside of the coffin lid. Rosemary had me exactly where she wanted me.

I'm the first to admit that she was provoked. As husband material goes, I was pretty threadbare. My obsessive personality was the problem. When I was obsessed with Rosemary, she was happy enough, but when she was displaced by the game of golf, a contented wife was transformed into a vengeful harpy. She kept my crime sheet scrupulously up to date. I was accused of ignoring her, neglecting our daughter and refusing to take on any family obligations. Since I was playing or practicing on a golf course in order to feed, clothe and house the three of us, I felt that some of the allegations were a trifle unfair, but Rosemary allowed me no defense counsel. My irregular income was another strike against me. The higher the peaks in a golfer's career—and I've been fortunate enough to have several—the deeper the valleys. During adverse times when those valleys broadened out into wide, arid, poverty-stricken plains, Rosemary was at her most scathing about my choice of profession.

Divorce solved nothing. It simply made my dealings with her even more fraught. That's why it took me the best part of a week to screw up the courage to ring her. When I discuss our daughter with her, I have to weigh my words with care. Taking a deep breath, I dialed the fatal number. Rosemary snatched up the telephone at the other end.

"Yes?" she demanded with crisp politeness.

"Rosemary?" I began tentatively. "Is that you?"

"Alan!" Her voice softened. "How nice to hear from you!"

"I've been meaning to give you a buzz."

"How are you?"

"Fine, fine," I said with feigned enthusiasm.

"Keeping your head above water?"

"Just about. And you?"

"Oh, everything is going splendidly at the moment."

"Good."

"Where are you?"

"In Carnoustie."

"But where is Carnoustie parked?"

"In Wiltshire."

"Which part of Wiltshire?" she pressed. "I know that your motor caravan needs plenty of room but it doesn't take up an entire county."

"I'm in Chippenham."

"Can't you be more specific?"

"Okay," I said, shifting my mobile phone to the other ear. "If you want chapter and verse, I'm in the car park of the Angel Hotel, stuck between a metallic blue Honda Accord that needs cleaning and a red Volvo with a teddy bear in the rear window. Would you like their numbers?"

"No, thanks." She laughed. It was an infallible warning. "I'm in transit, Rosemary."

"As ever."

"My life is one long list of parking places. I'm a true vagabond."

There was a reflective pause. "Are you alone?" she asked.

"Completely," I replied. "Apart from the flock of sheep, the band of the Royal Marines and the sixteen casual acquaintances I invited in for afternoon tea. Of course, I'm alone! Why do you think I *live* in a motor caravan? Carnoustie is hardly big enough for me, not to mention all my gear. I *like* being alone, Rosemary. I thrive on it." I gave a nervous chuckle. "Besides, I'd never dare to ring you while someone else was about. It would inhibit me."

Another well-bred laugh came down the line. Her good humor was unnerving.

"So what did you want, Alan?" she went on.

"The pleasure of chatting to you, Rosemary. That's all."

"Oh, come off it. I know you better than that. You only ever ring if you have to."

It was true and I didn't attempt to deny it. Put on the spot, I gabbled my request like a child pleading with a stern parent. "I want to take Lynette on holiday with me," I said, feeling my heart pound. "A week in Bermuda, just before she goes back to college. I mentioned it to her and she was thrilled with the idea but I wanted to clear it with you first. It's ages since I've spent any quality time with her and this is the ideal opportunity."

Rosemary kept me waiting for an answer. Strictly speaking, there was no need to involve her at all. Lynette is nearly twenty-one, old enough to vote, bear arms for her country and make her own decisions. But I didn't want to complicate an already tense situation between my ex-wife and me by going over her head. Since our daughter lives with her, Rosemary has certain unspoken rights. It was only a courtesy to let her know what my plans were. She eventually spoke.

"Why did you choose Bermuda?" she wondered.

"It chose me."

"Are you playing in a tournament?"

"Not this time."

"So why are you going?"

"To design a new golf course."

She was impressed. "All on your own?"

"No, I have a partner, Peter Fullard. He's a genuine course architect. They felt that his experience and my practical know-how would be a winning combination. It's a great challenge for me."

"Does it pay well?"

"Extremely."

"That makes a change," she said with slight bitterness. "And will your work leave you much time to spend with Lynette?"

"Oh, yes."

"She won't enjoy trailing around a non-existent golf course behind you and this partner of yours. Lynette needs attention."

"Just like her mother."

"I was denied it."

"That won't happen to Lynette in Bermuda. She'll get lots of attention."

"And protection, I hope."

"Against what?"

She clicked her tongue. "Alan, for heaven's sake! Use your eyes. Lynette is a desirable young woman. She turns heads."

"Have no worries on that score," I assured her. "I'll take care of her."

"It'll require more than fatherly vigilance."

"What do you mean?"

"We'll come to that in a moment." Her voice hardened. "Is Clive Phelps going to be in Bermuda with you?"

"No, Rosemary."

"Are you sure?"

"Absolutely," I asserted. "I'm not familiar with Clive's travel plans but he has to cover the next tournament on the European Tour. That's what golf writers do, you see. They write about golf."

"Clive Phelps has other strings to his bow as well."

"Rosemary!"

"We have to face facts," she insisted. "He's a complete menace to women."

"I thought you liked Clive."

"I do, Alan—in the right place. But the right place is not on a holiday island with our daughter. Lynette is an impressionable girl."

"She's a full-grown adult."

"Females of any age should be protected from Clive Phelps."

"Stop exaggerating."

"Alan, he's a compulsive lecher."

"Not with the daughter of his best friend. He'd never make a pass at—"

"Oh, yes, he would," she interrupted. "Clive can't help it. It's an automatic reflex. If he can make a pass at his best friend's wife, he won't have any compunction about stalking his nubile daughter."

My anger stirred. "Are you saying that Clive—?"

"Yes," she confirmed.

"The bastard!"

"I thought that you knew."

"I knew that he turned on that battered charm of his whenever you were around but he does that with every woman he meets."

"I rest my case."

"Let me get this straight," I said, trying to fight off rising jealousy. "Clive made a pass at *you*? Was this before or after we split up?"

"Both."

"Two passes?"

"I'd rather not discuss it."

"Rosemary, this is important to me."

"Why?" she asked. "It happened a long time ago. I've buried it along with all the other unpleasant memories associated with the game of golf. Clive was never a serious threat to me. In Lynette's case, however, it might be different."

"Look," I said firmly, "I promise you that Clive Phelps will not be within three thousand miles of Bermuda. This trip has nothing whatsoever to do with him. Except indirectly, that is."

"Indirectly?"

"He introduced me to Peter Fullard."

"You mean that this course architect knows Clive?"

"They're close friends."

"Birds of a feather, no doubt."

"Of course not!" I said irritably. "Peter lives for his work and for his family. He's squeaky clean. I've got a horrible feeling that he's a committed Christian. Probably rings the bells in church on Sundays. In any case," I added, trying to put the issue beyond further question, "his wife will be in

Bermuda with him. Peter and Denise are the perfect married couple. Denise is a saint."

"That wouldn't stop Clive from making his obligatory grab at her."

"Forget him, will you? He's nothing to do with this."

"I'm glad to hear it. Where will you stay?"

"At the Blue Dolphin Hotel. It only opened for business a year ago," I explained. "It's not far from Elbow Beach."

"I remember that," she said fondly. "We stayed there once." A sigh of regret came down the line. "You played golf. Non-stop."

"That won't happen on this trip, Rosemary."

"I loved Bermuda."

"So will Lynette."

"Yes, I'm sure she will."

My hopes soared. "She can come?"

"Of course," said Rosemary. "I couldn't stop her even if I wanted to, and I've no reason to do that. Lynette's been working so hard at college. She deserves a break."

"Thank you!" I said with relief. "It would mean so much to me."

"Then I've no objection."

I slapped my thigh in triumph. But even as I was celebrating, I knew that there had to be a catch. Rosemary is never that agreeable without a purpose. There's always a dagger hidden up the sleeve of her generosity.

"Just one thing, Alan..."

Here it comes, I thought.

"...I'd feel happier if Lynette took someone with her."

"But she'll have me there, Rosemary. Her doting father."

"She needs someone of her own age," she argued. "As it happens, we have a college friend staying with us at the moment. Her name is Jessica Hadlow. She's a lovely girl— bright, sensible and good company. Just the right type for our daughter. Lynette would be thrilled if you could take

Jessica along with you as well. She said as much over breakfast today."

I was checked. "Lynette has already *spoken* to you about Bermuda?"

"Of course. She tells me everything."

"But I asked her to keep quiet until I'd had a word with you myself."

"She was far too excited to do that," said Rosemary. "I knew that something was in the wind and she eventually let me in on the secret."

"Why didn't you say so?" I complained. "Instead of letting me ramble like that?"

"I wanted to see how you presented it, Alan. And to make sure that Clive Phelps wasn't going to be there to pounce on Lynette at the first opportunity. I give the trip my blessing," she said bountifully. "Now that I know that Lynette can take a friend, I have no qualms at all about the holiday."

"Hang on a minute!"

"All three of you will have a lovely time."

"I was expecting that only two of us would be going," I told her. "My employers are happy to pay travel and accommodation for Lynette but I doubt if their philanthropy will stretch to a complete stranger."

"There's a simple answer to that."

"Is there?"

"Yes," said Rosemary. "You can pay for the flight yourself. Lynette and Jessica can share a room at the hotel so the additional costs there will be small. Excellent!" she continued, giving me no chance to protest. "It's all settled. I'll go and tell them the good news. Goodbye, Alan."

Before I could even gurgle a farewell, she hung up. Rosemary had done it again. Without even trying, she had left me thoroughly jangled. I felt so stupid at having to pussyfoot through a conversation that need never have taken place. Since she already knew about the projected holiday,

Rosemary could easily have rung me to signal her consent, but that's not her way. She let me go through the usual agony before calling her, then pretended to be hearing about Bermuda for the first time. It was typical of her. She let me roast on the spit while she basted me expertly. The way that she had introduced a third person into the equation was especially maddening. When I first put the proposal to Lynette, there was no mention of any college friend coming with her. That was clearly my ex-wife's doing. Whatever plans I have, Rosemary always has to alter them. The one consolation was that she hadn't decided to include herself in the trip.

I left Carnoustie and adjourned to the lounge bar of the hotel for a stiff whiskey. It rallied me at once. When all was said and done, my main aim had been achieved. Lynette was going to spend a whole week on holiday with her father for the first time in years. It would give us chance to catch up on each other's news, to repair a few fences and to have some real fun together once again. It's rather strange. Lynette left school two years ago, yet I still haven't got used to the idea of having a daughter at Oxford. As someone who fled from the British educational system at the earliest opportunity, I can't understand why anyone would wish to remain within it longer than necessary. It was one of the many things I intended to discuss with Lynette and—lo and behold—I'd now be able to do it. Having survived another bruising exchange with my ex-wife, I'd secured my objective.

Lynette was coming to Bermuda with me. So, alas, was someone called Jessica Hadlow. The name was new to me. I'd met most of Lynette's friends on my visits to Oxford but I didn't recall a Jessica. What sort of person was she? How well would she fit in? Rosemary had described her as "the right type." That sounded ominous. I decided to order another whiskey.

I dislike noise, I detest crowds, I hate the curiosity of the Great British Public and I simply loathe hanging around in a dangerous place. Gatwick Airport has been carefully designed to incorporate all my aversions. Its relentless clamor is swelled by a series of booming announcements, its concourse is as busy as Epsom on Derby Day, and its swirling chaos throws up dozens of nosey travelers who half-recognize Alan Saxon and therefore feel entitled to invade my privacy with insulting questions ("You mean, you still play golf for a living? At *your* age? Haven't they pensioned you off yet?") My gray hair is partly to blame but it's still humiliating for someone in his early forties to be taken for a decrepit old man. All I can do is to maintain a dignified silence.

What makes it worse is that this army of occupation is equipped with lethal weaponry. Indiscriminate attacks come from all sides. Steel trolleys will smash your legs, swinging flight bags will crack your ribs and other items of luggage can inflict even worse injury. Look the wrong way for two seconds at Gatwick and you can be steam-rollered by excess baggage or impaled on a pair of skis. It's like running the gauntlet. For a person of my delicate sensibilities, the airport is continuous torture.

"Daddy!"

One word made all the suffering worthwhile.

"Daddy! Over here!"

I spotted her at once. Lynette was sprinting across the concourse towards me, weaving her way between the aimless groups of holiday-makers with sublime ease. Her face was shining, her fair hair bobbing, her whole body animated by excitement. I revived instantly. Lynette flung herself into my arms for an embrace that momentarily reconciled me to the hostile surroundings. I was a father once more. I stood back to appraise her properly. It was months since I'd last seen her and Lynette seemed to have aged subtly. Tall, willowy and beautiful, she looked even more like her mother

and I was forcibly reminded of what made me fall in love
with Rosemary all those years ago. I, too, was under scrutiny.

"You look tired," observed Lynette.

"It was a long drive."

"How is Carnoustie?"

"Still chugging along."

"Are you ever going to have a proper house again, Daddy?"

"I've got one," I said proudly. "Carnoustie."

My motor caravan bears the name of the course where I
achieved my greatest success with a set of golf clubs. I can't
expect my daughter to appreciate what it means to win the
Open Championship, but it's the reason I'd never part with
my home on wheels. Carnoustie is my refuge. It's only during winter months that its shortcomings are obvious, and
I'm usually playing tournaments in warmer climes then.
Lynette thinks I'm mad to live in such a confined space, but
unlike her mother, she's very tolerant of my multiple luna-
cies. As I studied her afresh, I noticed a perceptible difference
in her. It was not so much in her appearance as in her manner. The girlish exuberance had gone to be replaced by a
distinctive poise. Lynette was wearing a dark blue T-shirt
and a pair of pink shorts. I also detected more make-up than
usual. I felt a stab of guilt as I found myself wondering if
my daughter was still a virgin. The question was surely redundant. Were *any* girls of that age still virgins? Not if they
were as gorgeous as Lynette, I suspected. Suddenly, I was
very grateful that Clive Phelps was not coming to Bermuda
with us.

"Where's your luggage?" I asked.

"Jessica's got it."

"That's a bit unfair, isn't it? Dumping it on her."

"She sent me on ahead so that I could meet you alone."

"I appreciate that," I said, hugging her again. "Jessica is
obviously considerate."

Lynette beamed. "I'm so glad you let me bring her, Daddy. She's such fun. You'll like Jessica. She's rather special."

"Why haven't I met her before?"

"I only met her myself last term," she explained. "We were in *Love's Labour's Lost* together at the Playhouse. You missed the production because you were in Spain. Jessica and I just hit it off."

"Is she at St. Hilda's?"

"Heavens, no! Jessica would never go near a women-only college. She doesn't believe in single sex education. She's at The House."

"The where?"

"Christ Church—the biggest and the wealthiest of the colleges. It was founded by Cardinal Wolsey in the sixteenth century so it's positively oozing with tradition. It's the ideal place for Jessica."

"Why?"

"You'll see when you meet her."

I glanced round. "Where is she?"

"Searching for a porter, I expect. When I left her, the chauffeur was unloading our luggage from the Roller."

"You came in a chauffeur-driven Rolls Royce?" I said, gasping at the thought.

"Of course. Jessica's father is seriously rich."

"I see."

I was glad that I'd changed my original plan to pick the two of them up in Carnoustie. A motor caravan of rattling antiquity is no match for the kind of transport that Jessica's father could lay on. Lynette would have been compromised. Street cred is so important among the young. She read my mind and gave me an affectionate squeeze. It was the last moment we had on our own.

"Here I am!" called a voice.

Jessica Hadlow was bearing down on us with a porter at her heels. She was shorter, darker and shapelier than Lynette, with a cosmopolitan confidence radiating out of her. The crowd seemed to part obligingly for her, as if recognizing a superior. She had the relaxed grin of someone who was completely at home in an airport. After giving me an approving glance, she extended a hand.

"Hello, Mr. Saxon," she said amiably. "I'm Jessica Hadlow."

"Pleased to meet you," I replied, shaking her hand.

"It's so kind of you to take me with you."

"Not at all, Jessica. Any friend of Lynette's is very welcome."

"Thank you."

We moved across to join the queue at the check-in desk. The porter unloaded the suitcases and Jessica tipped him handsomely. She was a striking young woman. Every father likes to think that his daughter is a vision of beauty, but I had to concede that Lynette's classical loveliness was over shadowed by her friend. Wearing white shorts and a white cheesecloth shirt, Jessica was stunning. A necklace of multicolored beads dangled down to the deep cleavage. Her long-brown hair was brushed back and held in place by a red ribbon tied in an elaborate bow. Dark green eyes sparkled in a face of almost doll-like prettiness. Though her voice and manner were decidedly English, there was something faintly Mediterranean about her. Jessica was glowing with a kind of educated sexuality. I doubted very much if she was the sort of student that Cardinal Wolsey had in mind when he founded her Oxford college.

I caught myself staring at her and felt constrained to ask a question.

"Have you been to Bermuda before, Jessica?"

"Oh, yes," she said. "Many times."

Lynette giggled. "Jessica's father has business interests there."

"Daddy has business interests all over the place," confirmed her friend. "He's a real globe-trotter. He uses Bermuda as a tax shelter."

"What does he do?" I asked foolishly.

Jessica shrugged. "He makes money."

Lynette noticed that it was now our turn to check in. She heaved her case forward. I hauled my luggage off the trolley. Jessica looked admiringly at my golf bag.

"I hear that you're a marvelous golfer," she said.

"He's the best in the world," claimed Lynette.

"Don't oversell me," I told her.

"You are, Daddy. I've seen you play."

Jessica grinned up at me. "I've always wanted to play golf," she confessed. "Will you give me some tuition, please?"

"I may not have the time," I said, uneasy at the very notion.

"An hour a day is all that I'd need."

"We'll see, Jessica."

"I'm quite happy to pay, Mr. Saxon."

I almost blushed. "There'd be no question of that."

"How much do you charge?"

She gave me no time to reply. Her attention was diverted by something that put quiet outrage into her voice. She saw the sign on the desk in front of us and realized that the travel arrangements fell short of perfection.

"This is Club Class!"

"That's right," I said. "I managed to buy you the last ticket on the plane."

"But I've never flown Club before," she went on, her face puckering with distaste. "Daddy always takes me First Class."

"Does he?"

"He says that we're First Class people."

"Don't be such a snob, Jessica," chided Lynette, giving her a playful nudge. "You can slum it for once, surely?"

"Well, I suppose so."

I tried to conceal my annoyance. Thanks to Rosemary, I'd been forced to pay for an additional ticket out of my own pocket. When you part with over two and a half thousand pounds, you're entitled to a modicum of gratitude, but all I was getting from Jessica was a mutinous pout. I did my best to make light of the situation.

"I tell you what," I said with a wink. "Next time we go to Bermuda, I'll arrange for you to sit next to the pilot. Is it a deal?"

She managed a smile and gave a nod of agreement. Lynette nudged her again.

"You're getting a free hol, Jessica," she said. "What more do you want?"

"Nothing," replied Jessica blithely.

But I could see that she was lying.

Bermuda is only seven hours away by British Airways jet, but the flight seemed to take an eternity. Jessica Hadlow had a way of elongating time that made a nonsense of airline schedules. She hardly ever stopped talking. She monopolized Lynette until I was seething with jealousy, then threw an occasional remark in my direction. During the two films that were shown, I put on my headphones and turned up the reception to full volume but even that did not block out the sound of her commentary on the movies. She was irrepressible. I could easily understand what Lynette saw in her new friend. Jessica was lively, attractive and highly intelligent. Her family background had given her a sort of mirthful arrogance that set my daughter off into peals of laughter, and she was a distinct advance on all those polite, conventional, well spoken Rachels and Emmas and Charlottes with whom Lynette spent her time when she was at Benendon. Jessica had—as my dear mother would have put it—something about her. The trouble was that she had far too much of it.

What puzzled me was how readily Rosemary had given her a seal of approval. Jessica had much to recommend her in my wife's eyes, but her easy sensuality would be a huge obstacle. Rosemary believed that sex was something that should be kept hidden at all times and only enjoyed in the strictest privacy. She is the only woman I know who can make love with glorious abandon, then pretend that nothing happened immediately afterwards. Such an attitude can be very off-putting for the man. I lost count of the number of times when I was still basking in the afterglow, only to be ordered off the bed so that Rosemary could strip the sheets and put them in the washing machine to remove the evidence of carnal delight. Jessica seemed to have no such hang-ups. As she chatted on to Lynette, I caught the names of at least half-a-dozen young men with whom she cheerfully admitted to have had intimate relations. I could only assume that, when she stayed with Rosemary, she kept that aspect of her character well concealed. There's no place at all for promiscuity in my ex-wife's concept of the right type of friend for our daughter.

Jessica concealed nothing from me. As soon as Lynette went off to the toilet, her friend moved across to sit next to me. Her smile comprised friendliness, curiosity and boldness in equal parts. She put a hand on my arm.

"I'm terribly sorry, Mr. Saxon," she said.

"Why?"

"For talking non-stop to Lynette."

"She obviously enjoys it."

"I know," she said, "but it does rather exclude you. Daddy hates it when I rattle on in what he calls that hideous undergraduate lingo. He can't understand a word of it."

"Neither could I, Jessica. It might have been Greek to me."

"Oh, Daddy could understand that. My mother was Greek, you see."

It explained a lot. "What does she make of your Oxford slang?" I asked.

"Who know? She and Daddy split up years ago. He never keeps his wives all that long," she said airily. "I'm on my third stepmother at the moment."

"What nationality is she?"

"Italian." Her smile broadened. "I must say, I loved meeting Mrs. Saxon."

"She was impressed with you as well."

"Why has she never re-married, do you think?"

"I've no idea."

"Lynette says that she was engaged once, to a psychiatrist. Dreary David, that's what Lynette used to call him. Apparently, he was a big disappointment in bed. That was Lynette's guess, anyway. She found him rather creepy."

I'd found the man highly objectionable for a number of reasons but I was not about to discuss him with Jessica. There was a directness about her questions that was unsettling. I found myself wishing that Lynette would soon come to my rescue.

"There is another explanation, of course," suggested Jessica.

"Is there?"

"Yes. It may be that Mrs. Saxon never intended to marry him at all. She was only testing the water, so to speak. Trying out the idea of being with another man before she actually committed herself."

"You sound like something of a psychiatrist yourself."

"Hell, no! I'm reading English."

"Just like Lynette."

"Yes, we have so much in common. I'm so glad we met in the play. We're sisters under the skin." Her hand tightened on my arm. "Do you know what I think?"

"About what?"

"Your ex-wife," she said. "The reason she ditched the psychiatrist is that she's still carrying a torch for you." I shook my head. "She is, I swear it. Why else does she have so many framed photographs of you in the house? And why does she speak so fondly of you? She still loves you, Mr. Saxon." She leaned in closer. "I can see why."

It was bad enough to have Rosemary's name introduced into the conversation. When it was coupled with the absurd claim that she was still yearning for me, I felt my stomach churn. Compounding my discomfort was the fact that a twenty-year-old student was daring to flirt with me. She had certainly kept that look in her eye hidden from Rosemary. It belonged to the wrong type altogether.

"Have you never wanted to marry again?" she probed.

"No, Jessica."

"Lynette says that you have lots of girlfriends."

"I'd rather not discuss my private life."

"Is there anyone special at the moment?"

"Yes," I said, noting with relief that Lynette was about to rejoin us. "Here she is."

Jessica laughed. "You didn't answer my question."

"What question?" asked Lynette, sitting the other side of her.

"We're talking about sex."

"No, we're not," I said pointedly.

"There's nothing to be ashamed of," said Jessica, finally removing her hand from my arm. "People of all ages are entitled to sex lives. Look at my father. Daddy must be ten or fifteen years older than you and he's always on the prowl. I admire him for that. It's refreshing to be with someone who's so honest about his desires."

My one desire at that moment was for the cabin crew to grab Jessica violently and lock her away somewhere for the remainder of the flight, but my wish was not granted. Instead, I had to listen to that extraordinary voice as she treated Lynette to yet another of her monologues on the pleasures and perils of life at Oxford. The pair of them laughed conspiratorially. A century later, we touched down in Bermuda.

Chapter Two

There are so many things to dislike about Bermuda that I can never understand why I love it so much. On paper, it's not my kind of place at all. I recoil from its nauseating whiff of colonialism, from its air of quiet refinement and from its deep-seated parochialism. Its remorseless beauty always makes me feel that I've stumbled upon the outright winner in a Best Kept Island competition. Bermuda is altogether too neat and tidy. Its quaint limestone houses with their cedar doors, brightly painted shutters and distinctive white tiled roofs are far too photogenic. Its views are breathtaking, its leisure facilities are overwhelming and its sense of privilege is tangible. Hordes of lotus-eaters bask on its spotless beaches or recline beside its myriad swimming pools, luxuriating in their wealth. Bermuda is expensive, elitist and irritatingly close to perfection.

The island paradise does have its problems. Thousands of mopeds and scooters buzz continuously along like swarms of bees. Hundreds of taxis, cars and buses are in perpetual motion around its narrow roads and hazardous bends, making it a danger zone for the careless driver or the ambling pedestrian. The weather, too, can be menacing. High winds and driving rain occasionally scour Bermuda as a blustery storm blows in from the Atlantic. Tempests that used to wreck so many helpless vessels in the days of sail still visit the citizens to remind them of their human frailty. And there are deeper causes for concern, hidden from the naked eye.

Notwithstanding all this, I adore the place. As soon as I step on to the soil of Bermuda, I feel inspired. It's not only a community with a handful of excellent golf courses, it's a premier golf course in itself. Designed by Nature to the very highest specifications, it lies invitingly in the ocean to offer a supreme test to anyone with a real feeling for the game. I've always said that, when I die, I want my ashes to be scattered over my spiritual home, the eighteenth hole at Carnoustie, which, coincidentally, is named Home. But there'll be a post script in my will, urging my nearest and dearest to discard the last few remaining specks of Alan Saxon at the Mid-Ocean Golf Club in Tucker's Town, Bermuda. I can think of no two better final resting places.

Geared very largely to tourism, the island has streamlined its welcome. Airport officials greet you with a smile and whisk you through Customs without delay. The doors of the baggage hall spill out on to a huge car park that's filled with serried ranks of taxis. There are well over six hundred in Bermuda and every one of them seemed to have assembled for our benefit. The one that I was interested in was a shining new dormobile with the name and logo of the Blue Dolphin Hotel on its bodywork. Its driver was a large, shambling, black Bermudian in his fifties with a fringe beard. Wearing blue pants and white short-sleeved shirt, he was leaning against his vehicle and puffing at a cigarette. As I turned in his direction, he recognized me and sauntered across to take charge of our luggage. He assessed me through narrowed lids before giving a curt nod of welcome. While he loaded the cases and the golf bag into the rear of the dormobile, we climbed inside, the girls choosing the middle seat, leaving me to sit directly behind the driver.

Jessica voiced her first cheerful criticism of the accommodation.

"I've never heard of the Blue Dolphin," she said. "That's bad."

"It's new," I explained tolerantly. "Built on the site of two old hotels and a beach club. It's state of the art. You'll like it, Jessica."

"We always stay at the Southampton Princess."

"You'll have to make do with the Blue Dolphin this time."

"How many guests can it handle?"

I pursed my lips in thought. "Seven or eight hundred."

"The Princess has room for a thousand."

"Oh, stop boasting, Jessica," said Lynette happily. "I don't care if we have to sleep on the beach. We're here, aren't we? I can't imagine a better way to prepare for the hard slog of Michaelmas term. Our friends will be green with envy."

Jessica beamed. "So they should be." She tapped me on the shoulder. "Excuse me, Mr. Saxon. Do they have any real dolphins at the Blue Dolphin?"

"Not as far as I know," I said.

"Well, they do at the Princess."

"Jessica!" chided Lynette.

"It's true. I've seen them. They have this two-acre holding pen that's separated from the open sea by underwater netting. Last time we were here, they had seven Atlantic bottlenose dolphins there. I actually swam in the water with them. I must take you there, Lynette," she continued. "It's the most amazing experience."

Still puffing on his cigarette, the driver clambered into his seat and turned on the ignition. As the vehicle pulled away, smoke drifted over his shoulder. I objected to being in his firing line.

"Do you mind not smoking?" I asked pleasantly.

The man grunted in reply and tossed the cigarette through the open window.

"Thank you," I said.

It was a typical autumn afternoon with a brilliant sun hanging in a cloudless sky. The blue pennants on the bonnets of the other taxis and courtesy cabs fluttered in the stiff breeze. Freed from the intrusive cigarette smoke, I inhaled deeply. I could smell the golf already. It was invigorating. The airport is on St. George's Island at the eastern end of Bermuda. As we went over Long Bird Bridge, I glanced left for my first view of Castle Harbor with its scattering of small boats, bobbing lazily on the turquoise sea. Jessica pointed them out to Lynette and began her commentary.

Guide books invariably remind you that Bermuda was the island that gave old Will Shakespeare the idea for *The Tempest,* but the author who always pops into my mind is Robert Louis Stevenson. I feel as if I've discovered a Treasure Island with all mod cons. Names like Whale Bone Bay, Shark Hole, Spanish Point, and Wreck Hill are straight out of a pirate yarn. Clarence Cove and Flatt's Inlet positively beckon the longboat. Two Rock Passage and Tobacco Bay echo with sea shanties. Gibbet Island would be an ideal hiding place for Long John Silver and his men. Out in the Great Sound, there is even a Hawkins Island for Jim and the rest of them. It all serves to bring out the boy in me.

The presence of Jessica Hadlow was less oppressive now that we were on dry land again. When she and Lynette began to discuss what they'd do in arrival at the hotel, I was able to switch off, enjoy the scenery and muse foolishly about the delights of sailing the Seven Seas under a pirate flag. My buccaneering was soon interrupted.

"Youbinformissaxon."

The driver spoke so quickly out of the side of his mouth that I had no idea what he said. What I did catch was the slight hint of aggression in his voice.

"Could you repeat that, please?" I said.

"Youbinfor."

I separated the words out and realized that he was telling me that I'd been to the island before. Since I'd stayed at the Blue Dolphin on a number of occasions, it was there that he had probably seen me. He slowed his diction down a little.

"You like it?"

"Very much," I replied.

"O.K. for you," he said bitterly. "You don't have to live here."

"That's true, my friend."

"Mo. My name is Mo."

"I don't have to live here, Mo," I agreed, "but I wish I did. If there's one place in the world I'd love to retire to, it's Bermuda."

"Retiring's not *living* here. It's not working on the island."

"Maybe not."

"Some us were born here," he emphasized "We got no fucking choice."

"Don't you like the place?"

He gave a hollow laugh then lapsed into a sullen silence. Taxi drivers on the island tend to be uniformly courteous. In Mo, obviously, we had the exception to the rule. I ignored him and went back to thoughts of Blind Pew and cheese-loving Ben Gunn. After spitting through the window, the driver started to talk to himself. We were coming down Collector's Hill and turning into South Road when he decided to favor me with his thoughts once more.

"Knowmuchbouteltroncs?"

The speed and manner of his delivery again gave me difficulties. Getting no reply, he repeated the question with a more truculent edge. I inserted gaps between the words and found out that I was being asked if I knew anything about electronics.

"Electronics?" I said. "Nothing at all."

"Me do."

"Do you?"

"Me an expert."

"Are you, Mo?"

"Yes," he said, raising his voice. "Me took exams, see. Me studied two fucking years. They said me should have studied more but me think me done enough. Don't you? Me good at lectronics. That's what me should be doing, not driving round the island like this." He slapped the dashboard with the flat of his hand. "Me got a skill, see. That's what it's all about. Having a skill. Me deserve better than this shit. Me a skilled man."

The outburst brought the girls out of their debate. Jessica was blunt.

"Can you ask him to shut up, please, Mr. Saxon?" she said loudly. "We're trying to have a conversation back here. We don't want to listen to him, swearing like that."

"Mo was only expressing an opinion," I said with a defensive note.

"Well, we don't want to hear it."

Her brutal comment made our driver twitch with anger. I could see his shoulders stiffen. Instead of replying, he went off into another mumbled soliloquy. Evidently, Mo had not read any of the guide books. The link with *The Tempest* was unknown to him. Where he should have been playing Prospero, he opted for the part of Othello, burning with jealousy. He made me feel as if I'd just stolen Desdemona's handkerchief.

A signpost indicated that Hungry Bay was off to the left. To stave off further exchanges with our surly chauffeur, I joined in the girls' chatter. Lynette and Jessica were planning so many treats for themselves that they would need a month, rather than a week, in order to include them all. We were still sweeping along South Road. I tried to point out a few landmarks but everything I said was edited and extended by Jessica. She knew the island better than I and had an acquaintance with its flora and fauna that was truly impressive. Listening to her voice, surging on with unassailable confidence, I suspected that she would be a difficult student

in tutorials. Nobody else could get a word in. It was an uncomfortable journey to the hotel. I was trapped between a
Bermudan with a chip on his shoulder and a garrulous young
woman who sounded as if she owned the island.

We were almost there when Mo came out of his sustained
sulk.

"Longyouaying?" he asked.

When I'd translated the question into "How long are you
staying?", I told him that I'd be on the island for the best
part of three weeks and explained that the girls would only
be there for the first week. He glanced over his shoulder.
Jessica was still in full flow. Mo gave a snort of disapproval.

"Do she ever shut up?"

"I heard that," snapped Jessica. "I'll thank you to mind
your own business."

"Oh, me will, missie," he said with mock humility. "Me
only the driver. Me don't count. Me just take you from one
place to another, that's me."

She asserted her authority. "Well, we'd prefer you to do
it without comment, please. This is a private conversation.
You shouldn't be listening."

Before Mo could reply, I jumped in to smooth over an
awkward moment.

"Here we are!" I announced, spotting the hotel ahead of
us. "Welcome to the Blue Dolphin! This is where the fun
really starts."

"Not with *him* around," observed Jessica tartly.

Mo growled something under his breath that I was grateful I didn't catch.

The vehicle turned in through the gates of the hotel and
the girls got their first view of the Blue Dolphin. To her
credit, even Jessica was complimentary. The main building
was a five-story structure that was set on the crest of a hill.
Its brilliant white stone glistened in the sun and its vast
expanse of glass gave it additional dazzle. Each room at the

front had a private balcony with its own blue and white striped awning. A giant version of the hotel logo soared from the roof like a dolphin leaping out of the sea. There were larger and more luxurious hotels on the island but few had such a superb position. Surrounding the hotel were dozens of neat white cottages for guests who liked a measure of independence. At the bottom of the slope was a glorious beach of fine white sand that was dotted with multi-colored sunshades. There was a large beach pavilion and a landing stage for small boats.

Lynette and Jessica had already made their first decision of the holiday.

"Look at that sea," said Lynette. "It's so blue."

"Wait until you get in the water," advised Jessica. "It's warm."

"I *knew* I was going to enjoy this holiday." She leaned forward to kiss me. "Thanks, Daddy! This is such a treat."

"Yes, Mr. Saxon. Thank you." Jessica waited until Mo went to open the rear door before hissing in my ear, "Don't give him a tip."

"Leave that to me, Jessica."

"He doesn't deserve it. If you ask me, Mo stands for Moron."

Unfortunately, our driver opened the door at that precise moment and heard the remark. He glowered at Jessica, then at me, then he began to unload the luggage. We got out of the dormobile and stood in Bermuda sunshine. A porter arrived with a baggage trolley. After tipping the peak of his cap deferentially, he turned to our driver.

"How are you, Mo?" he asked.

"Not too good, man," replied Mo.

"Why? What's the problem?"

"Bad company."

I didn't think that Jessica caught his last comment because she was already striding off towards the hotel entrance with Lynette. But I heard it and left Mo a stern glare in lieu of a tip. He had the grace to look sheepish. As I walked after the girls, he rid himself of a litany of complaints to the porter. I was relieved when I was out of earshot. Whoever drove us back to the airport, it would not be the failed electronics expert.

They had put a few more potted palms in the lobby since my last visit and the furniture had been rearranged to give a more decorative effect. I sensed that other changes had taken place but I had no time to work out what they were because Calvin Reed came clicking across the marble floor to greet us.

"How nice to see you again, Alan," he said, pumping my hand. "I trust that you had a good flight?"

"Yes, yes," I lied.

"And this must be your daughter," he went on, studying Lynette. "The family likeness is unmistakable."

I introduced both girls and they shook hands with him. Calvin Reed was the hotel manager, a tall, slim, sleek man in his thirties with one of those all-purpose smiles that people in his line of business can conjure up at the touch of a button. He was an arresting figure in an immaculate suit, with the good looks of a male model enhanced by an air of unforced authority. The Californian accent had a charm that won over Lynette instantly, but Jessica reserved her judgment. Calvin Reed had never been less than friendly, yet I couldn't bring myself to call him by his first name. There was something about him that I distrusted. Like the island itself, he was almost too good to be true.

Easing us across to the reception desk, he kept up simultaneous conversations with all three of us as we checked in. That evening, he insisted, we would dine in the hotel restaurant with him and his wife. Lynette was patently disappointed that he was married, but it did not deter Jessica. Having decided that she liked him, she gave him a grin of frank admiration. I shuddered inwardly. In terms of sexual confidence, she was light years ahead of Lynette. When she

struck that pose with a hand on one hip and tossed her hair
back provocatively, Jessica Hadlow was jail bait. Into what
sort of wild adventures would she lead my darling daughter,
I wondered. It's rather alarming to discover, at my age, that
you still have moral standards. It was Jessica who brought
them bubbling to the surface. Watching her in action made
me feel like a Mother Superior who's just found out that her
nuns work as strippers in a nightclub.

"I'll see you later then," said Calvin Reed, distributing a
smile between the three of us. "I hope you find everything
to your satisfaction."

Jessica's grin broadened. "I'm sure that we will, Mr. Reed."

I was tempted to register a complaint about our taxi driver
but I let it pass. A hotel manager is far too exalted a person
to deal with the problem of a minor employee. Besides, I
wanted to forget Mo and his doomed passion for electronics.
Wheeling our luggage ahead of us, the porter took us into
the elevator and up to the top floor. We had adjoining suites
that gave out on to separate balconies, commanding a spectacular view of the ocean. Since the girls were eager to take
a first dip in the sea, I unpacked my bags and took the
opportunity to slip into a pair of Bermuda shorts and a golf
shirt. Through the connecting door between the rooms, I
could hear Jessica's voice raised in excitement. She was not
simply Lynette's friend. After less than a day in her company,
I came to see her as a curse placed on me by Rosemary. Somewhere back in England, my ex-wife was laughing quietly in
her sleep.

I was hanging the last of my things in the wardrobe when
the telephone rang.

"Hello?" I said into the mouthpiece.

"Alan?" asked an anxious voice.

"Peter, how are you?"

"All the better for hearing you. Thank God you've come."

"Why?"

"We've got problems, Alan."

"What kind of problems?"

"I'll tell you when I see you."

"Calvin Reed said that everything was under control."

"He would."

"You sound uneasy."

"I'm desperate!"

"Calm down," I soothed. "The cavalry had just arrived."

"How soon can we get together?"

"Give me ten minutes."

"Right. I'll be in the Flamingo Bar."

"See you there, Peter."

Peter Fullard hung up and I put my receiver down. I wasn't troubled by his tone of alarm because it's his normal mode of speech. Peter thrives on worry. If they awarded degrees in it, he'd get a First before going on to gain his M.A.—Master of Apprehension. Peter Fullard is a brilliant course architect who is highly paid for his services. He earns every penny in sustained disquiet. No matter how successful a project is, he's never satisfied. No matter how smoothly things are running, Peter always discerns a host of nagging setbacks.

There was a tap on the connecting door then it opened to admit Lynette.

"Are you there, Daddy?" she called.

"Yes," I said, going out of the bedroom. "All ready for your swim?"

It was a redundant question. Lynette was wearing a pink toweling robe over her bikini and a pair of flip-flops. She carried a pair of sunglasses and a bottle of sun tan lotion. When she saw my legs, she gave an involuntary giggle at their deathly pallor.

"Don't mock," I said. "It's the only pair I've got."

"I'm so glad you brought us, Daddy. Being here is pure magic. Don't be fooled by Jessica's manner. She's as thrilled as I am to be here."

"Good."

"And she thinks you're marvelous."

"Does she?" I replied, torn between surprise and concern at the news.

"Jessica has a thing about older men."

"Thanks for the warning."

"I know that she takes a bit of getting used to," said Lynette, glancing over her shoulder, "but she's a wonderful friend. Never a dull moment when Jessica is around."

"So I noticed."

"Please try to like her, Daddy."

"I do like her," I said through gritted teeth. "In small doses. So far, the doses have been rather on the large side. But we've rubbed along happily enough."

"Why don't you join us for a swim?"

"No, thanks, Lynette. I have a date with Peter Fullard."

"Oh, of course. I forget that you're here to work."

"There'll be time to play as well, I promise."

"I hope so."

I lowered my voice. "What does Jessica intend to do?"

"Have a ball."

"I don't mean here, Lynette. What happens when she graduates? Is she going into business or merely setting up as a tour guide in Bermuda?"

"Nothing like that, Daddy. She's a star. Jessica's going on the stage."

"Really?"

"If you'd seen her in *Love's Labour's Lost*, you'd understand why. Jessica stole the show. She had rave reviews in all the papers. One critic said that it was the best performance of Rosaline he'd seen outside Stratford. Jessica is a natural."

"What part did you play?"

"The Princess of France."

"Then I bet you were every bit as talented as her," I said loyally.

Lynette smiled. "It's sweet of you to say so, Daddy, but it's just not true. Jessica was in a different league from the rest of us. She was so *professional.*"

"I'd still cast you ahead of her any time."

"Thank you," she said, giving me a kiss on the cheek. "But you may change your mind when you get to know Jessica better. She grows on people. Wait until you give her that golf lesson. She'll soon win you over."

Right on cue, Jessica Hadlow came into the room without knocking. The door swung open and she glided through it like a contestant in a beauty contest. She didn't believe in hiding her charms. Wearing a skimpy red bikini and red beach shoes, she was carrying a towel over one arm. Her sunglasses were perched high on her head. Taken aback by her sudden entrance, I goggled at the supple young body with its bronze sheen. Jessica enjoyed creating an impact.

"I just rang down to complain," she said.

"Complain?" I repeated. "I thought you were happy with the room."

"Oh, I am, Mr. Saxon. Delighted. Especially as we're so close to you," she added with a glint in her eye. "What I was complaining about was the village idiot they sent to drive us here from the airport."

"Mo?"

"He was appalling."

"I didn't think he was too bad, Jessica."

"We don't have to put up with that kind of thing," she insisted. "He was rude and disgusting. Mr. Reed was shocked to hear about it."

I quailed. "You rang Calvin Reed?"

"Naturally. It's the Hadlow family motto. If you want something done, you always go to the top. Mr. Reed said that he'd look into it straight away. A driver like that shouldn't be working for the Blue Dolphin. It gives the hotel a bad name." Having achieved her effect, she slipped on her beach robe and turned to Lynette. "Come on. I'm dying to get in that water."

"Me, too," said Lynette.

After an exchange of farewells, they scampered off together and I was left to reflect on the danger of having a sex siren on the other side of a connecting door. My daughter would be my salvation. When I first invited her to come on the trip, I assumed that I'd be acting as Lynette's chaperone but, in fact, it would be the other way round. It was her presence that would guard me against the very real temptation of Jessica Hadlow.

The Flamingo Bar opened out on to a large oval-shaped patio that was a forest of sunshades. Most of the people lounging beneath them were relaxed and happy but Peter Fullard was the odd man out. Bolt upright in his seat, he looked like a condemned man in the electric chair, waiting for the switch to be thrown. A glass was clutched between both hands. When he saw me approach, Peter swallowed the last of his drink and leapt up to greet me. He shook my hand as if I'd just saved his life in the nick of time

"You're a sight for sore eyes, Alan," he said.

"My daughter thinks the shorts are a mistake."

"Who cares what you're wearing?"

"Lynette does. Fathers are supposed to keep up appearances in front of friends."

We sat down at the table. Short, stout and balding, Peter should have been one of those cuddly middle-aged men who are always popular at parties among more discerning ladies. Instead, he was a nervous wreck with a face like a map of the Amazon delta. There was a hunted look in his eyes.

"They're trying to get at us, Alan," he wailed.

"Who is?"

"It's one damn thing after another. There's a definite pattern."

"To what?"

"I think it's deliberate. Calvin Reed says it's pure coincidence but I don't believe that. I have this gut feeling, Alan, and I don't like it. I don't like it one bit."

"Like what?"

"Any of it."

I was bewildered. "Could you be more specific, Peter?"

"This morning," he said, wagging a finger. "Take this very morning. Or last Wednesday. That's an even better example." He jumped to his feet. "Do you mind if we talk somewhere else, Alan? I feel nervous in here."

Peter Fullard felt nervous wherever he was, but I humored him nevertheless. Since he was worried about the golf course, I guided him in that direction.

"What's going on?" I asked.

"I wish I knew."

"You mentioned problems over the phone."

"Yes, Alan. Lots of them. Someone is trying to stop us."

"What do you mean?"

"It's sabotage."

"Surely not?"

"There's no other word for it."

I was mystified. "When I spoke to you a month ago, work was ahead of schedule."

"It was, Alan—a month ago. Then the trouble started."

"What trouble?"

He wiped the back of his hand across a sweating brow. "One of the bulldozers has been vandalized. Badly."

"When was this?"

"Last Wednesday."

"Bored youths, probably," I suggested. "Looking for kicks."

"And was it the same bored youths who stole a mower and who pulled up some of the saplings we planted along the first fairway? This is not merely a case of adolescent high spirits," he argued. "We're under concerted attack. To be honest, I'm beginning to wish that I'd never heard of the Blue Dolphin Hotel."

"Don't be so defeatist, Peter."

"I can't work in this kind of situation."

"Yes, you can," I assured him. "With me beside you."

"Who is it, Alan?" he demanded. "What are we up against?"

"A run of bad luck, by the sound of it."

"It's much more than that."

"Give me the details."

He let out a moan. "Difficult to know where to begin."

"Try the bulldozer."

Peter Fullard managed a semblance of composure, then reeled off a list of crimes. Most of them were very minor and could easily have been the work of careless tourists. The attack on the bulldozer and the uprooting of the saplings might also have been part of some ill-conceived holiday fun, but the theft of the mower was not. It cost thousands of pounds and was a vital piece of equipment. I wondered how something so large and conspicuous could disappear into thin air. What rattled Peter most was the loss of his supply of Bermuda grass seed, a hybrid strain that he'd developed himself. He'd sooner have parted with his false teeth.

"What are they going to steal next?" he cried.

"Nothing," I affirmed.

"It's this hotel. Denise says that the Blue Dolphin is jinxed."

"Rubbish!"

"It is, Alan."

"We had no trouble during our last visit."

"They were biding their time."

"Don't let it get to you."

"I can't help it," he said. "Denise and I stay awake at nights."

That was not unusual. From what I could judge, the Fullard marriage was one long sleepless night. Peter's wife was a true companion in misery, one of those indefatigable anxiety-mongers who can be relied upon to view everything in the worst possible light. If Peter Fullard was shaken, Denise would be quivering uncontrollably. As his distress threatened to burn itself out, she would be there to fan the flames into another inferno. On my mental list of people to avoid in Bermuda, I put the name of Denise Fullard only just below those of Jessica Hadlow and Mo, the irascible chauffeur. None of them did much to nurture my holiday spirit.

Peter ran a hand through the tufted remains of his hair.

"What are we going to do, Alan?" he bleated.

"Our job."

"In these circumstances?"

"In *any* circumstances."

"There are limits."

"Let's walk the course."

It was an inspiration. Allow him to voice his concerns and he would wallow in his anguish for hours on end. Get him on a golf course and you could distract him with questions about this fairway or that cluster of trees or those bunkers. I addressed his mind to our shared passion for the game of golf. Reminded why we had come to the island in the first place, he began to sound some positive notes at last.

"You were right about the lake, Alan," he conceded.

"I'm always right."

"It now comes into play on three holes instead of two. I've moved the tee on the tenth and changed the line of attack on the green. The water is now just waiting for that hooked tee shot." A quiet smile changed the Amazon delta into something approximating a human face. "They're going to need a full-time diver to get all the balls out of that lake."

"What about the sixteenth?"

"It'll meet all your specifications."

"That's the hole that really interests me."

"There's not a lot to see as yet."

"Except a dream."

Of all the holes that had exercised our mind, the six teenth was my favorite because it was virtually a carbon copy of its equivalent at Carnoustie—known to its friends as Barry Burn—a 235-yard par three that calls for a long shot of unerring straightness. Like the green in Scotland, ours would be set on a plateau beyond a narrow gap between two bunkers. It would examine the skills of every golfer in the closing stages of a round and it was a personal act of homage to the Scottish golf course that is tattooed indelibly on my mind and the name of which is emblazoned across the front of my motor home.

The course was at the rear of the hotel. We stepped over the ropes that guarded it and began our tour of inspection. It was well over eighteen months since we'd been given the commission and our plans had long since moved off the drafting-board. Work had been proceeding steadily. The growl of bulldozers and the hum of rotary ploughs could be heard in the distance. Fairways were being created. Mounds and slopes were being added. Bunkers were being cut in strategic positions and filled with sand. Thousands of new trees and shrubs had already been planted. Grass seed had been sown, turf had been laid. Millions of dollars were turning our common vision into an eighteen-hole reality. It was both uplifting and terrifying. Sheer pleasure competed with immense responsibility.

Peter's faith in the project was revived. As we strolled along what would be the first fairway, he put his woes aside and heaved a sigh of satisfaction.

"We were so lucky, Alan."

"I know."

"The last course I designed was built completely from scratch," he recalled. "They gave me a hideous wilderness and expected another St. Andrews by the end of the year. It took us that long to drain the land properly." He looked around. "We had a head start here. One of the hotels they demolished already had a nine-hole course so we were able to incorporate and extend that."

"We made some pretty radical changes to it," I noted. "Nobody who played it in the past would recognize it now. What used to be the first hole is now the sixth on the Blue Dolphin course. But I agree, Peter. It was a huge advantage to have a base from which to work."

"There's another huge advantage."

"Having me as your partner, you mean?"

"No," he said with a grin. "Operating in such a friendly climate."

"It makes all the difference."

"Every time we've been here, the weather has been beautiful."

The Blue Dolphin was the brainchild of an American consortium that owned an international chain of luxury hotels. Having bought the adjoining properties of the Neptune Colony Club and the South View Hotel, they leveled both to the ground and raised the Blue Dolphin in their place. A major attraction of South View had been its nine-hole golf course. The Neptune Colony Club, by contrast, had large stables that brought in a steady flow of horse-lovers who could ride in the extensive parkland that surrounded the place. Their needs were not even considered by the new owners. With the two properties, they acquired a combined acreage that could support a 5000-yard eighteen-hole golf course, and everything was subordinated to that end. The Neptune Colony Club and its horses were wiped from the face of the earth and the associated talents of Alan Saxon and Peter Fullard moved in.

The Blue Dolphin Golf Course was born. It would never rival the majesty of Mid-Ocean or the undulating beauty of Port Royal, the two premier courses on the island, but it would be the only course in Paget Parish and it would enhance the appeal of the hotel enormously. Holiday hackers and seasoned golfers alike would enjoy playing on the course. The fun factor was important, but there were no easy holes. I was touched by the thought that, when players came to grief on the sixteenth, my name would be mentioned somewhere in the torrent of expletives.

"It looks such a mess at this stage," said Peter.

"It's coming. I feel it."

"As long as there are no more setbacks."

"There won't be. I'm here now."

"I'm glad about that. So is Denise."

"The pair of you can sleep soundly for once."

"I feel better already, Alan."

"It's the effect I have on people," I boasted.

He chuckled. "I hope that it lasts."

An hour in Peter's company restored his confidence and lifted his spirits. Though I would've preferred to take a shower before adjourning to the bar for a long, cool drink, I felt that it was time well spent. I'd got my partner temporarily off my back. When he returned to his wife, I feared, Denise would lower his spirits once again, but there was nothing I could do about that. I'd brought a measure of relief to his febrile mind. The other bonus was that I got to see something of our golf course and that put a spring in my own step. While a rejuvenated Peter Fullard went off in search of his wife, I headed for the Flamingo Bar. I could almost taste that first piña colada.

Before I could even order it, however, I was ambushed. A menacing figure came out of nowhere to block my path. Mo snatched the cigarette from his mouth and hurled it to the ground before confronting me. Hands on hips, he gave me a challenging stare.

"Whyat?" he snarled.

"Could you try that again in English?" I requested.

"Why you do that?"

"Do what?"

"You know, Mr. Saxon."

"I'm sorry, Mo. But I don't."

"What did me ever do to you?"

"Nothing," I replied with a shrug. "Except drive me from the airport."

"Got you here in one piece, didn't me?"

"Yes."

"So why you complain?"

I finally understood what he was on about. Jessica's phone call to the manager had obviously had consequences. While she was frolicking in the sea, I was left to face the anger of a hotel driver who had been severely disciplined. If his manner was anything to go by, he might even have been sacked. He confirmed my diagnosis.

"Me lose my job 'cos of you, Mr. Saxon," he asserted.

"That's not quite true, Mo."

"Yes, it is. My boss say you complain about me."

"But I didn't, I promise you."

"Then who did?"

"It was Jessica," I admitted. "My daughter's friend."

The information only served to increase his ire. "Why didn't you stop the bitch? She got no right to do something like that. Not fair. Me only doing my job and now it's been taken away."

"I'm sure that she didn't mean that to happen."

"You sure you didn't put her up to it?" he said, squaring up to me.

"Quite sure," I replied, meeting his gaze.

"All I did was talk about lectronics."

"Yes, but your manner was too aggressive."

"What you mean?" he demanded.

"Only this, Mo," I said, raising my palms to calm him down. "You may be an expert at electronics but you'd never win a prize at charm school."

"Fuck you!"

"My point, exactly."

I thought that he was going to strike me and got ready to parry the blow, but it never came. After breathing heavily through his nose, he controlled himself and changed his tack slightly. Closing one eye, he fixed me with the other.

"Sort it out, Mr. Saxon," he said.

"In what way?"

"Speak to my boss. Tell him the truth. Get me taken on again."

"But I can't do that."

"Why not?"

"Because I have no right to interfere in the matters regarding hotel personnel."

"Then why you get me sacked?"

"I didn't, Mo. That was Jessica's doing."

"Then get *her* to talk to the boss."

"Keep her out of it," I advised. "She's already said far too much on the issue."

"Me want an apology from that little cow."

"I'll thank you not to call her names."

"You should hear what me *like* to call her."

"As long as I don't have to listen," I warned, losing my patience with him. "If I have any more of your obnoxious behavior, I'll complain to the management myself, then you won't even be allowed on hotel premises."

Mo looked hurt. "You're not going to help me, Mr. Saxon?"

"I'm in no position to do so."

"Yes, you are. You could get my job back."

"Switch to electronics," I urged. "You'll find that a lot more rewarding."

"Me want to be a driver," he whined.

"Then you need to do something about your temperament."

"Fuck you!"

"And I'd rule out the Diplomatic Service, if I were you."

"Fuck you, Mr. Alan Fucking Saxon. Alright," he said, nodding vigorously. "Me ask you nice. Me gave you a chance to help and you say piss off. Alright, alright, if that's way you want it, that's the way you get it. Just wait. That goes for *her* as well," he added. "That little bitch with the big mouth. Tell her from me. Me be back, Mr. Saxon. You watch. Me make you wish you never came anywhere near Bermuda."

"Don't you dare threaten me," I retorted, "or there'll be big trouble."

He gave a cruel laugh. "Big trouble? Oh, yes. There'll be big trouble, alright. That's one thing you get lots of here, Mr. Saxon. Big, big trouble. You and that Jessica bitch. I teach you both."

Still laughing harshly, he turned on his heel and ambled slowly away.

Chapter Three

Dinner that evening was a battle against jet lag. The meal was delicious, the conversation bright and the mood friendly, but a long day was slowly sapping my strength. Lynette and Jessica, on the other hand, were as alert as ever and showed no sign of fatigue. High on adrenalin, they made me feel ancient. There were seven of us around the table in the Blue Dolphin restaurant. Calvin Reed and his wife, Melinda, were our gracious hosts. Melinda Reed was one of those faultless American beauties you see on the covers of glossy fashion magazines, a study in cosmetic perfection that is quite dazzling for the first few minutes but which then becomes curiously irrelevant. She had brushed her dark brown hair severely back and held it in place with a multi-colored bow. Considering how tantalizingly little there was of it, her dress was needlessly expensive. Dignified yet vivacious, Melinda was a standard issue wife for someone like Calvin Reed and their double-act was carefully rehearsed.

The same could not be said of the other couple in the party. They made everything up as they went along. Peter and Denise Fullard used each other like emotional Zimmer frames. Every time one of them spoke, he or she would turn to the other for support and ratification. Their attitudes were so similar and their tone of voice so identical that their comments were largely interchangeable. I wondered if they'd ever been seized by a spirit of novelty just once in their lives and actually disagreed. Denise Fullard was a plump, pale-faced woman of middle years with horn-rimmed eyeglasses providing a focal point for her mobile features. Her taste in clothes was woeful. Melinda Reed's cool elegance made Denise's baggy floral dress look ridiculously dowdy. The girls' colorful attire all but obliterated her.

To their credit, the Fullards manage to snap out of Despair Mode for once. Denise maintained a toothy grin and, on his subject, Peter was lively and entertaining. It was Lynette who gave him his opportunity. Picking up on a chance remark, she sought to clarify something.

"You brought Bermuda grass to Bermuda?" she asked.

"That's right," said Peter.

"Isn't that rather like carrying coals to Newcastle?"

"No, Lynette. What I brought was a hybrid strain that was grown in my own nursery. I was very keen to sow some of it here, you see. Bermuda grass is ideal for golf courses if the climatic conditions are favorable. Its proper name is *cynodon dactylon*," he explained. "It's tough, crisp and hardy. Alan's the best person to tell us why golfers are so fond of Bermuda grass."

"It's firm to the tread and always gives a good lie," I said.

"It has wiry, creeping rootstocks," continued Peter, "that make it ideal for lawns, pasturage and binding sand dunes. On a golf course, it needs to be cut judiciously. Allow it to grow too high and you'll see why it's sometimes called wire grass."

"Yes," I agreed. "I once played on a course in Oklahoma where the rough was ankle high. It was like walking through steel wool."

My colleague took over again. "Bermuda grass doesn't have to be like that. There are dwarf and hybrid strains that are less wiry. Grasses have always fascinated me," he went on with a beatific smile. "I remember talking to one of the greenkeepers at Royal Calcutta. He told me they sowed dhoob grass on the course at first, then experimented with hariali, Bermuda, Australian couch and creeping dog's tooth."

Lynette giggled. "Creeping what?"

"Dog's tooth."

"What does it do—bite you?"

"Not exactly, Lynette."

I would not have believed that anyone could hold six people entranced with a description of various grasses but Peter Fullard did. Proud of her husband's expertise, Denise beamed happily throughout but even Calvin and Melinda Reed were genuinely interested. Jessica Hadlow was so enthralled that she stopped speaking for all of ten minutes. After rhapsodizing about the virtues of Pencross bent on the putting surface, Peter glanced around apologetically.

"Oh, I'm sorry. I don't want to bore you all."

"You were wonderful!" cooed Denise.

"Yes," said Melinda, "I had no idea there were so many different grasses."

"You certainly know your stuff, Peter," noted Reed admiringly. "In a couple of years' time, thanks to you, the Blue Dolphin will have some of the finest greens and fairways on the island."

"As long as they don't steal any more of my seed," observed Peter.

Jessica was about to make a comment when she caught sight of a young man at the door of the restaurant. He waved to her. Responding with a nod, she gave Lynette a nudge then rose from her seat. Jessica smiled at our hosts.

"Thank you so much," she said effusively. "You've given us the most marvelous welcome to Bermuda. It's been an absolute treat. And it was lovely to meet *you* as well," she added, turning to Peter and Denise. "I hope we see lots more of each other. But you'll have to excuse us, I'm afraid. We promised to have a drink with friends."

"Friends?" I echoed.

"Yes, Daddy," said Lynette, getting up. "We met them on the beach."

"Good night," said Jessica, raising a hand.

Lynette smiled at the Reeds. "Thank you again. Goodbye."

We waved them off as they went to join their new friends. Peter and Denise also decided it was time to leave. After thanking our hosts, they stood up in unison. Denise put a grateful hand on my shoulder.

"I'm so glad you've come at last, Alan," she said. "Peter's been worried to death."

"Unnecessarily," I suggested.

"Now that you're here, everything is fine."

"You can rely on it, Denise."

"We can have a decent night's sleep at last."

"Thanks, Alan," said Peter. "I feel as if you've waved a magic wand."

I grinned wearily. "I always wanted to play the Good Fairy."

They went off hand in hand, weaving their way swiftly between the tables as if desperate to get to bed. I watched them go. Calvin Reed waited until they were out of earshot before he spoke.

"I had no idea that Peter got upset so easily," he said.

"He's always been a bit nervous."

"I'm glad that you've arrived to steady the ship."

"Does it need steadying?"

"Not really, Alan," he said smoothly. "We've had a few minor problems on the course but nothing to get anxious about. Peter Fullard just over-reacted. To calm him down, we've increased security on the site and we're installing electronic surveillance soon. That should put his mind at rest."

"Peter's mind is like the sea," I said fondly. "It ebbs and flows. I'm afraid that it doesn't take much to create waves. The same goes for his wife."

Melinda nodded. "Denise is a nice lady. She and Peter are well suited. And it was great to meet your daughter, Alan. She's a charming girl."

"Delightful," said Reed. "What does Lynette aim to do?"

"You mean, here in Bermuda?" I asked.

"No. When she finishes at Oxford. She's obviously very bright."

"Oh, she is. She's been tipped to get a good degree. But the truth is that I'm not sure what her career plans are, Mr. Reed. She hasn't decided yet. Lynette's talked about various things in the past but she wants to keep her options open. Unlike her friend," I said. "Jessica knows exactly what she wants to do."

"I'm sure she does."

"Jessica intends to act."

"I'd have thought she has all the qualifications."

"She has such tremendous confidence," said Melinda. "Jessica is the kind of girl who's at home wherever she goes. I wish I could be like that."

"You *are*, honey," said Reed, fondling her arm.

"No, I'm not, Cal. Out of my own environment, I'm lost."

"Don't listen to her, Alan," he said. "Melinda is the most resourceful woman I've ever met. She can handle any situation."

His wife was frank. "I reckon I'd meet my match in Jessica Hadlow."

"So would I, Melinda," I confessed.

"That girl is so much like her father," said Reed.

"You *know* him?"

"Let's just say that I bumped into him once and it wasn't an entirely pleasant experience. I was general manager of a hotel in Barbados when he stayed there," he recalled. "I'd been warned about Bernard Hadlow. He likes to throw his weight around and, unfortunately, there's rather a lot of it to throw. As soon as he checked in, we had the first round of pointless complaints and it went on from there."

"He was playing power games, Cal," said Melinda.

"Well, he can play them somewhere else. I was so relieved when he and his wife checked out. That's why I didn't mention anything to Jessica," he admitted. "I prefer to forget my association with Bernard Hadlow."

"In what way is she like her father?" I wondered.

"It's that I-want-it-now attitude. Call it a forceful personality."

"Jessica's also pretty good at making pointless complaints. Just like her Dad, it seems. I understand she talked to you about our drive from the airport."

Reed rolled his eyes. "If only she had, Alan! But, in circumstances like that, members of the Hadlow family don't talk. They bully, badger and insist. In fairness, Jessica does it in a nicer way than her father but she has the same iron will."

"What was the complaint about?" asked Melinda.

"One of our drivers, honey."

"His name was Mo," I said, remembering my earlier confrontation with him. "He wasn't the most amiable of chauffeurs but I didn't think he was too unbearable. I had the feeling he was a man with personal problems. He is *now*," I pointed out, "that's for certain. Jessica had the man dismissed."

"Is that true, Cal?" she said. "Did you sack the guy?"

"Of course not," he replied with a hint of irritation. "It was far too trivial a matter for me to handle. I passed it on to Frank."

"Frank?" I repeated.

"Frank Colouris. My new deputy manager. You haven't met him yet, Alan, have you?" I shook my head. "You'll like Frank Colouris. He's a pro. He gets things done."

I fell asleep the moment that my head touched the pillow but my biological clock refused to adjust itself to the new time zone. When I came fully awake, I was distressed to see that it was still only four-thirty in the morning. My first thoughts were about Lynette. Was she safely tucked up in her bed? What time did she get there and was she its only occupant? I was hardly in a position to check, even though the connecting door between the two suites was unlocked. There was an insurmountable barrier—fear of entering a bedroom that contained Jessica Hadlow. She had the look of someone who always sleeps naked and I had no wish to get anywhere near a nude Jessica. Seductive enough in her clothes, she'd be lethal out of them.

Unable to get off again, I switched on the light and read for a bit from the Gideon Bible, a volume that's helped me on more than one occasion in a lonely hotel room. It finally did the trick and I dozed off with the Gospel of St. Luke still open across my lap. Awake again at seven, I gave up all hope of further sleep and took a shower instead. By the time I'd shaved, dressed and gone downstairs, the whole hotel was stirring. I was surprised to see how many people were having an early breakfast. Luckily, Peter and Denise Fullard were not among them. At the start of the day, I need sustenance before I can face their joint melancholy. I chose a quiet table in a corner and kept my head down. A glass of freshly squeezed orange juice revived me and two soft-boiled eggs made me feel almost chirpy, but it was the arrival of my daughter that really perked me up. In white shorts and T-shirt, she came bounding across to me.

"Good morning, Daddy!" she said, giving me a kiss. "Can I join you?"

"Of course, darling."

"Did you sleep?"

"Yes, but not long enough."

"Nor me," she said, sitting beside me. "I woke at six and that was that."

"What about Jessica?"

"Oh, she's still fast asleep. She got to bed much later than I did."

"Why?"

"Because she went for a walk with Rick and Conrad," she said, sipping the orange juice that had just been poured for her by the waitress. "They wanted me to go with them but jet lag finally caught up with me. I've no idea what time Jessica came into the room. I was fast asleep."

"Did you check to see that she was on her own?"

"Daddy!"

"Well, she is rather gregarious."

"She likes to enjoy herself, that's all. Besides, we've only just met Rick and Conrad. Even Jessica doesn't work that fast."

"Who are these friends?"

"They're Canadians. Great fun."

"What are they doing in Bermuda?"

"Having a good time," she said, glancing through the menu. "Rick has just graduated from Toronto. He's having a year off to see something of the world before he starts work. Conrad decided to tag along."

"They can't be short of money if they can afford to stay here."

"We didn't discuss their financial situation. The four of us just hit it off." When she saw the concern in my eyes, she laughed. "Relax, Daddy. I'm not a child. I'm old enough to look after myself. So is Jessica."

"I'm sure about that."

"In any case, Rick and Conrad are only here for a few days. They'll be off to the Bahamas soon. I do envy their sense of freedom." The waitress returned and Lynette gave her order before turning back to me. "By the way, I never got round to telling you that Mummy sent her love."

"Did she?" I said guardedly.

"Yes. She thought it was so considerate of you to ask her if I could come."

"Apparently, you'd already told her about the idea."

"I was too excited to keep it to myself and you know how good Mummy is at worming things out of you."

"Oh, yes! She could have taught the Inquisition a few tricks." Lynette giggled and drank some more orange juice. I tasted my coffee then tried to sound casual. "Is your mother seeing anyone at the moment?"

"Dozens of them. She has her toy boys on a rota system."

"Lynette!"

"The answer is no, Daddy," she said. "As far as I can judge, anyway. And it's not the kind of thing Mummy talks about. After that scare she had with Dreary David all those years ago, she's much more careful. Mummy had a lucky escape there."

"So did he!" I said under my breath.

It was always faintly embarrassing, trying to find out information about Rosemary from our daughter, but she's my only reliable source. On the few occasions when we speak, my ex-wife is deliberately vague about her private life though she feels impelled to ransack mine over the telephone. ("Are you still with that dental nurse, Alan, or has that sordid little affair finally run its course?" One of her kinder inquiries.) I'd be happy if I never saw or spoke to Rosemary ever again yet somehow, whenever I'm with Lynette, in defiance of a hundred warning bells, I find myself asking about her mother. I daresay that a psychiatrist would have word for the syndrome.

"So," I resumed, "what have you got lined up for today?"

"Jessica wants us to hire motor scooters and tour the island."

"Be careful. Those things can be dangerous."

"I'll be fine."

"Calvin Reed was asking what you intended to do when you graduate."

"Collapse in a heap, probably."

"You must have some plans."

"I do, Daddy. Thanks to Jessica."

My stomach lurched. "You're not going to follow her into the acting profession?"

"No, I haven't got the temperament. Or the talent."

"Then how does Jessica come into it?"

"She's been a tremendous help," said Lynette. "She's so focussed. What I'd really like to do is to get into publishing, you see, but so do lots of other people in my position. There are far too many of us, chasing too few jobs. I've written over a dozen letters but I haven't had one positive reply. I was beginning to lose heart so I confided in Jessica. She solved the problem at once."

"Did she? How?"

"Jessica spoke to her father. It turns out that he's got friends in some of the big publishing houses. In fact, he has contacts everywhere. Mr. Hadlow said he'd pull a few strings for me."

I was worried. "And you accepted his offer?"

"Of course."

"Was that altogether wise, Lynette?"

"What do you mean?"

"Well, nobody is as keen as I am to see you get a head start in your career but I'm not sure I like the idea of relying on Mr. Hadlow. You'd be beholden to him, Lynette."

"So?"

"What happens if you and Jessica fall out?"

"That could never happen, Daddy."

"Are you sure?"

"We'll always be friends."

"Not if she disappears off to Hollywood to be the next Catherine Zeta-Jones."

"Jessica and I will keep in touch somehow."

"It's wrong to let her make your decisions for you."

"That's not how it is. I want to go into publishing. Jessica is simply helping."

"Wouldn't you rather get a job on merit?"

"It will be on merit," she insisted. "Nobody will take me on unless they can see my potential. I'm not being smuggled in by the back door, Daddy. I'll be a graduate, remember. Even today, an Oxford degree still counts for something. At long last, I'll actually be *employed.* You ought to be pleased."

"Oh, I will be!" I said with feeling.

It would bring to a merciful end the constant drain on my erratic income. When Lynette left Benenden, I felt as if a rock had been lifted from my shoulders, but the crippling school fees were quickly replaced with exorbitant tuition fees. Since they only have three eight-week terms at Oxford, I'd foolishly assumed that my financial commitments would ease, but that was an illusion. The bills were worse than ever. If it helped to set my daughter up for the career of her choice, I wouldn't begrudge one penny of the money that I spent on her education, but the latest development was like a slap in the face. I struggled for over a decade to give her the best possible start in life and along comes Bernard Hadlow to pull the appropriate strings and get her into publishing. It didn't seem right somehow. I was about to explain why to Lynette when her friend came tripping across the room with that unassailable buoyancy.

"Good morning!" said Jessica with a grin. "I don't know about you two but I feel fantastic this morning. Something tells me we're going to have the most *amazing* day…"

Her vitality was almost frightening. I reached for my coffee.

Breakfast with Jennifer Hadlow was followed by a long session with Peter Fullard. It was like going from the blistering heat of the Sahara into the icy chill of the Antarctic. Instead of being burned to a frazzle by a sizzling monologue about the joys of her moonlit walk with Rick and Conrad, I began to shiver. Peter had no warmth at all in his voice. A night in his wife's capacious arms had left my partner wallowing once more in the Slough of Despond. I tried to pull him out.

"You look wonderful this morning," I said, clapping him on the back.

"I don't feel wonderful, Alan."

"Anyone else in your position would. Count your blessings, man. You've got a plum assignment to design a golf course in the Garden of Eden. As a bonus, you've got your lovely wife to play Eve to your Adam. What more do you want?"

"Peace of mind."

"I'd hoped that *I* was providing that."

"Only up to a point," he said. "When we went to bed last night, Denise and I began to have a few doubts. We talked things over for hours. The truth is that we still feel that we're victims of a conspiracy."

"You are, Peter, but it's of your own making."

"I don't follow."

"You and Denise are the conspirators."

It took me ten minutes to banish the worst of his fears and another twenty to address his mind to the project in hand. We were in my suite, seated at the table with the plans for the Blue Dolphin Golf Course set out on front of us. Though Peter had done the actual designs, I had, in effect, guided his hand while it held the pencil. The results were very much a team effort and he was the first to acknowledge that. We both knew that a good course must have the capacity to test golfers of all abilities and neither of us made the mistake of treating the holiday golfer as a lower order of creation, a dreadful hacker who needs cosseting with benign fairways, generous greens and mild rough. Many of the people who'd check into the Blue Dolphin would be highly competent golfers, men and women who played regularly throughout the year and who expected a challenge when they stepped on to a tee.

Peter Fullard and I had given them a course that would examine the very best of them. It would require long, accurate tee shots, skilful iron play, a good short game and precise putting. Water hazards existed on three holes, bunkers and heavy rough dotted all eighteen. Trees had been planted to create blind shots or to vary the angle of approach on a green, and the greens themselves were relatively small so that the art of chipping was encouraged. Peter believed in strategic design rather than penal. Instead of dangerous traps, he liked to set a golfer problems. Not everyone who played at the Blue Dolphin, of course, would be an experienced amateur golfer, so we provided forward tees for beginners and a first hole with a fairway so wide that it was almost impossible to go astray with a tee shot. At the start of a round at least, the novice would be spared instant humiliation. We tried to offer a little consolation to even the worst hackers

Having arrived in Bermuda before I did, Peter had been able to inspect progress and mark it on the plans. He'd been characteristically meticulous. Detailed comments on every hole had been inked neatly in. Though we had reshaped it substantially, the bulk of the nine-hole golf course that we had incorporated was more or less playable. It was the new holes that had yet to evolve properly. During our walk the previous day, I'd been too preoccupied with cheering up my partner to give the course more than a cursory glance. It was only when I saw Peter's progress report that I realized how much had been done since my last visit. While it inspired me, it only served to depress my colleague.

"I hoped we'd have got further than this by now," he sighed.

"The contractors have been working flat out, Peter."

"Until the sabotage began."

"It's not sabotage."

"Then what is it?"

"Why don't we go and find out?" I suggested.

Armed with his plans, we went out to walk the course in its entirety and make a thorough inspection. The shift of locale once again transformed Peter's mood. As soon as we stepped on to the first tee, his dejection slowly began to fade. One more excellent golf course would soon be added to Peter's Fullard's CV. I was honored to have my name coupled with his on the project, conscious that it might be the start of a whole new career for me. The strange thing was that Peter was such an indifferent golfer. Though he practiced continuously, he never seemed to lower his handicap. Somehow he lacked coordination. His fierce love of the game had therefore been channeled into course architecture. Peter didn't merely design a hole, he played it endlessly in his mind until he felt that he had mastered its subtleties.

We were on the third fairway when I remembered a name that I had heard.

"Have you met Frank Colouris yet?" I asked.

"Yes, Alan. He's the deputy manager."

"Calvin Reed seemed to have great faith in him."

"He's been very kind to us, I know that," said Peter. "Mr. Colouris went out of his way to help. He's a nice man, youngish, dedicated, not quite as suave as Calvin Reed, if you know what I mean."

"That's a relief. I'd hate to be dealing with two Calvins."

"It's his wife who unsettles us."

"Melinda?"

"She always makes us feel so shabby."

"Mrs. Reed dresses to impress, that's all. It's part of her stock-in-trade."

"Denise can't believe that she keeps her waist as slim as that."

"Perhaps her husband doesn't feed her," I joked, "but tell me a bit more about Frank Colouris. I got the feeling that he was Calvin's hatchet man."

"Oh, no, Alan. He's far too polite for that."

"Polite hatchet men are the worst. They throw you completely off guard."

"I think you've got the wrong idea about Mr. Colouris."

"We'll see."

"Why did you bring up his name?"

"Because he was the person who kicked Mo out of his job."

"Mo?"

"Our chauffeur from the airport," I said. "He had an unfortunate manner. It upset Jessica so much that she reported him to Calvin. The problem was handed over to Frank Colouris who promptly gave Mo his marching orders. I'd like to know exactly what the deputy manager said to him."

"Why?"

"Because Mo seemed to think that I was the one who'd complained about him."

"Instead of which, it was Lynette's friend."

"Yes."

"I'm not surprised, Alan," he said seriously. "She looks the type. I don't think I'd ever be brave enough to take Jessica Hadlow on holiday. That girl likes to be in charge."

"That's the least of her virtues," I said with gentle sarcasm.

It was a productive morning. Though there was still much to do, I was thrilled by the advances that had already been made. The major setbacks had occurred on four of the holes and the site foreman was pleased that we were both there to discuss them. After an hour with him, we broke off for lunch, promising to return for a longer meeting that afternoon. Peter was fired with enthusiasm once again. On the walk back, he never even mentioned the vandalism and the thefts that had occurred. Fearing that his new optimism would hit the rocks once he and his wife got together again, I declined his invitation to lunch with them. Besides, Lynette had agreed to have lunch alone with me so that we could have a proper conversation at last. That had priority over everything.

"I'm sorry, Daddy. Change of plan."

"Oh?"

"Rick and Conrad have hired a boat. We're going to have lunch onboard."

"But we had an arrangement," I protested.

"I know but I could hardly refuse."

"These two Canadians rate higher than a father, do they?"

"Of course not," she said, squeezing my arm. "But they're leaving Bermuda soon. We'll probably never see them again. You and I can have lunch together any day this week."

"Unless I'm displaced by the next Rick and Conrad."

"What do you mean?"

"Well, Jessica only has to crook her finger to attract men," I said bitterly. "She probably has the next pairing already on the substitutes' bench. What happens if *they* decide to hire a boat and whisk you off for lunch?"

"I thought you wanted me to have fun, Daddy."

"I do, Lynette. But I did promise your mother that I'd spent some quality time with you. Actually," I admitted, "it was a promise to myself. I don't intend to spend the entire week trudging around the Blue Dolphin Golf Course. I want to be with you, darling. Why don't we make a date for dinner this evening?"

She gave an apologetic shrug. "Rick and Conrad wanted to take us out tonight. Jessica thinks we should go dancing somewhere. She knows this place that has a great band. You don't mind, do you?"

"No, Lynette," I said, hiding my disappointment behind a smile. "You go off and enjoy yourself. As long as you can fit your long-suffering father into your schedule at some point. Is it a deal?"

"Yes," she said, giving me a kiss. "Of course, it is. See you later, Daddy."

And she went racing off like a greyhound just let off the leash. I watched her run toward the beach. It was churlish to complain. In ten days' time, Lynette would be attending her lectures in Oxford as she started her final year at the university. Bermuda was the calm before the storm. She was entitled to make the most of it while she could. As for Jessica, she may not have endeared herself to me but my daughter clearly loved being with her and that would be an education in itself. Lynette should be allowed to learn the ways of the world in the way that she chose.

I was about to adjourn to my room when I heard a voice at my elbow.

"Mr. Saxon?"

I turned to face him. "Yes."

"I just wanted to introduce myself," he said with a smile. "My name is Frank Colouris. I'm the deputy manager here. Mr. Reed may have mentioned me."

"Yes, he did," I said, shaking the proffered hand. "Pleased to meet you, Mr. Colouris. Actually, I'm glad we've bumped into each other. I wanted a word about that driver you dismissed yesterday—Mo."

"I'm very sorry that he was so rude to you, Mr. Saxon."

"Mo had poor social skills, that's all. It wasn't really a hanging offence."

"Yours wasn't the only complaint, I fear."

"But I didn't complain."

"So I understand. A young lady did so on your behalf."

"Without my permission."

"Be that as it may, Mr. Saxon, I'm afraid that we had to let that particular driver go. He'd been warned twice in the past. It was a case of three strikes and out."

Peter Fullard was right about the man. Frank Colouris was effortlessly polite. The deputy manager was a stocky man of middle height with a swarthy complexion. He was in his early thirties at most but the gleaming bald head made him look much older. Smartly dressed in a blue mohair suit, he had none of Calvin Reed's urbanity. His face was pleasantly ugly, his smile disarming. There was a solidity about Colouris, a down-to-earth quality that I liked immediately.

His Brooklyn accent and open manner were reassuring. I had the feeling that he'd give me the straight answers that Reed always twisted slightly out of shape.

"I gather that you've had a few problems on the course," I said.

"One or two, Mr. Saxon."

"My partner seems to think there's a plot against us."

"Oh, I wouldn't go that far," he replied. "I'm not even sure that the incidents are connected. Mr. Fullard is too pessimistic. It's almost as if he *wants* to believe the worst."

"What upset him was the theft of that gang-mower."

"It upset us, too, Mr. Saxon. When such a valuable piece of equipment vanishes from our property, it's bad news. That's why we stepped up security." He gave me a confiding grin. "Much to the dismay of some of our guests."

"Dismay?"

"Yes, sir. Strictly speaking, the golf course is out of bounds, but that didn't deter amorous couples from slipping under the ropes for midnight trysts. The favorite spots were around the lake. I guess it looks real romantic with the moon shining on the water. Anyway," he went on, "the first time one of our security men patrolled that area with his dog, he reckons the best part of a dozen naked couples suddenly leapt up and fled into the trees. Since then, we've had far less trespass."

"Mr. Reed said that you were going to install security cameras."

"That's right. They'll be in position by the end of the month."

"That'll frighten away the lovers for good."

"I doubt it," said Colouris with a twinkle in his eye. "Some people have an exhibitionist streak. If they know they're being filmed, they'll turn it into a real production number. The guy in charge of the monitors is going to see some pretty lively stuff on some of those TV screens. Anyway," he continued, "I don't want to hold you up. I just wanted to say hello. If there's anything you need, just holler. I'm usually easier to get hold of than Mr. Reed."

"Thanks. I'll bear that in mind."

"Goodbye, sir."

"Cheers."

Colouris strode off and left me with the feeling that I could trust him. If there was an emergency of any sort, I would certainly turn to him first. Ever since we had met, Calvin Reed had been extremely helpful, yet there somehow remained an invisible barrier between us. Frank Colouris was different. I sensed that he was on our side.

After a dip in the hotel pool, I got dressed and had a quick snack in the Calypso Bar. When I met up with Peter Fullard again that afternoon, I expected him to have been dragged back into Stygian gloom after lunch with his wife, but he was unusually upbeat. In the course of his meal, he'd managed to think of a way to solve some of the problems that had cropped up on specific holes. They were ingenious compromises.

"Congratulations!" I said. "I think you've hit on the answers, Peter."

"Let's hope the contractors agree."

"They have to. We're the pipers so we call the tune."

"I should have anticipated some of these headaches," he confessed. "Designing courses in Europe has spoiled me, Alan. I can create mounds, hollows and ridges at will, digging out subsoil to my heart's content. It's not so easy here. Bermuda is essentially solid rock. There's a limit to how far you can go down before you hit limestone."

We strolled off to resume our meeting with the site foreman. On our way, we passed the lake that would swallow up any wayward shots on three separate holes. I couldn't resist teasing Peter.

"Have you brought Denise out here yet?"

"No, why should I?"

"According to Frank Colouris—I met him earlier, by the way—this is the designated spot for nocturnal lovers. I thought you might have brought your wife out here for a moment of madness in the moonlight."

Peter was appalled. "This is a golf course, Alan!"

"It wouldn't be the first one to be used for assignations."

"That's a form of sacrilege to me," he said. "We've designed a course that will be a joy to play for the enthusiast. That's its exclusive function. I didn't go to all the trouble in order to further the sex lives of promiscuous holiday makers."

"We don't want to be spoilsports."

"They've got hotel beds for that kind of thing."

"Some prefer doing it *al fresco*."

"Not on my golf course," he affirmed. "Sorry, Alan—*our* golf course."

I regretted raising the topic, even in fun. Peter has many virtues but a sense of humor is not one of them. I manoeuvered him back to a discussion of the problems we'd encountered on the course. He calmed down immediately. When we met up with him again, the site foreman was very impressed with the adjustments Peter had made in the design of the holes in question. They involved a sacrifice of some of the features we'd been eager to include, but my partner had found ample means of compensation. All three of us talked at length about how the changes could best be made. Apart from anything else, we would be shaving valuable time off the work on the designated holes and the contractors were as pleased about that as we were. Our afternoon session was infinitely satisfying and we rounded it off by watching the men carve a wondrous new golf hole out of what had once been overgrown parkland. On the long walk back, Peter was as close to elation as I'd ever seen him. He was at last convinced that the Blue Dolphin Golf Course would actually be built.

We arranged to meet for dinner then went off to our respective rooms. There was no sign of Lynette or Jessica in the adjoining suite. They were obviously still enjoying their mixed foursome elsewhere. Deciding that there was safety in numbers, I tried to fight off my anxiety and took a nap instead. I was still suffering the effects of jet lag and slept soundly for a couple of hours. When I awoke, it was almost time to dress for dinner. Hoping for at least a glimpse of the girls and of the two young Canadians who were monopolizing them, I kept my eyes peeled. I scoured the Calypso Bar, the pool and the patio in vain. Evidently, they had already left. I had to settle for the ambiguous pleasure of dinner with the Fullards. A delightful surprise awaited me.

"I'd like to introduce you to a friend of mine, Alan," said Denise, beaming at me. "This is Nancy Wykoff. She's so keen to meet you."

"I'm thrilled to make your acquaintance, Mr. Saxon," said the newcomer.

"How do you do?" I replied, shaking her hand.

The arm that was extended towards me was long, slender and beautifully tanned. There was an expensive gold bangle around the wrist. As we sat down at the table, I glanced at her other hand but saw no wedding ring.

"Divorced," she explained, reading my mind. "For the second time."

"Goodness!" exclaimed Denise.

"Oh, that's par for the course where I come from, Denise. I don't know anyone in my circle who hasn't split up with a husband at least twice. One friend of mine has just completed her fifth divorce."

Nancy Wykoff clearly enjoyed scandalizing the Fullards. She was a tall, slim, elegant woman with close-cropped fair hair. Her face was long and interesting rather than handsome but she knew how to make the most of her charms. Her earrings matched the color both of her blue silk dress and of her large, inquisitive eyes. Around her neck was a pearl necklace that made Denise's jewelry look dull and artificial. It was difficult to put an age on Nancy Wykoff. At most, she was in her early forties and might well be a lot younger. I liked her easy sophistication and her soft Texan drawl. What puzzled me was how she had befriended Denise Fullard. They were hardly sisters under the skin. Once again, she seemed to read my thoughts.

"I'm a golf fanatic," she explained. "My first husband and I used to play three times a week at least. Whenever we came to Bermuda, we used to stay at the Belmont. Do you know their course, Mr. Saxon?"

"Yes, I've played it a number of times."

"I love its undulations. The eleventh hole is the tricky one."

"And the seventeenth," I said. "A lot of golfers come to grief there."

"Nancy is a big fan of yours, Alan," said Peter.

"Yes," added his wife, "she's watched you play."

"Mostly on TV," confessed Nancy, "though we were at the Masters the year when you came within a stroke of winning. You played brilliantly. You were so close to going home with that green jacket."

"The story of my life," I said sadly. "Near misses and hair's breadth failures."

"Nobody could describe your performance at the Masters that year as a failure. For two whole days, you led the finest golfers in the world. That takes courage as well as skill." She gave me an admiring smile. "You've obviously got both."

The situation was explained. Nancy Wykoff had taken an interest in the Fullards when she learned that Peter was helping to design the new course at the Blue Dolphin. They were a means of meeting me. She had clearly kept tabs on my career and reminded me of tournaments I'd entered and shots I'd played that I'd long since forgotten. Her knowledge of the game was profound but she was no armchair pundit. She and her first husband had played on courses all over the world. Nancy had even managed a round at Augusta National, the home of the U.S. Masters.

"I soon realized why it was called Amen Corner," she said with a laugh. "I lost two balls in Rae Creek. I said 'Amen' to my round there and then."

"You're in good company," observed Peter kindly. "The bones of many golfers' high ambitions are buried between the eleventh and thirteenth holes at Augusta."

"Mine are among them," I said. "I've fallen foul of that water on more than one occasion and had to kiss my chances goodbye."

Nancy Wykoff was good fun. She was also very considerate. Mindful of the fact that Denise had never played the game, Nancy took care not to exclude her from the conversation by limiting it solely to golf, introducing subjects of general interest so that Denise could contribute her opinions. Peter, too, was careful to involve his wife. To my relief, neither of them even touched on the sensitive topic of alleged sabotage at the Blue Dolphin. Time slipped gently by. The more I got to know of Nancy Wykoff, the more I liked her. We were soon on first-name terms. I even heard myself offering to show her around our course at some time in the future. She was delighted with the offer. When the meal finally came to an end, she shook my hand in parting and held it a moment longer than was necessary. Minutes after she'd gone, my palm was still tingling and I could still smell her exquisite perfume. Nancy Wykoff had been a most welcome addition to the table. She had not only kept the Fullards amused, she had reminded me that I was, in a sense, on holiday. My new friend had also contrived a small miracle. During the three hours I was in Nancy's company, I hadn't once thought about Lynette.

I hoped I'd made as good an impression on the leggy Texan as she'd made on me. Staying in the same hotel as Nancy Wykoff could turn out to be an unexpected joy.

While the others went off to their beds, I lingered in the Calypso Bar over a meditative drink. My real reason for staying up was to be there when my daughter finally came back from her night out with the Canadians, though there was no guarantee that I'd last out long enough. If Jessica was allowed to set the pace, the girls might not return until dawn and I'd be wasting my time in staying up. It was all very well my telling myself that Lynette knew what she was doing and that I should let her get on with it. But parenting doesn't operate by the rules of common sense. I felt guilty about my lack of vigilance as a father. The simple fact was that I missed her. I was honest enough to admit that I wouldn't have wanted her around while I was dining with Nancy Wykoff, but that pleasant interval was over. Lynette now took precedence in my mind. She and Jessica had gone out dancing with two young men who were, in essence, complete strangers. The girls were taking a risk.

One thing was certain. They hadn't returned to the hotel as yet. If they had, Lynette would certainly have let me know. There was no danger of my going back to my room and hearing noises of passion from the adjoining suite. As midnight approached, more people began to drift away from the bar. I was left to brood in a quiet corner. Tiredness competed with fatherly concern. Should I go up to bed or keep my vigil? After finishing my drink, I elected to take a walk in the hotel grounds before turning in. It was a beautiful night for a stroll and my feet took me in the direction of the golf course. It crossed my mind that it would be much nicer if I had Nancy Wykoff as my companion, and I even allowed myself fleeting fantasies about a moment of lakeside abandon with her beneath the stars. When I remembered that the security firm had dogs, such seductive notions evaporated at once. Canine teeth have no place whatsoever in a romantic assignation.

What I could luxuriate in were thoughts of playing the first ever round on the Blue Dolphin Golf Course. It was a co-designer's privilege. Written into our contract was the stipulation that Alan Saxon would launch the course in the most appropriate way, and I looked forward to tackling the various obstacles that Peter and I had so cunningly set up. On paper, they posed a definite challenge. It remained to be seen how they fared in reality. When I reached the rope that guarded the first tee, I was tempted to duck under it and go on to the course itself, but I drew back. It was late and I needed my sleep. I was about to turn round when I heard the scream. It was difficult to make out from where it actually came, but I distinctly heard the fear in the woman's voice. My immediate thought was that it might be Lynette, lured into the trees by one of her new friends and resisting his advances. Whoever it was, she was patently crying for help.

I responded immediately. Jumping over the rope, I ran towards the first fairway. I was halfway along it when I heard a second scream. It seemed to come from way over to my left so I plunged off into the undergrowth. The third scream was the loudest yet, high, piercing and filled with sheer terror. It was followed by the barking of a dog. Was my daughter being savaged by one of the Alsatians? I quickened my pace but my ears played tricks on me. The barking seemed to come from a different direction and I had to veer back to the right. I blundered on, hoping that I was going the right way. Having run almost a quarter of a mile, I paused to catch my breath beside a clump of cedars. It was then that I heard another sound altogether, a slow, rhythmical, swishing noise that came from somewhere nearby. My mouth went dry. I listened more carefully and tried to identify the noise. In the gloom, it sounded distinctly sinister. Fearing that someone was in distress, I went darting into the trees.

My haste was my undoing. As soon as I reached a clearing, I was knocked off my feet by a heavy object that struck

me hard in the chest before continuing on its way. The swish
ing sound was much quieter now and less regular. Picking
myself up, I soon saw why. There above me, silhouetted
against the night sky, was the body of a man, swinging to
and fro on a last pointless journey in this world. A stout
rope had been used to hang him from a high branch, then
he had been set in motion. Leaping to my feet, I caught his
legs and brought the human pendulum to a halt. The man's
arms were pinioned behind his back. It was too dark to see
his face clearly, but I sensed that I knew him.

It was Mo, our taxi driver from the airport. I felt sick.
My mind was reeling. All that I could think of was a remark
I had made about Mo when I spoke to Frank Colouris.

"It's not a hanging offence."

Someone had decided that it was.

Chapter Four

I was completely dazed. I just stood there for several minutes, my stomach churning and my head pounding as I wondered what I should do. Even in the semi-darkness, I could see that Mo was beyond help. His head was twisted at an unnatural angle and his body was limp. The man was comprehensively dead. It was equally obvious that he had not taken his own life. I know that some people go to extraordinary lengths to stage manage their suicides in order to gain maximum shock effect, but Mo was not one of them. Nobody could pinion his arms behind his back like that, then hang himself from such a high branch. The man with whom I'd had the abrasive encounter at the hotel was a murder victim. I was overcome with sympathy. I remembered his tirade against the world of electronics for keeping him at bay because he lacked sufficient qualifications. In a sense, it had let him down again. Arrangements had been made to put surveillance cameras in every part of the course. Had they already been installed, those responsible for the murder would never have dared to commit it there for fear of being seen on the CCTV monitors. The electronics industry, which Mo felt had cruelly rejected him, might conceivably have saved his life.

I was too scared to try to get him down and, in any case, I knew that it was best to disturb the scene of the crime as little as possible. The alarm had to be raised. I lurched out of the clearing and broke into a run. As I jogged back towards the hotel, I wondered if the female screams that I'd heard had in some way been connected with the murder. Had the woman been forced to watch the execution? Or had she stumbled on the corpse by accident? At all events, she was quiet now and so was the barking dog. The whole golf course was eerily silent as if aware of the horror that had taken place at its heart. I lengthened my stride and tried to ignore the sweat that was now trickling down my face. My stomach was still churning, my mouth dry, my mind in turmoil. The last time I'd seen Mo, he'd threatened me with revenge. I took no solace from the fact that he was no longer in a position to implement his threat. All I could think about was the hideous nature of his death. Did he have a wife and children? He would certainly have friends and former colleagues. They would all be utterly devastated.

When I came to the rope that marked the start of the course, I leapt over it like a hurdler and put in a final sprint. I was panting stertorously by the time I finally reached the hotel, and I steadied myself for a moment on one of the chairs on the patio. The place was almost deserted but my sudden arrival did not go unnoticed. A figure came walking purposefully out to join me.

"Is that you, Alan?" asked Calvin Reed.

"Yes," I said, gasping for air.

"I saw you from the bar. Are you all right? You look exhausted."

"Never mind about me, Mr. Reed. Call the police."

"Why?"

"Just call them."

"Has something happened?"

"The worst thing possible. We've got a murder on our hands."

Reed was aghast. "Are you *sure?*"

"No question about it."

"Who's the victim?"

"Ring the police," I implored. "I'll tell you the details afterwards."

He pulled out a mobile phone and pressed the memory button. A number rang immediately. He was icily calm as he requested immediate assistance. Crisp and authoritative, Calvin Reed talked to the police in a way that suggested he had done so many times before. After putting his mobile away, he helped me into a chair and looked at me more carefully.

"Is there anything I can get you, Alan? A brandy, perhaps?"

"No, thanks."

"I can roust out the hotel doctor, if you like."

"I'm not that bad," I replied. "The shock is starting to wear off."

"Do you feel up to telling me the details?"

"I think so."

"Go on," he encouraged.

I took a deep breath. "You're not going to like this," I warned.

ᴡꞁꞁꞃᴠꞁᴜᴡᴠᴠꞁᴠᴡꞁᴠᴡꞁꞁᴠꞁ

The police arrived with commendable speed. After taking a statement from me, they asked me to guide them to the clump of cedars where I'd found the body. Calvin Reed came with us and so did Frank Colouris, hauled out of bed by a call from the manager and stunned to learn that the murder victim was Mo.

"Maurice Dobbs," he murmured.

"Who?" I asked.

"That was Mo's real name. Maurice Dobbs."

"It's not his week, Mr. Colouris," I said.

"What do you mean?"

"Sacked one day and murdered the next."

"Poor guy!"

"Does he have a family?"

"Not any more."

When we got to the scene of the crime, the police acted with the detached efficiency of true professionals. Lights were set up, the body was lowered carefully to the ground, then a doctor conducted an initial examination but was, to my surprise, reluctant to give his opinion as to the cause of death. The whole area was cordoned off by police tapes and the search for forensic evidence began at once. I watched from the sidelines with Calvin Reed and Frank Colouris. All three of us were grateful that I'd been the one to discover the body and not Peter Fullard. The loss of his treasured Bermuda grass had thrown my partner into gibbering incoherence. Had he been knocked flying in the middle of the golf course by the body of a hanged man, he would have had an apoplectic fit. I didn't relish the idea of passing on the bad tidings to him. In Peter's fevered mind, Mo's death would be conclusive proof that someone was determined to sabotage our project. Work would certainly come to a sharp halt now. The police would want the whole course cleared while their investigation was in progress.

The manager and his deputy were anticipating the problems ahead and making contingency plans. When the major decisions had been agreed, Calvin Reed turned to me and put a consoling hand on my shoulder.

"This has knocked you for six, Alan," he said gently.

"I'm still turning somersaults."

"We'll try to spare you even more upset. I don't think you should be the one to tell Peter Fullard about this. We can both guess how he'll react. Naturally, he'll want to know the full details from you at a later stage but I feel that someone else should actually break the news to him. Is that OK with you?"

"Yes, Mr. Reed," I said with relief. "Will you speak to him yourself?"

"No," he replied, indicating his deputy. "Frank will handle it."

"I get on pretty well with Mr. Fullard," said Colouris quietly. "But I know he needs careful handling. This is going to come as a terrible blow to him."

"And to his wife," I suggested. "Denise will be shattered. They'll get even less sleep from now on. Peter will see it as a bad omen."

"It's an unfortunate setback, that's all," said Reed firmly. "Our police are very efficient. I have the greatest faith in them. Once they track down the person or persons behind all this, we can carry on as if nothing has happened. In the meantime, alas, we have to do a lot of damage limitation. I hardly need tell you that murder is bad for business, Alan. The news will go round the hotel like wildfire. I'd advise you to keep your head down."

"In what way?"

"You were the person who found him. Some people take a ghoulish interest in these things. You're bound to be pestered by endless questions from other guests. Frank will do his best to keep people off your back."

"I don't need a bodyguard."

"You may change your mind about that."

"I doubt it, Mr. Reed."

"Let's just say that I'll be there if you need me, Mr. Saxon," said Colouris with a helpful smile. "We simply want to protect you from any undue pressure, that's all."

"Fair enough," I conceded.

Having supervised the preliminaries, the senior officer broke away from the activity in the clearing to take me aside. Inspector Troy Morley was a black detective with a compact frame and a head that seemed slightly too small for his body. His handsome face boasted a neat moustache and a square chin with a small dimple. I've always had severe problems with policemen. Because my father was—and still is, even

in retirement—one of the breed, I've no liking for law
enforcement officers of any kind or nationality, but in Troy
Morley I fancied that I might have found the exception to
the rule. He felt no need to intimidate or to let me know
that he was in charge. When he took my statement, he could
see how shaken I still was. He was patient and understanding. In a voice that was low and measured, he'd coaxed out
details in the most painless way.

"Thank you, Mr. Saxon," he said. "You did the right thing."

"It seemed so indecent to leave him hanging there," I
recalled.

"Getting him down was our job, sir. The body will be
taken off for an autopsy. When the pathologist has examined
him properly, we'll have a much clearer idea of what we're
up against."

"Do you need me any longer?"

He shook his head. "I don't think so, Mr. Saxon, though
I'd like to take a fuller statement from you tomorrow, if you
don't mind. There may be small details that you'll remember
later on. At the moment, we are, literally, working in the
dark." He leaned in closer. "Just one last thing, sir. You
mentioned a woman screaming."

"Yes, that's what brought me here in the first place."

"Are you sure that the screams came from this spot?"

"No, I'm not, Inspector," I admitted. "Sound is very
deceptive. I could easily have been misled. It wasn't even
possible to make out if the screams and the barking of the
dog came from the same place."

He gave a dismissive nod. "We'll look into it, sir."

"Am I free to go, Inspector?"

"Yes, sir. You've had a nasty experience. Try to get some
sleep."

"With *this* on my mind?"

In the glare of the lights, I saw him give a wan smile
before moving away to talk to Calvin Reed about what steps

it would be necessary for the police to take. There was no point in staying. If I remained any longer, I feared, I might be horrendously sick and wanted to avoid that embarrassment. I trudged away from the depressing scene. Frank Colouris caught me up and fell in beside me.

"Mr. Reed wants me to see that you get back safely, sir," he explained.

"I can find my own way, thanks."

"You must still be feeling groggy."

"I've had better days, Mr. Colouris," I said, "but, then, so have you, I daresay."

He grimaced. "Oh, yeah. Much better."

"Have you ever had to deal with a murder before?"

"No, sir," he replied, "and I never expected to do so. Not in Bermuda, anyway. We did have a stabbing in a Manhattan hotel where I once worked but, luckily, the victim pulled through. New York is a dangerous city. You allow for a certain amount of violent crime there. It's so different here. The island is very law-abiding."

"It's always had that reputation."

"Since I've been at the Blue Dolphin, we've only called the police in for things like petty theft and guests who try to sneak off without paying their bill. Oh, and we did have one guy who trashed the bridal suite in a fit of anger because his wife ran out on him during their honeymoon. I suppose there were mitigating circumstances in that case." He gave a shrug. "Apart from that, there's been nothing."

"You're forgetting the trouble on the golf course."

"Yes, that was worrying," he said.

"Mr. Reed tried to shrug off the incidents. He might change his mind now."

"We'll all be forced into a major re-think, sir."

"Then it *could* be deliberate sabotage?"

"Too early to say, Mr. Saxon. We'll have to see what the cops come up with."

"Why should anyone want to stop a golf course being built?" I wondered. "It doesn't make sense. Surely nobody hates the game *that* much. If they do, why pick on us? Why not go for the existing courses on the island?"

"I wish I knew, sir."

"Do you have any theories at all?"

"None, I'm afraid," he said wearily. "As Mr. Reed told you, our main concern is to cope with the fall-out. A brutal murder is the last thing we need. Our job is to make our guests relax and have a good time. They won't be able to do that when they hear what's happened on our golf course."

I began to feel sorry for Frank Colouris. Dragged from his bed by the manager, he was flung into the middle of the crisis and would get very little sleep that night. The whole of his next day would be devoted to calming people down and smoothing ruffled feathers. I didn't envy him the task of passing on the grim tidings to Peter Fullard. It would require tact and discretion. Though I'd wanted to be on my own, I became grateful for the deputy manager's company on the walk back. In sympathizing with him, I forgot my own worries. I no longer felt quite so queasy and light-headed. We parted in the hotel lobby and I took the elevator up to my floor. As I let myself into my suite, I heard sounds of laughter through the connecting door. Relieved to recognize Lynette's voice, I didn't stop to ask myself if their Canadian friends might be in the room with them. I simply banged hard on the door.

Jessica Hadlow flung it open. She was still grinning broadly.

"Hello, Mr. Saxon," she said affably. "Would you like to come in?"

"Yes, please."

Lynette came across. "What's the matter, Daddy? You look worn out."

"I think your father's had a night on the tiles, Lynette," said Jessica with a teasing laugh. "Just like us. Am I right, Mr. Saxon?"

I shook my head. "We need to talk," I said.

Calvin Reed's prediction was accurate. Word of the crime spread through the hotel at an alarming speed. By the time I came down for breakfast, the place was buzzing. Some of the catering staff had obviously known Mo and the news of his death had rocked them. The waitress who served me had tears in her eyes and moved around in a daze. Neither Lynette nor Jessica joined me for the meal. When I told them what had happened, both had been deeply upset. Lynette had been sobered instantly and, to her credit, Jessica was overcome with regret. She wished that she hadn't complained about Mo's conduct during the drive back from the airport. When I finally left them, they were still very disturbed. I suspected that they'd have stayed up for hours, discussing the implications. I was grateful to have breakfast alone. A taxing night had left me tired, dispirited and in no mood for conversation. My fear was that Peter and Denise Fullard would descend on me to demand the full details, but they never showed up. In the event, it was someone else who came across to my table.

"Hi, Alan," she said softly.

"Oh, good morning."

"Listen, I've heard the news and I'm terribly sorry that you had to be the one to find him. It must have been dreadful for you. Anyway, I'm sure you'd rather be alone with your thoughts so I won't bother you."

"No, please," I said, lifting a hand. "Don't go. Join me, if you wish."

"Are you sure?"

"Quite sure."

"As long as I'm not in the way."

"You could never be that, Nancy," I said with an attempt at gallantry.

Nancy Wykoff took a seat opposite me and reached out to give my arm a sympathetic squeeze. Her white lace blouse had the most elaborate pattern down the front and her red skirt matched the color of her sandals. She was not wearing any perfume but she still gave off the most pleasing aroma. It was odd. I'd only met the woman the night before yet I felt as if we were old friends. There was an unforced familiarity about her.

"You're a brave man, Alan," she remarked.

"Am I?"

"Everyone knows you discovered the dead body. That's why they're all looking at you. Most people in your position would have barricaded themselves into their room."

"That's not my style, Nancy."

"Nor mine."

"If anyone tries to corner me, I'll tell them I have no comment to make."

"Does that include me?"

"Of course not."

"Thank you," she said, reaching for the menu. "But, don't worry, I'm not going to bombard you with questions. I just want to enjoy the pleasure of having breakfast together. Let's not even mention the subject, shall we?"

"That suits me."

When the waitress came over, Nancy ordered breakfast then sat back in her chair to appraise me. She arched a compassionate eyebrow.

"Something tells me you didn't get too much shuteye last night."

"Almost none at all."

"Try to fit in a nap during the day."

"As many as I can," I promised, stifling a yawn. "What are your plans?"

"They're in limbo right now. I was intending to go into Hamilton with Denise Fullard to do some shopping, but in the circumstances I imagine that we'll have to cancel that. Denise will be too upset."

"Afraid so. I don't see Denise or Peter venturing out for days."

"They're such sensitive people."

"Denise is," I said. "The problem is that her sensitivity rubs off on Peter."

"Will you be able to carry on with your work, Alan?"

"I doubt it, Nancy. The police want to stop all activity on the course until they've finished their search. Peter and I were due for another session with the site foreman today, but that's out of the question. To be honest," I confessed, "I don't think my partner will be eager to do anything concerned with the Blue Dolphin Golf Course."

"In other words, you'll be free," she said hopefully.

"Not entirely. The police want to interview me again and I owe it to Peter to spend some time trying to soothe him. Also," I went on, pouring some coffee, "I'd like to have a moment alone with my daughter. That's been difficult to arrange so far."

"So you were telling us over dinner."

"Lynette and Jessica were out until the small hours with their Canadian friends. They clearly had a high old time. I felt cruel having to bring them back down to earth with a bump. They were distraught—especially Jessica."

"I thought you said that she was such a robust character."

"She is," I said, "but she had a link with the murder victim, you see." I added milk to my cup. "Maurice Dobbs—or Mo, as he's known—drove us from the airport and made some remarks that were decidedly out of turn. I was ready to ignore it. Jessica wasn't. She complained so loudly to the management that Mo was sacked on the spot."

"No wonder she's feeling guilty."

"I don't think the two events are in any way related, Nancy. I mean, even if he'd kept his job here at the hotel, Mo might still have ended up hanging by that rope. That's what I told Jessica, but she didn't seem too convinced. She still feels herself somehow responsible." Nancy's breakfast arrived and I waited until she started on her blueberry muffin. "I hope this doesn't ruin their holiday."

"Or yours, Alan."

"Strictly speaking, I'm here to work."

"When you can't even get onto your golf course?"

"A temporary problem, that's all."

"What will you do in the meantime?"

"Try to relax a little."

"And fit in a round of golf, perhaps?" she asked, looking me in the eye.

I met her gaze. "Not at the Blue Dolphin."

"There are other courses on the island."

"And very good, they are. That's what puzzled me about you, Nancy," I said. "If you're such a keen golfer, why do you stay at a hotel that doesn't have its own course?"

"Call it loyalty, Alan."

"Loyalty?"

"Melinda Reed is an old friend of mine. When I heard that she and Cal had moved here, I couldn't come to Bermuda without staying at the Blue Dolphin, could I? Besides, Melinda told me that you were involved in the design of the new course here. The chance of meeting Alan Saxon at last was quite a draw."

"I hope you're not disappointed."

"Not one bit."

Nancy Wykoff offered me the kind of smile she would never have dared to give in front of the Fullards. They would have been shocked by its sophisticated boldness. I, on the other hand, was both intrigued and enchanted. I smiled back.

"Well," she said easily, "if you're going to have some time on your hands, we'll have to think of ways to entertain you, won't we?"

ᴡⅼⅼⅼⅼⅴⅼⅼⅴⅰⅴⅴⅰⅴⅼⅴⅰⅴⅴⅰⅴⅴⅰⅴⅴⅰⅼⅼⅼⅼⅴ

"What did you do then, Mr. Saxon?"

"I told you."

"Tell me again, sir, if you don't mind."

"I just stood there, trying to take it all in."

"And?"

"I was rooted to the spot by the sheer horror of what I'd seen."

"That's not quite what you told me last night, is it?"

"Isn't it?"

"You said that you were wondering if you should get the body down."

"Oh, yes," I recalled. "That, too, of course, Inspector. My mind was racing. Things were flashing through it at a hundred miles an hour."

"Yet you claim that you were dazed."

"Who wouldn't be?"

"Exactly, Mr. Saxon. In your position, most people would have felt the same. But when you're so shocked that you're rooted to the spot, your brain doesn't usually function that well. It goes numb. It's almost as if you're concussed. Yet you say that your brain seemed to be working overtime. Which is it, sir?" he probed. "Were you genuinely dazed or fully conscious?"

My confidence in Troy Morley had been misplaced. When he interviewed me late that morning, he embodied some of the qualities that had made me hate my father so much. He was relentlessly inquisitive, picking me up on every tiny inconsistency in what I said, remaining on his feet while I was seated, exerting steady control. Though the Inspector was scrupulously polite, he still managed to make me feel as if I were a suspect instead of an innocent witness who had stumbled on the crime. He looked bigger and stockier in daylight and his handsome features were disfigured by an expression of grim determination. If he hadn't been so racist, my father could have recognized Troy Morley as a kindred spirit. The one consolation was that the meeting did not take place at the police station, an establishment that has always unnerved me even when I've just crossed its threshold to hand in a wallet that I happened to find. In effect, I spent the whole of my boyhood and adolescence in a police station. In whatever country I come across them, the real thing always reminds me of home.

Morley had set up an incident room at the Blue Dolphin so that he could be close to the scene of the crime. While the Inspector questioned me, his colleague, Sergeant Derek Woodford, took notes in a pad. Woodford was a pale, stringy detective with the lean and hungry look of a potential assassin. His eyes sparkled appreciatively whenever his superior caught me out. Occasionally, Woodford tossed in his own questions.

"Tell us a little more about your relationship with the murder victim, sir."

"I didn't have a relationship, Sergeant," I said. "Until the man drove us here from the airport, I'd never set eyes on him."

"Yet you mentioned a confrontation with Mr. Dobbs."

"That was after we arrived."

"You said that he was aggressive towards you."

"Yes, he was."

"In what way did you provoke him, Mr. Saxon?" he asked.

"I didn't provoke him at all," I replied, losing patience. "Mo had got hold of the idea that I'd been the one to complain about him and he blamed me for his dismissal."

Morley took over again. "Can you recall his exact words?"

"They weren't very pleasant, Inspector."

"He swore at you?"

"Yes," I recalled. "He gave me a real mouthful then told me that I'd be sorry I ever came to Bermuda. That little prophecy is turning out to have some foundation to it."

The detectives had a long, silent conversation. I felt like a erring pupil, waiting outside the headmaster's office before being summoned in to face my punishment. I'd hoped the interview with the police would be a mere formality but it had already gone on for an hour. When he turned back to me, Morley contrived an appeasing smile.

"I'm sorry that we kept you so long, sir," he began, "but we have to sift through every detail. I hope you understand."

"Only too well, Inspector."

"We don't need to detain you any longer, sir."

"Thank you," I said, rising from my seat.

"But I do advise you to take care, Mr. Saxon."

"Of what?"

"Yourself, of course. Not that I think you're in imminent danger or anything like that," he added, "but we can't take any chances. The fact remains that someone is doing all they can to halt progress on your golf course."

"So?"

"I'd hate to think that you were their next target, sir."

I was alarmed. "The thought never occurred to me, Inspector. Why should they pick on me? I'm not the brains in the outfit, you know. Peter Fullard is. If someone wants to scupper the Blue Dolphin Golf Course, then he's the man they'd go after."

"I made that point to Mr. Fullard."

"Then you probably gave him a heart attack."

"He was a little agitated," said Morley with the ghost of a smile. "Sergeant Woodford had to escort him back to his room. I don't think he'll be stirring out of it very much for a while. He was demanding police protection."

"Well, that's something *I'd* never ask for," I assured him. "Am I really in danger?"

"I think it unlikely, sir. On the other hand…"

"Go on."

"There's something we can't ignore," he explained. "You see, Mr. Dobbs did not die at the end of a rope. According to the pathologist, he was killed hours earlier. Some sort of injection seems to have been used. We know he wasn't murdered at the spot where you found him because the security guards patrolled that area every half-an-hour. On their last sweep before you got there, they saw nothing and nobody in that stand of cedars. Do you hear what I'm saying, Mr. Saxon?" he said pointedly. "The murder occurred elsewhere, then the body was taken to the golf course for the sole purpose of causing a disruption in your work."

"Wait a moment," I said. "Mo was swinging from side to side."

"What do you deduce from that, sir?"

"That someone—the killer, perhaps—was in that clearing shortly before I was. He must have set the body in motion before leaving the scene. Otherwise, Mo would just have been hanging there. Then there are the screams I heard, not to mention that dog barking. Have you followed all that up yet?"

"Yes, Mr. Saxon." Morley turned to his colleague. "Derek."

"We managed to track down the young woman, sir," said Woodford, referring to some notes in his pad. "She was at the side of the lake, less than a hundred yards away from the murder scene. It transpires that she and her boyfriend had gone there for a walk in the moonlight. He'd had rather too much to drink and fell accidentally into the water. That's when you heard her scream. She thought he was going to drown."

"As for the dog," resumed Morley, "it belonged to one of the security men on patrol. He was alerted by the screams as well and went to investigate. In other words, neither the young woman in question nor the dog is in any way linked to the murder."

"So who made the body swing to and fro like that?"

"The person who strung the victim up."

"The man who saw you coming, Mr. Saxon," emphasized Woodford. "It may even be that he recognized you. It was a clear night and you're a distinctive figure. There aren't many people in Bermuda as tall and angular as you."

"I bet he couldn't believe his luck," said Morley. "At the very moment when he has just hanged Mr. Dobbs from that tree, he saw one of the designers behind the Blue Dolphin Golf Course actually hurrying in his direction. That's why he gave the body a shove. He wanted to surprise you."

"He certainly did that!" I agreed.

"To surprise you and to give you a gruesome warning."

"That's why we think you should take precautions, sir," said Woodford seriously.

"Sensible precautions, that's all," added Morley, easing me towards the door. "I hope they'll be unnecessary, but we can't take that risk. They know who you are, sir. I daresay they've had an eye on you from the moment you arrived in Bermuda."

Entering the Fullard suite was like going into a morgue. The atmosphere was charged with grief and the occupants had a funereal air about them. Lying on the table, like a dead body on a slab, were the plans of the Blue Dolphin Golf Course. Peter was crouched over his designs, a bereaved father, mourning the loss of a favorite child. His wife had let me in. When he glanced up at me, there were tears in his eyes.

"Now will you believe me, Alan?" he asked.

"Try not to upset yourself," I replied, knowing that it was futile advice. "Who told you? Frank Colouris or the police?"

"Both," said Denise, wringing her hands. "Mr. Colouris called on us first thing to put us in the picture. We were appalled, Alan. Utterly appalled."

"Yes," said Peter, dabbing at his eyes with a handkerchief. "Of course, we didn't dare to leave the suite. Mr. Colouris suggested that we have room service but neither of us could eat a thing. Then this detective came up to see us, an Inspector Morley. He did his best to reassure us but he couldn't hide the truth. It was an act of sabotage."

"It was a case of murder," I corrected, "and our first concern ought to be for the unfortunate victim. He didn't volunteer to be hanged from that tree. Let's remember him before we start to wallow in self-pity."

"You're right," he said, nodding soulfully. "I'm sorry."

"But what about you?" asked Denise. "You were the one who actually found that poor man. How did it happen? What were you doing on the course in the first place?"

I gave them a concise version of events, omitting the uglier details and playing down the effect that it had had on me. I stressed that it had only made me more committed to the notion of seeing the golf course built to our specifications. Peter traded a look of despair with Denise. She seemed on the verge of a nervous breakdown.

"I want out, Alan," he decided.

"What do you mean?" I said.

"I want to cut my losses and get out of this damned hotel."

"But we've got a contract, Peter. You can't renege on that."

"It's not safe to stay here."

"Of course, it is. We're not in Miami. This is no homicide capital. Bermuda is one of the friendliest and most crime-free places in the world."

"It hasn't been very friendly to us."

"You can't just turn tail and flee," I argued. "We have obligations."

"My main obligation is to Denise. As long as we stay here, we feel under threat. We want to fly home until the police have solved the crime."

"But that could take weeks, even months. We've no guarantee that the killer is still in Bermuda. Look, Peter, we agreed to come here to sort out any last problems. They need us on site."

"I know that. I hate to let them down."

"Think of the effort it's cost us, the endless meetings we had, the time we spent on your drafting board, the haggling with our employers, the disputes with the contractors, the flights to and from Bermuda. Are you going to throw all that away?" I asked in tones of disbelief. "We were hired to do a job here and I intend to do it. Nobody is going to frighten me off the island."

If my words didn't exactly instill some courage into Peter Fullard, they did at least shame him. Running for cover was an act of cowardice and he accepted that. At the same time, he had a wife to consider. I indicated a compromise.

"Denise doesn't have to stay," I pointed out. "If you're worried about her, put Denise on the next plane to England and take a load off your mind." I turned to her. "You'd rather Peter stayed to finish his work, wouldn't you, Denise?"

"Well, I don't know," she said uncertainly.

"You can rejoin him when this business has blown over."

"But Peter and I go everywhere together."

"Then stay and give him moral support."

"It's not as simple as that, Alan," said Peter, shaking his head.

"Well, there's no point in arguing about it," I concluded. "The decision is yours. Why don't I leave you to think it over? All I ask is that you consider every aspect of the situation. Walk out now and you forfeit the respect of Calvin Reed, not to mention the contractors. You also delay the whole project."

I took my leave of the unhappy couple, hoping that I'd planted enough doubt in their minds to make them think again. The trouble was that Peter took it all so personally.

The discovery of a murder victim was seen as a direct threat to him. It was almost as if Mo's body had been found with his pockets filled with the stolen Bermuda grass seed. On his own, I would have convinced Peter that he had to stay on the island. With the neurotic Denise at his side, it was a different matter. They talked each other into a state of terror.

It was truly a marriage of two anxiety-mongers.

My own anxieties were directed at my daughter. I hadn't seen Lynette or Jessica all morning and wondered how they were coping with the news that I'd sprung on them. Our respective suites were on the floor above the Fullards, so I skipped up the stairs on the off-chance that the girls were still there. My timing was perfect. As I came out into the corridor, Lynette was pressing the button on the elevator. She and Jessica were in T-shirts and shorts. Both were carrying sun hats.

"Hold on a minute!" I called, quickening my pace.

"Good morning, Daddy!" said Lynette.

"Hello, Mr. Saxon," welcomed Jessica.

They were beaming happily as if nothing untoward had occurred. I wished that they could have given lessons in resilience to Peter and Denise. Filled with remorse in the early hours of the morning, the girls were now raring to go again.

"We're meeting Rick and Conrad for lunch," said Lynette.

"Oh," I replied. "I rather hoped you'd eat with me."

"It's their last day in Bermuda," explained Jessica. "We can't let them down."

"No, no, of course not."

Lynette was ambivalent, wanting to see her friends yet unhappy about having to disappoint me again. "Why don't we arrange to have lunch tomorrow, Daddy?"

"Is there no chance of dinner together this evening?"

"I'm afraid not," she said, clearly torn. "We're not sure when we'll be back."

"Rick and Conrad have no sense of time," said Jessica with a tolerant grin. "They're crazy people. That's why we like them so much. Knowing them, we can't even promise to be back by midnight."

"Don't burn the candle at both ends," I warned.

"Why not? That's what we came for, isn't it?"

Lynette kissed me. "Sorry, Daddy. Lunch tomorrow. It's a date."

"I'll hold you to that."

"You'll have her all to yourself, Mr. Saxon," said Jessica with an arm around Lynette. "I've got a hair appointment at twelve-thirty. Besides, I think it's only fair that you two should have some time alone."

"Thank you, Jessica."

The elevator arrived and they got into it. As the door slid back into position, I felt suddenly envious of the two young Canadians with whom the girls would clearly spend the rest of the day. Statistically, they had already notched up substantially more time with my daughter than I'd managed to spend with her since we met at Gatwick airport. The fact that it was their last night on the island worried me. Strange things happen on last nights. Emotions can run high between friends who are about to part. Fond farewells can escalate out of control. I've been known to take advantage of the fact myself and yield to impulses that might not otherwise occur. Which of the two Canadians would be trying to make my daughter yield to an impulse? It was odd. I'd heard so much about Rick and Conrad yet I had no idea what they looked like or how they paired off with the girls. In a sense, of course, it wasn't my business. But that didn't stop me from fretting. I needed the distraction of lunch.

Exactly how it happened, I'll never know, but a few hours later I found myself standing on the first tee at the Port

Royal Golf Club with Nancy Wykoff as my playing partner. She was one of those clever women who get what they want while convincing you that the decision was really yours. This isn't meant as a criticism. I admired the way that she operated. She was no crude predator. Everything was done with such style. Seated alone at a table in restaurant, she'd beckoned me over for a chat then invited me to join her. During the meal, I'd been gently manipulated into suggesting a round of golf together. Nancy responded with controlled enthusiasm. It was almost as if she'd already booked our slot at Port Royal. The truth is that I was a one hundred percent volunteer. Apart from enjoying her company immensely, I wanted to escape from the prying eyes of the other hotel guests. At the Blue Dolphin—because I'd discovered Mo's body—I was under constant surveillance. It made me uneasy. I felt the need to retreat to my habitual refuge with fourteen clubs and a strong desire to block out all else but the magic of the game. It was only when we stepped onto the course that I began to wonder if Nancy was up to the challenge ahead of us.

Port Royal is in Southampton Parish, at the western end of the island. Designed by no less an architect than the celebrated Robert Trent Jones, the course is built on high ground that sweeps down to cliff edges above the Atlantic. Scenically, it's up there with the best of them and is a joy to behold. The greens are vast but their contours create all kinds of problems. Three small lakes offer a variety of water hazards, but the real test of nerve and skill comes on the sixteenth hole, a spectacular 153-yard par three that's featured in the obituaries of many a professional. The tee-shot has to be played across a yawning gap to a promontory that holds nothing more than a green that is all but encircled by bunkers. Did my partner realize what was lying in wait for us?

"Have no qualms on my account, Alan," she said cheerily. "I've never lost a ball on this course yet and I've played it half-a-dozen times."

"I'm impressed, Nancy."

"Not as much as I am. I never thought I'd play alongside the great Alan Saxon."

"I'm feeling rather less than great at the moment," I confessed.

"Only because of that horrible experience last night. You'll soon forget that."

"Will I?"

"Yes, Alan," she said confidently. "I'll make sure of that."

Nancy was as good as her word. Like me, she was there to play a game she loved and she did so with a quiet tenacity. She was no hacker. Nancy was a talented golfer who rarely strayed off the fairways and who found the greens with regularity. There was little flair to her game, however. She invariably chose the safest option so that she avoided any big disasters. It was percentage golf of a very effective kind. What she lacked in power, she made up for with accuracy. Her real weakness was bunker play. After the first nine holes, my card made far better reading but she was by no means disgraced. I was grateful. Nancy Wykoff was helping me to play exactly the kind of game that I needed—pleasant, unhurried and quietly competitive.

"This is fantastic, Alan," she said as we arrived at the tenth tee.

"Best thing that's happened to me since I came to Bermuda."

"Thank you so much for suggesting it."

"I had the feeling that you did."

She laughed. "What the hell! We're here, aren't we?"

Nancy marked the occasion by getting her first birdie. It was refreshing to play the game for the sheer fun of it. Pulling my golf cart along, I was struck by the thought that it must have been almost four years since I'd last dispensed with a caddie. I was playing majority golf, the kind enjoyed by millions of people all over the world, free from the pressures of professionalism and filled with the sort of uncomplicated pleasure that I'd sorely missed. Without a hint of fear, Nancy drove straight and true at the treacherous sixteenth. It was I who found sand from the tee and dropped a shot. My one serious mistake of the round didn't seem to disappoint her at all. She was there to learn. Though she concentrated hard on her own shots, she watched every one of mine with great interest, noting my technique and offering sincere praise whenever it was due. The whole experience was so enjoyable that time stood still throughout its duration.

It was not until we left the course that she referred to the murder.

"How do you feel now, Alan?"

"Annoyed at my tee shot on the sixteenth," I replied.

"I was talking about the traumatic events in the night. There aren't many guys who could play such a faultless round of golf after going through an experience like that."

"Except that it wasn't entirely faultless, Nancy."

"It was by my standards," she said. "You're obviously feeling better."

"That doesn't mean I've forgotten what happened," I confided. "I doubt if I ever shall. What I can't understand is why they hanged Mo where they did. According to the police, he was murdered elsewhere, then strung up some time later from that cedar."

"I guess that someone wanted to make a statement."

"But who? And why?"

"I can't help you with the first question, Alan," she said. "I've no idea who'd do such a thing. But I might be able to tell you why."

"Oh?"

"It was something that Melinda Reed let slip a few nights ago. She and Cal were thrilled to take charge of the Blue Dolphin when it opened, but not everyone wished it well. Apparently, there was a lot of friction behind the scenes."

"Between whom?" I asked, pricking my ears.

"The consortium who built the hotel and other interested parties. Disappointed rivals wanted to strike back. According to Melinda, there were sabotage attempts during the actual construction. They had to turn the Blue Dolphin into Fort Knox in order to get it built on time."

"Calvin Reed said nothing of this to me and Peter."

"He didn't want to alarm you," she reasoned. "Having met your partner, I can see why. Peter Fullard is flaky enough already. In any case, once the hotel was open for business, the problems seemed to fade away. It was almost as if the would-be saboteurs had given up."

"Evidently, they hadn't. They were biding their time."

"Waiting to strike at the golf course instead."

"Probably because it's far more difficult to protect," I observed. "A hotel of that standard is bound to be a huge success in Bermuda. When it's equipped with its own golf course, it could turn out to be a gold mine."

"That's who you're up against, Alan."

"Who?"

"Someone who wants to halt the Gold Rush."

When I got back to the hotel, there was a message on my answering machine from Calvin Reed. He asked me to join him and his wife for dinner in a voice that made it sound less like an invitation than a courteous order. I was happy to accept. It would give me the chance to find out more about the background to the Blue Dolphin. The manager had obviously been keeping certain things from us. There was another good reason to join the Reeds. According to the message, Nancy Wykoff would be at our table as well. She and I already had a tacit agreement to dine together, so matters were simplified. As I lay in the bath, I reflected on my afternoon in the company of the long-legged Texan. It had been the perfect antidote to the hassle and upset that I'd endured. At a deeper level, it had aroused a feeling in me that was more honorable than sheer lust while falling well short of true devotion. Under other circumstances, I'd have done my best to get on more intimate terms with Nancy and she'd made no secret of her readiness to comply. What held me back was the presence of Lynette and, even more, of Jessica. I was worried about my daughter's reaction and feared the barbed comments of her friend. Between them, the girls were a most effective contraceptive. Nancy would have to wait. When the girls flew home, she'd still be in Bermuda. That was the time to strike.

Curiosity about the murder had reached boiling point. No sooner had I stepped outside my room than I was subjected to a battery of questions from two people waiting for the elevator. I made an excuse and took the stairs instead. Heads turned as I entered the lobby. Comments followed me all the way across its marble floor. I could hear my name on dozens of lips. Before I went into the restaurant, I glanced across at the Flamingo Bar and was rewarded with an unexpected sight. Lynette and Jessica were sitting in a corner with two young men whom I assumed must be Rick and Conrad. Which was which I couldn't discern, but I was reassured by their appearance. Neither of them fitted my stereotyped idea of a Canadian. Anything less like a bearded lumberjack or a handsome Mountie was difficult to imagine. One of them was tall, rangy and sporting a Che Guevara mustache to compensate for his rapidly thinning hair, while the other was a chunky character of medium build who looked more like a bank clerk on his day off than a rampant lecher in search of a lay.

Rick and Conrad—or Conrad and Rick—seemed to be eminently respectable. The seating arrangements indicated their preferences. The tall one was on one side of the table with Jessica, his arm draped lazily across the back of her chair. Lynette sat beside the bank clerk, who peered at her earnestly as if checking a twenty pound note for signs of forgery. When she saw me watching them, Lynette gave me a cheerful wave. I wondered if she'd deliberately arranged for them to be there in the hope that I'd spot them on my way past and realize that I need have no fears on her account. If every picture told a story, the one that I'd seen in the Flamingo Bar contained no hint of danger. I blew her a kiss and walked on to the restaurant.

"I hear that you played a round at Port Royal," said Calvin Reed.

"Word travels."

"This is a small island, Alan. If you sneeze loud enough at one end of Bermuda, someone at the other end will say 'Bless you!' It's the first thing we noticed when we came here. Privacy is at a premium."

"It reminds me why I could never live in an English village," I said. "Everyone knows everyone else's business."

"Did you have a pleasant afternoon?"

"Very pleasant, thanks."

"Good. Oh, by the way, I did invite Peter and Denise Fullard to join us but they declined. Recent events have given them a fortress mentality. They prefer to have room service." He rolled his eyes. "Ideally, they'd like the food to be pushed through a hatch."

"At least, they're still here, Mr. Reed. They were talking of leaving Bermuda."

"Yes, I know. I spoke to Peter on the telephone. Apparently, you persuaded them to stay. Thank you, Alan. We have enough on our plate without losing one of our course architects. Frank Colouris said they went into a flat spin when he broke the news."

"They'll calm down in time," I said. "Denise is the real problem."

Calvin Reed had been alone at the table for four when I reached it. Eager to keep me out of the limelight, he'd selected a quiet corner that was largely obscured by artificial palm trees. I seized my opportunity to ask a few straight questions.

"Have the police made any progress?"

"Not yet. Early days."

"Do you have any idea who's behind it all, Mr. Reed?"

"Not really," he sighed. "I wish that I did."

"There are rumors floating around about vengeful rivals. I understand that there was a lot of bitterness involved in the battle to purchase this site."

"It's in a prime position. Competition was bound to be fierce."

"But the consortium for whom you work finally won the day."

"Yes, Alan. By fair means."

"Then why is someone trying to hit back at you?"

"We've no proof that they are," he said with his bland smile. "It may look as if all the incidents on the course are connected, but that may not be the case at all. Inspector Morley isn't jumping to the sort of conclusion that you are, Alan. He's keeping an open mind. That's why he's investigating Dobbs' background more carefully."

"Mo?"

"He does seem to have made a few enemies on the island."

"Jessica was one of them."

"His murder may yet turn out to be the result of a personal grudge."

"Then why go to the trouble of hanging him in the middle of our golf course?" I asked. "Killers usually try to conceal the body, not run it up the flagpole like the Union Jack. Mo was in that spot for a purpose."

"Only the police can determine what that purpose is."

"What exactly happened when this site came up for sale?"

"A number of bidders threw their hat into the ring."

"How did your consortium beat off the opposition?"

"That's a confidential matter, Alan," he said crisply. "To be honest, I'm rather more concerned about the immediate future than about the past. Right now, our main task is to pour oil on troubled waters. We've already had two people moving to another hotel because of what happened last night. It's unsettled everyone."

My inquiries had been comprehensively rebuffed. Whoever told me the truth about the building of the Blue Dolphin, it would not be Calvin Reed. He was either too loyal to his employers or too careful to keep off a delicate subject. I'd have to probe elsewhere. Before we could continue our conversation, the ladies arrived and we stood up to welcome them. Clad in an evening gown of green satin, Melinda Reed looked even more like a model on a catwalk. There was something so studied about her every movement. Yet it was Nancy Wykoff who really caught my attention. She was wearing a plain white dress of the finest silk that was held in place over one shoulder by a gold clasp, exposing the other shoulder and most of her back. Her bronzed body looked shapelier than ever. Nancy's make-up was understated and she'd applied just the right amount of that bewitching perfume. After accepting a welcome kiss from Reed, she leaned forward so that I could give her a peck on the cheek. As she drew back, her eyes momentarily met mine.

The decision I'd made in the bath suddenly vanished down the plughole. It was clear that Nancy Wykoff had no intention of waiting until the girls had left Bermuda. Why should I? To postpone the delight of becoming more closely acquainted with her wasn't only foolish, it was akin to masochism. I liked her and needed her. Why hold back? The Reeds saw nothing of what passed between us, but the message in Nancy's eyes was unmistakable.

The time to strike was now.

Chapter Five

During the meal, it was Calvin Reed who set the agenda. Determined to keep us off the subject of the murder, he initiated a variety of discussions on neutral topics that allowed for pleasant and relaxed conversation. It suited me to be spared any reminders of the horror I'd witnessed on the previous night. I was able to concentrate on learning more about Nancy Wykoff. She was on good form, witty, alert and full of diverting anecdotes. She also managed to bring Melinda Reed out of her shell. The two women were clearly good friends even though there were such obvious differences between them. Nancy was older, more intelligent, more interesting and far more seasoned in the ways of the world. She was also completely at ease. Melinda, by contrast, always seemed to be holding a calculated pose. Whenever she showed her teeth in a smile, she did so as if advertising a new brand of toothpaste. Mirrors evidently played a large part in her life.

"How did the two of you meet?" I asked them.

"Quite by accident," said Nancy, turning to Melinda to cue her in.

"It was in the ladies' room at a tennis tournament in San Diego," said Melinda, flashing her perfect smile. "It was years ago. I was dating this guy who had hopes of following in the footsteps of Pete Sampras. Unfortunately, Larry got knocked out in the first round by some complete unknown. That seemed to happen in most tournaments. It was Nancy who talked some sense into me."

"There's nowhere like a ladies' room for doing that," said Nancy with a grin. "Someone had accidentally spilled a drink down Melinda's dress and I helped clean her up with some tissues. We got talking and she told me how fed up she was with watching her boyfriend lose. I told her to start dating Pete Sampras instead."

Melinda took up the story. "That was asking too much, but at least I took the first important step towards it. I ditched my boyfriend that evening. He took it badly."

"I don't blame him," I said.

"Pretty soon after that, Cal came on the scene so I lost all interest in tennis stars." She gave him her full beam. "And I've never regretted it for a moment, have I, sweetie?"

"I hope not, honey," he said.

"What were you doing at a tennis tournament, Nancy?" I said, looking across at her. "I thought that golf was your passion."

"It is, Alan," she agreed, "but not to the exclusion of all other sports. What took me to that particular tournament was nostalgia."

"Nostalgia?" I echoed.

"Yes. Believe it or not, I was the tennis correspondent on the *Houston Post* in my younger days. I majored in journalism in college, you see. If you can stand the traveling, it's a great way to get around and to meet the top players," she went on. "My first husband and I were staying in San Diego when that particular tournament was on, so I dragged him along. As Melinda explained, I went to her rescue in the ladies' room and ended up interfering in her private life."

"Thank heaven you did!" said Melinda.

"I'll go along with that," added Reed. "Otherwise, I might never have met my future wife. She might still be stuck with that loser."

Melinda touched his cheek with her fingertips. "Oh, no, Cal. What I really wanted was a winner and I was lucky enough to find one in you."

"That's how we met, Alan," concluded Nancy. "We've been friends ever since."

"Nancy came to our wedding," said Melinda. "I felt that she had a stake in it."

As the two women reminisced, I began to see how their friendship could work to my advantage. Calvin Reed would divulge nothing about the ferocious infighting that lay behind the purchase of the site for the Blue Dolphin, but his wife was another matter. If I could prevail on Nancy to question her discreetly, Melinda might unwittingly furnish me with the sort of details that I was keen to get. The manager's wife was no mere attractive appendage. She knew how the hotel world ticked. At the time she met Reed, she was working for a PR company that handled the contract for the five-star Los Angeles hotel where he had been employed. Looking at Melinda Reed now, it was difficult to believe that she'd once been a tennis groupie. In the sumptuous surroundings of the Blue Dolphin, she was in her natural habitat.

The meal was exceptional and the service brisk. As the wine flowed, I came to enjoy the evening more and more. Reed was an expert host. For all its formality, his charm seemed to work on both ladies, but he reserved most of his attention for me. I'd never known him so excessively nice and it was a little unsettling. I had the feeling that he was softening me up so that I'd continue to keep Peter Fullard on board. If I left the island, any changes to our golf course could be supervised by Peter, but if he and Denise fled, the whole project would grind to a halt. Reed was operating to a very tight schedule. It was vital that the Blue Dolphin could offer its guests a round of golf the following summer. Color brochures had been printed to that effect. Several reservations had already been made. Millions of dollars were in the balance. Because I had influence with Peter Fullard, I was crucial to the enterprise.

"You'll always be welcome here, Alan," he said expansively.

"Thank you, Mr. Reed."

"Come any time—and bring that lovely daughter of yours."

"I'll bring Lynette," I said, "but I can't promise you'll see anything of her. She's got to the age where going on holiday with your father means dumping him at the earliest opportunity so that you can party with the younger set."

"I was the same at her age," admitted Nancy. "My parents embarrassed me."

"That's not Alan's problem," noted Reed. "His daughter idolizes him. Anyone could see that. She just wants to be let off the leash, that's all. And why not?"

"No reason at all," I agreed.

"You're an understanding father."

"I do my best, Mr. Reed."

"Yes," said Melinda, "your daughter is a credit to you."

"How did you get on with your own father, Alan?" asked Nancy.

"I didn't," I said, shaking my head. "We loathed each other."

"Why?"

"He could never leave his job behind when he came home."

"What did he do?"

"He was a policeman."

Mention of the law brought that phase of the conversation to a swift end. Since the meal was almost over, Reed jumped in to invite us back to their house for coffee. Nancy was happy to go and I was about to join them when we were interrupted. Frank Colouris glided up to our table, exchanged niceties with everyone, then bent over to speak in my ear.

"Excuse me, Mr. Saxon," he said, "but there's someone who wishes to see you."

Reed was irritated. "Can't it wait, Frank? We're just leaving."

"The woman is very anxious to see Mr. Saxon."

"Woman?" I repeated.

"Yes, sir," said Colouris. "Her name is Angela Pike. She's actually a member of our catering staff but this is her night off. Just as well, in the circumstances."

"Why?"

"She used to live with Maurice Dobbs."

The mood of the evening changed immediately. Reed's bonhomie evaporated and he took his deputy aside for a moment. Melinda shot a meaningful glance at Nancy. The idea of meeting Mo's partner was not very appealing to me. Uncertain what to expect, I knew that she hadn't come to offer me congratulations. Part of me wanted to dodge the woman altogether but another part accepted that I had an obligation to see her. Reed turned round with a forced smile.

"You don't have to bother with her now, Alan," he said airily. "Why spoil a nice evening? Frank can tell her that you're far too busy. Put her off until tomorrow."

"But I *want* to see her now, Mr. Reed," I said.

"Oh?"

"The least I can offer the poor woman is common courtesy."

"We can't have her bothering one of our honored guests."

"It's no bother." I looked at Colouris. "Where is she?"

"Waiting in my office, sir."

"Then let's go. I'll catch up with the rest of you later."

I could see that Reed was unhappy with the arrangement, but he didn't protest. While he escorted the two ladies out, I went off in the other direction with the deputy manager. As we passed the Flamingo Bar, I scanned the tables for a sign of Lynette, but she and the others had gone. Colouris took me across the hotel lobby.

"It might be better if I stayed with you, Mr. Saxon," he suggested. "Angela is understandably upset. She wants to see you alone but it may not be such a good idea."

"I don't need you to hold my hand, Mr. Colouris."

"Things may get a little heated."

"We'll see."

"What if she starts to get hysterical?"

"I'm quite used to handling distraught females," I said. "I married one."

"It's not quite the same thing, sir."

I was adamant. "If she wants me on my own, that's what she'll get."

Colouris was torn between concern and relief. Though he was worried on my behalf, I had the feeling that he did not really want to face the woman himself. After all, it was he who had dismissed Mo from his job at the hotel. He settled for a compromise.

"I'll wait outside the door," he said.

Angela Pike was waiting for me in the deputy manager's office, pacing the floor like a caged animal. I could see why Colouris had qualms about her. She was a black woman of medium height and spreading girth with a pretty face that was besmirched by a scowl. What startled me was the fact that she was at least twenty years younger than Mo. It required an effort of will to picture them as lovers. She'd obviously been crying but her eyes were now blazing with anger.

"Is you Mr. Saxon?" she demanded.

"Yes," I said, holding my ground. "I believe you wanted to speak to me."

"Mo told me all about you, he did."

"I'm terribly sorry about what happened."

"You helped to get him the sack."

"That's not true," I said gently. "Look, why don't you sit down so that we can discuss this properly?" She folded her arms in defiance and remained on her feet. "OK," I went on, "have it your way. But let's get the facts straight, Miss Pike. I made no complaint at all against Mo. I didn't approve of his behavior when he drove us from the airport, but I was ready to let it go. It was Jessica, a friend of my daughter's, who lodged the complaint with the management."

"You still responsible, Mr. Saxon."

"I'm sorry you feel that way."

"Mo hated you."

"Why?"

"He liked his job. He was good at it."

"That's a matter of opinion," I said. "According to Mr. Colouris, there'd been one or two other complaints made about him."

She became defensive. "Only in the last couple of weeks. Before that, Mo had no trouble. Everyone liked him. You ask them, Mr. Saxon. Go on."

"I'll take your word for it, Miss Pike. You knew him far better than I."

"I loved him!"

The declaration produced a flood of tears but she spurned the handkerchief that I offered her, using the back of her hand to stem the flow instead. She surveyed me through moist eyes. I tried to look contrite.

"Tell me how you found Mo," she said.

"I'd rather not."

"He was my man, Mr. Saxon. I got a right to know."

"I'd prefer to spare you the anguish."

"Mo's dead. My man been murdered. Tell me what you saw."

"Only if you agree to sit down," I said, indicating the chair. "Please, Miss Pike. It'll make it easier for both of us. What happened last night was a tragedy. I wish to God that I hadn't been a witness."

She glowered at me before lowering herself slowly onto the chair. I sat opposite her, wondering how I could tell my tale without either provoking her ire or distressing her even more. I glanced around the office. It was a small, featureless room with little furniture beyond a table and three chairs. A green filing cabinet stood up against one wall. A notice board, bedecked with charts and information sheets, covered the wall opposite. On the desk was Frank Colouris' computer. Locked away in its memory, I felt sure, among the details of the rest of the hotel staff, were the names of Maurice Dobbs and Angela Pike, but what brought the pair together was a mystery. They seemed an unlikely couple. The place was functional and cheerless. I could have wished for a more comfortable venue in which to discuss such a harrowing subject, but I had no choice. Hands clasped tightly, Angela Pike waited with impatience.

I cleared my throat. Speaking slowly, I gave her as simple and unvarnished an account as I could manage, pausing whenever she winced and offering my handkerchief twice in the course of the narrative. On the second occasion, she took it from me and I saw that as a sign of progress. Angela Pike would never like me. Because of my brush with Mo, I'd always be seen as an enemy, but at least she was listening to me without adopting the aggressive stance I'd seen earlier. I was strangely nervous in front of her. Giving my statement to the police had been far less grueling than describing events to the lover of the murder victim. I trod with extreme care every inch of the way. When I'd finished, she needed a couple of minutes before she could speak.

"Thank you," she mumbled.

"Nobody deserves to die like that," I said.

"Mo was a good man. Who could do such a thing to him?"

"That's what the police want to find out."

She gave a snort. "The police! All they wanted to do was to search the house. For clues, they said. Mo was the victim. They should look for clues that lead them to the killer, not bother me like that. What they after in our house?"

I was asking myself the same question but I didn't think that she would have liked some of the answers that suggested themselves. Mo may have been a wonderful partner to Angela Pipe, but he had been distinctly unpleasant to me. I hadn't forgotten the threat that he'd issued at our last meeting. It made me probe for information of my own.

"How long did you know him?" I asked.

"Almost a year," she replied. "Ever since I come to work here."

"You'd never met him before?"

"No, I live in St. George's Parish then."

"Had he always been a driver?"

She was evasive. "Mo do lots of jobs. He was a quarry worker in Hamilton Parish then he was on the ferry. Oh, and other things. He study electronics," she said proudly, "Mo was very clever. He know about electronics but they say he not study enough."

"Yes, he told me. It rankled with him."

"Not fair, Mr. Saxon. They were never fair on Mo."

"Who weren't?"

"Everyone."

"Is that why he was so angry?" Belligerence flared momentarily in her eyes but it soon faded. She stared ahead of her. "I can only speak as I find, Miss Pike," I continued. "On my short acquaintance with Mo, I'd say he had a chip on his shoulder. Am I right?"

She nodded her head. "My fault," she murmured.

"Why?"

"Mo blame himself but it was me."

"How could you make him so angry?"

"I try. I try ever so hard."

"Try what?"

"Mo was hurt. He think it him."

"I'm not with you, Miss Pike."

"Until then, we were happy."

"I'm sure."

"No problems. Nice, new house. Money coming in. No worries, until then."

"When?"

"A couple of weeks ago. When we hear."

"I'm sorry," I said, "but I don't quite understand."

Angela Pike looked at me with a mixture of dislike and curiosity. While she would always resent me, I'd earned some respect from her for the honest way in which I'd told her about my discovery of the dead body. It made her study me on her own account instead of looking at me through Mo's eyes.

"He talk about you a lot," she confided.

"We only met the day I arrived in Bermuda."

"Before you come, Mr. Saxon. Mo mention your name."

"Why?"

"You famous man."

"Not any more, I'm afraid. I'm near the end of my career as a golfer."

"Mo say you were famous."

"What else did he say?"

"Nothing you like to hear."

"Go back to what happened a few weeks ago," I urged. "Mo was hurt by something, wasn't he? Something that went very deep with him. That's why he was so angry. What was it?"

She gave a shrug, "Report."

"What report?"

"From the hospital."

"Was he ill? Was he in pain?"

"Report about me, Mr. Saxon. Tests were negative." She bit her lip and lowered her eyes. "Doctors say I never have children. We want a baby so much. Mo think of nothing else. We *pray* for a baby but it impossible. I let Mo down."

"It's not your fault," I assured her.

"I think it is."

"No. These things happen. It's just bad luck."

"Mo believe it to do with him. It change him completely, Mr. Saxon. He behave like he never behave before. I frightened for him."

"Frightened?"

"Yes, Mr. Saxon," she said, looking up at me. "Mo so upset, he even talk about giving up. What's the point? he ask. When the police tell me they find him dead, I think at first Mo carry out his threat."

"What threat? *Suicide?*"

"Yes," she wailed. "I think that he take his own life because of me."

I was alone in the room with Angela Pike for so long that Frank Colouris eventually knocked on the door and came in. He looked as if he expected the carpet to be stained with my blood and was amazed to find me kneeling in front of the woman and holding her hands as I tried to console her. In recounting her personal tragedy, she had lost all sense of rage. She was at last available for sympathy and I gave it unequivocally. The sight of the deputy manager made her pull herself together. Conscious that she was still a minor member of staff, she rose guiltily from the chair and muttered her thanks. Before I could offer to see her off the premises, she thrust my handkerchief back at me, gave Colouris a dutiful nod, then went out.

"How did you get on?" he asked.

"I'm still breathing."

"She was quite fired up when she banged on my door."

"I think that she was entitled to be, Mr. Colouris," I said. "Mo was her man. She loved him to distraction. I can't think why, but there must have been a reason."

"What did she say?"

"Very little. I was the one who did the talking."

"I see."

"What she really wanted to know was how I discovered the body. The police had given her their version but she doesn't have too high an opinion of them. She needed to hear it from the horse's mouth, so to speak. I was treading on eggshells. Give me a police interrogation any day."

"Did she threaten you in any way?"

"Of course not, Mr. Colouris."

"That's a relief," he said with a sigh. "After what happened to Mo, I'd hate to have to discipline her as well. Angela is a nice woman and an experienced waitress. We don't want to lose her."

"It's not for me to tell you how to do your job," I said, gazing through the open door, "but I do think compassionate leave is in order."

"I've already spoken to her about that, sir. Angela can have as much time off as she wishes. The time to come back here is when she's good and ready."

I was glad that Colouris was in charge of the situation rather than Calvin Reed. The manager might not have been so accommodating. He would certainly have kept Angela Pike away from me. Colouris was more considerate. After thanking him for the loan of his office, I made my way towards the Reeds' bungalow, making a detour so that I could check both the Calypso Bar and the restaurant. Lynette and her pals were in neither. Clearly, she was off having fun somewhere with the Canadian bank clerk. The meeting with Mo's partner had been enlightening. I'd approached it with a measure of trepidation, yet I'd come away with some intriguing pieces of information as well as some insight into the man's character. Mo had obviously talked to her about me before he picked us up at the airport. I wondered why.

It was not difficult for me to understand why he'd blamed himself for her failure to conceive. Angela Pike was still relatively young. He was middle-aged, worn down by years of hard work and nagged by fears of flagging potency. His urge to have a child with her had turned to desperation. The report from the hospital must have been soul-destroying for both of them. I could imagine all too well the arguments that had ensued. Having seen how irascible Mo could be, I felt sorry for his partner. She would certainly have come off worse in the exchanges. Given the situation, it was very brave of her to confront me the way she did so soon after his death. If I'd relieved her suffering in even the tiniest way, my efforts had been well worth it.

"Sorry to drop this in your lap, sir," said Colouris.

"I'm glad you did."

"It was kind of you to see her."

"It would have been cruel not to, Mr. Colouris."

"You obviously brought her some comfort."

"Not really," I sighed. "The only comfort she'll get is when the police catch the man who killed Mo. I'd like to be around when that happens as well."

When I got to the bungalow, I said very little about the encounter with Angela Pike. It was hardly the stuff of polite chitchat. Since they'd already made and drunk their coffee, I moved straight on to the next stage and accepted the offer of a brandy. After my session in the deputy manager's office, I felt that I needed it. Nancy Wykoff was reclining in an armchair, rolling her glass between her palms to warm it. I admired her readiness to take her time. She had already signaled her intentions to me and knew that I was hers at some point that night. But there was no hurry. Preliminaries were there to be savored.

The house was the largest and most luxurious on the site. Situated at the rear of the hotel, it was sheltered by palms and featured a kidney shaped pond in the middle of its lawn. A bronze flamingo stood at the edge of the water. The living room was a true reflection of Calvin Reed's taste. It was neat, tidy, well organized and expensively furnished. In spite of the fact that Cubist prints hung on the walls and *objets d'art* were scattered around on every surface, the place was almost characterless. It had an almost clinical feel to it. Reed and his wife fitted in it perfectly. Like the flamingo, they, too, might have been well-polished bronze statues.

They listened with amusement as Nancy described our round of golf.

"The guys playing ahead of us lost ball after ball into the lakes," she recalled. "Their language was appalling. In the end, they had the grace to let us through."

"Only on condition that I gave them some tips," I said.

"And did you?" asked Reed.

"Yes, I told them to abandon golf and take up water sports."

Melinda laughed. "You sound as if you had some fun at Port Royal."

"Alan was a real gentleman," said Nancy fondly. "Whenever I hit a bad shot, he pretended not to notice."

"You didn't hit any bad shots," I argued.

She smiled at the others. "See what I mean?"

"Nancy is a good golfer. Don't believe a word she says."

"Let's face it, Alan. I'm hopeless in sand. Put me in a bunker and I create a Desert Storm before I manage to hack the ball clear. Whereas you just chip it out as if it's second nature to you."

"I've played dozens of links courses in England, remember. I'm used to dealing with sand. Except when there's a high wind, of course," I added ruefully. "If it doesn't go in your mouth when you use your sand wedge, it either goes down the front of your shirt or it blinds you. Golf has many hazards."

We talked on until Nancy excused herself to visit the bathroom. Melinda put the coffee cups back on the tray and took them into the kitchen. Reed took advantage of their absence to touch on the murder for the first time.

"What did that woman want, Alan?"

"To hear how I found the body."

"She'd no right to bother you like that."

"I think she has every right, Mr. Reed. The police had given her their story but she doesn't seem to have the same faith in them that you do. Did you know that they searched Mo's house? That really upset her."

"They were only looking for evidence."

"It depends how they did it," I said, recalling my father's brutal search technique as he ransacked my room. "Nobody likes to have their personal possessions thrown all over the place."

"Is that what happened?"

"I'm not sure, but Angela Pike was jangled by the experience. I know that."

"You won't be troubled by her again."

"She was no trouble, Mr. Reed."

"I'll tell Frank to keep her away from you."

"There's no need."

"Anyway," he said, changing tack, "let's forget her. She's irrelevant. Our main problem is keeping Peter Fullard here. There's been a development."

"Oh?"

"When we got back here from the restaurant, there was a message from him on my answerphone. He and his wife have had second thoughts. They want to fly home, after all. You know what that means, Alan."

"Further delays."

"His presence is vital."

"Not at the moment," I reminded him. "Work has been suspended on the course until the police have finished sniffing around. Peter and I are just cooling our heels."

"He's not prepared to wait until they've finished their search."

"Why not?"

"He seems to think that his life is in danger."

"That's ridiculous!"

"Try telling him that."

"I did, Mr. Reed. I thought I'd brought him and Denise to their senses."

"Apparently not." We heard the noise of the toilet being flushed. "Look, I don't suppose you could have another go at them, could you, Alan?"

"Tonight?" I asked, glancing at my watch. "It's late."

"They'll still be up, I'm sure."

"That's one thing we can count on. Sleepless nights in the Fullard bedroom."

"Talk to them, Alan. They listen to you."

"Don't bank on it."

"We simply mustn't let Peter disappear now. Supposing the murder investigation drags on and on? We may never be able to get him back."

"Tell him you'll sue him for breach of contract."

"I prefer to use a softer approach," he said. "His name is Alan Saxon."

Nancy rejoined us in time to hear the tail end of our conversation.

"What's all this about breach of contract?" she asked.

"My partner is getting cold feet," I explained. "He and his wife are so shaken by what's happened that they want to run away from Bermuda. I have to talk them around."

"*Now?*"

Something in her voice hinted at fear of another breach of contract—the one that I'd willingly signed the moment that we met again that evening. I tried to reassure her with a smile.

"It won't take long," I said confidently. "And it is important."

"Very important," added Reed as his wife came in from the kitchen.

Nancy collected her purse. "Time for me to leave, anyway," she said casually.

"Must you?" asked Melinda.

"I need my beauty sleep, honey."

"Not from where I'm standing," said Reed appreciatively.

"You're a sweetie, Cal."

Melinda beamed. "That's what I keep telling him."

We exchanged farewells with our hosts then walked back to the hotel. The sky was clear. A gentle breeze was blowing. The sound of music wafted out of the Calypso Bar. It was a night for romance, not for another exhausting debate with the Fullards. Nancy let her shoulder brush gently against my arm.

"I thought for a moment that you were pulling out on me," she said.

"Business before pleasure, I'm afraid."

"Can't it wait until morning?"

"They may be on their way to the airport by then."

"Is it that serious?"

"Yes, Nancy."

"As long as you don't keep me waiting too long."

"Where will I find you?"

"Third Floor. Room 333. Think you can remember that?"

I grinned broadly. "I'm working on it."

It took minutes of patient negotiation before Peter and Denise Fullard would even let me into their suite. When they finally opened the door, the first thing I noticed was that their bags were standing in the middle of the room, already packed.

"Are you planning to do a moonlight flit?" I asked.

"We're leaving tomorrow morning," said Peter, embarrassed by what he was forced to do. "The direct flight to Gatwick is fully booked so we'll take whatever we can get.

We'll fly to New York or somewhere. We can pick up a plane to the U.K. there."

"Don't you think you're being too hasty?"

"No, Alan. We've talked it through. Denise and I came to a decision."

They'd also come to a decision to wear matching dressing gowns of white cotton with a floral design on them. They probably had identical toothbrushes as well. That was my problem. I was up against two people who spoke with one voice. My only hope lay in separating them. Peter and Denise looked so ridiculously vulnerable in their night attire. I felt sorry for them but I didn't let pity deflect me.

"Denise," I began, "I wonder if I might have a word alone with Peter?"

She blinked nervously. "Why?"

"Because he and I are partners in this venture."

"You can say anything you like in front of Denise," said her husband loyally.

"But I'd appreciate a moment alone with you, Peter. Is that too much to ask?"

There was a long pause before he nodded his approval. After a muttered conversation with his wife, he ushered her into the bedroom and closed the door behind her. He made an effort to look adamant.

"Don't waste your time trying to talk me out of it, Alan," he warned.

"You're the one who's wasting time," I countered. "Valuable time, at that. If you take to the skies tomorrow, vital decisions about our course will be delayed."

"That can't be helped."

"Yes, it can."

"I'm sorry, Alan."

"Do the job for which we're being paid."

"There was no mention of sabotage in the contract."

"No," I said, appealing to his sense of pride, "but there was the stipulation that the power of decision lay with a certain Peter Fullard. They didn't choose you because they admired your taste in dressing gowns, you know. They wanted the best, Peter, and they know your reputation. What will happen to that reputation if the word gets round that you ran for cover when the project hit a few snags?"

"A murder victim is rather more than a snag."

"Granted."

"Then that's the end of the discussion."

"Oh no, it isn't," I insisted. "I had an interview with his girlfriend earlier on. Angela Pike, that's her name. The poor woman is in a terrible state and with good reason. I wish that you and Denise could have met her," I said, glancing at the bedroom door. "She's lost the person she loved most in the world. All that you and Denise have lost is your nerve." He had the grace to look slightly ashamed. I capitalized at once. "There are two ways to do this, Peter. You can wash your hands of the whole project and fly home to safety or you can stand by your partner and tough it out. Actions have consequences. Go now and you know what will happen."

"What?" he bleated.

"Calvin Reed won't be able to hold things up forever. He has deadlines to meet. If he wants the course finished on time, he'll be forced to give the contractors a free hand. They're bound to look for short cuts and make significant changes. It won't be the course that we designed."

"Yes, it will—if you stand over them."

"I don't have the experience. You do. You know how to deal with contractors."

"I'll talk to them on the phone from England."

"It's not the same thing, Peter."

"It's better than nothing."

"You can't do this by remote control."

He walked away. "Stop trying to blackmail me, Alan."

"I only want to help you," I said, going after him. "And myself, of course. We're in this together, remember. Both our names appear in the hotel brochures for next year. 'A magnificent new golf course, designed by Peter Fullard, the internationally acclaimed course architect, and Alan Saxon, renowned golfer, former winner of the British Open.' I don't want people playing on a course that's two-thirds ours and one-third improvisation by contractors who are told to hurry things along." When he turned to face me, I could see that I was at last getting through to him. I played my final card. "Then there are the personal implications."

"In what way?"

"Well, I thought we were friends."

"We are, Alan. You know that."

"What I know," I said with unfeigned sincerity, "is that working with you on this project has been one of the most exciting things I've ever done in my career. It's been a revelation, Peter. Thanks to you, I've learned things about designing a golf course that never even crossed my mind. You're a genius."

"Don't undervalue your own input," he said. "It was crucial."

"So crucial that you were eager to continue the partnership."

"I still am."

"You mentioned a course in Spain."

"That's the one I've been approached about," he said, "but there are some people in Thailand who've been putting out feelers as well. I'd be thrilled if you agreed to be my partner on either of those projects."

"Not if you walk out now and leave me holding the baby."

"That's not what I'm doing, Alan."

"Well, it's what it feels like to me."

He became more agitated. "If I was here on my own, I'd stay," he said. "I would, honestly. Nothing would scare me off. But I have to think about Denise."

"I'm responsible for Lynette and Jessica," I argued, "but that doesn't stop me from staying at my post. Get one thing into your head, will you? We're not in the slightest danger. Especially here in the hotel, where they have their own security." I patted him on the arm. "Raise the portcullis. Lower the drawbridge. Come out and join the rest of us."

"It's easy for you to make light of this."

"Oh, I'm not making light of it," I said with sufficient to anger to make him take a step back. "I was the one who found Mo hanging from that tree. I was the one who was grilled by the police this morning. I was the one who had to face a sticky interview with Mo's girlfriend." I strode to the door. "If you or Denise had been through any of that, you might have cause to complain. As it is, you're behaving like a pair of frightened rabbits."

It sounded like a good exit line so I left before he could reply. Instead of walking away, however, I waited outside the door and listened. I heard Denise come hurrying out of the bedroom to join her husband. Their voices were soon raised in anxious discussion. My hopes rose. I had the feeling that my strategy may have worked.

I was relieved that Nancy Wykoff had invited me to her room. It would have been awkward for me to lure her into my suite. Even if the girls were not there, I'd have felt inhibited by the fact that they had the adjoining suite. What if they should decide to knock on the connecting door when they got back from their night out? I could be caught in a compromising position. Jessica, I fancied, would hoot with laughter, but Lynette was bound to be embarrassed. I wanted to spare her that. Nancy had to be protected as well. There were rules to be observed. No woman wants a nervous lover who is looking over his shoulder throughout. On my way to the third floor, I made a resolve. I was no longer the father of a twenty-year-old daughter. I was simply the man on whom Nancy Wykoff had graciously bestowed a favor. She deserved all of me.

When she let me into her room, she gave a smile of surprise.

"That was quick, Alan."

"I'd have been here much sooner," I joked, "but I forgot your number."

"We'll have to think of a way to make you remember it." She waved me to the sofa and I sat down at one end. "What can I get you? More brandy?"

"No thanks. A glass of water will be fine."

"Coming up."

She crossed to the drinks cabinet and unscrewed a bottle of spa water. After filling two tumblers, she handed one of them to me then sat at the other end of the sofa so that she could tuck her legs up on it. Nancy was still wearing the toga-like dress that I'd admired earlier, but she'd kicked off her shoes. She raised her glass.

"Cheers!" I said, then took a long sip of water.

"How were Peter and Denise?"

"Teetering on the brink of total collapse."

"What did you say?"

"I appealed to Peter's better instincts."

"And?"

"Keep your fingers crossed."

"I'm sure you did the trick, Alan." She sipped her own water. "What happened earlier, when you went off to see that woman?"

"It was a bit stressful at first but I think I offered her some solace."

"Good."

"Mo was a lucky man, to have someone like her."

"Why?"

"She was an attractive woman and considerably younger."

"What did she see in him?"

"That's what I can't work out, Nancy. The main thing is that I managed to calm her down. She was quite aggressive when I arrived but it soon wore off."

"Sounds to me as if you've been a regular Boy Scout this evening," she said with approval. "Soothing the grief-stricken girlfriend of a murder victim. Using your magic on Peter and Denise Fullard. I hope you haven't used up your stock of Good Deeds."

"Oh no. I've come prepared."

"That's what I was hoping." She appraised me shrewdly. "Tell me when."

"When what?"

"When you decided that you wanted this to happen."

"I suppose it was on the sixteenth green at Port Royal."

"I thought you were concentrating on your game."

"I was, Nancy," I replied, "but I took an interest in yours as well. I may be the pro but you played the better tee shot at the sixteenth. Yet you didn't tease or crow over me. You simply admired the way I got out of that bunker."

"And *that's* when you made the decision?"

"Not exactly," I confessed. "If you want to know the precise moment, it was when you bent over to retrieve your ball from the hole. Those blue shorts really suit you."

Nancy laughed. "You're way off the pace, Mr. Saxon. I'm years ahead of you. I started having lewd thoughts about Alan Saxon when I saw you playing golf on TV. There's something so sexy about the way you swing that driver. When I met you in person, I was bowled over. In spite of the way it looks, I'm very selective where guys are concerned. It usually takes me months to make up my mind."

"I don't have months."

"You don't need them, Alan."

"So when did *you* decide we might get it together?"

"Halfway through that meal with the Fullards."

"You kept it well hidden."

"I didn't want to upset the others." She drank some more water then toyed with the glass. "How honest do you want me to be?"

"As honest as you like."

"OK," she said with a lazy grin. "By the time we reached the dessert, I was ready for you to take me across the table."

I grinned. "Peter and Denise would really have freaked out then!"

"Do you think they spotted anything?"

"Only each other, Nancy. It's the secret of their success." She uncurled a leg so that she could rub my thigh with her naked foot. "How honest do you want *me* to be?" I asked, thinking it was time to put my cards on the table. "Because there's something you should know before we go any further. I think you're a marvelous woman and there's nowhere I'd rather be right now then here with you. But, in view of your personal history, I do hope you haven't got me lined up as a potential third husband." She went off into peals of laughter. "What's so funny?"

"You are, Alan."

"I'm only telling you the truth. I can't ever marry you."

"Nobody marries me," she said, rubbing my thigh again. "I marry *them*."

"Does that mean I won't have to buy an engagement ring tomorrow morning?"

"You'll be too busy having breakfast in bed with me."

"Sounds tempting."

"Then why don't we make a start?" she suggested, getting up from the sofa and handing me her glass. "I could use some more water. Will you see to it, please?"

I hauled myself to my feet. "Of course."

"And try to relax. You're quite safe with me."

"Safe?"

"You're not being lined up, I promise you," she said, toying with the clasp on her dress. "I like to call the shots in a relationship. I could never hook up with a guy who was so much better than me at golf. It would upset the balance of power."

She went into the bedroom and left the door ajar.

Breakfast in bed was a rare treat for me, especially since it was fed to me by a naked woman with a beautiful all-over tan. Nancy Wykoff seemed determined to spoil me in every way. She'd boasted about being in control of her relationships but she was gloriously submissive in bed. While she peeled a banana, I admired the contours of her body. She offered me the banana. When I bit off a slice, she began to eat the rest of it herself, tossing the skin onto a plate.

"Any regrets?" she asked.

"Yes," I said. "I had my eye on the whole banana."

She nudged me playfully. "About last night, I mean."

"None at all, Nancy. What about you?"

"I'm still floating on Cloud Nine."

I snapped my fingers. "So that's why you asked for room 333!"

We shared a laugh then drank from our respective cups of coffee. I was both revived and awakened to my responsibilities. She saw the concern in my eyes.

"Problems?"

"I'm afraid so. I need to make sure that Peter and Denise haven't flown the nest."

"You did your best to stop them."

"Calvin Reed will expect a report. Also," I said, "I'd like to slip back to my room for a shave and a change of clothes. I think you deserve more than this designer stubble."

"That's not all, is it?"

"Yes, it is, Nancy."

"Why try to hide it?"

"Hide what?"

"The real reason you want to go is to check on the girls."

"Well, yes," I admitted, "I suppose it is. I'd like to know that they got back safely."

"Where did they go?"

"Who knows? They made friends with two young Canadians. It was their last night in Bermuda so Lynette and Jessica decided to give them a send-off. The girls are probably still fast asleep in bed. I'll just peep in on them."

"Then what?"

"I'll see if I can remember how to find my way back here." She smiled invitingly. "Take the card key. I'll be in the bath."

"Anything I can get you while I'm gone?"

"A clean-shaven Alan Saxon."

"I'll be a new man," I promised, getting out of bed and moving the breakfast tray to the table. "And thank you for your hospitality. I'm grateful."

"Show me *how* grateful."

I kissed her on the lips. "That's just a deposit," I explained, breaking away. "I'll pay the rest of the installments when I get back. Don't go away, will you?"

"I wouldn't dare."

She lay back against the headboard and watched me dress, then she pointed to the card key that lay on the dressing table. Scooping it up, I gave her a wave and went out of the bedroom. Before I let myself out into the corridor, I put my head out to see that it was deserted. Once across the threshold, the rules changed. Inside her suite, I'd relished the sense of freedom and exhilaration. Outside, I was a man with a daughter and a paranoid partner. I was also involved in a murder investigation. I had serious obligations. There was another important consideration. For Nancy Wykoff's sake as well as my own, I didn't want to be seen sneaking out of her room. People might get the right idea.

My first instinct was to make my way to the Fullards' suite to see if my words of wisdom had had the desired effect. Peter had been visibly shaken by what I said. In a sense, our friendship was at stake, and he valued that as much as I did. Denise was the critical factor. Could he persuade her to stay or would he succumb to her fears and take her off the island? There was nothing else I could do to sway their decision. All the buttons that could be pressed had been well and truly pushed home. I was better off ignoring Peter and Denise for a while. I'd soon know which way they'd jumped. In any case, Lynette and Jessica were my primary concern. I not only wanted to make sure that they had got back to their room, I was anxious that they didn't catch me slipping into my own with a growth of beard on my face. I didn't want either of them to *know*.

After walking up two flights of steps, I came out into a deserted corridor and trotted along the carpet. Once inside my room, I felt that I was over the first hurdle. I put my ear to the connecting door but heard no sound from the other side. I tapped gently on the door before inching it open. They were not there. Since their bedroom door was wide open, I walked across to it to look in, expecting to find both girls fast asleep after a late night. Neither of the beds had been slept in. When the initial shock wore off, I chided myself for being so narrow-minded and hypocritical. Lynette and Jessica were old enough and intelligent enough to make decisions about their sex lives, and I could hardly take a moral stance after spending a night of abandon with Nancy Wykoff. The likelihood was that the girls were still curled up with their Canadian friends. The most sensible thing for me to do was to forget that I'd seen their empty bedroom and say nothing about the matter when we next met.

It was only when I went back into my own suite that I saw the light flashing on the telephone. Someone had left me a message. I lifted the receiver and pressed the button. The man's voice was curt and explicit.

"Hello, Mr. Saxon. We have your daughter and her friend. Do as you're told and they will not be harmed. We'll be in touch very soon."

Chapter Six

My first thought was that it must be some sort of hoax, a cruel joke played on me by the two Canadians. The notion that Lynette and Jessica had been abducted was too ludicrous to take seriously. They were strong and capable adults who could look after themselves very well. Then I remembered the sequence of events on the Blue Dolphin golf course, culminating in the murder of Maurice Dobbs. It seemed that whoever wanted to sabotage the course had decided to increase the pressure markedly. Because the sight of a hanged man hadn't scared me off, they'd kidnapped my daughter and taken her friend along as well. I was overwhelmed with guilt. In bringing Lynette to Bermuda, I'd placed her in a position of great danger. Worse than that, at a time when I should have been protecting her, or at least checking that she was safe, I was lying in the arms of a woman whom I'd met only days earlier. It was unforgivable. What sort of a father was I? Something else pricked my conscience. I didn't know how long the message had been waiting for me to pick it up but valuable time had definitely been wasted. Because I delayed the return to my room, the girls' ordeal was probably already several hours old.

My mind was ablaze. Assailed by all sorts of fears, I simply couldn't think straight, and a clear head was vital at such a time. Rushing to the bathroom, I turned on the cold water tap then used both hands to scoop up the water and drench myself. When I caught sight of myself in the mirror, I saw a haggard face, lined with anguish, pitted with remorse and in desperate need of a shave. Was this really the man who'd been lying so contentedly in bed with Nancy Wykoff only five minutes ago? I'd been transformed. I dried myself with a towel and hurried back to the telephone. I needed to hear the message again before I was absolutely sure that it was not someone's warped idea of fun. When I pressed the button once more, the voice was as brusque and peremptory as before.

"Hello, Mr. Saxon. We have your daughter and her friend. Do as you're told and they will not be harmed. We'll be in touch very soon."

The man had an American accent but I could neither place it geographically nor make an accurate guess at his age. He did, however, sound somewhat older than the two Canadians whom the girls had befriended. Were they involved in the abduction? Had their attentions merely been a clever front for ulterior motives? The first thing I needed to do was to chase them up immediately. Lynette had said that they were leaving the hotel today. I prayed that they'd not already departed. Snatching up the receiver, I dialed the number for reception. A bright young female voice came on the line.

"Reception here. How may I help you?"

"I want to know if two guests have checked out yet," I said.

"Were they due to leave today?"

"I think so."

"What are the names, sir?"

I realized that I only knew them as Rick and Conrad. What their surnames were, I could only guess. I wished that I'd found out more details from Lynette at the start. I'd been far too lax. My sense of guilt deepened.

"Are you still there, sir?" asked the young woman.

"Yes," I replied, "but I have a slight problem. The guests are two young Canadians and I only know their first names. I could describe them to you, if you like."

"That's not much help, I'm afraid."

"They're young, early twenties. One of them is tall and—"

"I'm sorry, sir," she said, interrupting politely, "we have almost eight hundred guests staying at the Blue Dolphin. Several are from Canada. Unless you can tell me their surnames, I can't say if they've left the hotel or not."

"Well, has *anyone* checked out so far today?"

"Quite a few people, sir," she said. "Some of them went to the airport by taxi but most of those leaving this morning are waiting in the lobby for the hotel courtesy bus. It departs in twenty minutes."

"I'll be right down!"

I was out of my door within a second. The elevator seemed to take an age coming and I cursed it audibly until it eventually arrived. When it took me down to ground level, I darted out into the lobby. With their luggage stacked on a trolley, well over a dozen people were waiting for the courtesy bus, but neither Rick nor Conrad was among them. My heart sank. I was afraid that they had either left for the airport by taxi or were implicated in the kidnap. If the latter were the case, they would be holding the girls captive at some secret address. I couldn't bear to think about what they might be doing to Lynette and Jessica. It was enough to know that both my daughter and her friend were being held against their will. The voice message had told me they would not be harmed, but they already had been. Abduction would have terrified the pair of them. Resilient as they might be, the psychological wounds would be deep and lasting. Even Jessica's over-confidence would be reduced to shreds by their predicament.

What was I to do? Inform the police? Seek help from Calvin Reed? Sit by the telephone in my room until I was contacted again? Or conduct a more thorough search for the two Canadians? Another problem reared its head. Up in room 333, Nancy Wykoff was waiting for me in her bath. What was I going to tell *her?* I was in a quandary. Feeling an urgent need for fresh air, I went out on the patio and took several deep breaths. My change of location was fortuitous. As I looked to my left, I was able to see through the windows of the restaurant. A number of guests were enjoying their breakfast. One of them, seated in a corner, caught my attention at once. He was a tall, stringy young man with thinning hair and a Che Guevara mustache. It was either Rick or Conrad. I didn't stop to speculate which. Dashing back into the lobby, I made my way to the restaurant with my heart pounding. By the time I reached his table, I was starting to sweat.

"Excuse me," I said, looming over him. "My name's Alan Saxon."

"Oh, sure," he replied, glancing up at me through bleary eyes. "Heck, I know that. I've seen pictures of you in the sports pages. You're Lynette's father."

"Where is she?"

"Fast asleep in bed, I guess. We had a late night."

"How late?" I said, lowering myself into the chair opposite him. "And before we go any further, do you mind telling me your name?"

He extended a hand. "Conrad, sir. Conrad Biedemeier."

"And your friend is called Rick, I believe," I said, giving him a token handshake.

"Rick Ransley. He's still dead to the world."

"I thought you were leaving today."

"Not until late afternoon. What's the trouble, Mr. Saxon? You look upset."

"What exactly happened last night, Conrad?"

He chuckled. "That's not for me to say, sir. You'd better ask your daughter."

"I had the feeling that you and Jessica had paired off."

"Sort of. Jessica had first pick."

"Did the four of you stay together?"

"Of course."

"So Lynette didn't peel off alone with your friend?"

"What is this?" he said, sitting upright. "When I date a girl, I don't usually get the third degree treatment from a parent. The four of us just went out together and had a great time. Nothing wrong in that, is there, Mr. Saxon?" His eyelids narrowed. "The girls haven't made any complaints about us, have they?"

"No, Conrad."

"So what's the problem?"

"They've disappeared."

"Aren't they in their room?"

"No," I said, "and the beds haven't been slept in."

"That's funny. They said they were going straight back to their suite."

"From where? Where did you last see them?"

He gave a shrug. "Does that matter?"

"It matters a great deal, Conrad. My daughter and her friend have vanished. I'd like to know where they were when you parted with them."

"Inside the hotel."

"In other words," I said, understanding his reluctance to tell me the truth, "they were in your room. If that's the case, I'm not blaming you. I just need to know the time they left. Now, please! This is very important."

"Then, yes," he admitted, "we did finish up in our room. But only because it was on the ground floor," he added, as if it were an extenuating circumstance. "It was closer, you see. When we came up from the beach."

"The beach?"

"Jessica had this crazy idea we should have a midnight swim. I'm not into skinny-dipping myself but she bullied us into it. Luckily, there was nobody else about. Anyway," he went on, "we stayed on the beach till we dried off and, you know, did the usual things, smoked some grass, fooled around a bit."

"You gave my daughter cannabis?" I protested.

"Heck, no, Mr. Saxon. It was Lynette who offered it to us. Good quality stuff as well. She gets it from some guy in Oxford, apparently."

I was shaken. Although I see her infrequently, I like to think that I know my own daughter very well. I'd have said categorically that she neither smoked, drank to excess nor took drugs of any kind. A new Lynette suddenly came into view. She'd not only been smoking pot with her friends. If Conrad's story was correct, she'd also been the supplier, which meant that she must have brought the cannabis illegally into Bermuda.

"A little grass does nobody any harm," he said, trying to calm me down. "I daresay you've smoked a bit yourself in your time. We're not talking hard drugs here, Mr. Saxon. Jessica was the only one interested in those."

I gaped. "Did she have any with her?"

"Of course not. She likes to boast about what she's tried, that's all."

I was even more alarmed. If Lynette was firmly under her friend's influence, how long would it be before she was drawn into experimenting with heroin or cocaine? It was an additional fear but it was dwarfed by my horror at their immediate plight.

"What time did you leave the beach?" I asked.

"Who knows?" said Conrad, scratching his head. "Must have been close to two o'clock, I guess. We walked up to the hotel together."

"Was there anyone about?"

"Only the night staff."

"Nobody else? Did you have the idea that you were being *watched*?"

"No, sir. But, then, we were still a bit high. Especially Rick. He was way out."

"So the four of you went to your room, you say?"

"Only for a nightcap," he explained, "except that it didn't turn out that way. We had a drink or two, then Jessica decided to teach us this game of cards. She had a pack with her. Didn't last long, though, because Rick passed out on the sofa." He gave a confiding chuckle. "He doesn't have much staying power at the best of times. Then Lynette said she felt sick and went into the bathroom. We had the feeling she might be in there some time," he said easily, "so I took Jessica into the bedroom and we made out."

"While your friend was asleep and my daughter was sick?"

"You have to take your chances when you can, sir. And Jessica was dead keen."

"I'm sure she was."

"By the time we came out of the bedroom, Lynette seemed much better but she was very tired. She insisted on going back to their own suite so off they went."

"Alone?" I said. "You didn't even see them to their door?"

"I was pooped, Mr. Saxon. Just waved them off."

"So what did they do? Take the elevator?"

"I guess. It's only ten or fifteen yards from our room."

"Where was Rick all this time?"

"Snoring on the sofa. He still is."

"I'll need to speak to him."

"He can't tell you any more than I did, sir."

"Nevertheless, I want a chat with him, especially as he and Lynette seem to have got quite close. He may remember things that have slipped your mind."

"Don't count on it. Rick is not the brightest guy on the block."

"What does he do?"

"Do?"

"Yes," I said. "If the pair of you can afford to stay at a luxury hotel like this, you can't be short of money. Do you or Rick have a private income or something?"

He burst out laughing. "Private income? You gotta be joking. This is the only part of the trip where we treated ourselves. When we get to the Bahamas, we start work as ski bums. We teach water-skiing there and in other places before going on to the French Alps to teach the real thing. We're qualified ski instructors," he said, stroking his mustache. "That's how I worked my way through college." A note of envy intruded. "Private income? Rick and I don't have a spare cent between us. We're not like Jessica with a rich Daddy to indulge our whims and pay all the bills."

The picture became clearer. If Conrad and Rick were ski bums, they'd be experts in the art of picking off attractive female tourists. In all probability, Lynette and Jessica were just the latest in a long line of conquests in the sun or on the slopes of some skiing resort. I didn't know whether to feel hurt or relieved by the information. At least, I told myself, Rick Ransley, the counterfeit bank clerk, would not be my future son-in-law.

"What time are you checking out?" I asked.

"There's a bus leaves for the airport at three o'clock."

"Don't go out of the hotel until then."

"We hadn't planned to, Mr. Saxon," he said. "We'd hoped to have a last lunch with the girls. Where have they gone?"

"I wish I knew, Conrad."

"Probably just wandered off somewhere, that's all," he reassured me. "Jessica's an impulsive girl—I can vouch for that. Once she wants something, she has to have it now. They'll turn up soon, I'm sure."

"I hope so. Meanwhile, I need to know where to find you."

"Room 108."

"Warn your friend," I said. "I'll be along to see him shortly."

Further interrogation would get me nowhere. I was convinced that Conrad Biedemeier had nothing to do with the kidnap. Given the fact that an angry father was glaring at him, he'd been remarkably honest and laid back. He seemed a decent, amiable, easy-going young man with no cause to harm either Lynette or Jessica. What he had done was to place the girls on the ground floor of the hotel some time after two in the morning. The abduction must have occurred somewhere between Room 108 and the suite next to my own. I was jolted by the thought that someone might have been lying in wait in the girls' own suite. My inspection of it had been very cursory. I should have looked for signs of a struggle or clues that pointed to an intruder. It was not too late. I took the elevator back up to our floor, let myself into my own suite then went through the connecting door to theirs. The place seemed dreadfully empty. Clothes, books and magazines were lying untidily about, but they had been since the girls moved in. The room was very much as it had been when I called on them to tell them about my grisly encounter with Mo's lifeless body on the golf course.

It was in the bedroom that I found the evidence I feared. When I put on the overhead light and took a proper look, I saw that a bedside lamp had been knocked to the ground. A small table was on its side in a corner, items that had lain on it now scattered across the carpet. Among them, I noted, was a pack of cards, perhaps the one that Jessica had produced earlier in the Canadians' room. What caused me real pain was the sight of a gold chain on the floor, and I bent down to retrieve it at once. I'd bought it for Lynette's seventeenth birthday and she almost never took it off. Since the clasp was broken, I could only assume that the damage had occurred during a fight. Even though they must have been tired, Lynette and Jessica were still fit young women. They would have resisted any attack on them. My guilt was intensified. Had I been in my own suite, I might have been roused by the commotion and gone to their aid. Lynette would surely have cried out for me. I'd let her and Jessica down badly.

After checking the bedroom thoroughly, I went into the bathroom and saw that the girls' sponge bags had gone. They weren't on the shelf in front of the mirror or in any of the cupboards. Whoever had kidnapped them had shown some forethought. They'd taken the sponge bags with them and perhaps items of clothing. I wondered if it was a sign of compassion on their behalf or an indication that they expected to hold their victims for some time. I was still puzzling over it when I heard the telephone ring in my suite. I shot back through the connecting door as if my life depended on it. I didn't want to miss a call from the kidnapper this time.

"Hello," I gasped, after snatching up the receiver.

"Alan," said a familiar voice, "I'm ringing from the airport. Wanted to thank you."

It was Peter Fullard. I was pulsing with disappointment. At a time of crisis like that, the last person I wanted at the end of a telephone was my partner. I needed a moment to collect myself before speaking.

"Thank me for what?" I said.

"Putting everything in perspective last night."

"Is that what I did?"

"I think so. And so does Denise."

"Good."

"I've changed my mind. Denise is going alone. I'm staying here."

"Great," I said without enthusiasm. "Mr. Reed will be delighted."

"You were so right, Alan. I'm not in any personal danger. I've got to stop being so timid. It's not as if someone is going to murder me in my bed."

At that moment, I'd willingly have committed the crime myself. Peter and Denise were suddenly irrelevant. With an emergency hanging over me, I wanted to forget that they and their multiple anxieties even existed. While they were stoking up each other's paranoia, I was the one who'd been targeted. Not that I intended to tell Peter that. In the short term, I had to keep him in the dark.

"Are you all right, Alan?" he asked.

"Fine, fine," I replied. "Late night, that's all."

"Your voice sounds funny."

"To be honest, I'm expecting an urgent phone call."

"This one is urgent enough, isn't it? I thought you'd be pleased."

"I am, Peter. Overjoyed."

"When you put our friendship on the line, the choice was easy."

"Glad to hear it," I gabbled. "Listen, I'm sorry this isn't the ideal time to talk. Later on, maybe. I need to keep this line clear, Peter. I hope you don't mind. Thanks for ringing. Give my love to Denise, won't you? Hope she has a good flight."

I hung up and dropped down on the sofa. In my desperation, I'd completely forgotten about my late-night embassy to Peter and Denise Fullard. It no longer impinged on my consciousness. My partner is an intelligent man but he's not a student of irony. I don't think he'd appreciate the fact that, while he was worrying about his own safety, it was my daughter and her friend who were now in danger. He'd have to know the truth sooner or later but not at this stage. It would either frighten him away from Bermuda or prompt him to help me, and that would be an unbearable handicap. Before I confided in anyone, I needed to consider whom to tell and what exactly to say.

The telephone rang again. I grabbed it and gasped into the mouthpiece.

"Yes?"

"Alan, it's me," said Nancy Wykoff.

Disappointment flooded through me again. Hoping for contact with the kidnapper, I'd had my second let-down. This one was potentially more embarrassing than the first. Peter Fullard had not been left in a bubble bath, waiting for a lover to return.

"Oh, hello, Nancy," I said meekly.

"You do remember me, then?"

"Of course, of course."

"I thought you were coming back."

"Yes, I was. Honestly."

"So what's keeping you?" she asked. "You've been gone almost an hour."

"Have I?"

"It doesn't take you that long to shave, does it?"

"No, no."

"So what happened. Second thoughts?"

"Nothing like that, Nancy."

"I'm feeling neglected."

"Look, I'm sorry about that. I came back to find a crisis."

"Oh?"

I couldn't stall any longer. Even though our acquaintance had been short, I knew that I could trust Nancy. She was more than a friend. Besides, after spending the night in her bed, sharing secrets along with an immense amount of pleasure, I couldn't, in all fairness, hold out on her. Nancy Wykoff would offer positive support of a kind that was beyond Peter and Denise.

"Lynette and Jessica have been abducted," I told her.

"*What?*" She was shocked. "Are you sure?"

"Dead sure. The kidnapper left a message for me."

"But why would anyone want to touch them?"

"Why else, Nancy? They want to sabotage the new golf course, good and proper."

"Who's behind it?"

"That's what I'm waiting to find out."

"What about those so-called friends? The two Canadians?"

"Rick and Conrad are nothing to do with it," I said. "I'm certain of that. I've just spoken to Conrad in the restaurant. He was as baffled as me."

"What do the cops think?"

"I haven't told them yet."

"Then you must, Alan," she insisted. "Right away. Call the cops. You need to bring in the professionals. Give me five minutes to get dressed and I'll come up."

"This is not your problem, Nancy."

"I know. It's *ours*."

She rang off and left me wondering what the police would think if they found her in my suite when they arrived. I dismissed the thought contemptuously. My daughter and her friend had been abducted. It didn't matter if Inspector Troy Morley found me with a naked woman on each arm. The safety of Lynette and Jessica was paramount. When I made the call, the Inspector was still at the police station in Hamilton. Like me, he made an immediate link between the abduction and the earlier crimes on the golf course. Troy Morley told me to stay in my room in case a second call came from the kidnapper. He promised to be with me as soon as possible. I sighed with relief. Calvin Reed would also need to be informed, but there was another priority. Nancy Wykoff would be knocking on my door within a matter of minutes. She didn't want to see a bearded and hollow-eyed version of the man with whom she'd spent the night. I needed a shower and a shave.

There were so many people in the room that we were in danger of running out of chairs. Inspector Troy Morley arrived with Sergeant Derek Woodford and another detective, a somnolent young man called Steve Hills, who attached a small machine to my telephone so that any incoming calls would be both recorded and simultaneously broadcast to anyone else in the room. Calvin Reed was also there with Frank Colouris in attendance. As soon as they heard what had happened, both men leapt into action and roused the night staff to make preliminary inquiries. Having met the girls, Reed expressed great sympathy and apologized on behalf of the hotel, fearing that the Blue Dolphin had inadvertently placed Lynette and Jessica in danger. In addition to Nancy Wykoff and myself, Conrad Biedemeier and Rick Ransley were also present, summoned by Morley for cross-questioning. When I saw him in action, I realized how perfunctory my own interrogation of Conrad had been. After demanding to see their passports, the Inspector told the young detective to check that the addresses given in them were genuine. Hills went off into the bedroom to make the calls on his mobile.

On closer inspection, Rick Ransley looked less like a bank clerk than one of those irritating know-it-alls you often find behind the desk of airport car rental firms. He was annoyingly over-helpful, spraying the police with details about the girls that were totally irrelevant and even suggesting where they should start looking. Troy Morley eventually shut him up. The story that Conrad Biedemeier told was substantially the one he'd given me, with one significant difference. He made no mention of the cannabis that had been smoked on the beach or of the fact that my daughter had supplied it. Rick Ransley, too, wisely suppressed that particular piece of information. I was grateful. I remembered how indignant I'd been to hear that the four of them had been smoking pot. Peter Fullard and I now had something in common. Both of us had been alarmed at the fate of some Bermuda grass.

Steve Hills was thorough. He could not only confirm the names and addresses of the two Canadians, he knew their destination in the Bahamas and their rates of pay as instructors. Worried by the fate of the girls, Rick and Conrad volunteered to cancel their flight and stay around to offer further assistance, but the Inspector had no reason to detain them. I had the feeling that, if he'd had to listen to Rick Ransley for another minute, he'd have had him forcibly deported. The Canadians were warned to say nothing of the kidnap to anyone else and sent on their way. I raised the thorny problem of how to break the news to Peter Fullard, and the manager came to my rescue. He deputed Frank Colouris to take on diplomatic duties once more. The latter was confident that he could speak to my partner without provoking another dash to the airport. Once he and the young Canadians had left, the room seemed less crowded. Morley did some more pruning. A whispered command sent Steve Hills on his way, then the Inspector turned to Reed.

"We don't need to detain you, sir," he said. "I'm sure you have plenty to do."

"Yes, Inspector," replied Reed, "but you can always get me on my mobile."

"Thanks."

"When do you want to speak to the night staff?"

"Right now." He gestured to the Sergeant. "Derek?"

Woodford made for the door. "I'll come down with you, Mr. Reed."

"Nobody saw anything, I'm afraid," said the manager.

"I'll double-check just in case."

They went out together. As soon as one door closed, another immediately opened. A head popped into the room from the adjoining suite. It featured a neat black mustache and a pair of mobile eyebrows. The man's tone was respectful.

"We've finished in here, Inspector," he said, "but we'll need to take Mr. Saxon's fingerprints as well so that we can eliminate him." Morley nodded. "Could you spare us a moment, sir?" asked the man, opening the door fully and beckoning me across.

"Yes, of course," I said.

While I was having my fingerprints taken in the other suite, I could hear the Inspector talking to Nancy Wykoff. One glance had been enough for him to establish our relationship. He didn't try to invade our privacy. He merely wanted an idea of the exact time when I returned to the room. After wiping my fingers clean, I rejoined them.

"Is there no way of tracing the call from the kidnapper, Inspector?" I wondered.

"I'm afraid not, Mr. Saxon," he replied. "It was made from a mobile."

"There must be a way to find out when he actually telephoned."

"We've already done that, sir. It was at 4:18 a.m."

Nancy and I exchanged a rueful look. At that time of the morning, we'd had other priorities. They seemed so trivial now. Almost five hours had elapsed before I came back to my room to pick up the message. I was both uneasy and reassured to have Nancy with me, embarrassed that I'd dragged her into a family crisis yet glad to have the visible support of a friend on whom I could rely. Unlike Peter, she wouldn't have a fit of the vapors or threaten to flee from the island. She was there for me. In thinking about her, I'd overlooked a rather more important person in the equation. Morley jogged my memory.

"Have you called home yet, sir?" he asked.

"Home?"

"You mentioned that your daughter lives with your ex-wife."

"Yes, that's right."

"I believe that she ought to be made aware of the situation."

"I was hoping we might resolve it before Rosemary needed to be brought in," I said, discomfited by the need to talk about her in front of Nancy. "I don't want to cause her unnecessary upset."

The Inspector was firm. "That may be so, Mr. Saxon, but she has a right to be told. Imagine how much more upset she'll be if you delay contacting her and if," he paused to search for an euphemism, "the situation doesn't end satisfactorily."

"Ring her, Alan," ordered Nancy. "You've got no choice."

"Keep this line free," said Morley. "Make the call from next door."

"Wait a moment," I said as something else dawned on me. "It isn't only Rosemary who needs to be contacted. There's Jessica's family as well. I'm sorry, Inspector, but I don't have their phone number. I'll have to ask Rosemary for it."

"No need for that, Mr Saxon."

"Why not?"

"Mr. Hadlow already knows about the abduction."

I was astonished. "But how?"

"His daughter must have told the kidnapper his whereabouts. He was contacted in Chicago not long ago. I took his call at the police station shortly after receiving yours. You'd better brace yourself, sir."

"Brace myself?"

"Bernard Hadlow is catching the first plane he can get to Bermuda. He wasn't too complimentary about you, I'm afraid. He blames you for what happened."

ᴧᴧᴧᴧᴧᴧᴧᴧᴧᴧᴧᴧ

I stared at the telephone in the adjoining suite as if fearing electrocution from the instrument. Thousands of miles away, at the other end of the line, was a quiescent Rosemary. I had never felt such a strong urge to let a sleeping dog lie. Even from that distance, I'd hear the bark and feel the bite. There's never a good time to ring my ex-wife. One of the worst, I now saw, was when I had appalling news to impart, a task made even more difficult by the presence in the next room of a lover and a senior policeman. Nancy might be blasé about her discarded husbands but my indifference to Rosemary was only ever feigned. In spite of myself, I still cared and that was fatal.

When I finally rang the number, I hoped that she wasn't there. If I left a message on her answerphone, I'd be spared her initial reaction. But I was out of luck. She picked up the receiver as if she'd been standing over it in wait for a call.

"Yes?" she asked

"Rosemary?"

"Alan, what a lovely surprise! Where are you?"

"At the hotel."

"Lynette rang me yesterday. She said that she and Jessica are having the most marvelous time. Thanks to you, that is. You're such a brick to take the pair of them. Do you know what Lynette said about you?"

"No."

"Then let me tell you."

As she gushed on about our daughter's phone call, the full poignancy of the situation hit me. The previous day, Lynette was an elated young woman who rang her mother to say what a wonderful time she was having in Bermuda. Now she was a kidnap victim, imprisoned somewhere with her friend. I interrupted Rosemary's flow.

"Sorry to cut you off," I apologized, "but I didn't ring for a friendly chat. There's an emergency. A serious one."

Rosemary was alarmed. "Lynette's not ill, is she?"

"No, not ill."

"Injured, then?" My hesitation put more distress in her voice. "Has she had an accident of some sort, Alan? Has she been hurt?"

"I'm not sure about that."

"Then what? Tell me, for heaven's sake!"

"The girls have been abducted."

Back in England, there was a pained silence. I took advantage of it to give her the outline facts, mentioning the incidents on the golf course and telling her about the girls' night out with Rick and Conrad, but omitting any incriminating detail. It was not the moment for her to hear about Lynette's supply of cannabis or about my dereliction of parental duty. With luck, she might never know where I'd spent that particular night. I did my best to sound optimistic.

"Inspector Morley has high hopes," I said. "The island is very small. There aren't all that many places they can hide. Also, as you know, it's terribly parochial. Bermuda is like a glorified Neighborhood Watch. People like to know what's going on here. In other words, somebody must have seen *something*. Take heart."

I broke off and waited for the storm to break. It never came. Instead of hurling blame and abuse at me in equal measure, Rosemary was calm and decisive.

"I want to be there, Alan."

"But there's no point."

"There's every point. I'm Lynette's mother."

"You won't be able to *do* anything, Rosemary."

"I'll be at the center of the action," she argued, "and that will reduce my anxiety. When my daughter's in such danger, I'm not going to stay here at home. The wait would be excruciating."

"But it might all be over by the time you got here."

"Then Lynette will need me to comfort her. I'm coming, Alan."

I tried to head her off. "You won't get a direct flight at short notice."

"Then I'll fly to the States first and change planes there. I seem to remember that there are daily flights to Bermuda

from places like New York and Boston. I'll see what they
advise." I heard tears in her voice. "Thank you for letting
me know, Alan. It can't have been easy for you. When I've
booked my flights, I'll ring back with details."

"Why put yourself to all that trouble?" I asked.

But I was talking to thin air. Rosemary was already dialing
another number. She would be out of the house and on her
way within the hour. So much for taking Lynette away so
that we could have quality time together. What had been
planned as a holiday for two now included four people—
five, if I counted Bernard Hadlow. In practical terms, Nancy
Wykoff had a claim as well. Six people in all. Two kidnapped
daughters, an anxious mother, an irate father, a neglected
lover and me. Even the most skillful author couldn't make
that line-up sound attractive in a travel brochure. When I
factored in Mo, the murdered driver, along with Peter and
Denise Fullard, I saw that I was enjoying a veritable holiday
from hell. I wondered if the hotel had one of those little
cards that invite you to make comments about your stay.

Before I rejoined the others, I took some time to compose
myself. In the course of my conversation with Rosemary,
my friendship with Nancy Wykoff had undergone a subtle
change. It had flourished in the absence of my daughter and
her friend. There was no way that it would blossom in the
presence of my ex-wife. Delicate negotiations of a personal
nature lay ahead. I was going to have to rely on Nancy's
worldliness. My hope was that she'd read this particular green
perfectly and know exactly how and when to putt.

I went through the connecting door and saw that Steve
Hills had returned. He was handing a sheet of paper to Troy
Morley. After scanning through it, the inspector folded it
and slipped it into his pocket.

"I have to go to the Incident Room, sir," he said. "Constable Hills will remain here in case you get another call. If you need me, I won't be far away."

"How is the murder investigation going?" I asked.

"Too early to say, Mr. Saxon."

"Have you established how Mo actually died?"

"By lethal injection. The chances are that he didn't feel a thing. Mr. Dobbs had been drinking heavily that evening."

"Do you have any leads at all?"

"We're pursuing various lines of inquiry," he said with that stonewall technique favored by policemen the world over. "Please excuse me. The murder must take precedence at the moment, though I'm treating the kidnap as a related crime. That doesn't mean it will get no attention. Search teams have already been dispatched all over the island. If your daughter and her friend are still here, we'll find them."

"I want to be out there, taking part in the search."

"It's more important for you to stay here, sir. You're the contact point for the kidnapper. He obviously wants to work through you. Next time he rings, I expect him to make his demands." He paused at the door. "Did you manage to get through to England?" I nodded. "How did your ex-wife take it?"

"On the chin, Inspector. She's coming to Bermuda at full speed."

"I had a feeling that she might."

"Any mother would do the same," observed Nancy.

"I agree, Mrs. Wykoff."

Troy Morley glanced at Hills then let himself out of the room. The detective constable sat in a corner and tried to look inconspicuous, but he still made a private conversation impossible. I gestured to Nancy and we slipped into the adjacent suite. She gave me an affectionate hug.

"How are you feeling?"

"Rotten," I confessed.

"Do you still think you should have been here to protect the girls?"

"Actually, I'm feeling rotten about you."

"Me?" she said with a laugh. "Why?"

"For dumping all this in your lap."

"But you did nothing of the kind."

"Yes, I did, Nancy. I hate bothering you with my family problems."

"It's no bother, Alan."

"There's the other thing as well," I pointed out.

"Other thing?"

"Yes. Last night was very special, but I don't believe that either of us wanted to shout about it from the rooftops. It's no longer a secret. As soon as Calvin Reed saw you in here, he guessed what must have happened."

"So what?"

"I don't want to injure your reputation."

She laughed again. "Injure it? Hell, last night you made it. Just wait until Melinda gets wind of it. She'll be so jealous. Next time we meet, she'll want a detailed account."

"What will you say?"

"Nothing that would compromise you."

She slipped her arms around me and I kissed her gently on the forehead. I felt awkward in the embrace. It was in the wrong place at the wrong time. It was not all that long ago that two young women were taken by force from that same suite. Sensing my reluctance, she broke away.

"What's wrong, Alan?"

"Nothing."

"Would you rather I disappeared?"

"Of course not."

"It may be different when your wife gets here."

"My ex-wife," I corrected. "A relic from the distant past."

"They can sometimes be the worst kind."

"Nancy," I said, taking her shoulders, "I can't tell you what to do."

"You must have some kind of preference."

"Oh, I do. I'd prefer that every British airport was closed until we get this whole business sorted out. I don't want Rosemary anywhere near Bermuda. She'll only complicate things."

"It sounds to me as if I should melt into the background."

"Play it by ear, Nancy. Is that too much to ask?"

"Precious little. Count on me, Alan," she said, kissing me on the cheek. "I'll either be totally invisible or hanging off your arm. Whatever the occasion demands."

"I'll settle for that."

"But I do have one request…"

Before she could tell me what it was, the telephone rang in the other room. I darted back through the connecting door with Nancy at my heels. Steve Hills was on his feet, jerked out of his somnolence by the loud ring.

"You'd better answer it, sir," he counseled.

Gritting my teeth, I picked up the instrument and spoke into it.

"Yes?" I said.

It was not the voice of the kidnapper this time, but the message was equally chilling. Nancy and Steve Hills heard it as well on the speaker. They didn't know the voice in the way that I did but they recognized at once that it was recorded.

"Daddy," she said clearly, "it's Lynette here. Please do as they say. They haven't hurt us yet but they will if you disobey them. Just do as you're told. *Please.*"

If the hotel chain for which he worked gave awards for services above and beyond the call of duty, Frank Colouris deserved one. He somehow managed to tell Peter Fullard about the kidnap without making him feel that he was next in line for attack. Indeed, so skillfully did he present the situation that Peter didn't even consider himself. All he wanted to do was to offer me sympathy. Colouris had to stop my partner from rushing to my suite. He gave me a wry smile.

"I had the feeling he'd be something of an impediment, sir," he said.

"Thanks, Mr. Colouris. You're a friend."

"You've got your hands full enough, as it is."

"So have you and Mr. Reed. This is turning into an ordeal for the pair of you."

"All part of the rough and tumble of hotel life."

"How often have you had a murder *and* a kidnap on your doorstep?"

"Never, luckily. Until now."

"What's next—an armed invasion?"

"They'd be wasting their time, sir. We're fully booked."

"The suite next door has suddenly become vacant."

"We're reserving that for some very special guests, Mr. Saxon."

I liked Colouris more each time I saw him. Cool in a crisis, he had a dry sense of humor. I remembered how sympathetic he'd been to Angela Pike.

"Are they any nearer catching Mo's killer?" I asked.

"Who knows?"

"The police must have made *some* progress."

"Difficult to say," he replied, shaking his head. "Inspector Morley doesn't give much away, I'm afraid. No disrespect to him, but I'd hate to play poker with that guy."

"I'd certainly draw the line at a round of golf with him."

"Mr. Reed says he's very able, and he's met the Inspector before."

"We'll have to trust to his judgement."

It was mid-morning and Colouris had called in to give me a report on his visit to Peter Fullard, who'd just returned from putting Denise on a plane. Colouris spent almost an hour with him, explaining and soothing. During that time, I'd been stuck in my suite, reflecting on the recorded message from Lynette and promising myself what I'd do to the people responsible for her kidnap if I ever got my hands on them. Hills rang the inspector on his mobile to inform him of the latest development, but Morley didn't appear. Nancy had made all three of us a reviving cup of coffee. We'd just finished drinking it when Colouris turned up. Preoccupied as I was with the kidnap, I'd not forgotten the murder victim nor the poor woman he'd left behind. If the crimes were in any way linked with the rivalry behind the purchase of the hotel site, I wanted to know. I tried to fish.

"How do you like working at the Blue Dolphin?" I asked.

"I love it," he said. "After Manhattan, it feels like a rest cure. At least, it did until the last couple of days. That's when the tornado struck."

"From what I hear, Mr. Colouris, this place has already been hit by several tornadoes. Metaphorically speaking, that is. The site is in such a prime position that there must have been intense competition to acquire it. I gather that the fight turned nasty. No holds barred. No prisoners taken."

"The business world is a jungle, sir."

"Nature red in tooth and claw," I commented. "Who lost out?"

"You'd have to ask Mr. Reed that. It was before my time."

"But you must have some idea of what went on."

"I'm in senior management, Mr. Saxon," he explained. "That means I work at least ten hours a day and I'm on call for the other fourteen. That doesn't leave me much time to look into how the Blue Dolphin site was bought and who got muscled out. I simply work here and—in spite of all that's happened recently—I like it. You meet interesting people."

I winked at Nancy. "Yes, I found that out as well."

"All I hope is that we can get your daughter and her friend back safe and well so that you can give us a second chance." He smiled wanly. "We'll do everything we can to prove that the Blue Dolphin is not quite as bad as it seems."

It was a fair comment. There was no future in trying to pump information that the deputy manager didn't have. Colouris had only been at the hotel a few months. He was still finding his way around the place. I saw him to the door and thanked him for keeping Peter Fullard away from me. Nancy had the same opinion of him as I.

"Nice guy."

"The human face of the Blue Dolphin."

"Now, now," she scolded, "I'm not having you criticizing Cal. I know he can be something of a stuffed shirt at times but he's sweet when you get to know him. He's devoted to Melinda and, believe me, she needs a lot of devotion."

Steve Hills was still with us in case there were any more calls from the kidnapper, and his presence made relaxed conversation impossible. Even when he sat in a corner, he couldn't blend into the background. Nancy had to wait until the detective slipped off to the bathroom before she could ask the question that she'd been saving up.

"Why do you want to know about the hotel site, Alan?"

"Because I think it will explain a lot," I replied. "My guess is that we're up against someone who lost out in a big way when the sale for this land was agreed. Mo was the first victim of their revenge. Lynette and Jessica may well be next on the list."

"Would you like me to find out what I can from Melinda?"

"Yes, please. Only, be discreet," I cautioned. "We don't want that sweet husband of hers realizing that we're digging up the past. Calvin Reed seems to have reasons of his own for keeping it well buried."

"Leave it to me," she said. "I'm known for my tact."

"It was the first thing I noticed about you," I teased.

"What was the second?"

"Ask me when all this is over."

"I will." She looked towards the bathroom. "I'll slip away and see if I can track down Melinda. She'll be agog to hear what happened last night. I won't be long," she added, blowing me a kiss. "Think you can manage without me for a while?"

"I'll probably collapse in a heap."

"That's how I like to leave all my guys!"

She let herself out of the room and I missed her immediately. At the same time, I was glad that she'd gone, and not only because she might be able to root out crucial information from a friend. I needed time to think and that was difficult with Nancy around. She wanted to share everything. I was denied the luxury of independent thought. Where were Lynette and Jessica? That was what I continued to ask myself. What did the kidnapper hope to achieve by spiriting them away? My promise to turn my back on the Blue Dolphin golf course? Our instant departure from Bermuda? It didn't make sense. In keeping the girls, he was simply extending the delay caused by Mo's death. My daughter and her friend were powerful bargaining tools. I just wished I knew what the bargain really was.

The ringing of the telephone jerked me out of my reverie. It also galvanized Steve Hills, because I heard the toilet flush. I gave him time to come out of the bathroom before I approached the instrument. After a nod from him, I picked it up.

"Yes?" I said.

"Let me speak to Alan Saxon," demanded a rasping voice.

"You're talking to him."

"Then let me introduce myself," he said. "My name is Bernard Hadlow. You were supposed to be looking after my daughter, Jessica, but I'm told she's been kidnapped. What the fuck's going on there, Saxon? You're in deep shit, my friend."

"My daughter was abducted as well," I reminded him.

"Can't you even protect *her*?"

"Mr. Hadlow—"

"You failed miserably and, if there's one thing I hate, it's failure."

"The kidnap took place in the middle of the night."

"So?"

"You can hardly expect me to sit outside Jessica's door with a loaded shotgun."

"Don't get funny with me, Saxon, or you'll regret it. Believe me." I heard a booming announcement in the background. "I have to go. That's my connecting flight."

"Where are you?"

"Kennedy Airport, New York."

"You'll be here this afternoon, then."

"Yes, I will," he warned. "And let me tell you this, Saxon. I've got some hard fucking questions for you. You'd better have the answers."

The line went dead and I put the receiver down. Hills had the grace to turn away, though I suspected that he was smirking. When Bernard Hadlow and I came face to face, it was not going to be the friendliest encounter. It was an open question whether he or Rosemary would cause me more grief. In the space of twelve hours, everything had been turned on its head. Instead of sharing a holiday with two young women, I'd be confronted by an enraged father and a distraught mother. Bermuda was giving me a poor exchange rate. I'd think twice about visiting the island again.

Chapter Seven

I was beginning to develop a phobia about my telephone. Every time I picked it up, it seemed, it brought me bad news. If the kidnapping of Lynette and Jessica was not painful enough, I now had to contend with wild accusations from Bernard Hadlow. He had the kind of voice that told you exactly what he looked like—large, ugly and overbearing. Everything I'd heard about him seemed to fit. He was not the sort of person I'd care to meet at any time. In the present circumstances, he was supremely unwelcome, but, I reminded myself, he was Jessica's father and therefore directly implicated. How well did he know her? She obviously inherited her bossiness from him, but was he aware that his daughter was promiscuous and dabbled with hard drugs? And if he did, would Bernard Hadlow care? What I'd resented most was his supercilious tone. He talked to me as if I was some minor employee of his who'd been caught with his hand in the till. Poverty has its own integrity. I'd rather be destitute than work for someone like Bernard Hadlow. I decided to make that point crystal clear to him.

At the moment, he held the whip hand over me. He knew who I was, what I did and where, in his opinion, I'd slipped up. He was judge, jury and executioner. The least I could do was to prepare some sort of defense, and the best way to do that was to know exactly what I was up against. All that

I had to go on were comments that Jessica, Lynette and Calvin Reed had made. I needed more data. The name of Clive Phelps popped straight into my mind. He owed me a favor, and because he'd introduced Peter Fullard to me, he was, to some extent, involved in the chain of events. Clive was the golf correspondent for a British national newspaper. The sports editor would know where to get hold of him.

"I'm sorry that you chose the short straw, Constable Hills," I said, noting his glum expression. "Staring at a telephone for hours on end is not exactly the sharp end of law enforcement."

He was resigned. "Someone has to do it, sir."

"It's worse than watching quiz shows on television."

"There may be some action further down the line."

"Is that why you joined the police force? For some action?"

"No, sir," he said gloomily. "I couldn't think of anything else to do." He gave a secret smile. "Well, I could but I was never good enough to become a pro at that." He tried to sound more positive. "Police work is interesting. You're always learning something new. It keeps you on your toes."

"My father is, or rather was, a copper. He spent most of his time treading on my toes."

"Oh, I see."

"What sort of a governor is Inspector Morley?"

"A good one, sir. Knows his stuff."

"I hope so," I said, searching for my address book. "Look, I'm going to use the phone next door. Keep an eye on mine while I've gone, will you?"

"I'm not allowed to answer it, Mr. Saxon."

"I know that. I'll be back in a flash, if it rings."

Having found my address book under a magazine, I went through into the other suite. It took me three separate phone calls to run Clive Phelps to ground. Having covered a golf tournament and dutifully written his column, he was having a few days off in the Algarve. Not surprisingly, I caught him in the bar of his hotel. From the sound of his voice, I guessed that he'd been there for some time, sampling the local vino.

"Alan!" he exclaimed with delight. "I thought you were in Bermuda."

"I am, Clive, but I need your help."

"Peter's Fullard's not cracking up on you, is he?"

"No," I lied, "he's a picture of self-control."

"How's your new golf course coming along?"

"Swimmingly."

It was Troy Morley who'd suggested that we keep news of the kidnap to ourselves for the time being or the local media would be all over us like a nasty rash. I was more than happy to agree. I had no intention of letting Clive Phelps in on the story either. He'd have me splashed all over the front page of his paper in no time at all, and I preferred to stay in the familiar surroundings of the sports coverage. Private traumas are easier to cope with when they remain private. TOP GOLFER'S DAUGHTER IN KIDNAP ORDEAL was not the kind of headline that would help anyone. There was a gurgling sound in my ear as Clive drained his glass.

"So what's the problem?" he asked.

"Bernard Hadlow."

"Never heard of him."

"That's because you don't read the business pages," I said. "He's an international businessman. One of those bloated plutocrats who jets round the world from one tax haven to another. Does the name ring a bell now?"

"Only a very distant one. What's this bugger got to do with you?"

"He's on his way to meet me, Clive. His daughter, Jessica, is a friend of Lynette's. I brought the pair of them with me for a short holiday before they go back to Oxford."

"Nice of you."

"I was feeling fatherly."

"How is Lynette?"

"Fine, fine," I said, swallowing hard.

"Give her my love. Ages since I've seen her. Thank goodness she doesn't take after you," he said with a derisive chuckle. "She's got her mother's beauty and it doesn't come much better than that. How is Rosemary, by the way?"

"The same as ever. Though while we're on the subject," I said acidly, recalling a snippet that I'd picked up from my ex-wife, "I must say that I was rather peeved to hear that you once made a pass at Rosemary."

"That was after you'd split up with her."

"And before. She was very explicit about the timing."

"Well," he said airily, "that's all water under the bridge."

"Not in my book, Clive."

"But I only did it on your behalf, old son," he claimed, before ordering another drink from the barman. "I was like a burglar, testing a friend's alarm system to make sure that it worked properly. And it did, believe me. Rosemary clanged away until I was deafened by the noise. I wouldn't care to repeat some of the things she called me."

"If I'd known about it, I'd have done much more than call you names."

He went on the defensive. "Now, don't be like that, Alan."

"I'd have punched you on the nose for starters."

"But it was ages ago."

"There's no statute of limitations on this one, Clive."

"Can't we just forget the whole thing?" he pleaded.

"Only if you come to my rescue."

"Why? What's the trouble? Is Denise Fullard trying to vamp you?"

"I need some information about Bernard Hadlow."

"Well, don't ask me for it, Alan. This may be a four-star establishment but all they give you with your room is a hotel brochure and a Gideon Bible in Portuguese. I doubt if Bernard Hadlow is mentioned in either."

"Get on to the business editor of your paper," I instructed. "Ask him to haul everything he has on Hadlow out of his files and fax it to the number I'll give you when you find a pen to write it down. *Please*, Clive. I wouldn't ask if it wasn't very urgent. If I've got to meet Hadlow, I need to know what I'm letting myself in for. I have the feeling he wants to have the gloves on with me. Forewarned is forearmed." I looked at the card beside the telephone. "Ready for that number?"

"Alan, I'm supposed to be on holiday."

"So am I."

"Do you know what you're asking?"

"A very big favor," I said, "but I think I deserve it, don't you? Think how many times I've helped you to fill that column of yours. You'd be lost without me, Clive. Now, come on. Take this number then ring your colleague. It'll only take five minutes."

"That's what I said to Rosemary."

"No wonder she turned you down!"

"What's the fax number?"

I gave it to him, exchanged a few niceties, then rang off. It was a long shot but it was worth trying. Give or take a few dramatic lapses, Clive Phelps was a good friend. He knew that I'd only ask such a favor if it was really important to me. There was always the chance that he'd be given a flea in his ear by his business editor, but that wouldn't deter him. Clive would do his best for a pal. One day, over a drink, assuming that the girls were safely returned to us, I'd tell him why I made the request. And I'd forget all about his bungled attempt to get Rosemary into bed. I'd made a few of those myself when I was supposed to be her husband.

Luckily, the hotel was paying for any phone calls that I made, but the real bonus was the private fax machine. I'd never stayed anywhere before that provided them. It meant that any material sent to me would arrive in the girls' suite and not have to go via Reception. When he got there in person, the Blue Dolphin would be more than aware of Bernard Hadlow's presence. They didn't need advance publicity. I did. Hoping that Clive Phelps would click into action at once, I went back into my own suite. Steve Hills was doing the crossword in a paper while keeping one eye on the telephone. The instant I stepped through the connecting door, it rang again. He tossed the paper aside.

"Go ahead, sir," he urged.

"This is starting to get habit-forming."

"If it's the kidnapper, try to keep him talking as long as possible."

"Right."

After licking my lips, I picked up the receiver once more.

"Yes?" I said.

"Alan, it's me," said Rosemary, almost out of breath. "I've just got to Heathrow. I managed to get a flight to Boston and a connecting flight to Bermuda. Have you got a pen? I'll give you the details"

"Shoot," I said. Snatching up the ballpoint provided by the hotel, I wrote on the pad beside the telephone. I was impressed. "You did well to fix all this up so quickly."

"It's an emergency, Alan."

"I know that."

"Any developments?"

"Not as yet."

"I'm on my way. Incidentally," she added, as if issuing a royal decree, "I expect you to meet me at the airport in Bermuda. Is that understood?"

I suddenly felt very cold. "Yes, Rosemary."

"I'll try to ring from Boston."

"Right."

"Something may have happened by then. Goodbye."

"Goodbye, Rosemary."

I hung up and turned to my companion. He noticed the change in me at once.

"Are you all right, Mr. Saxon?" he asked. "You're shivering all over."

Whoever was holding Lynette and Jessica knew how to make me suffer. Silence was his weapon. After the initial phone message in the early hours of the morning, I'd been given nothing but that brief recording of my daughter's voice. Since then, there hadn't been a peep out of the kidnapper. I was being roasted on the spit of my imagination, fearing for the girls' safety, speculating on what sort of horrors they might be undergoing. In her recorded message, Lynette spoke clearly but with understandable strain. She sounded as if she was reading words that someone else had written for her. Had she been forced to make the recording? Was any coercion involved? I'd twice been assured that the girls were unharmed, but the signs of a struggle in their bedroom suggested otherwise. Something else gnawed away at the back of my mind. The recording could have been made shortly after the abduction then replayed hours later to give me the impression that Lynette was still alive and well. What if she and Jessica had already been killed? Was someone playing a sadistic mind game with me? Why on earth didn't he *ring*?

There was a tap on the door and Hills went to answer it. Hoping that it would be Nancy Wykoff with some valuable information, I was disconcerted to see that it was Inspector Troy Morley. He had a whispered conversation with Hills before turning to me.

"How are you bearing up, sir?" he asked.

"I've had better mornings."

"When did you last eat?"

"Who cares?"

"You have to keep your strength up, Mr. Saxon. I'm told that room service is very efficient here. Would you like Constable Hills to order something for you?"

"Only the safe return of the girls."

"I'm afraid that's not on the hotel menu," he said solemnly, "but it's at the top of our own. We're doing all we can to track down your daughter and her friend."

"I thought the murder inquiry took precedence."

"Yes and no, sir."

"Well, that's the feeling I'm starting to get," I complained. "The big guns are deployed downstairs in the Incident Room while I have to make do with a solitary constable. That's no reflection on you," I said to Steve Hills, "but I would like more visible evidence that the police are doing something."

"I understand your disquiet," said Morley, "but in cases like this, there's little we can do but watch and wait. Would it make you feel any better if you had twenty officers in here instead of one? I doubt it, Mr. Saxon. We're not idle, I assure you. Patrol cars have been out searching all morning. Every way into and out of Bermuda has been alerted. We've thrown an iron ring around the island." He was starting to sound horribly like my father. "Until we know what the kidnapper's demands are, there's not much else we can do. As for concentrating on the murder, that's not to your detriment. If, as we believe, the two crimes are connected, then the sooner we solve the murder, the sooner we locate the missing girls. Find the killer and we have the kidnapper."

"You don't seem to be making much headway on either front."

"That's not true at all. As a matter of fact, we've had an important breakthrough in the Incident Room. I came up here to tell you about it."

I was relieved. "Thank goodness you didn't ring. I'm starting to hate that phone."

"A witness has come forward," he said. "On the night in question, he claims that he saw a vehicle driving down the third fairway not long before midnight."

"What sort of vehicle?"

"A large van, sir."

"Don't tell Peter Fullard. The third fairway was his pride and joy. If he knows his Bermuda grass has got tire tracks all over it, he'll burst every blood vessel in his body." I became serious. "I'm sorry, Inspector. Where was this witness of yours?"

"Some distance away, unfortunately."

"What was he doing on the golf course?"

"Trespassing," explained Morley. "That's why he didn't come forward when we made our appeal. He says that he was only taking a short cut but I fancy that he had another reason for being there. However, the point is that he observed a vehicle moving slowly towards the part of the course where you found the body of Maurice Dobbs."

"What else did he see?"

"The vehicle stopped and two men got out. They unloaded a wheelbarrow then lifted something heavy into it."

"The dead body," I concluded. "It must have been Mo."

"That's a strong possibility, but the man was unable to see all that much in the half-dark. According to him," Morley continued, "one of the men went into the trees with the wheelbarrow then brought it back empty. When they'd put it back in the van, the vehicle was driven off by one man while the other went back into the trees."

"Didn't the witness go to investigate? Wasn't he curious?"

"He assumed that someone was just dumping rubbish, sir. Besides, he had reasons of his own for not wanting to get caught on private property. So he continued on his way. But the timing fits," he noted. "All this happened not long before you heard that scream on the course. The witness heard it as well. The reason you didn't see the van was that it had gone off in the other direction."

"What about the man who hanged Mo from that tree?"

"He'd just finished his work when he saw you coming."

"So he set the pendulum in motion."

"And watched from nearby, I suspect," said Morley with a sigh. "My guess is that he was probably only yards from you when you made the discovery."

The thought made me jump. Had one of the killers really been lurking in the trees? I was grateful that I didn't know it at the time. Morley tried to reassure me.

"This could be the break we need, Mr. Saxon," he said. "When we saw those tire tracks, we thought they'd been made by one of the contractor's vehicles. We should be able to identify that van in due course. We know the make already." He saw my surprise. "That's our other stroke of luck. Our witness is a motor mechanic. Unemployed, as it happens, but, even in silhouette, he can tell one van from another." He was pleased by the new development. "As you see, we're making definite progress, sir."

I nodded my approval. "All we need now is the make of that wheelbarrow."

"The trail is warm. We'll get them."

"As long as the trail leads to Lynette and Jessica."

"There's every indication that it will."

"I don't want *them* to end up hanging from a cedar."

"Quite so." He touched my arm in sympathy. "It's been a long morning, sir. Get some food inside you. I'm sure you'll feel better for it."

"All this waiting has robbed me of my appetite," I said wearily. "In any case, it seems awful that I should be enjoying a meal while my daughter and her friend are locked away somewhere. What about *them*, Inspector? Are they being fed? Do they have access to quality room service? Or are they being deliberately starved?"

My questions hung in the air. From the adjoining suite came a series of beeps followed by a long buzzing sound. The inspector snapped his fingers and Hills went to investigate. When he came back, he seemed rather excited.

"It's for you, Mr. Saxon."

"What is?"

"The World's Longest Fax."

Clive Phelps had done his stuff. So much material had been faxed through from his newspaper that it took me the best part of half an hour to go through it. I wondered how he had worked such a miracle, then I remembered an attractive young female journalist he'd once introduced to me. I think her name was Barbara. She was a financial analyst on his paper. My bet was that he'd rung her to remind her of nights they'd spent together and to slip in my request when she was in no state to resist. It's a mystery to me why any woman should fall for Clive's seedy charm, but they keel over like ninepins. Barbara was clearly among them. She'd ransacked the files on his behalf and sent me articles about Bernard Hadlow that went back almost ten years.

It was not pleasant reading. While Hadlow seemed to have had an unbroken record of success, his methods were highly questionable. Essentially, he was a smash and grab merchant. Small companies who had struggled to improve themselves suddenly found themselves hit for six by hostile takeover bids. Rivals were ruthlessly put to the sword in savage price wars. He specialized in horizontal and vertical integration. He wanted every link in the chain. Hadlow was also an indefatigable litigant. If someone so much as sneezed in his presence, he'd slap a writ on them. In the courts, too, he was almost always the winner. Libel juries, in particular, found in his favor. It made people extremely wary in their choice of words about Bernard Hadlow, and this was nowhere more evident than in the articles before me. Framed in elegant prose, they dropped vague hints or drew gentle inferences without ever committing themselves to outright condemnation. I had the impression that the articles were composed with the in-house lawyer looking over their authors' shoulders. It was not difficult to read between the lincs. Hadlow was an unashamed pirate. In the seven seas of international business, nobody was safe from his grappling irons.

My mental image of him was close to reality. I had dozens of photographs of the tycoon, showing the way that he'd fleshed out over the years. He was a big man who towered over anyone else in the shot. Even when lit by a smile, his features were unpleasant. He had a prominent nose, heavy jowls, a slit of a mouth and eyes that looked as cold as stone. Yet the peculiar thing was that I could still see a faint resemblance to Jessica. In repose, her father was almost grotesque, but when he was animated, as in some of the photographs, he somehow reminded me of her. The exercise had worked. Not only had I been given some useful ammunition against Hadlow, I'd been distracted from my fretful meditation about the girls. Time had passed swiftly. No more phone calls came.

Steve Hills had taken the opportunity to order himself some club sandwiches. While I wrestled with the faxed material in one suite, he had his lunch in the other. When he finished, he popped in to see how I was getting on.

"I've never seen a fax with so many pages," he said.

"It was a love letter from an old flame," I explained. "Unfortunately, she wasn't an old flame of mine, but I'll give her a big kiss if ever I meet her again."

"I thought they were some newspaper articles about Mr. Hadlow."

"They are, officer. But I only got them as a result of a love affair. Never mind," I said, as I gathered the pages up. "It would take too long to explain. How was lunch?"

"Better than usual, sir."

"You see? This job does have perks, after all."

He brightened. "Meeting you is one of them, Mr. Saxon."

"Why me? Do tormented fathers hold a weird fascination for you?"

"No, sir."

"Then what's the attraction?"

He shifted his feet. "I play golf."

I understood at last. Steve Hills was not as downcast as he looked. He was simply shy. Assigned to look after the father of a kidnap victim, he couldn't believe his good fortune when I turned out to be a well-known golfer. He'd been slightly over-awed by me. I recalled his saying that he wasn't talented enough to make a living at what he really wanted to do. Hills had yearned after life as a pro golfer. Now that the truth was out, he gave me a hopeful grin. I had a sinking feeling that he expected me to give him a few tips. It was ridiculous. He was part of a police team that was supposed to help me, not to seek for ways to improve his swing. A tap on the door of my room sent him scurrying back into it. It was Nancy Wykoff. My detective fan showed her in, then, withdrew to maintain his vigil beside the telephone. Nancy looked at the fax.

"What's that?"

"The Life and Times of Bernard Hadlow."

"Where did it come from?"

"London."

"Why?"

"Hadlow rang earlier," I explained. "From the anger in his voice, I got the idea that he's going to take me outside for a fight. I just wanted to make sure we were in the same weight division."

"And are you?"

"Oh no! He's a real bruiser. I wouldn't last one round."

"When will he get here?"

"Pretty soon, Nancy. He was leaving New York when I spoke to him."

"Anything else happen?"

I shook my head. "Afraid not."

"No more calls from the kidnapper?"

"He must have lost my number."

"He just wants to make you sweat, Alan," she said. "What a bastard!"

"Forget about me. How did *you* get on?"

She sat on the sofa beside me. "With mixed success."

"Tell me all."

"Well," she said, "I called on Melinda and found her at home alone. So far, so good, I thought. Cal had obviously spoken to her about us because she couldn't wait to hear what had happened. Needless to say, I drew a veil of decency over the whole affair."

"How did that go down with her?"

"Not too well. Melinda was counting on a re-run in glorious Technicolor. You know the kind of thing. Grand passion, shot from fifteen different angles. The part of Nancy Wykoff played by Julia Roberts with Sean Connery as Alan Saxon."

"He's too old!" I protested.

"I managed to fend her off and guide the conversation around to the Blue Dolphin. She was very helpful. Melinda's not just a trophy wife. She's got a keen brain when she chooses to use it. She remembered everything. Unfortunately," she sighed, "just as she got to the interesting bit, Cal walked in on us. I had to shelve the topic at once. When he learned what we'd been talking about, he was very uptight. I've never seen him like that."

"But you did find out something?" I prompted.

"Oh, lots."

"Give it to me."

"The Blue Dolphin is owned by a consortium which operates under the name GGM—it stands for Griffin, Grein, Mortlake. They have a chain of luxury hotels, stretching from Bermuda to Bangkok. Their stock is worth billions."

"How did they manage to acquire this site?"

"By fair means and foul, Alan."

Nancy's training as a journalist was sound. She knew what questions to ask and how to pin back her ears and listen. Thinking it was just a chat with a friend, Melinda Reed had talked openly about the battle to secure the site. It had resembled the early stages of World War Three. A host of companies had put in offers but the small fry had been burned off at once. Only the big boys remained, upping the stakes and stopping at nothing to spike the guns of their rivals. GGM clearly had a very inventive Dirty Tricks Department. They'd gone to amazing lengths to discredit their competitors in the eyes of the vendors. I lapped it all up greedily. Nancy's grasp of detail was astonishing and she knew how to pick out salient facts.

"So there are three companies with a reason to hate GGM?" I concluded.

"Four, if you count the late bidder."

"Who was that?"

"A company that came in at the last moment," she said. "I think they waited for the others to tear each other to pieces before they stepped in. Griffin, Grein, Mortlake were not having that. They went for the jugular at once."

"What was this new company called?"

"Redfurst Leisure."

I frowned. "I've heard that name before."

"They're part of a some multi-national group."

"I know," I said, leafing through the fax. "It was mentioned in here somewhere."

"In what context?"

"I can't remember."

I knelt on the floor so that I could put the pages out in sequence. Nancy laughed as I moved slowly forward on my hands and knees, scrutinizing each sheet as I did so. Bernard Hadlow's face stared up at me from the floor in a variety of poses. I gave myself the pleasure of squashing his nose with my palm. Jessica, too, appeared in some photographs. The articles had been arranged in chronological order, so I had to work nearer the present day before I finally spotted the name.

"Redfurst Leisure?" I checked.

"That was the name."

"Then my theory may have been right all along."

"What do you mean, Alan?"

"Look here," I said, jabbing a finger at the article. "The company is part of a global corporation that's headed by a certain Bernard Hadlow. One more part of his mighty empire. That's what I'd call an intriguing coincidence. Wouldn't you?"

Nancy Wykoff stayed long enough to persuade me to order some food and make sure that I ate it when it arrived. It was a sunny afternoon and Hadlow's plane would probably have touched down on the runway by now. I didn't tremble at his approach. In fact, I was glad that he was coming. Thanks to the fax, I believed I might have stumbled on a vital clue. Instead of handing it to the police, I kept it for my own use against Jessica's father. I sensed that I'd need it. Nancy had an appointment in the hotel health spa that afternoon. She offered to cancel it in order to stay with me, but I insisted that she keep it. When Hadlow came bursting in, I wanted to face him on my own.

Left alone with Steve Hills once more, I came to see that abduction turns the victims' families into prisoners as well. They're also held captive in a given place, unable to move, at the mercy of commands from someone else. My discomfort didn't compare with that endured by Lynette and Jessica, of course. Constable Hills was an officer of the law, quiet and unthreatening—until the game of golf was mentioned, that is. The girls, on the other hand, were being held hostage by a complete stranger. They were unlikely to be in a hotel like the Blue Dolphin. They'd probably be locked up in a confined space, perhaps even tied up and gagged. My heart went out to both of them. They'd be absolutely terrified. Yet still no call came from the kidnapper. Why the delay? Had something happened? Could I dare to hope that the girls might have escaped and be on their way back?

A loud knock on the door made me believe for a fleeting moment that the fantasy was true and that they'd somehow made it back to me. Before the detective could get there, I rushed to the door and pulled it open. But there was no Lynette to fling herself into my arms and no Jessica to collapse gratefully against me. Instead, I was staring into the face of Calvin Reed. I stood aside to let him in.

"I just came to see how you're getting on, Alan," he said.

"We're still waiting for another call."

"You look all in."

"It's not the most relaxing way to spend a morning."

"I'm sure. I can't tell you how distressed we at the Blue Dolphin are by all this."

"It's not your fault, Mr. Reed."

"If there's anything—anything at all—that we can do, just ask."

"Well," I said, "there is something, actually. My ex-wife will be arriving in Bermuda tonight. Could I have a driver to take me to and from the airport, please."

"Of course. No problem."

"And I'd like a quiet one this time. Not another Mo."

"I'll ask Frank Colouris to arrange it. Anything else?"

"Yes. Rosemary will need a room."

"There's nothing left on this floor, I'm afraid."

"That's OK," I replied, glad that there'd be distance between us. "We don't have to sleep cheek by jowl. As long as Rosemary has somewhere to lay her head when she arrives. She's flown from England, remember. She'll have been in transit for the best part of eleven hours. Jet lag will hit her with the force of a baseball bat."

"Leave it to me, Alan."

"Thanks."

Reed was hovering. I could see that he wanted to speak in private. Steve Hills was now standing at the window, gazing soulfully at the hotel pool, perhaps reflecting on his failure to become a professional golfer. I took the manager through into the other suite so that we were not overheard. I'd gathered up the sheets of fax paper and put them away. There was no need for Reed to see them. He tried to cheer me up.

"Have you spoken to Inspector Morley?" he asked.

"He came up to see me earlier."

"This new witness has been a great help."

"So I hear."

"He's given the police so much to go on. It won't take them long to find that van. The inspector has every confidence that an arrest will soon be made."

"All I'm concerned about is the safety of Lynette and Jessica."

There was a long pause. "Not quite," he said.

"What do you mean?

"I think you know only too well."

"No, I don't."

"You may not have noticed," he said smoothly, "but we have an excellent police force on the island. Now, I know that you have profound reservations about the guardians of the law, but I'd advise you to put them aside. You can't do their job for them, Alan."

"I'm not trying to."

"Yes, you are. You set Nancy Wykoff on to my wife."

"You make her sound like a watchdog."

"She looked more like a bloodhound to me," he went on with a reproving glance, "and Melinda confirmed it. Apparently, all that Nancy wanted to talk about was the purchase of this site. That couldn't possibly have any interest for her, so she must have been acting on your behalf. Am I correct?"

"I was curious, that's all."

"Well, your curiosity is not appreciated."

"What have you got to hide?"

"Nothing," he returned, "but that's not the point. There's such a thing as loyalty, Alan. I respect my employers. When I took this job, I signed a confidentiality agreement to the effect that I wouldn't discuss with anyone the business affairs of the consortium that owns it."

"They're obviously determined to keep the lid on things."

"They want to do what every company does—preserve a degree of privacy."

"And you go along with that?"

"Naturally."

"Has it never occurred to you that the people who killed Maurice Dobbs might have been hired by one of the companies that lost out in the scramble for this site?"

"Of course."

"What have you done about it?"

"That's my concern."

"Have you raised the matter with the police?"

"I've given Inspector Morley every possible help."

"I hope so, Mr. Reed," I said, stung by his ability to remain so cool and unflustered during an argument. "Because there's a very real possibility that the kidnap is the work of the same people. In short, my daughter and her friend may be in jeopardy because the consortium for which you work adopted such vicious tactics when buying this site that one of their rivals wants revenge. Do you see what I'm getting at, Mr. Reed?" I asked, letting him see my anger. "I don't know how binding this confidentiality agreement of yours is, but if it means that you withhold vital information from the police, you won't only have to answer to Inspector Morley. I'll come looking for you as well."

"There's no need to get so worked up," he said, lifting both palms.

"Lynette and Jessica are in dire straits, man! For God's sake, help them."

"I told you, I've done what I can."

"While honoring your contract of employment."

"No, Alan!" he said, raising his voice for the first time. He composed himself before he went on. "Look, nothing will be served if we fall out. We both want the same thing. I'm not prepared to discuss the history of the Blue Dolphin with you but I can assure you of this. GGM are as anxious as you to have these crimes solved quickly. I haven't been gagged. On the contrary, I've been ordered to assist to the police in every way. And that's what I've been doing. So, please—call off your bloodhound."

"I simply want to get at the truth, Mr. Reed."

"Then you should start by reading your bank statements more carefully. Before you start accusing *me* of working for an unscrupulous consortium, you might remember that GGM are also paying you and Peter Fullard."

It was a telling point. I had no answer.

"We have to play by the rules, Alan," he said. "The leisure industry needs big men with big ideas. They may sail close to the wind at times but only because they have to in order to get ahead. GGM won the race to buy this site. Our job is to develop its facilities, notably its golf course. Someone is trying to stop us doing that and, unfortunately, Lynette and Jessica have been abducted as a warning. The way to get them released is to cooperate with the police, not to go sniffing around on your own account."

"That's a matter of opinion, Mr. Reed."

"It's all very well to talk about revenge as a motive here, but we have no proof."

"Aren't a murder victim and two kidnapped girls proof enough?"

"Proof that we have enemies," he argued. "That's all. Who they are, I honestly don't know. I have some knowledge of how this site was acquired yet I still couldn't give you a name of a possible suspect."

I had a strong suspicion that he was lying.

It was late afternoon before we got the call. By that time, I was so starved of conversation that I let Steve Hills tell me how he'd watched me play in the Bermuda Open some years earlier. The annoying thing was that he only seemed to remember the wayward shots that I'd hit. My eagle in the first round at Mid-Ocean's tricky par-5 fifteenth hole didn't even get a mention. He did, however, have the courtesy to recall that I'd actually won the event. Hills was telling me about his tendency to hook from the tee when his mobile phone rang. With a shrug of apology, he turned away to take the call. He nodded obediently then switched off the instrument.

"Inspector Morley thought you ought to know that Mr. Hadlow has arrived."

"Thank you," I said.

"He's on his way up here right now."

"Has he spoken to the inspector?"

"Yes, sir. Very loudly, it seems."

"That seems to be his style."

"I know, sir. I heard that call he made to you."

I was glad that Bernard Hadlow had gone to the police first. They would tell him how they were handling the case and what developments there had been. I'd be spared the trouble of having to explain everything in exhaustive detail to him. Troy Morley might have done me a favor. In dealing with Hadlow, he would, I hoped, have drawn some of the man's sting. When he came buzzing into my personal space, he would not be quite so angry. The early warning was helpful. It gave me time to prepare. Expecting Hadlow to bang on my door, I was surprised when he chose a different mode of entry. He was let into the adjoining suite by Frank Colouris' master key so that he could see for himself the suite from which his daughter had been abducted. We could hear his voice booming through the connecting door. I screwed up my courage and went in to confront him.

"Hello, Mr. Hadlow," I said.

He glowered at me. "You're Saxon."

"Only by descent. Anglo-Saxon, to be more precise. My name is *Mr.* Saxon."

"I'll be with you in a minute."

He went off abruptly and left me standing there while he went back into the bedroom again. Frank Colouris pulled a face. On the short journey in the elevator, he'd weighed up his companion very accurately.

"Would you like me to stay, sir?" he offered.

"No, thanks."

"I've arranged a room for your ex-wife."

"What about transport to the airport?"

"It'll be standing by for you. Just give me a time."

"We need to be there by ten."

"Joel will be ready from 9:15 onwards."

"Thanks, Mr. Colouris."

Hadlow came out of the bedroom, deep in thought. He was bigger than the photographs had shown and had a size-able paunch that even an expensive tailor could not entirely disguise. Yards of materials had gone into his white suit. His shoes cost more than my whole outfit. The face was as podgy and repulsive as I'd expected, but there was one surprise. His hair had been inexpertly dyed. In the photographs, its luxuriance had reminded me of Jessica's hair, but it had the most unconvincing color. Patches of gray showed through on the temples and there was an uneven hue on the top of his head. I felt almost sorry for him. Even with his money, he could not defend himself from the ridicule that his hair would invite.

"Was there anything else, Mr. Hadlow?" asked Colouris politely.

"What?" growled the other.

"I'll leave you now, if that's OK with you."

"Yes, yes. Off you go, Mr. Colouris. I don't need you any more."

"Goodbye."

The deputy manager gave me a look of sympathy before he let himself out. Bernard Hadlow studied me before speaking. He was very calm but I sensed that anger was rippling beneath the surface.

"What's going on, Mr. Saxon?" he asked.

"If you've spoken to the police, you know as much as I do."

"Tell me your version."

"First," I said, "let's get one thing clear. I don't like anyone swearing at me over the telephone. Especially when they have no real cause. I'm desperately sorry for what's happened but the fact remains that I brought Jessica along as a treat. She and Lynette get on so well together. I wanted your daughter to enjoy herself."

"Anything else?"

"Stop treating me like an erring employee. I don't work for you."

He gave a grunt that I took to be a sign of consent.

"Look, wouldn't it be easier if we sat down?" I suggested.

While I lowered myself onto the sofa, he opted for the armchair. He almost filled it but he looked less menacing now that he was sitting down. I was relieved.

"I'm waiting," he said.

"Well, the trouble really started on the drive from the airport…"

I'd been through the sequence of events so many times in my mind that I was able to give him a precise account. He listened without interruption, never taking his eyes off me and giving an occasional nod. It was an uncomfortable situation. I felt as if I were being interrogated by him in a police station. When I finished my recital, the questions came thick and fast.

"So you didn't pick up the phone message until hours later?"

"No, Mr. Hadlow."

"Why weren't you in your room?"

"That's a personal matter."

"My daughter's been abducted, man," he snarled. "I want to know everything."

"Where I was at the time is not relevant."

"What are you hiding, Mr. Saxon?"

"Nothing."

"Out with it, man!"

"Nothing!" I repeated, with more force. "Now, I know that you're very distressed by what's happened but you have to remember that we're in the same boat. My daughter was kidnapped as well. Can you imagine how I felt when I went into that bedroom and saw signs of struggle?"

"Yes," he said, pursing his lips. "I'm sorry."

"I'll do *anything* to get them safely back."

"Inspector Morley mentioned two young men."

"Rick and Conrad," I said. "Two young Canadians who befriended the girls. They spent a fair bit of time together. Conrad was the last person to see them before they were kidnapped." I anticipated his inquiry. "No, they weren't involved in it. I'm absolutely certain of that and so is Inspector Morley. They were genuinely horrified at the news."

"So they should be. It was their job to protect the girls."

"Not twenty-four hours a day, Mr. Hadlow."

"When their friends weren't around, Jessica and Lynette were in your care."

"Actually," I admitted, trying to introduce a lighter note, "it was the other way round. They looked after me. Jessica took charge the moment we stepped onto the plane. Once we got here, they teamed up with Rick and Conrad."

"Do you accept no responsibility at all?"

"Of course. I wish that I'd never brought them to Bermuda now."

"You'd heard the alarm bells, Mr. Saxon."

"Alarm bells?"

"Yes," he went on, shaking an admonitory finger. "Those acts of sabotage on your golf course. Heavens, man, according to the police, you actually found that murder victim yourself. How much more of a warning did you need?"

"I'd no reason to suppose that the girls would be the next target."

"These people had launched a direct attack on your work. Didn't it occur to you that they'd go on to strike at your weak spot? Namely, the girls."

"Frankly, no."

"You shouldn't have let them out of your sight."

"What sort of holiday would that have been for them?"

"A *safe* one, Mr. Saxon."

Bernard Hadlow glared at me with undiluted disgust. Having made up his mind that I was culpable, he was letting me feel the full weight of his displeasure. It was almost suffocating. Before he could resume his cross-examination, I sought to clarify something that had been puzzling me.

"I understand that the kidnapper contacted you as well?"

"That's right."

"What did he say?"

"Very little. He simply told me that he was holding my daughter and that, if I wanted to see her alive again, I was to come to Bermuda at once."

"At what time did you take the call?"

"Just after I'd got up. I was staying at a hotel in Chicago."

"Why the delay?" I wondered. "If they rang me in the middle of the night, why not get on to you straight away? I know there's a time difference between here and Chicago but there still seems to have been a gap between the two calls."

"Jessica didn't know where I was," he explained. "She would only have given them my home number. A man did ring the house. My wife confirmed that when I talked to her earlier. She says that he wanted to speak to me urgently on a business matter."

"Did he tell her about the abduction?"

"Fortunately, no. She upsets easily. Even though she's only her stepmother, she's very fond of Jessica. I still haven't told her. I want to keep her out of this."

"What about Jessica's mother?"

"The fewer people who know about this, the better."

"I still don't understand why there was a delay."

"My wife didn't have my number," he said evasively. "I'd moved on from a business meeting in Israel a few days earlier than anticipated. What she was able to give the man was the number of a close associate of mine. He eventually tracked me down in Chicago and passed on the number of my hotel to the caller."

"Did the kidnapper give a name?"

"Not to me. The person who rang my wife called himself John Loomis. You can bet anything that it's a false name. Anyway, that accounts for the time lapse in the calls," he said, running a hand through his hair. "First thing I did was to get myself a flight to Bermuda. Then I rang the police here."

"Shortly after I did, it seems."

I wasn't surprised that Hadlow's wife didn't know exactly where he was at any given time. A man as interested in women as he obviously was is very careful not to leave too incriminating a paper trail behind him. He would doubtless ring his wife at regular intervals to give her the impression that they were in constant touch. What he did not want from her was a phone call at night in a Chicago hotel room, because the chances were that he was not alone. He went back on the attack.

"Didn't you check that the girls got back safely last night?"

"They've gone beyond the age when you have to tuck them in, Mr. Hadlow."

"You should have taken sensible precautions."

"Against what? How was I to know that they'd be kidnapped?"

"Wasn't the murder sufficient warning for you?"

"It shook me rigid," I confessed, "but I didn't expect a follow-up."

"You should have. In your position, I'd have taken precautions."

"Neither Jessica nor Lynette would have thanked me for that."

"They certainly won't thank you for letting them be abducted."

"I did nothing of the kind," I said, jumping angrily to my feet. "I simply gave them the freedom that young women of their age are fully entitled to expect. If you must have a scapegoat, Mr. Hadlow, don't look at me."

"Then where do I look?"

"Try the nearest mirror."

"What are you on about?"

"A company called Redfurst Leisure," I said, watching his eyebrows shoot up. "Yes, I thought you would recognize the name. They're part of your far-flung empire, aren't they? And they just happen to have been in the race to purchase the site on which the Blue Dolphin was built. They were knocked out of the reckoning by GGM."

"What's this got to do with the abduction of my daughter?"

"I'm not sure, Mr. Hadlow, but I'd hazard a guess that there is a connection."

"How?"

"Suppose—just suppose—that someone at Redfurst Leisure was so furious at losing the deal that they wanted revenge? What better way than to try to sabotage the golf course that will turn the Blue Dolphin into a real moneymaker?"

"This is nonsense," he roared, hauling himself out of his chair.

"Is it? How can you be so sure?"

"Because I keep tabs on the activities of every company I own."

"Even though there are so many?"

"Yes," he boasted. "If the tea lady in one of them goes down with flu, I get to hear about it. I'd certainly be told about any plans for sabotaging a golf course and I'd cancel them right away. Redfurst Leisure had nothing whatsoever to do with this, Mr. Saxon," he yelled, bunching a fist. "For fuck's sake, man, why should anyone in one of my own companies want to kidnap my daughter?"

"Perhaps you're not the model employer you think you are."

I thought for a moment he was going to strike me, and I got ready to parry the blow. Clenching his teeth, he breathed heavily through his nose and brought his eyebrows together in an angry chevron. I could see the veins standing out on his forehead like lengths of whipcord. Thanks to the fax from London, I'd been able to catch him on the raw. He was furious. I held my ground. Tall as he was, he was still inches shorter than me. The physical intimidation he used on business colleagues simply didn't work on me. Instead, he fell back on a throaty denunciation.

"You're to blame for all this, Saxon!" he affirmed.

"*Mr.* Saxon," I corrected.

"You were the target and they snatched your daughter away. Because Jessica was with her, she got taken as well. Can't you at least show some remorse, man?"

"I've been overcome with it."

"If it hadn't been for that fucking golf course of yours," he cried, pointing a finger at the window, "my daughter would be safe and well."

"So would mine, Mr. Hadlow."

"Jessica is an only child."

"So is Lynette."

"If she's harmed in any way, I'll lay it at your door. This is all your doing," he insisted. "If you'd heeded the warning, none of us would be in this predicament. Nobody upsets me with impunity, Mr. Saxon, and I'm extremely upset. I'll get back at you for this. By God, I will, I swear it!"

When the telephone rang in the other room, it took us a moment to realize what it was. The mood was broken. I went swiftly through the connecting door to pick up the receiver. Hadlow was on my heels. Steve Hills waited expectantly.

"Yes?" I said.

"Mr. Saxon?" replied the curt voice I'd heard earlier.

"Yes, who's this?"

"Never you mind. I'm sorry that your daughter got caught up in this, Mr. Saxon. We weren't really after her at all. It was Mr. Hadlow's daughter we wanted and yours got in the way. Is he there? We know he's arrived at the Blue Dolphin."

"What about Lynette?"

"I need to speak to Bernard Hadlow."

"Is she all right?" I asked.

"Give it to me," snapped Hadlow, wrenching the telephone from my grasp. "Hello," he barked into the mouthpiece. "Bernard Hadlow here."

"Listen carefully," warned the voice.

Hadlow struck back viciously. "No, you listen to me, whoever you are. Do you know who you're dealing with? If you don't return my daughter immediately, unharmed, then you'll live to regret it for the—"

The line went dead and stopped him in mid-threat. Hills stepped forward.

"That was a bad mistake, sir," he said, taking the receiver from his hand to replace it. "Never antagonize someone in a situation like this. It could have dire consequences for your daughter. I'm sure that you don't want to imperil her. We have to try to build a relationship with the kidnapper."

"Damn it, man!" howled Hadlow. "What was I supposed to do? Invite the bastard to dinner?"

"Constable Hills is right," I agreed. "You have to remain calm. All you've done is to lose contact with him. What use is that to our daughters?"

Though he couldn't rise to an apology, Hadlow did manage to look shamefaced. His outburst had not only been prompted by the fact that he was talking to the kidnapper. What had goaded him was the information that he'd been the real target and not me. Instead of Jessica, it was Lynette who was the innocent bystander. Had she not been with her friend, she would have been left alone. Deprived of his main excuse to blame me, Hadlow paced the room restlessly. It was five minutes before the telephone rang again. When Hadlow lumbered across to it, Hills stood in his path.

"Why not let Mr. Saxon answer it?" he said. "It's his room, after all."

I suddenly warmed to the detective. Maybe I *would* give him some golfing tips. With a tense Bernard Hadlow breathing down my neck, I lifted the receiver once more.

"Hello," I said. "Alan Saxon here."

"Is Mr. Hadlow still with you?" asked the same voice as before.

"Yes, he's right here."

"Is he prepared to discuss this sensibly?"

I looked at Hadlow. "Yes, I'm sure he is. He regrets losing his temper like that. He's under great stress. We both are. Just assure us that the girls are unharmed."

"One moment."

There was a long pause before Jessica's trembling voice came on the line.

"Do as they say, Daddy!" she begged. "*Please!*"

Hadlow lunged forward but I held the instrument from him this time.

"Before I give this to you," I cautioned, "just remember that you're bargaining for my daughter's life as well. Stay cool, Mr. Hadlow. Hear the man out."

He nodded then took the telephone from me. "Hello. Bernard Hadlow here."

"Welcome back," said the voice with light sarcasm.

"Who are you?"

"That's immaterial."

"May I speak to my daughter, please?"

"When she's released, Mr. Hadlow."

"And when will that be?"

"When you do exactly what you're told," said the man coldly. "Otherwise, you'll never see either of the girls again. Go to Reception. There's an envelope waiting there for you. It contains your instructions. Do you understand?"

"Yes," he said quietly.

"Obey them, Mr. Hadlow, or you can kiss your lovely daughter goodbye. And the same goes for Mr. Saxon's daughter," he added with a chilling laugh. "You'll have *her* death on your conscience as well. Goodbye."

Chapter Eight

Bernard Hadlow was visibly rocked. He was so used to giving orders that he'd forgotten what it was like to take them. For once in his life, he wasn't in total control and it left him bewildered. At the risk of losing his daughter, he had to obey a command. If he didn't, Lynette would suffer along with Jessica. I was shaking with impotent rage. While the two of us were trying to absorb the shock, Steve Hills turned away to make a call of his own on his mobile. I could hear him talking to Inspector Morley in the background. Hadlow seemed to be in a trance. It was only broken when the detective rejoined us.

"I've just told Inspector Morley about the call," he said. "He's coming at once."

Hadlow blinked. "There's a message for me," he remembered, moving towards the door. "He said it was in Reception. I must go at once."

"There's no need, sir," said Hills, intercepting him before he reached the door. "The inspector will collect it on his way up here. He wants to hear the phone call with the kidnapper for himself."

"I see."

Still trying to take it all in, I perched on the arm of a chair and gestured at the sofa. Hadlow flopped down on it, giving me an aerial view of his head and allowing me to see a small bald patch. Conflicting emotions flitted across his face. He was, by turns, dejected, angry, rueful, optimistic, resigned and vengeful as he tried to find the right face to fit the occasion. Eventually, he looked across at me with a grudging reluctance.

"I think that I owe you an apology, Mr. Saxon," he said.

"Thank you."

"Jessica is in danger because of me. So is your own daughter."

"We must do everything humanly possible to get them back," I emphasized. "You can't browbeat your way out of this, Mr. Hadlow. We must cooperate."

"We will, Mr. Saxon," he murmured. "We will."

He went off into another reverie. The irate man who'd abused me over the telephone was now a frightened father, wondering if he'd ever see his daughter alive again. Just like me. The ordeal didn't exactly unite us but it broke down some of the barriers between us. He reached into his pocket for a silver cigarette case and flipped it open. Both Hills and I declined the offer of the cigarette, but Hadlow slipped one between his lips, then lit it with a gleaming lighter. He inhaled deeply. We sat in silence until there was a knock on the door. Hills went across to admit Troy Morley and Derek Woodford. The inspector was carrying a white envelope.

"This is addressed to you, sir," he said, giving it to Hadlow. "It was delivered by hand earlier this afternoon."

Tearing open the envelope, Hadlow read the contents and blenched.

"May I see it, please?" asked Morley.

Hadlow passed it over. "Of course."

The inspector read it before showing it to Woodford. They traded a glance.

"They don't give you much time, Mr. Hadlow," said Morley. "Can you get this sort of money together at such short notice?"

"I'm not sure," said Hadlow.

"We'll have to discuss our strategy."

Hadlow became decisive. "Our strategy is that we do what they tell us, Inspector. For the moment, that is. When the girls are released," he said rancorously, "it's a different matter. That's when they'll realize how big a mistake they made. However long it takes, and however much it costs, I'll pursue them to the ends of the earth."

"That's our job, sir."

"It'll take more than a Toytown police force to catch these bastards."

"Don't underestimate our abilities, sir," said Morley, stung by the remark. "I venture to suggest that our record compares very favorably with anyone else's. We're proud of it. While you're on the island, you might care to visit our prison. It's full of people who took us for a Toytown outfit. They know better now."

"I'm sure that Mr. Hadlow didn't mean it as an insult, Inspector," I said.

"I hope not, sir. Constable Hills?"

"Yes, Inspector?" said the detective.

"Can you replay the last two calls, please?"

"One moment, sir."

Hills bent over the miniature tape recorder that was plugged into the telephone and pressed the rewind button. He estimated the amount of time the calls had taken and stopped the machine. When he switched on, we heard the end of my conversation with Rosemary. The call from the kidnapper was then played. It was cut short by Hadlow's foolish outburst. Morley said nothing but I could read the disapproval in his eyes. He listened to the next conversation with the kidnapper, then asked Hills to play both calls through once more. Familiarity did not breed contempt as far as I was concerned. It only sharpened my anguish. The more I heard the kidnapper's voice, the more frightening it became. The man was cold and merciless. Our daughters were in his power.

"How much is the ransom demand?" I asked.

"That's my business," said Hadlow sulkily.

"Not when my daughter is involved as well."

"Let's just say that it's for a large amount of money, Mr. Saxon," explained the inspector, picking up the discarded envelope. "If Mr. Hadlow can get it in time, the exchange will take place tomorrow evening."

"Tomorrow?" I exclaimed. "The girls have to endure another twenty-four hours?"

"Unless we find them first."

"No," said Hadlow sharply. "Back off, Inspector. You read what the note said. If the police get anywhere near them, they'll cut and run. I can't take that risk."

"We'll be discreet, Mr. Hadlow."

"Play it their way."

"Only up to a point." Morley held up the envelope and letter. "May I hang on to these, sir? I'd like our lab to give them the once-over." Hadlow gave a curt nod. "Well, I daresay that you want to pick up a telephone to try to rustle up the money."

"I'll get it somehow," asserted Hadlow.

"Constable Hills will show you to your room, sir. In your haste to find me as soon as you arrived, you forgot to check in. Sergeant Woodford did so on your behalf. Your luggage has been sent up. Hills?"

"This way, sir," said the young detective, moving to the door.

Bernard Hadlow was unsure what to do. He looked at me as if wanting to say something but the words wouldn't come. Instead, he turned on his heel and flung his departing comment to Troy Morley.

"I'll see you later, Inspector."

"I'm sure that you will, sir."

Morley waited for them to leave before speaking. "I'm sorry about that, sir," he said to me. "Mr. Hadlow is not the most amenable of gentleman."

"It was like having an army of occupation in the room."

"At least, we now know where we stand."

"Do we, Inspector?"

"You won't have to sit beside that phone any longer. They won't ring here again. Mr. Hadlow is the point of contact. We'll have to transfer the recording equipment to his room instead. You don't need to have Constable Hills in here with you any more."

"He was no bother."

"It would be stupid of me to tell you to relax, I know," he said with an apologetic smile. "The situation is far too tense for that. All that I can advise is that you try to find some distractions."

"I don't really feel in a mood for a game of golf, Inspector."

"Of course not."

"In any case, my ex-wife is arriving this evening. Rosemary concentrates the mind like the threat of execution. And I know exactly what such a threat sounds like," I went on with a grimace. "We heard it over the telephone."

"Quite so, sir."

"What do you propose to do, Inspector?"

"Play a waiting game."

"I hope that doesn't mean we take second place from now on," I protested. "When you thought the murder and the abduction were linked, you said that the arrest of the killer would solve the kidnap as well. But it won't. The crimes are unrelated."

"So it seems."

"We've been working on the wrong assumptions."

"Yes, sir," he conceded. "That's true. But, at least, we've got our bearings now. And you have my assurance that the kidnap will have our full attention."

"I hope so." I recalled something. "What happened about that van?"

"We traced it, sir," said Derek Woodford. "It was stolen from a building firm in Pembroke Parish. The van was found abandoned near Burton Bay. That's in Sandys Parish at the western end of the island. Our lads are going over it right now."

"In other words, the breakthrough may not be as important as you believed."

"That depends on what we find on the vehicle."

"We're also exploring other avenues, Mr. Saxon," resumed the inspector. "We won't rest until the killer is behind bars."

"What about the kidnapper?"

His eyes flashed. "Oh, I want him just as much, I promise you."

"So do I, Inspector."

"I understand that, sir. Well," he said briskly, "you'll have to excuse us. Sergeant Woodford and I have to get back to work. There's a lot to do. If there's any news, you'll be informed straight away."

"Thank you."

"Anything else before we go, sir?"

"Yes," I said as the face of Angela Pike suddenly popped into my mind. "After the murder, one of the first things you did was to search Mo's house. That upset his partner terribly. Why did you do it?"

"We wanted an explanation, Mr. Saxon."

"Of what?"

"How they could afford to live where they do," he replied. "It's a very nice house. Miss Pike is a waitress at the hotel and Maurice Dobbs was a driver. Their joint income was fairly low. Yet they could somehow afford a new house."

"Did you discover how?"

"Not yet, sir. But we will."

I don't know what they did to Nancy Wykoff at the health spa but it left her looking wonderful. When I called on her, she was positively glowing. Unfortunately, I wasn't in a position to appreciate her attributes properly. I felt numb and detached. Nancy and I had spent a most delightful night together, yet there was no *frisson* when I met her again. For the time being, my heart and mind were elsewhere.

"I was just about to come to your suite," she said.

"No need."

"What's happened, Alan?"

"We got another call from the kidnapper."

"And?"

"He wanted to speak to Bernard Hadlow."

"Has Mr. Hadlow arrived?"

"Oh, yes. In an explosion of red flame."

I told her the details of the calls and she listened with interest. Though I mentioned everything else, I couldn't bring myself to repeat the death threat that was leveled against the girls. It would have been like twisting a dagger in a raw wound. When I'd finished, she led me across to the sofa.

"What a dreadful experience!" she said, helping me to sit. "You must be going through hell. But there are two tiny consolations."

"I can't see them, Nancy."

"Well, you don't have to stay chained to your telephone, waiting for a call."

"That's not exactly a consolation," I argued.

"The other news ought to be."

"Other news?"

"Yes, Alan," she said. "The fact that your daughter was not the target, after all. I know how guilty that made you feel. You thought that you'd put Lynette and her friend in danger because of the golf course, but that wasn't the case at all. It was

Jessica Hadlow they wanted, not your daughter. If she hadn't been with her friend at the time, Lynette would be free."

"That won't make me sleep any easier," I said. "For whatever reason, both girls are in jeopardy because I brought them to Bermuda. If there *is* a consolation, it's that Peter Fullard will be relieved to know the kidnap is nothing to do with our work. There's no solace at all for me."

She was disappointed. "Oh, I rather hoped there was."

"So did I, Nancy."

"Since the person they wanted to get at was Bernard Hadlow and not Alan Saxon, I hoped that your conscience would be eased a little with regard to me. I know how much you've blamed yourself for not being in your own room last night."

"That's no criticism of you."

"Maybe not, but it does rather take the shine off things."

I squeezed her hand. "It's still shining pretty brightly for me."

"And me." She kissed me lightly on the lips. "What I can't understand is how they knew that Hadlow's daughter was in Bermuda in the first place. She'd only been here a couple of days before they pounced."

"The answer to that was contained in the fax."

"What did those articles say?"

"It's what they showed, as much as what they said," I explained. "Jessica Hadlow is a dreadful exhibitionist. She can hear a camera clicking half a mile away. Jessica never misses a photo opportunity. I'll show you the fax. The photos are not very clear but you'd be surprised how many times she manages to get in them, even though her father is the ostensible star."

"So everyone in the business world would know what she looks like."

"Exactly. She's the beautiful daughter of Bernard Hadlow."

"There has to be a connection with Bermuda as well."

"There is, Nancy," I continued. "Apart from the fact that one of his companies failed to secure this site, that is. It was a rare failure. According to one article, Hadlow has considerable business interests here and he was utterly ruthless in the way that he acquired them. In short, he has lots of enemies in Bermuda with scores to settle. I think that one of them spotted Jessica here and saw a means of hitting back at Hadlow."

"By the sound of it, she's not exactly a shrinking violet."

"Not our Jessica. Within twenty-four hours, she made almost everyone on the island aware of her presence. Look at the way she roped Rick and Conrad in," I said, thinking of the two Canadians. "She had the pair of them in tow immediately. They went everywhere together, out and about, whooping it up. Jessica has the kind of looks you remember, even if you've only seen her photograph."

"Didn't you say she'd been here before?"

"Yes, a number of times. She's quite proprietary about Bermuda. The chances are that the person who abducted her had seen her on the island before. When she was with her family, she didn't present such an easy target. This time, alas, it was different."

"Do the cops have any leads?"

"I don't think so."

"But they must be aware of Hadlow's links with Bermuda."

"Oh, yes, Nancy," I said with a wry smile. "I think they know all about Bernard Hadlow. I saw the look in Inspector Morley's eye. It verged on polite contempt. The person I feel sorry for Constable Hills."

"Why?"

"He'll have to sit beside the telephone with Hadlow, as he did with me. I wasn't in the ideal mood for company—especially from a policeman—but at least I was civil to the man. I doubt very much if Bernard Hadlow will be."

"So what's the next step?"

"Watch and pray."

"Is there anything more practical you can do, Alan?"

"I'm afraid that there is."

"Your ex-wife?"

"Her plane touches down at ten."

"I didn't expect her until tomorrow."

"Rosemary is at her best in an emergency," I admitted. "If anyone can get the last seat on a flight, it's her." I glanced at my watch. "Talking of whom, I ought to get back to my suite. She said she might ring from Boston when she changed planes. I don't want to be out of the room again at the wrong time."

"Is that all last night was?" she said, a hand on my knee. "The wrong time?"

"Of course not."

"I have my own share of guilt, you know."

"That's ridiculous."

"Is it?"

"You've nothing to reproach yourself with, Nancy."

"I took you away from a place where you might have saved your daughter."

"We don't know that," I said, touching her cheek. "Besides, you didn't take me away. I came willingly—and gratefully. I can't tell you how sorry I am that this has overshadowed our time together."

"No regrets, then?"

"Only about that bad tee shot of mine at Port Royal's sixteenth hole."

She laughed. "You're a lovely man, do you know that?"

"That's what they all say," I joked.

"And so they should."

I became more wistful. "I just wish that I was a good father as well."

"You *are*, Alan. Nobody could love his daughter as much as you do."

"I hope that I get the chance to prove that to Lynette," I sighed. "When something like this happens, all you can think of are your own deficiencies. Things you should have told her, places you should have taken her, advice you should have given. Loving your daughter is not enough, Nancy. You have to translate that love into something tangible and I don't feel that I've done that." I clicked my tongue. "This holiday was an attempt to make up for my lapses. I was desperate to spend time alone with her."

"Why didn't you?"

"Because of Rosemary. She hung Jessica around my neck like an albatross."

"You can't blame it all on your ex-wife, Alan. The fact remains that Lynette was very keen to bring her friend, though, from everything you've told me about Jessica, I'm bound to wonder why."

"I don't follow."

"Well, Lynette sounds like a bright, sensitive, charming young lady with a great future ahead of her. Why did she hook up with someone like Jessica Hadlow?"

"That's what I wondered at first," I said ruefully. "But it soon became clear. It's a kind of infatuation. Jessica has real charisma, even though it's not the kind that I appreciate. Lynette is dazzled by her talent, by her sophistication and by the lifestyle she enjoys because of a rich father. We've all met people like that in our time. Performers. They sweep us away before we have time to take their proper measure."

A knowing smile. "Is that what you did to me?"

"All that I intended to do was to play a round of golf with you."

"One shot follows another."

"You won't hear any complaints from me."

"Then let's postpone this conversation until a time when we can take things further," she suggested, brushing her lips against my cheek. Nancy stood up. "Come on, Mr. Saxon. Back to your room. We don't want you missing another vital call."

I got to my feet. "Rosemary may not ring."

"Oh, I'm certain she will. She'll be desperate for news."

"Then I'll go. Meanwhile," I warned, "don't press Melinda Reed for any more details about the Blue Dolphin."

"Did Cal complain to you?"

"Bitterly. He called you a bloodhound."

She grinned. "Is that all? I've been called far worse than that."

"Not by me." I looked at her face, shining up at me. "There *is* a consolation," I said, "but it's nothing to do with the kidnap. If Lynette and I had come together, we'd have been together for a whole week and I'd have been the happiest man on the island. But I can't claim that she'd have been the happiest daughter. Lynette likes company of her own age. Having her friend here made the holiday for her."

"Even though it ruined it for you."

"But it didn't, Nancy. That's the consolation, you see. Because the girls went off together, I was free to spend time with you. On and off the golf course."

"Which did you prefer?"

"This is not the right time to answer that."

"I know. Sorry I asked."

"No, it's a fair question," I said. "Ask me again when this is all over."

"I will, Alan—and good luck!"

I gave her a warm hug and a final kiss.

Thanks," I said, "I need it."

ᴠᴧᴧᴠᴧᴠᴧᴠᴧᴠᴧᴠᴧᴠᴧᴠ

Frank Colouris obeyed my instructions to the letter. Having reserved a room at the hotel for Rosemary, he had a car and driver waiting at the designated time. Colouris walked me solicitously out to it.

"You'll have no problems with Joel," he promised. "He's an ideal chauffeur. The kind of guy who won't speak unless he's spoken to."

"That'll be a pleasant change."

"The flight is on time. I checked with the airline."

"So did I, Mr. Colouris. My ex-wife rang from Boston to say it was leaving on schedule. I was able to bring her up to speed on developments."

"I hope that everything works out satisfactorily, sir."

"That depends on Mr. Hadlow."

"He should be able to raise the amount of money demanded."

"That's not my worry," I said, fearing that Hadlow might do something impetuous when it came to handing the ransom over. "Still, I can't do anything about that just now. I wonder if I could ask you a favor, Mr. Colouris?"

"Sure. That's what I'm here for."

"Could you possibly go on another diplomatic mission to Peter Fullard?"

"If need be, sir."

"I do think he'd feel slightly better about things if he realized that the kidnap is not connected in any way to the golf course. Peter might even stop blaming himself for getting me involved in the project and—as he thinks—putting my daughter in danger."

"I'll go up there right away."

"Has Peter set foot outside his room today?"

"Only when he took his wife to the airport," he said. "He wouldn't even let the maid in to change the bed until they saw me standing beside her. Mr. Fullard is taking no chances."

"Put his mind at rest about the abduction, anyway."

"I will, sir."

"Thanks."

My chauffeur was standing beside a sleek limousine, hold-ing the rear door open for me. Joel was a black Bermudan in his thirties, a short, tubby man with an amiable face and a deferential smile. I climbed into the vehicle and sat back. When the engine started up, it was no more than a faint purr. We glided forward. Joel was clearly under orders to keep quiet. He drove along at a comfortable speed and left me alone with my thoughts. We were halfway there before I realized that he might be useful to me.

"You must have known Maurice Dobbs," I said.

"Yes, sir. We all knew Mo."

"Was he popular?"

"Mo was Mo, sir. You had to take him or leave him."

"I understand he lived with one of the waitresses."

"That's right. Angie Pike."

"They had a new house, didn't they?"

"A very nice one, sir. We passed quite close to it."

"He must have been well-paid if he could afford to buy a house like that."

Joel gave a dry laugh. "Well, he wasn't well paid for driving, sir. It's a steady job and I like it, but you won't get rich doing this."

"So where did the money come from?"

"That's what we all wanted to know. Then Mo told us."

"Oh?"

"Gambling, sir. He'd had a big win. Mo like to gamble."

"Did you know him well?"

"Not really, but I sorry about what happened to him."

"So is everyone."

"Bad business, sir. Real bad."

"What about his partner?"

"Angie? I spoke to her once or twice, that's all. Pretty woman."

"Yes," I agreed. "I met her myself. She was devastated by his death."

"I not surprised."

"Mo meant everything to her. She worshipped him."

"So did Ella, sir."

"Who?"

"Ella," he said. "Mo's wife. She was a lovely woman. Mo was lucky to have a wife like that. She stood by him through thick and thin. Ella keep him afloat, then he goes and takes up with Angie instead. His wife still mad about him."

"In her shoes, I'd have been mad *at* him."

Joel gave a throaty laugh. "That's what my wife said, sir. She not taken in by Mo's charm but lots of women were. He had a way with him."

"It didn't work on me, I'm afraid."

"Ella was a special lady," he said. "Angie is nice but she's not a patch on Ella."

"Did they have a divorce?"

"No, sir. She keep hoping he might go back to her one day."

"You mean, she'd forgive him enough to take him back?"

He nodded. "Ella have a lot of practice at forgiving. Mo gave that woman a rough ride but she never let him down. Angie's not the only woman who'll mourn him," he said quietly. "I think Ella will shed far more tears."

The chat with Joel was enlightening and I wished that I'd initiated conversation earlier so that it could have gone on longer. He talked at length about Mo, but his tone was noncommittal. I had the feeling that he'd never really liked, and certainly not trusted, the man. Yet he wouldn't be drawn when I asked about Mo's background. Out of loyalty to a dead colleague, there were certain things he simply wouldn't tell me. I was bound to speculate on what those things might be.

Crises play havoc with our emotions. There have been times in my life when I'd have looked forward to the imminent appearance of my ex-wife with the horror I'd reserve for the approach of the bubonic plague. Yet here I was, standing in the arrivals lounge, waiting for Rosemary with something akin to enthusiasm. Lynette's plight had dissolved all differences between us. Ours was a shared pain. My anguish was intense but at least I had some idea of what was going on. Rosemary had flown thousands of miles in a state of continuous apprehension, wondering what was happening, fearing the worst, frightened that she might be too late to see our daughter alive again. When she'd phoned from Logan Airport, I hadn't been able to offer much comfort. The second leg of her long journey would have been another exercise in sustained torment.

I waited at the barrier with a small crowd as the passengers began to come out. Some were native Bermudans, returning home from business trips or holidays. Others were about to start a vacation on the island. All had the anticipatory delight of people who were glad to be there, who could rely on a cordial welcome at their homes or at their hotels and guest houses. There was no pleasure involved in Rosemary's visit. She was coming out of need and desperation. Yet there was no sign of her. Expecting her to be among the first in sight, I was puzzled when the main batch of passengers streamed out and she was not among them. Had she missed the flight in Boston? Or—the thought was even more alarming—had the anxiety been too much for her? Was it possible that she'd collapsed under the strain? I had to resist the urge to jump over the barrier and go in search of her. Having tried at first to stop her from coming to Bermuda, I now accepted that I wanted her there. We needed each other.

Eventually, she came through the door. Instead of pushing a heavily laden trolley like everyone else, she simply pulled a small case behind her on wheels. It was the clearest indication of the scale of the emergency. Rosemary has been known to pack three large suitcases and a travel bag for a weekend stay in the Cotswolds. To bring so little showed how speedily she must have got herself ready. When she saw me, she gave a brave smile and waved. I hurried forward through the stragglers and we met in an involuntary embrace. Her eyes were darting nervously.

"Any more news?" she asked.

"No, Rosemary. Things are as they were when we spoke earlier."

"So Lynette is still being held?"

"Along with Jessica."

"I want you to tell me *everything*, Alan."

"I will," I promised, "though not on the drive to the hotel. As I told you, the police want to keep this whole thing under wraps. If the media got to hear of it, they'd only get in the way and that might imperil the girls. It's not something we want shouted from the rooftops. So—not a word about the kidnap in front of Joel."

"Joel?"

"Our driver. He's waiting outside."

I took charge of her luggage and was pleased when she slipped a hand through my other arm. We were nominally a couple once more. Given the circumstances, Rosemary was holding up very well. She looked tired but there was no hint of the grief that was whirling around inside her. When we came out into the fresh air, she tightened her grip on my arm as if needing my support before facing the trauma ahead. Joel was there to relieve me of the case and to open the car door. We were soon easing away from the curb. It was a strange journey. Eager to hear about the calls from the kidnapper, Rosemary was reduced to filling the time by updating me on the activities of various relatives that I'd shed as a consequence of our divorce. The social trivia must have bemused Joel. He heard about Uncle Eric's retirement from the Parish Council, Cousin Amy's engagement to a twice married accountant from Chichester and Great Auntie Maud's hip replacement operation at the William Harvey

Hospital in Kent. All that I could throw in by way of reply
was the information that Clive Phelps had sent his love. It
was received with icy indifference.

Calvin Reed was waiting to greet us at the Blue Dolphin.
He'd arranged for the formalities of checking in to be
dispensed with and simply handed Rosemary her card key.
He was as unperturbed as ever. Nobody would have guessed
that one of his employees had been murdered and that a
kidnap had taken place in the hotel. As we waited for the
elevator, his face was impassive, his voice calm.

"Call on me personally for anything, Mrs. Saxon," he
offered.

"Thank you, Mr. Reed."

"I daresay you're too exhausted to come down for supper,
but I can recommend our room service. The response time
is exceptional."

"Then it's far better than my own," she said.

Reed turned to me. "No problems on the drive this time?"

"None at all," I said. "Joel was an ideal choice."

"That's what Frank thought."

"Please thank him on my behalf."

The elevator came and the manager waved us off. Rosemary had been given a room on the fourth floor. I was
relieved that it was not on the floor below, in proximity to
Room 333. Though I was sure that Nancy would handle
the situation with aplomb, I wasn't sure that I could cope
with a chance meeting with her while Rosemary was still on
my arm. My ex-wife let us into the room and gave it a cursory glance. I set her case down and played the host.

"What can I get you?" I asked. "Tea? Coffee? Something
stronger?"

"A glass of tonic water, if they have one," she said, drop-
ping into an armchair and kicking off her shoes. "It's all
that I can manage. I seem to have been on the go all day."

I opened the cabinet and poured her a drink. "Try this," I said, handing it over.

"What about you?"

"I'm fine, thanks."

She sipped the tonic water gratefully. "Oh, that's nice."

"Do you feel up to some food?"

"I had far too much on the plane, Alan. Comfort eating. I was a real pig."

"I don't believe that. You never over-indulge on anything. Moderation is your middle name." I sat opposite her. "Sorry about the car journey. Fascinating as it was, I didn't really want to hear about Great Aunt Maud's hip operation."

"Tell me everything," she begged. "From the beginning."

"You know most of it, Rosemary."

"Tell me again. I couldn't take it all in over the phone."

I gave her as detailed an account as I could without causing undue upset. Once again, I kept any mention of cannabis on the beach out of the story. Rosemary had enough to worry about without being hit with the fact that our daughter smoked pot. Where I did speak more frankly was on the subject of Bernard Hadlow. I thought she'd object to some of my trenchant comments about the man, but she took them in her stride.

"So that's where Jessica gets it from," she concluded.

"What?"

"That arrogance of hers. Oh, she kept it well hidden when she was with me. In fact, I now see that she was on her best behavior. Jessica took the pair of us in." She smiled contritely. "Forgive me for foisting her on to you."

"She was Lynette's friend. That was enough for me."

"And for me. They seemed so well suited and they'd had some wonderful times together at Oxford. Jessica is a splendid actress," she said. "I've seen her in action. She tends to hog the limelight but we're all a bit like that at her age."

"Lynette isn't. She's more level headed."

"I know. And the cracks were starting to show in their friendship. When we spoke on the phone, Lynette said what a marvelous time they were having but that Jessica was getting rather out of hand."

"Out of hand?"

"That was the phrase she used."

"I can think of more accurate ones."

"Apparently," said Rosemary, "she insisted on making all the decisions. Lynette went along with it at first because Jessica had been to Bermuda before, but she began to long for a breathing space after a while."

"Jennifer Hadlow does tend to suffocate," I agreed.

"She was charming when she stayed with us."

"Oh, she can be very charming. Conrad Biedemeier found that out. However," I said, "I'm not going to run the girl down. I feel desperately sorry for her. She's in the same predicament as Lynette and deserves all the help we can get."

"Of course."

I leaned forward. "How do you feel now?"

"All the better for seeing you."

"It's a long time since I heard you saying that."

"Let's not score points off each other, Alan," she said wearily. "I haven't the strength. We've got to pull together, that's what I meant. It was agony on the plane, thinking about what might be happening to the girls. Not knowing is such a torture."

"Would you like me to go and let you get some sleep?"

"I think I'll take a bath first."

"Shall I run it for you?" I offered, getting to my feet.

"Please."

I went into the bathroom and turned on the taps, adjusting them to the right temperature before drying my hands on a towel. When I went back into the other room, Rosemary was sitting on the edge of the bed, undoing the buttons on her dress. I felt embarrassed, as if I was intruding on her privacy. I walked towards the door.

"I'll leave you to it, Rosemary."

"But I don't want you to go."

"I thought you were exhausted."

"I am," she said, "but I won't be able to sleep if I'm on my own. I want you to stay, Alan. *Please*." She indicated the other bed. "You can sleep there. I know it's a lot to ask but it would mean so much to me. Will you do that for me?"

The implications were unnerving. My first instinct was to refuse politely and to get out of the room. Separate beds brought back too many searing memories from our time together. I tried to make an exit but I heard myself saying something else.

"Yes, Rosemary. Of course, I will."

I've spent some weird nights in hotel rooms but few could compare with this. Six feet from where I lay was the woman I'd once loved, and often hated, enjoying the deep sleep that only comes from exhaustion. Rosemary was both familiar and a stranger, someone who'd been close to me yet who was now impossibly apart. What she gained from my presence, I can only guess, but there was certainly no advantage for me. I was on edge for most of the night, sleeping only fitfully and bombarded with the kind of dreams that make you sit up in bed with silent terror. Lynette and Jessica featured largely in my nightmares, but so did Maurice Dobbs. During wakeful periods, I reflected on what Angela Pike had said about him and what Joel, my driver, had told me about Mo's wife. Both women would be distraught. Rosemary and I had suffered a hammer blow but there was the hope—God willing—that Lynette would be returned alive to us. Angela Pike and Ella Dobbs had no such hope to sustain them. Each had lost a man on whom they doted. In one of my dreams, I saw the dead body, high above me, swinging rhythmically from the branch of a giant cedar. Mo seemed to get bigger and bigger until the rope snapped and he fell on top of me. I woke with a start to discover that it was not Mo who'd touched me, but Rosemary. She'd slipped into my bed while I was asleep. One hand rested lightly on my shoulder. There was no attempt to snuggle up to me. Wearing a silk nightdress, she lay well apart and snoozed on quietly. Since I was naked, I felt somehow vulnerable. She seemed even more of a stranger now. Wanting to comfort her, I was unable to reach out. Instead, I edged away from her until her fingers no longer touched me.

It was a long time before I finally dozed off. My nightmare this time consisted of various marital disasters we'd endured. Rosemary castigated me fiercely for not spending enough time with our daughter, then Lynette herself appeared at her side to heap blame on me. The two of them were still accusing me when Lynette was suddenly grabbed from behind by unseen assailants and spirited away. Crying in vain for me to help her, she was dragged out of sight. Rosemary turned on me with a viciousness that brought me awake with a shout. I reached out for her but she was no longer there. She was slumbering peacefully in the other bed. Had I *imagined* that she'd climbed in beside me? I was unsure. What was clear to me was the fact that I had no desire whatsoever to get under the sheets with her. I felt as if I was trespassing. I was afraid that she'd suddenly come awake and reprimand me. It was morning. A finger of sunlight was poking through a gap in the curtains. It was time to go.

When I tried to get out of bed, however, I had the most odd sensation. I felt shy. In the company of a woman who'd been my wife for many years, I was overcome with embarrassment. My clothes had been hung up in the wardrobe. To get to them, I had to walk naked around Rosemary's bed. Supposing the noise of the wardrobe door opening brought her out of her slumber? I dreaded being seen like that. I'd never experienced such an attack of maiden modesty before and couldn't understand it. But it nevertheless defined my behavior. Instead of going straight to the wardrobe, I got out of bed and inched my way to the bathroom. Once inside, I grabbed the white toweling robe with the hotel logo emblazoned on one shoulder. When I'd put it on, I felt more confident. Moving as quietly as possible, I tiptoed around Rosemary's bed to open the wardrobe in which I'd hung my clothes. She came briefly awake.

"Where are you going?" she asked.

"Nowhere."

She stifled a yawn. "What are you doing?"

A white lie was needed. "Just getting a handkerchief from my trousers."

"There are tissues in the bathroom."

"Never thought of that. I'm sorry to wake you, Rosemary. Try to get some more sleep," I urged. "You must be dog-tired."

"I am. Thank you, Alan."

"For what?"

"Staying. It helped."

"Good."

"Did you get any sleep?"

"Yes, but I had some terrible nightmares."

"So did I," she said, putting a hand to her forehead. "This business is preying on my mind. I'm worried to death, Alan."

"I know."

Eager to leave, there was something I wanted to know before I went. I adjusted the curtains to keep out the chink of light then went over to kneel beside her bed. She gave me a tired smile.

"Rosemary," I said.

"Yes?"

"Can I ask you something?"

"Of course."

"Did you slip into my bed in the middle of the night?"

The smile vanished. "Of course not," she said indignantly. "What an appalling thing to suggest! Why on earth should I do that?"

After dressing in the bathroom, I let myself out of the room. Rosemary had dozed off to sleep again. It saved me having to explain my departure. I walked furtively along the corridor. Without quite understanding why, I feared that someone might see where I'd spent the night. I breathed a sigh of relief when I got inside my suite and leaned with my back against the door. My respite was brief. The light on my telephone was flashing to indicate that I had a message. My heart began to pound once more. Was it a call from the kidnapper or a complaint from Nancy Wykoff that I'd not been in my room when she rang? Either possibility rattled me. If there was word about Lynette, I'd be mortified that I hadn't been there to receive it. If it was Nancy on the line, I'd feel that I'd betrayed her by sleeping in the same room as Rosemary. I grabbed the receiver and pressed the replay button. The voice was low and nervous.

"This is a message for Mr. Alan Saxon," said the woman. "My name is Ella Dobbs and I'd like to speak to you, please. It's very important. Please ring me back, if you can."

I jotted down the number she'd left then replayed the message. Mo's wife had none of the aggression I'd seen in Angela Pike. There was a pleading note, a sense of desperation that touched me. I had no notion why she should want to contact me, but she deserved the courtesy of a call. I dialed the number on my pad. The telephone was picked up instantly at the other end.

"Yes?" said a tearful voice.

"Mrs. Dobbs?" I asked. "My name is Alan Saxon."

"Oh, thank you. Thank you for ringing, Mr. Saxon."

"It sounded urgent."

"It is, sir. I need to speak to you. Can I?"

"Go ahead."

"Not on the phone, sir. I want to see you, please. Is that possible?"

"I don't see why not."

"One thing, sir," she implored. "You no bring the police with you, will you?"

"I wouldn't dream of it, Mrs. Dobbs."

"Thank you. I tell you how to get here."

I wrote the details on the pad and assured her that I'd be there before too long. After what Joel had told me, I was intrigued to meet her, all the more so because she had made the approach. The fact that she didn't want the police involved was significant. I fancied that I was about to get privileged information about Mo and the idea excited me. His widow had turned to me. I wanted to know why. Ella Dobbs only lived a couple of miles away. It would not take me long to get there and back. Rosemary might be asleep for hours yet and would not even know that I'd gone. As for the kidnapper, it was to Bernard Hadlow that he'd direct any calls. I had a quick shower and shave, changed into clean clothes and went down to the lobby. Calvin Reed was chatting beside the Reception desk to Frank Colouris. We exchanged greetings.

"You're up early, Alan," said Reed. "You must be hungry."

"I have to pop out, actually," I replied. "I'll need a taxi."

"Frank will organize that."

"Of course," said Colouris obligingly. "By the way, sir, I had a quiet word with Mr. Fullard, as you requested. I won't say that he was reassured but he did stop twitching quite so violently. I'll have a car at the door for you in two minutes."

Colouris strode off and I found myself subjected to the searching gaze of Reed.

"How is Mrs. Saxon?" he inquired.

"Fast asleep, I expect."

"Is she bearing up?"

"Oh, yes. Very well. I wonder if could you do something for me, please?"

"Just ask."

"Well, if she does come looking for me, could you tell her that I won't be long. I had to pop out to see someone."

"Can I tell her whom?"

"No," I said. "It's nobody that Rosemary knows."

I could see that his curiosity was aroused but I had no intention of satisfying it. If I told him where I was going, word of my visit would very quickly get back to the police. Ella Dobbs wanted them kept out of it and so did I. Frank Colouris reappeared and waved to me. He had conjured up my transport already.

⸻ ❧ ⸻

The house was one of a cluster of dwellings off a winding track. Small and rectangular, it had recently been painted and glowed in the sunlight. Since we approached from the side, I could see washing on the line in the little garden. It flapped in the stiff breeze. There were plenty of people about and I collected some suspicious looks when I got out of the car. One man, cleaning his windows on a stepladder, spat onto the ground. I'd been recognized. The driver volunteered to wait but I sent him back to the hotel. I had no idea how long I'd be and I could always ring for transport if I needed it. What occurred to me on the journey there was that I might actually walk back. I'd have some glorious views from the coast road and longed for some thinking time away from the Blue Dolphin. In the hotel, I'd be at the behest of Rosemary, the police and the kidnapper. I needed to get away for a while.

When Ella Dobbs let me into the house, she seemed embarrassed at first, but she had no need to apologize. The living room was immaculate. A wedding photograph stood on a piano that was gleaming as if just polished. Other photos of Mo were set on the mantelpiece and a shelf. She waved me to a chair and offered to make me a cup of tea. I accepted gratefully, hoping that she would relax if she was given something to do. Mo's wife was not simply an older version of Angela Pike. She was a slim black woman of medium height with close-cropped hair framing a handsome face that was now drawn. Ella Dobbs had to be ten or fifteen years younger than her husband. Evidently, he looked well outside his own age group for partners. While she busied herself in the kitchen, I took stock of the living room. Mo was still a real presence, but there were no photographs of children.

Her hands were shaking as she served the tea. I was glad when she sat down.

"Thank you for coming, Mr. Saxon."

"You said it was important."

"It could be."

"Is it about Mo?"

"Yes, sir."

"Why ring me and not the police?"

Her face clouded. "I got no time for the police. They not welcome here."

"Oh?"

"You see why, in a minute. I prefer to speak to you."

"Because I was the one who found his body?" I asked.

"Yes," she said, biting her lip. "That one reason. I talk to Angie. She tell me you were honest with her. She think that Mr. Alan Saxon could be trusted."

"As I remember, she had little time for the police as well."

"That was Mo's doing."

She sipped her tea and watched me for some while, trying to weigh me up, wondering if I really was a person in whom she could confide. I drank my own tea. It was strong and invigorating. Eventually, I passed whatever test I was undergoing.

"Mo was my man," she said with a mingled pride and resignation. "I loved him but I not blind to his faults. He drank too much, he gambled, he did other things I not like. But I was always there for him. When he went to Casemates, I stood by him."

"Casemates?" I repeated.

"It's our prison, Mr. Saxon."

"Why was he sent there?"

"For stealing," she said with a sigh. "He lost his job at the quarry, couldn't find another. We fell behind on payments. Mo got desperate. He always swore he'd provide for me. When he couldn't earn the money, he stole it. He tell me he have a job in Warwick Parish. I know he lying to me," she said without bitterness, "but I say nothing. Mo have a temper. Then one day, the police come banging on the door."

"When was this?"

"Years ago, Mr. Saxon. It shake him up. He promise to turn over a new leaf. No drinking, no cards, no betting, none of those things. He keep his word for a while," she recalled with a faint smile. "Got a job on the ferry. We happy then. I think the trouble was over. Then the drinking started again."

She described her domestic troubles with such frankness that I felt I was prying into areas where I had no right to be. Mo emerged as a much more complex person than I'd imagined. Full of good intentions, he had a habit of going astray from time to time. Most wives would have walked out on him but Ella had weathered it all without protest. I admired her stoicism in the face of continuous provocation. There was another side to Mo. He was a caring man, who wanted the best for his wife. He'd nursed her through illnesses, took his turn at the chores and maintained the property well. I was amazed to hear that, even after he'd gone off to live with another woman, he'd returned one weekend to paint the house for his wife. Except in the obvious sense, he'd never ceased to be her husband. Ella clung tenaciously to that thought.

"He would have come back to me one day," she said.

"I'm sure, Mrs. Dobbs."

"Angie thought he was hers, but he wasn't. She wasn't the only one. There were others. He always came back in the end. This was our home," she said, extending a hand to take in the whole room. "This is where Mo belonged."

"When did you last see him?"

The question brought a look of fear into her eyes. She drew back as if I'd raised an arm to her. I felt dreadful at the thought that I'd upset the woman.

"I'm sorry, Mrs. Dobbs. I shouldn't have asked."

"No, that's all right, sir. It's why I wanted to speak to you."

"You don't have to tell me anything you don't want," I said.

There was a long pause. "I must tell someone," she murmured at length. "It may help. I can't keep it to myself." Her brow furrowed. "As long as you promise not to say anything to Angie. I can never be friends with her but I no like to hurt her."

"I give you my word, Mrs. Dobbs," I said.

"Thank you." She took a deep breath. "After what they did to Mo, I no trust the police. That's why I tell them nothing. But you found him, hanging there. You part of this, Mr. Saxon. We all are."

"Go on."

"That night—before they kill him—he come here."

"Why?"

"Mo was so angry," she explained. "He lose his job at the hotel, they get bad news from the hospital. Mo want so much to have baby with Angie."

"Yes, Mrs. Dobbs, she told me."

"He not know which way to turn. He been drinking, not want to go home to her like that. So he come here." The faint smile returned. "Mo always come here when things are bad. She only had him for the good times. I was the one he turned to when he was in trouble, and Mo was in deep trouble. Not easy for him to find a job, with his record. He worried about paying the mortgage for the new house."

"I thought he bought it outright from a big win."

"Who told you that?" she said sharply.

"One of the drivers at the hotel. Joel."

"Joel Arnott? Yes, he may tell you that but Joel not taken in by Mo. He know the money must have come from somewhere else. So did I. But not Angie," she said with a sympathetic sigh. "I sorry for her. She believe all that he tell her. Mo didn't buy that house from any winnings, Mr. Saxon."

"Then where did the money come from?"

"Someone who paid him to steal things from the Blue Dolphin golf course." She saw my amazement. "Yes, Mr. Saxon, I know you help design it. Mo tell me your name. I'm sorry, sir. My husband told to make big trouble for you all. He earn lots of money. Then it stop. The night he come here," she remembered with a shudder, "Mo was in terrible state. He ashamed of what he done, sorry to let Angie down. He in tears, saying he wish he never left me."

"I'm beginning to understand why," I said.

"I frightened. I never see Mo so desperate before."

"What did you do?"

"I try to calm him down but it was no good. He keep saying that it was all over. No job, no money, no baby. Nothing to live for, he said."

"There was you, Mrs. Dobbs."

"That not enough any more. I try to hug him but Mo push me away and charge out of the house in despair."

"Did he tell you where he was going?"

"Yes, Mr. Saxon," she said, tears in her eyes. "To kill himself."

Chapter Nine

The visit to Ella Dobbs had been a revelation. It was bizarre. Her husband had confessed to the woman he'd walked out on what he'd kept back from the one with whom he was actually living. Angela Pike only ever heard the good news from Mo. He wanted to impress her. Bad tidings were saved for his wife because he knew that she alone could cope with them. Indeed, listening to her account of their troubled marriage, it seemed that she'd spent the greater part of it on the receiving end of his serious mistakes and false promises. I was touched that she felt able to confide in me and astonished that I came on the recommendation of Angela Pike. During our chat at the hotel, I didn't think that I'd made an altogether favorable impression on the young waitress, but something had caused her to adjust her jaundiced view of me. Whatever it was, I was thankful for it. The meeting with Ella Dobbs had not only helped me to understand Mo's state of mind when he confronted me after his dismissal from his job. It also explained a remark made by Troy Morley. The inspector had warned me that someone probably had his eye on me from the moment I arrived in Bermuda. He was right. That someone was Maurice Dobbs. It was no accident that he'd been sent to pick us up at the airport. While railing against the world of electronics, he'd also been keeping me under observation.

Unfortunately, his wife didn't know who'd been employ-
ing him to sabotage the Blue Dolphin golf course. Mo had
taken that secret to the grave. I wondered who his paymaster might be, and the long walk back to the hotel gave me
the opportunity to consider the problem. The fresh air was
stimulating. I was shocked to realize that the last time I'd
enjoyed a stroll in the sun was when I played a round of golf
with Nancy Wykoff. So much had happened in the inter-
vening period. We'd dined with Calvin Reed and his wife,
I'd been summoned by Angela Pike, I'd done all I could to
persuade the Fullards to stay in Bermuda, then spent an idyl-
lic night with my playing partner from Port Royal. Disaster
ensued. Lynette and Jessica had been abducted, I'd searched
in panic for their Canadian friends, and I'd been trapped in
my suite for hours on end with a golfing detective. Bernard
Hadlow had yelled accusations at me over the telephone,
Clive Phelps had arranged for one of his girlfriends to fax
material about the man, I'd made an unsuccessful attempt
to argue with Calvin Reed, and there was the impact of meeting with Hadlow himself. Then came the second and third
calls from the kidnapper, altering our whole perspective on
the abduction. When I threw in the arrival of my ex-wife
and the uneasy night I spent in Rosemary's room, I could
see why I felt so shell-shocked.

I welcomed the tug of the wind at my hair and clothing.
It was bracing. It also helped to remove a lot of irrelevant
clutter from my mind so that I could concentrate on the
matter in hand. I'd not forgotten the fate of the girls. How
could I?—but that didn't rule out an interest in the murder
investigation. Some time after he left his wife's house on the
night in question, Mo had been killed by lethal injection
before being taken to the Blue Dolphin under cover of
darkness. Ella Dobbs had told me that her husband had been
drinking heavily. It made him maudlin and suicidal. More
importantly, it lowered his defenses. He would have been

an easy target, too preoccupied to sense an impending attack, too drunk to resist it when it came. While he'd been opening his heart to his wife, someone had been lying in ambush for him. I stumbled upon their gruesome handiwork later that night.

I came to see how brave Ella Dobbs had been. It must have taken a great effort for her to contact me. Grieving over the death of a cherished husband, she nevertheless felt the need to pass on crucial information about him. In a sense, it was a serious betrayal, a posthumous breach of faith, an act of marital disloyalty, an unmasking of her husband as the saboteur who'd brought Peter Fullard close to total collapse. Unable to stomach the idea of confiding in the police, she was using me as a go-between, a messenger who'd take the new evidence to Troy Morley. That was where her real bravery lay. Others might see her as an informer, a snitch who sold out her husband, or, to use British slang, a grass. That was unjust. In revealing Mo's secret, she was not merely exposing his crimes. She was helping to solve his murder and that justified anything. Ella Dobbs was no Bermuda grass. She was a loyal and long-suffering wife whose belief in her erratic husband was somehow undimmed in spite of all that had passed between them. Her commitment was total, her love enduring.

I kept up a brisk pace, glad that I'd spurned a lift and enjoying the simple pleasure of being alone. My thoughts inevitably returned to Lynette and Jessica. How had *they* spent the night? Were they being treated well? What state were they in? Were they able to keep up their spirits in some way? There was no sense in trying to allot blame. It served no useful purpose if I pointed the finger at Rosemary for manoeuvering Jessica Hadlow into my travel arrangements, or to single out the girl's father as the true culprit. The three of us had some responsibility. Only by cooperation could we bring the girls safely back to us. If, that is, Lynette and

Jessica were still alive and well. All we had to rely on was the word of a kidnapper and he didn't sound like the sort of person who'd be overly concerned about the welfare of two young women. They were marketable goods to him. That was all. I tried to grapple with this harsh fact.

A steady trickle of cars, mopeds and other vehicles had gone past me in both directions but the road was now clear. I'd reached what I estimated to be the midway point and lengthened my stride for the second half of the journey. When a car came round the bend ahead of me, I paid it scant attention at first. It was rumbling along at a moderate pace on the opposite side of the road. Suddenly, it accelerated. I saw it jump forward in a fierce plunge of speed. There was a deliberation about the car that alerted me. Thirty yards from its target, it swung wildly across to my side of the road with a screech from its tires as it skidded. I had no option but to dive for cover. Flinging myself over a low stone wall, I missed being knocked down by a matter of inches. I rolled on the ground and felt the thick Bermuda grass dig into me like spikes. Simultaneously, there was a loud scraping noise as the wing and side of the car grazed the solid stone before the driver corrected his line. I didn't wait to see if he was going to stop and turn the vehicle round. I simply hauled myself up and fled across a field, vowing to find another route back to the hotel.

When I'd seen this kind of thing happen in films, our hero always eluded the oncoming car, then had the presence of mind to note the make, color and registration number as well as to get a good view of the driver, albeit from behind. I did none of these things. Everything had happened so fast. I had no idea what make of vehicle it was or even what its approximate color might be. Was the driver male, female, black, white, old or young? I didn't have a clue. I couldn't even say how many people were inside the car. The only information I could supply was that it had deliberately tried

to kill me. It was no freak accident. The vehicle had come
looking for me. I'd run a hundred yards before I paused to
ask myself why I was the target. It seemed very clear.
Someone had discovered that I'd been to see Ella Dobbs
that morning and feared what she might have told me. I
knew too much.

ᴡᴧᴍᴧᴡᴧᴡᴧᴡᴧᴡᴧᴡᴧᴡᴧᴡᴧᴡᴧᴡᴧᴡᴧᴡᴧᴡ

"Where exactly did it happen, sir?" he asked. "Can you point
out the spot?"

Sergeant Derek Woodford took me across to the large
map of Bermuda that was pinned to the wall. As I ran my
finger along the road I'd taken, my hand was trembling.

"Around about here, I think," I said, jabbing at a spot.

"Right. Thank you, sir."

Woodford gave orders to a uniformed constable and the
latter went swiftly out of the Incident Room. Having got
back to the hotel by a circuitous route, I reported at once to
the police. Troy Morley was not there but his assistant noted
the details. While we were talking, one of the young police-
women on duty in the room made me a cup of tea. It was
very soothing. Woodford took me slowly through the details
once more. I was in the middle of my recital when the
inspector returned. He was disturbed by the news of my
close shave on the road. I told them about my visit to Ella
Dobbs. They were puzzled.

"Mrs. Dobbs said nothing of this when we called on her,"
complained Morley.

"You're policemen," I said pointedly. "Some people don't
trust you."

"She withheld evidence."

"No, Inspector. Mrs. Dobbs was grief-stricken when you
broke the news to her. What wife wouldn't be? And the
situation gave his death an added poignancy. She didn't even
know that she *had* important evidence until the initial shock
wore off."

"I still think that she should have contacted us."

"She did," I indicated. "Through me. She knew I'd tell you what she couldn't bring herself to reveal. What does it matter how the information was obtained?" I argued. "We have it now. Mo was being paid to sabotage the golf course. He'd be a good choice. Someone who worked at the Blue Dolphin and who was used to being seen around the place. Mo could keep tabs on things from the inside. He'd know when and where to slip onto the course."

"Yes," said Woodford. "Dobbs wouldn't be hindered by the fact that he was breaking the law. If anything, that would have added spice. His wife didn't tell you the full story, Mr. Saxon. It wasn't a single visit he made to Casemates. Maurice Dobbs served three separate terms in prison for burglary."

"His criminal record might have got him the job as saboteur," I suggested.

"Then he was sacked and no longer any use to them. They ditched him."

Morley pondered. "There has to be more to it than that, Derek. They didn't have to kill the man. They could just have paid him off and sent him on his way."

"I agree," I said. "When I met him, he was unbelievably tense. His wife told me how much pressure he'd been under lately. Mo was starting to lose it. He was becoming a liability. I think that his paymaster was afraid he might give the game away. The fact that he lost his job showed how unreliable he'd become," I added. "They killed him to shut him up, then they hanged him on the golf course to cause more havoc there."

"A sound analysis," said Morley. "You should have been a policeman, sir."

"One in the family is enough."

"That's what my son keeps telling me."

"Did you want him to be a copper?"

"Yes," he admitted. "I'd have liked that."

"What does your son do?"

"Gerard runs small café in Hamilton, sir. Says it keeps him in touch with 'real people.' I'm not sure what that makes the people *we* deal with, but I take his point."

Woodford's mobile rang. He moved away to take the call but soon rejoined us.

"That was Constable Hodges, sir," he explained to Morley. "I sent him to check out the scene of the incident. He's found the tire marks where the vehicle skidded across the road and he says that the stone wall has been scored for several yards."

"Then so has the car," said the inspector. "There won't be many in Bermuda with damage like that along the bodywork. Put the word out, Derek. They won't be able to get that car off the island. We need to find it."

Woodford went off to issue instructions to his men. Morley and I were left alone with the two women police officers. One of them took a call and began to tap details into a computer. The other, also staring at a screen, was collating information about the murder that had already come in. The inspector took me aside.

"I'm sorry that I wasn't here when you arrived, Mr. Saxon," he said.

"That's OK. Sergeant Woodford was very efficient."

"I'd been up to see Mr. Hadlow."

"How is he?" I asked.

"The worse for wear, I'm afraid. He didn't get much sleep."

I thought of Rosemary. "None of us had a perfect night, Inspector."

"The good news is that he thinks he can get the ransom money in time."

"How much are we talking about?"

"Millions of dollars," he said. "I can't be more precise than that."

"What's the bad news? I have the feeling that there's a catch."

"There is, sir. He wants us out of the picture completely."

"No covert surveillance?"

"Nothing," said Morley with disappointment. "He won't even let us wire him up so that we can hear what happens when he hands over the money. Mr. Hadlow is obdurate. Could you talk to him on our behalf?"

"You've picked the wrong man as a police spokesman, Inspector."

"But it's in your interests as well, Mr. Saxon."

"Is it? My sole aim is to ensure the safe return of the girls."

"You want the villains caught and the money repossessed, surely?"

"I want the buggers more than caught," I affirmed. "I want to have a quiet chat with them myself. As for the money, that's Hadlow's problem. It's his dough."

"Don't be so flippant," he warned. "That money could save your daughter's life."

It was a timely reminder. "Of course," I apologized. "I spoke out of turn. You know, it was one of the reasons I was so surprised that they'd kidnapped Lynette. They could never have got that kind of ransom out of me. Only out of Bernard Hadlow."

"His financial assets are well known in the business world."

"Does he have any notion who the kidnapper might be?"

"Several, Mr. Saxon. He's trodden on a lot of toes along the way. Mr. Hadlow said he could name a dozen or more people in Bermuda with a grudge against him. The problem is that he refuses to tell us who they are."

"Why?"

"He fears that we'll go blundering in and upset the whole operation."

"Doesn't he trust you to make discreet inquiries?"

"No, sir. He's reached the same conclusion that we have."

"What's that?"

"Someone's watching our every move," he said, pursing his lips. "How do you think the girls were abducted in the first place? That could only be done by someone who knew his way around the hotel, perhaps even had a master key to their suite. And how do you think that ransom demand was delivered to Reception?"

"I assumed that someone just handed it in."

"They did. According to the clerk, it was given to her shortly after Mr. Hadlow arrived at the hotel. In other words," he went on, "the letter wasn't handed over until he was seen coming into the Blue Dolphin."

"Does the clerk remember who gave it to her?"

"Yes, sir. One of the pool attendants."

"Would she recognize him again?"

"She already has, sir. We questioned him earlier."

"And?"

"He was asked to hand the letter in to Reception by a young woman. She tipped him handsomely, it seems. All he could tell us was that she was wearing a bikini and a pair of sunglasses." He shook his head sadly. "Out in the pool at this moment, there are dozens of women who fit that description. He can't pick her out."

"She may not still be here, Inspector."

"Quite, sir. Or she might be just another intermediary. Someone who was told to give the letter to a third person for delivery. The kidnapper is being very careful. Either he or his accomplice is here at the Blue Dolphin, monitoring developments. We have to be seen to be doing exactly what he wants."

"Thanks for the warning."

"Watch your back, Mr. Saxon."

"Oh, I will," I said with feeling. "After that little encounter with a car on the highway, I'll be watching back, front and sides from now on."

It took me some while to find the driver who had taken me out to Ella Dobbs' house. When he got back to the hotel, he

was given the task of driving some guests to Tucker's Town.
I had to wait until he returned to his post at the Blue
Dolphin. He was a relatively young man whose bald head
and crinkly white face made him seem much older. When I
bore down on him, he gave me a broad smile.

"Where now, sir?" he asked.

"Nowhere, thanks. I just wanted to ask you something."

"Go ahead, sir."

"What happened when you dropped me off this morning?"

"I drove straight back here to pick up some other passengers."

"Nothing else?"

"What do you mean, sir?"

"Well, I wondered if anyone had asked you where you'd
taken me."

"As a matter of fact, they did," he recalled. "He was
waiting for me at the door."

"Who was?"

"The hotel manager, sir."

"Mr. Reed?"

"Yes, sir."

"What did he say?"

"Well, it was only a casual inquiry. He just asked me the
address I'd driven you to, then wondered why I didn't wait
to bring you back."

"What was your reply?"

"I told him what you told me, sir. If you needed a taxi,
you'd ring."

"And if I didn't?"

"Then you might walk back."

As I went up to the fourth floor, my brain was whirring
furiously. I couldn't believe that Calvin Reed was somehow
involved in the attempt on my life. He was my employer in
Bermuda, a man who'd given Peter Fullard and me every

assistance in our work. I remembered how kind he and his wife had been to Lynette and Jessica on our first night at the hotel. The Reeds had even invited us into their home when I dined with them in the company of Nancy Wykoff. Could the manager really have sanctioned the attack on me? What possible motive could he have? Besides, I reasoned, he couldn't be sure that I'd be walking back along the road at that precise time. All that he knew was that I'd sent the taxi back to the hotel. As I stepped out of the elevator, a thought hit me. To get Ella Dobbs' telephone number, Reed simply had to look it up in the directory. That was where Mo's former address would be listed. Reed might even have it in his employees' records. Could he have contacted Mo's wife to ask when I'd left?

Instead of going to Rosemary's room, I took the stairs up to the next floor and let myself into the suite. I dialed the number and Ella Dobbs came on the line.

"Mrs. Dobbs?" I said. "This is Alan Saxon."

"Oh, yes," she replied. "Thank you for coming, sir."

"It was good of you to contact me."

"I only want to help."

"That's why I rang," I told her. "I need a little more help."

She was reluctant. "Don't come again. Please, sir. I got no more to tell. Mo's funeral is tomorrow. I need all my strength to get through that."

"Of course, Mrs. Dobbs. Just answer one question."

"What is it?"

"After I left you this morning, did anyone ring?"

"Why, yes," she said. "Five minutes after you go."

"Who was it?"

"A man. He didn't give his name."

"Did he ask about me?"

"Yes, sir. He say he try to get in touch with Mr. Saxon. Where were you? I tell him that you walk back to the Blue Dolphin hotel." She was anxious. "Did I do wrong?"

"Not at all, Mrs. Dobbs. Have you ever heard the man's voice before?"

"Never. But he spoke well. He was educated."

"Thank you," I said. "I won't trouble you any further. Goodbye, Mrs. Dobbs."

"Goodbye, sir."

I rang off and revised my opinion of Calvin Reed. If he had rung the house, he'd have known when I left and roughly how long it would take me to get back. The car could have been dispatched so that it reached me at that particular stretch of road. I began to recall various things about the manager that had led me to distrust him in the past. The list was long. Nancy Wykoff claimed to have seen the human side of the manager, but he'd kept it concealed from me. In fact, he always seemed to be concealing something. Working on supposition rather than hard fact, I had no evidence with which to build a strong case against Reed. To confront him would be a grave error. I needed to gather more information first. Inspector Morley's advice was sound. I had to watch my back. Nobody got so close to it as Calvin Reed.

I was about to leave when there was a tap on the door. Fearing that it might be Reed himself, or some henchman of his, I applied my eye to the peephole in the door. Its lens distorted the face of Nancy Wykoff. I let her in at once and gave her a welcoming kiss.

"Caught you at last!" she said. "I rang a couple of times last night and again this morning, but there was no answer. I didn't want to leave a message in case your ex-wife was in the room when you picked it up."

"Thanks, Nancy."

"Also, of course, you've had a few scares already with your voice-mail. If you came in and saw the light flashing, you might have thought it was the kidnapper again. I wanted to spare you the anxiety."

"That's very considerate of you."

She grinned happily. "I'm a considerate person. Or hadn't you noticed?"

"Oh," I said, meeting her gaze, "I think I've spotted just about all your virtues."

"So where've you been hiding, Mr. Saxon?"

"Last night, I didn't get back until very late."

"Rosemary?"

"Yes," I said, uneasy at having to tell a lie. "She wanted to talk it through again and again. I had a job to get away from her. It was well past midnight when she finally keeled over out of sheer exhaustion."

"What about this morning? I rang around seven-thirty."

"I'd already gone, Nancy. When I got back from Rosemary's suite, there was a voice-message for me. And you're right. Seeing that light flashing did make me jump. But it wasn't the kidnapper," I went on. "It was Ella Dobbs, the widow of the murder victim. She was eager to see me."

"Why?"

"That's what I wanted to find out. So I rang and told her that I'd be there soon. I was probably on my way there when you rang my number."

"What happened?"

I gave her a shortened version of events and played down the incident with the car. Though I was pleased to see her, I had an obligation to Rosemary and didn't want to keep her waiting too long. Nancy was horrified to hear about my near miss with the car.

"He tried to kill you, Alan!"

"Maybe he just lost control of the car."

"Did you report it to the cops?"

"Yes, Nancy. They're out looking for the vehicle right now."

"So I should hope. You need a bodyguard."

"I'm safe enough in the hotel." I thought of Calvin Reed. "At least, I hope so."

"Who could want to bump you off?"

I tried to shrug it off. "A bad loser, perhaps. Some people just hate it when I beat them on the golf course. Well," I said with a wink, "you're one of them."

"Don't joke about it."

"Oh, I'm not joking. It frightened the living daylights out of me."

"Who could have known that you'd be walking along that road?"

"I hope to find out."

"Poor guy!" she said, stroking my arm. "You sure are having one hell of a vacation in Bermuda. The sabotage on the new course, the abduction and—now this!"

"My stay hasn't been without its high spots." She smiled at the compliment. "And, strictly speaking, I'm not on holiday. I came here to work. On my previous visits, Peter Fullard and I didn't have a whiff of trouble."

"You've made up for it this time. Still," she said, "I won't get under your feet. I know you've got lots to do. I just wanted to touch base and let you know that I'm thinking about you. Especially after what happened out there on that road."

"I survived, didn't I?"

"So did the man who tried to kill you."

Her comment jolted me. The driver of the car was still free to make a second attempt on my life. And if, as I was starting to fear, Calvin Reed was behind it all, he was in a position to choose the right moment for an attack. Nancy saw my distress.

"What's up, Alan?"

"Nothing, nothing."

"I get the idea there's something you haven't told me."

"Then you'll have to wait until I remember what it is," I said with a dismissive laugh, not wanting to voice my suspicions about Reed at this stage. "Thanks for coming, Nancy. I appreciate your concern."

She kissed me on the cheek. "It's more than concern, you dope."

"That's even better."

I opened the door and we stepped outside. Nancy looked up at me.

"You know where to find me, if you need me. I'll be standing by."

I wasn't listening. Over her shoulder, I could see a familiar figure, walking purposefully towards us. It was Rosemary. I felt as if the car had hit me, after all.

"I was shocked when you weren't there, Alan," she said. "What time did you leave?"

"Earlier this morning, Rosemary."

"Why didn't you tell me you were going?"

"You were fast asleep."

"So? You could have left me a message."

"I thought I'd be back long before you woke up."

"Then why weren't you?"

"I got distracted."

"That was obvious!"

"Nancy is just a friend."

"I wasn't born yesterday, Alan."

Further argument was senseless. When she came out of the elevator, Rosemary had supplied an instant caption to the picture that confronted her. Nothing I could say would amend that judgment. She'd been very gracious when introduced and Nancy had been equally polite. It was only when my ex-wife and I went back into my suite that she let her disapproval show.

"How *could* you?" she demanded.

"What am I supposed to have done?"

"You know very well. Lynette has been kidnapped and is probably undergoing the most terrible ordeal, yet you still find time to carry on your latest dalliance."

"Mrs. Wykoff is not a dalliance."

"Does that mean you're about to announce your engagement?"

"Rosemary!"

"How long have you known each other?"

"That's my business," I said, hitting back angrily. "Now why don't you sit down and shut up for a minute while I try to explain?"

Her laugh was sardonic. "I've heard your explanations before."

"Did any of them contain an attempt to kill me?"

The remark silenced her long enough for me to get the first few sentences out. To her credit, she made no interruption as I talked about my visit to Ella Dobbs and my foolish decision to walk back to the hotel. I omitted any mention of Calvin Reed, as I'd done with Nancy Wykoff, but I left her in no doubt about the seriousness of the attempt on my life. The least I dared to hope for was an expression of sympathy, but even that was beyond Rosemary. Her eyebrows rose meaningfully.

"Why on earth did you go to that house in the first place?" she asked.

"Because she wanted to see me."

"Alan, our daughter has been abducted!"

"Mrs. Dobbs' husband was murdered."

"I feel very sorry for the woman, but that doesn't mean you should go charging off there like that. Let the police handle the case. It's their job."

"Mrs. Dobbs wouldn't speak to the police. I was her intermediary."

"Well, you should have been *here*, thinking about Lynette."

"I've thought about nothing else, Rosemary, believe me. But you have to remember that I'm involved in the other investigation as well. I found the dead body. I have obligations."

"Your first obligation is to Lynette, And to Jessica, of course," she added. "What would they say if they knew that you'd gone racing off to see this Mrs. Dobbs when you should have been concentrating on securing their release?"

"Bernard Hadlow is the point of contact."

"That's another thing. I want to meet him."

"Now?"

Her sarcasm was effortless. "Unless you have another appointment with Mrs. Wykoff?" she said coldly. "Or perhaps you have to race off to see another discarded wife of the murder victim."

"Rosemary," I reminded her. "If I hadn't been so fit and agile, *you* would now be the discarded wife of a murder victim. So, no more nasty remarks—agreed?"

"I haven't made any nasty remarks."

"No, I suppose not. By your standards, you've been extremely pleasant."

"Alan!"

"I'm sorry," I said, biting back further comment. "That was spiteful. I'm not criticizing you, especially after that interminable journey you made yesterday. Your nerves are frayed, Rosemary. So are mine. We both need to be nice to each other." I contrived a smile. "Have you had any breakfast yet?"

"Yes. Room service."

"That's more than I've had."

"Order something now."

"I think I'd rather go down to the restaurant."

"But we can't talk in privacy down there."

"Exactly," I said. "I'd be safe from any further abuse."

Her face crumpled. "I didn't mean to turn on you like that," she said with enough sincerity to convince me. "But I was frightened when I woke up and found that you'd gone. I wondered if there'd been a new development, if you'd rushed off to try to get Lynette back without even telling me."

"I'd never have done that."

"We have to pull together, Alan."

"That's what we are doing."

"So why did you sneak out of my room?"

"I felt that I was in the way."

She lowered her head. "I suppose that I deserved that."

"It was wrong of you to ask me to stay."

"Why?" she said, looking up. "Did you have a commitment elsewhere?"

"No," I retorted. "How can I have commitments of any sort until Lynette and Jessica have been found? I've been tormenting myself with fears about them, but I wanted to be alone with those anxieties. Not tossing and turning in your room. I felt uncomfortable, Rosemary. As if I was an interloper."

"I didn't feel that."

"You were too tired to feel anything."

"Except despair." She reached out for my hand. "We're going to get Lynette back safe and sound, aren't we? I mean, you've talked to this man. You know what he wants. He's going to play fair with us, isn't he? We will see the girls again, won't we?"

But I couldn't give her the reassurance she craved. Only hard fact remained.

"That depends on Bernard Hadlow."

Waiving breakfast, I acceded to Rosemary's request and made the call. Bernard Hadlow was not exactly welcoming, but he agreed to see us. We made our way to his room. He let us in and I performed the introductions. We were offered the sofa.

"Thank you," I said as we sat down. I glanced round. "Where's Constable Hills?"

Hadlow was blunt. "I sent him packing, along with the detective who tried to relieve him for the night shift. I don't need policemen breathing down my neck."

"But they want to hear any calls you get."

"Then they can listen to the tape, Mr. Saxon. I had Inspector Morley up here earlier, daring to tell me that he had the right to insist that one of his men should be present. I wasn't having that. Damnation! I know how to answer a telephone. What's more," he declared, punching the arm of his chair, "it's *my* money, not theirs."

I was disturbed by his attitude. A man who could be so bullish with the police was likely to adopt the wrong tone with the kidnapper. It was unnerving to have the girls' fate in the hands of someone like Bernard Hadlow. He was no patient negotiator. At any moment, I sensed, he might lose his temper.

"Has there been any further word from the kidnapper?" asked Rosemary.

"No, Mrs. Saxon. He's leaving me to stew in my own juice."

"When is he likely to be in touch?"

"Your guess is as good as mine."

"He's giving you plenty of time to get the ransom money," I said.

"Not really, Mr. Saxon," replied Hadlow. "Even for someone like me, it's not easy to conjure that amount out of thin air. I was on the phone into the small hours, calling in favors, selling this, borrowing that."

"We're very grateful to you, Mr. Hadlow," said Rosemary. "Aren't we, Alan?"

"Yes, yes," I agreed, unable to think of any reason for gratitude.

Rosemary surged on. "You're making it possible to get Lynette and Jessica back. We love our daughter, naturally, but we're well aware of Jessica's virtues as well. She's got the most amazing talents. You must be very proud of her."

"I am."

"So must her mother."

"Her mother knows nothing about this and, I hope, never will. She'd only blame me," he sneered, "and I had enough of her whining when we were married."

"Nevertheless," said Rosemary, shocked at his attitude, "she has a right to be told. I'd have been appalled if Alan had tried to keep this from me. It's cruel to keep Jessica's mother in the dark like this."

"That's a matter of opinion."

"Well, I can tell you mine, Mr. Hadlow."

"Yes, Rosemary," I said, jumping in to head off a row between them, "I think we understand your position. But it's Mr. Hadlow who has to make the decisions here. That gives him certain prerogatives."

"Prerogatives!" she echoed. "Prerogatives? Holding back from a mother vital information about her daughter is not a prerogative. It borders on sadism."

Hadlow sighed to me. "Now you can see why I didn't tell my ex-wife."

Rosemary fumed in silence. He tried to appease her by offering refreshment but she declined. I, on the other hand, was more than ready for a cup of coffee and some biscuits. My brush with death had left me feeling decidedly peckish. Talk turned to how the two girls met at Oxford. Everything became far less contentious. Rosemary even felt able to turn on the well-bred charm that had first ensnared me. Hadlow slowly mellowed. He was patently short of sleep. The lines on his face had deepened and the bags under his eyes had taken on a darker hue. Beneath his surface pugnacity, he was suffering just as much as we were. There was one interesting revelation.

"The irony is," he said with a wan smile, "that Jessica e-mailed me that very evening. She never goes anywhere without her laptop. It's the one way she can be sure to reach me."

"You do seem to be ubiquitous, Mr. Hadlow," observed Rosemary.

"I have to be. According to the e-mail, Jessica and Lynette were just about to go out with someone called Rick and Conrad. They all got on famously, she said. And my daughter was full of praise for you, Mr. Saxon," he continued. "She said that you couldn't have been nicer to her. Thank you for that."

"It was a pleasure to have her with us," I said without blushing at the deceit.

"Only hours later, they were abducted. From their own room!"

"That what disturbed me," said Rosemary.

"Don't they have any security at the hotel?" he bellowed. "It's disgraceful. What kind of place allows people to get into someone else's room at night?"

"We don't know that that's what happened," I said reasonably. "The girls may have been surprised as they were letting themselves into their suite. They were obviously under surveillance that evening."

"Jessica will tell me the truth—when she's been released. If it turns out that someone was actually lurking in wait in their bedroom, I'll have some sharp questions to ask of the Blue Dolphin. I've warned Mr. Reed that I may sue."

"What did he say?"

"That he refused to believe the hotel could be at fault."

"He could be right."

"We'll see, Mr. Saxon. *Someone* is going to pay for all this, I know that."

"Let's not jump to conclusions," I said. "We did that earlier when we foolishly linked the kidnapping with the murder of Maurice Dobbs. It led us completely astray."

"Who on earth could the kidnapper be?" asked Rosemary. "When you come on a holiday like this, you don't expect there to be the slightest danger. What sort of man preys on two innocent young women?"

"Well?" I said, looking at Hadlow. "Can you suggest any names?"

"One or two have crossed my mind," he said grimly. Rosemary sat up. "Who are they, Mr. Hadlow?"

"Nobody you know, Mrs. Saxon."

"Have you given these names to the police?"

"I want them kept out of this."

"But that's impossible. Kidnapping is a serious crime. They must be involved."

"Only when Jessica and Lynette are safe," he asserted. "I'm not having Inspector Morley and his men rushing in and fouling everything up. We're dealing with professionals, Mrs. Saxon. They'll smell a policeman half a mile away."

There was a knock on the door. Annoyed at the interruption, Hadlow lumbered across to the door and pulled it open. I heard Frank Colouris' voice.

"Good morning, Mr. Hadlow," he said. "I'm sorry to disturb you but I understand that you lodged a complaint about room service."

"Yes, I did. I demanded to see Mr. Reed about it."

"I'm afraid that the manager is not available at the moment, sir. Mr. Reed is in conference with the police. He asked me to deal with the problem."

"I sent for the manager."

"My name is Frank Colouris, sir. I'm the deputy manager. Can I help you?"

"Yes," snapped Hadlow. "You can send Mr. Reed up to me."

Colouris was patient. "What seems to be the trouble with room service?"

"I'm more concerned about the trouble with your hearing. Are you deaf, man? When he's free, send the manager up here. I don't deal with underlings."

"Complaints about room service are normally dealt with by the restaurant manager," said Colouris. "Neither Mr. Reed nor I are usually involved."

"I haven't got time to argue with you. Just do as I say."

"Yes, Mr. Hadlow."

"One moment," I said, getting up to join them. "Before you go, Mr. Colouris, could I have a brief word with you, please?"

"Of course, sir."

"Out in the corridor," said Hadlow.

When I left the room, he closed the door hard behind me.

"I'm sorry about that," I said with a pained smile.

"No problem, sir. It goes with the territory."

"Mr. Hadlow is under a lot of pressure at the moment. It's got to him."

"You don't need to make excuses, Mr. Saxon. I understand the situation."

"I'm sure. Listen, what I'd like to know is this. Who is responsible for sending the hotel taxis and courtesy vehicles to the airport?"

"The transport manager, sir."

"So he'd have made the decision to send Mo to pick me and the girls up?"

"Under normal circumstances, yes."

"What happened in this case?"

"As I recall," said Colouris, running a palm across his chin, "Mr. Reed took personal control of the arrangements. He chose your accommodation, organized your transport, and made sure that he was there to welcome you when you arrived at the Blue Dolphin. Mr. Reed said that you were to be given the V.I.P. treatment." He shrugged. "We obviously let you down."

"I don't blame the hotel."

"Mr. Hadlow does. He's been threatening legal action against us. Although," he added with a grin, "from what I hear, he'd set his lawyers on to us if we put the wrong brand of soap in the bathroom. Who else demands to see the manager about something as trivial as his breakfast?"

"At least, he *had* a breakfast. That's more than I've managed."

"The restaurant is open all morning."

"I'll be down in due course, don't worry. One last question," I said. "What sort of hours do you and Mr. Reed work?"

He chuckled. "Highly unsocial ones. We're never off duty here."

"But you must have a rota of some sort."

"Yes, of course. During the day, Mr. Reed and I are at the helm. Then a duty manager takes over in the evening. In theory, we can put our feet up, but it never works out that way somehow. Why do you ask?"

"I'm thinking of taking up a career in hotel management," I said. "Anything is better than playing golf for a living."

"I thought you'd become a course architect."

"So did I, Mr. Colouris. Until I got here."

"Fair comment."

He took his leave and went down the corridor towards the elevator. I reflected on what he'd told me. It seemed odd that Calvin Reed should have chosen our driver from the airport and even more peculiar that he'd picked Mo. What interested me more was the fact that he'd been in the bar on the night that I found the man hanging from a cedar. If he went off duty earlier in the evening, why was the manager still around after midnight? With a beautiful wife waiting for him, he'd have every incentive to sign off for the day. Yet he was there when I staggered back to the hotel. Was it really a coincidence?

Before I answered the question, the door opened and Rosemary appeared.

"Quick!" she urged. "The kidnapper is on the line."

I rushed back into the room and we stood near Hadlow as he took the call. Amplified by the speaker, the man's voice was as curt and peremptory as before.

"Do you have the money, Mr. Hadlow?" he asked.

"I will have," said Hadlow.

"I hope so. One dollar short of the asking price, and the deal's off."

"As long as you keep to your side of the bargain."

"Have no fears on that score."

"But I do," said Hadlow. "I need reassurance. How do I know that my daughter is still alive? What guarantee do I have that this is not some kind of bluff?"

"You mean that you don't *trust* me?" asked the man with a hint of mockery.

"Not an inch. Let me speak to Jessica."

"Mr. Hadlow—"

"Let me speak to her," pressed Hadlow, "then we have a deal."

There was a lengthy pause before Jessica's tearful voice came on the line.

"I'm all right, Daddy," she said.

The kidnapper resumed. "Satisfied now?"

"No," said Hadlow. "I have Mr. and Mrs. Saxon with me. They need reassurance as well. Let them hear Lynette's voice, and I swear that I'll get the ransom."

There was an even longer silence. Tensing her body, Rosemary gripped my hand. The suspense was like a physical pain. We began to fear that something was awry. Eventually, to our relief, Lynette's voice was allowed a short sentence.

"I'm fine so far," she said before being cut off.

I put an arm around Rosemary. Our daughter was still alive. Lynette had been subdued but far less sorrowful than Jessica. I was deeply grateful to Bernard Hadlow. Having cursed him for the way he'd handled his first conversation with the kidnapper, I had to admire his performance this time. He was calm yet firm, taking orders without complaint yet wresting two important concessions. Both of our daughters had spoken. Instead of settling for a word from Jessica, he'd insisted that Lynette was heard as well.

"This is what you must do," said the man. "Get the money and wait for my next call. It will be at precisely seven o'clock this evening. Make sure you're standing by the phone and that you're able to tell me you've got the dough. Understand?"

"I understand," said Hadlow.

"You'll need Mr. Saxon there. He's coming with you for the exchange."

Rosemary clutched at me fearfully but I was delighted by the news. I wanted to be there when Lynette was released. She'd need comfort. I was also extremely anxious to meet the person or persons who'd abducted the girls in the first place.

"Are the cops there?" asked the man.

"No," replied Hadlow. "I'm handling this on my own."

"I hope so—for your daughter's sake. I know this call will be recorded and that the cops will hear the tape so here's some advice for them. Keep your distance. You can't see us," he stressed. "But we can see you."

The line went dead. Bernard Hadlow hung up and looked across at us.

"I still have calls to make," he said. "I'd appreciate some time alone."

"Of course," I agreed. "But I think you should let Inspector Morley hear that tape."

"All in good time."

"I'll be back well before seven, Mr. Hadlow."

"So will I," said Rosemary. "And thank you for what you did, Mr. Hadlow. It meant so much to us to hear Lynette's voice."

I put my arm around her. "We'll get her back—and Jessica."

"We'll get them both back," vowed Hadlow. "Along with my money."

Rosemary's presence stopped me from enjoying my late breakfast to the full. She was nervous and fatigued. True to type, she tried to drown her apprehension in a gushing stream of words. I was spared any mention of hip operations in the family this time, but I had to listen to meandering reminiscences of Lynette that left me hardly any room for comment.

My digestion was further impeded by the fact that Nancy Wykoff was seated at a table on the other side of the room, having a mid-morning coffee with Melinda Reed. I thought at first that Rosemary hadn't noticed them, but I was mistaken. She summoned up her sweetest smile and spoke with excessive politeness.

"Would you like me to leave, Alan?" she asked.

"Of course not."

"You could invite Mrs. Wykoff over."

"I don't wish to do so."

"Won't she expect it of you?"

"What Nancy expects of me is my concern," I said, buttering a last piece of toast. "Frankly, my social life is on the back burner until Lynette is handed over. I can't think about anyone else but her."

"Except for that murder victim."

"Well, yes," I admitted. "But that's a separate matter."

She glanced over at Nancy. "I'll leave you to another separate matter," she said, getting up. "I'm flagging. I'm going to take a nap. Would it be too much to ask for us to have lunch together?"

"I insist on it, Rosemary."

"Very well. But not here—we'll have room service."

"In my suite," I said.

"As long as you're there alone this time."

She sailed off and left me to munch my toast. I'd just swilled it down with coffee when Nancy Wykoff came over to me. Melinda Reed was going out of the restaurant by the other exit. There were mingled affection and worry in Nancy's voice.

"I hope that I didn't frighten your ex-wife away." she said.

"Only an exorcist could do that."

"Now, now," she scolded. "Show respect. Mrs. Saxon is a classy lady. I can tell."

"She's certainly out of my league."

"May I join you?"

"If you wish," I said. She sat down opposite me. "I was pleased to see that you and Melinda Reed are still friends. Or was she accusing you of trying to pump her?"

"I got a gentle rap on the knuckles, that's all."

"But no more background info about the Blue Dolphin?"

"Not a peep, Alan."

"Her husband has obviously told her to clam up."

"Cal has other headaches," she explained. "Apparently, he's getting a lot of hassle from Bernard Hadlow. Then there's the situation with your partner."

"What's Peter Fullard been up to?" I asked in surprise.

"Nothing at all. That's the point. The cops have finished on the course now and say that work can restart, but the contractors need you and Peter to make decisions."

"Count me out for the immediate future."

"That's what he's saying. Until your daughter is safe and sound, Peter won't even put his head outside his room. He told Cal it would be disloyal to you."

I finished my coffee. "How well do you know Reed?"

"Pretty well, I guess—though he doesn't make it easy."

"Has he always worked for the same hotel chain?"

"More or less. He's their blue-eyed boy."

"Running this place is a huge responsibility," I noted. "They must have great faith in him. So do his staff. You can see it in their manner whenever he passes them."

"Cal is certainly the boss around here, no doubt about that."

"Would you trust him, Nancy?"

"Implicitly. As a hotel manager, that is."

"And as a man?"

"Only up to a point," she said, "but, then, Cal Reed is not really my type."

"Who is?"

"The kind of guy who can play golf the way you do." She raised an apologetic hand. "Sorry, Alan, I know that golf is off limits for the time being. You've got other priorities. Any news, by the way?"

"We have to wait until this evening."

"Maybe I should vanish until this whole thing has blown over."

"There's no need."

"I think there is," she said. "Thanks to me, you got caught in a compromising position. We know it was perfectly innocent but she doesn't. Your ex-wife was pleasant enough to me, but I could hear the rumblings under the surface. I bet her manner changed completely when you were alone together."

"It did, Nancy."

"Weren't you amused?"

"Amused?" I said. "Why?"

"You split up all those years ago yet you can still arouse her jealousy. I thought you said she hated you, Alan. That's not the Rosemary Saxon that I saw. She hasn't let you go at all. She's far too possessive."

I was saved the trouble of a reply by the arrival of Constable Hills.

"Excuse me for butting in, sir," he said, "but the inspector wants to see you."

"Tell him I'm on my way." Hills went off. "It's only temporary," I said to Nancy. "The situation has put Rosemary under unbearable strain. That's why she seems a bit proprietary. When this business is finally over, she'll throw me away like an old glove."

Nancy laughed. "What a coincidence! I collect old gloves."

Troy Morley and Derek Woodford were waiting for me in the Incident Room. I was waved to a seat. The inspector's expression gave nothing away.

"I hear that you had another call from the kidnapper, Mr. Saxon," he said.

"That's right," I replied. "I'm glad I was there at the time."

"What else happened?"

"What do you mean, Inspector?"

"Well, Mr. Hadlow was reluctant to say very much," he explained. "All that he did was to let us listen to the tape of the call. I was hoping that you could fill in the gaps, so to speak. What were you talking about before the call, how did he react when it came, what did he say afterwards?"

I was cagey. "I doubt if there's much that I can add."

"Try, sir. It could be important."

"For instance," said Woodford, "what were you doing in his room?"

"That's an easy question, Sergeant."

I gave them a highly condensed version of events in Hadlow's room, omitting any reference to the visit from Frank Colouris. Brief as my account was, it clearly had more meat on it than that given by Hadlow. They probed for a few more minutes, then Morley shifted to another topic.

"We found your car, Mr. Saxon," he said.

"What car?"

"The one that tried to knock you down, sir. Derek?"

"It was found abandoned near Shelley Bay Park," said the sergeant, taking over. "The damage to the wing and bodywork was consistent with its having grazed that stone wall you dived over. The car was rented to a man who gave his name as Raymond Ziegel, but we now know that was an alias. Our lads worked at top speed on this one." A muted pride came into his voice. "They lifted prints from the car and got a match with those taken from the van that was seen on the golf course on the night of the murder."

"You were lucky, sir," said Morley. "The man driving that car was involved in the murder of Maurice Dobbs. He already had blood on his hands."

"Do you know who he is?" I asked.

"We do now, Mr. Saxon."

"Yes," said Woodford. "We had nothing in our own records so—thanks to the wonders of modern technology—we sent a copy of the prints to the FBI. They turned up trumps. They gave us a name, a photograph and a detailed criminal history."

"So who was he?" I said.

"Vincent Rodriguez. He lives in Manhattan. Lower East Side, to be exact. He started out as an enforcer for a loan shark before moving on to bigger things. Mr. Rodriguez has served two stretches in prison, one for attempted murder."

"Put the bastard away again, Sergeant. He tried to kill me as well."

"We know, sir. Unfortunately, the suspect is no longer on the island."

"No," said Morley. "As we speak, he's flying back to New York, thinking that he's got safely away from the scene of the crimes. Officers are waiting to pick him up at JFK. This is the man, Mr. Saxon," he said, passing me a photograph. "You'll be relieved to know that he's in no position to make a second attempt on your life."

I looked down at the mug shot of a thickset man with swarthy skin and dark, bushy eyebrows that met in the middle. He was around my own age. His eyes glared up at me from the photograph. I was pleased that I wouldn't have to meet him again. The inspector took the photograph back from me.

"So, you see, sir," he pointed out. "We have made some progress."

"I'm impressed, Inspector."

"Put in a word for us with Mr. Hadlow. We're not the hayseeds that he imagines. When we need to move fast, we do. And thank you, sir. You had a scare out there on the road this morning, I know, but it was you who helped us to net Rodriguez. That means we'll soon have one of the killers in custody."

"What about the other one?"

"We've reason to believe that he's still in Bermuda."

"Is he likely to have a go at me as well?"

"Who knows?" he asked. "But we've reached one conclusion, Mr. Saxon."

"What's that?"

"Our first guess may have been right, after all."

"First guess?"

"Yes, sir. Do you remember we thought the murder and the kidnap were linked?"

"But they're not, Inspector."

"Don't be so sure," he warned. "We're coming round to the view that there *is* a connection between the two crimes. What it is, we haven't worked out yet, but the evidence is pointing that way. Do you see what this means, sir?"

"You're telling me not to talk to strange men."

"I'm telling you more than that," he emphasized. "They may have another reason for wanting you involved in handing over the money. Take extra care, Mr. Saxon. They may be lining you up."

Chapter Ten

The long wait was excruciating. I felt so helpless. Instead of being able to do something positive and go in search of Lynette and Jessica, I was anchored to the hotel, assailed by horrid fears and clinging to faint hopes. After my chat with the police, I returned to my suite to absorb what I'd been told and to study its implications. Inspector Troy Morley had both impressed and disturbed me. I was astonished at the speed with which his men had matched two sets of fingerprints to learn the identity of the driver who'd tried to kill me. The fact that Vincent Rodriguez had left Bermuda and would soon be arrested was very heartening. Morley's other news was more alarming. If, as he now suspected, the murder and the kidnap were somehow connected, I might be in serious danger. That thought did not make the wait any easier. When the hand-over took place, Bernard Hadlow would be exchanging money for his daughter. I was bound to wonder if I'd be trading myself for Lynette.

A fruitless hour limped past. Nobody came, nobody rang. Rosemary, I assumed, was still sleeping in her room. Nancy Wykoff was filling her time elsewhere. In the normal course of events, the two women would never have met. It was my bad luck that they did so in the most unfortunate circumstances. Even without the debilitating anxiety of the abduction, my friendship with Nancy could never have developed with my ex-wife there. Whenever I'm in Rosemary's vicinity, my sex life withers on the vine. It's almost like being married to her again. She exerts a power that overrides the fact of our long separation and divorce. It's not simply possessiveness on her part. It's a kind of post-marital sabotage. Not wanting me herself, Rosemary nevertheless feels obliged to torpedo my relationships with other women, if they come within reach. It's one of the reasons I always keep such a respectable distance between the two of us. For Lynette's sake, that was now impossible. And when all was said and done, tolerating my ex-wife's idiosyncrasies was a small price to pay for the safe return of our daughter.

Unable to sit still, I paced the room restlessly. I'm too impatient by nature to wait for any length of time. It's rather like watching grass grow—Bermuda grass, at that—and only Peter Fullard could take any pleasure from such an exercise. He was still immured in his suite, desperate for news about developments. I was tempted to ring him in order to bring him up-to-date but I soon saw the folly of doing so. How would Peter react if I told him about my narrow escape from death or revealed that I was still a marked man? My partner would shake in his shoes. No, Peter Fullard had to be spared. The best thing was to forget him altogether. I had no room for him on my emotional worry list.

After walking up and down for what seemed like the best part of a mile, I grew very tired of the scenery. There's a limit to how many times you want to stare at a four-seat beige sofa, two matching armchairs, a mahogany wardrobe and chest of drawers, a drinks cabinet, a coffee table and the largest TV set in captivity. To break the monotony, I went through the connecting door into the adjoining suite. Suddenly, I was in a different world, that of carefree young womanhood. The girls' belongings were everywhere. When I took an inventory, I saw that the majority of things were Jessica's, tossed heedlessly onto a chair, a table or the floor by someone who treated a hotel room with the easy disdain of a veteran traveler. Lynette's discarded clothes, books and music tapes were concentrated in a much smaller area and there was a vague attempt at tidiness. The characters of the two girls were self-evident.

When I entered their bedroom, it was the same story. Jessica's bed, in a prime position beside the window, was littered with her possessions, and a veritable pagoda of books, papers, magazines, CDs and tapes stood on her bedside table. There was far less clutter on Lynette's bedside table. It upset me that it was my daughter's bedside lamp that been smashed during the kidnap. It showed that Lynette had resisted before being overpowered. Now that the police had finished in the room, I saw that the broken lamp had been replaced with a new one. Items that had been knocked to the floor had been put back on the bedside table. I noticed that Lynette was reading a novel by Margaret Atwood and that she had a tape of "Carmina Burana" in her personal stereo. Where, I asked myself, did she keep her stash of cannabis? How had she managed to smuggle it into the country in the first place? Assuming that she was released, what was I going to do about the fact that she smoked pot? Harangue her? Warn her about the health risks? Preach a sermon from the moral high ground? That would be ludicrous. I was hardly a candidate for sainthood myself. As I left the bedroom, I was bewildered.

My twin obsessions continued to smolder in my mind. Where were the girls? And was I really in danger? The fate of Lynette and Jessica was my immediate concern and I was still troubled that their release hinged on the behavior of Bernard Hadlow. He'd been far more controlled during his last conversation with the kidnapper, but that didn't mean he'd remain cool during the exchange itself. What if his notorious temper got the better of him? Worse still, what if he couldn't raise the full amount of money in the time allotted? It was a sickening possibility. Articles about Hadlow invariably described him as one of Britain's most successful businessmen, with commensurate wealth. Jessica had boasted of houses they owned in three different countries as well as about the family's constant globe trotting in First Class. Hadlow was patently a rich man, but most of his wealth was in the form of fixed capital. The ransom demand ran to millions of dollars. Even he couldn't pluck that sort of money out of a top hat. Where would he get it?

The question sent me back through the connecting door in search of the fax from Clive Phelps' erstwhile girlfriend. The pages were in the drawer of my bedside table. I read the material closely through again. Bernard Hadlow was a real presence on the international business scene. He liked publicity almost as much as his daughter did. I lost count of the number of times that his face beamed up at me in the wake of his latest takeover. He was pictured with the management teams of his various acquisitions, giving the impression that the change was beneficial to all parties. How long did some of those men and women retain their jobs, I wondered? Hadlow was proficient with the hatchet. He must have killed off hundreds of promising careers. It might even be that one of those faces, smiling bravely in the faxed photographs, belonged to the kidnapper. I was certain it was someone who'd been a victim of Hadlow's merciless business practices. They knew his weak spot and they struck accordingly.

What did emerge more clearly from a second reading of the articles was the extent of Hadlow's interests in Bermuda. He had a finger in several pies, but there was one company that even his ubiquitous digit had failed to penetrate. After a long war of attrition, Hadlow's hostile takeover bid had been repulsed. It was a Pyrrhic victory. As a result of the boardroom battles, it was implied, the chief executive of the targeted company was put under such intense stress that he died of a heart attack. His name was Grant Iliffe, a well-established figure in the leisure industry. I must have skimmed the article too quickly the first time to remember his name. Seeing it again, I recalled what Nancy Wykoff had told me about the fight to purchase the land on which the Blue Dolphin now stood. Among those engaged in the struggle was a company called ITH—Iliffe Temperley Holdings. The late Grant Iliffe must have been its overlord. ITH had cause to hate the consortium that eventually bought the site, and a reason to hold a grudge against Bernard Hadlow.

Could it be that Alan Saxon was also on their hit list?

I dismissed the notion at once. I'd been wrong about Redfurst Leisure and was probably even more adrift with regard to Iliffe Temperley Holdings. It was simply one more company that had stared into the gaping jaws of Hadlow. Most had been swallowed whole. ITH had escaped his shark attack. After reading the rest of the articles, I tossed the pages on the bed and pondered. A firm tapping on my door brought my meditation to an abrupt end. I guessed that it was probably Rosemary, roused from her sleep and feeling in need of lunch. I hoped that it wasn't Nancy Wykoff again. Her presence could be a profound embarrassment. If my ex-wife caught us together a second time, her comments would turn the air blue. Caution made me use the peephole and I saw a person who was less welcome than either of the women. It was Calvin Reed. I experienced a sudden tremor of fear.

Before he could knock again, I opened the door to confront him. Reed looked as composed as usual. There was nothing about his appearance or manner that suggested he could have been involved in the attempt on my life, but I was taking no chances. I was on full alert. He gave me his bland smile.

"I was hoping to catch you, Alan," he said. "May I have a word?"

"Why didn't you ring?" I asked.

"It's a private matter that needs to be discussed face to face."

"In that case, you'd better come in."

I stood aside to let him go past me, determined not to turn my back on him at any stage. When I invited him to sit down, he took one of the armchairs. I perched myself on the edge of the sofa. Concern registered on his face.

"How are you coping?"

"As well as I can," I replied.

"Anything more that we can do?"

"I'm afraid not, Mr. Reed. Unless you can snap your fingers and make the girls pop up in the adjoining suite. Then I really would praise Blue Dolphin room service. Talking of which," I went on, "I understand you'd had complaints from Mr. Hadlow."

"I've just come from him," he said, gritting his teeth. "He refused to let Frank Colouris sort out his problem. Only the manager would suffice, he said. So I had to listen to a tirade that lasted for at least twenty minutes."

"What happened? Were his soft-boiled eggs too hard?"

"I couldn't begin to tell you how trivial his complaints were at bottom. Mr. Hadlow didn't need me at all. He was just attention seeking," decided Reed. "What he really wanted to do was to hold the threat of legal action over me. He blames a lapse in hotel security for what happened."

"I know," I said. "He was sounding off earlier. I was with him when Mr. Colouris called. He gave your deputy short shrift."

"Frank took that in his stride."

"With luck, Bernard Hadlow won't be around indefinitely."

"That's my fervent hope."

"If his daughter is handed over this evening, my guess is that he'll be leaving Bermuda on the first available flight tomorrow."

"I'll willingly drive him to the airport myself."

"Don't expect a tip."

There was an awkward pause. I'd never known Calvin Reed to be lost for words before. In our discussions about the golf course, he'd always been highly articulate. He reached up to adjust his silk tie. I wondered why he was so uncomfortable.

"I'm not quite sure how to say this," he began.

"Take your time, Mr. Reed."

"You see? That's one of the reasons why this is so difficult for me, Alan."

"What is?"

"After all this time, I'm still 'Mr. Reed' to you, aren't I?"

"You employ us. It's a mark of respect."

"Respect or distrust?" he said. "Which one stops you from breaking through that barrier into friendship? Granted, I employ you on behalf of the consortium that owns the Blue Dolphin, but that doesn't set me up on Mount Olympus. I try to be approachable, Alan. Especially to people I like."

"I know. You've been wonderful to Peter Fullard and me."

"So why is there a glass wall between us?"

"I'm not sure, Mr. Reed," I said, "but I don't believe that you came all the way up here to discuss our personal relationship. It works well, as it is. Why change it?"

"If that's how you want it."

"I think it is."

"Then let's carry on as we are."

I could see that he was disappointed. I didn't know if his show of friendship was a ruse to make me lower my guard or a genuine attempt to prove that he was more affable than he seemed. Remaining alert, I bided my time.

"Forgive me for asking a personal question," he resumed.

"If you want to know if this is my natural color," I said, stroking my hair, "the answer's 'yes.' I went gray at an early age. My silver fox phase is yet to come."

"How close are you and Nancy Wykoff?"

I was jolted by his bluntness. "That's our business, Mr. Reed."

"I'm sorry that I had to ask you that."

"Then why did you?"

"Because it may be relevant to things that have happened around here."

"Nancy Wykoff and I are friends," I said defensively.

"I'd worked that out, Alan. I just wondered how deep that friendship was."

"This is not a psychiatrist's couch, you know."

"Look, don't misunderstand me."

"I think that you're the one with the misunderstandings, Mr. Reed," I said, starting to lose my patience. "Mrs. Wykoff and I happen to like each other, that's all. There's no crime in that, is there? We played golf and spent time together. It's what is known as enjoying a holiday. A hotel manager should know what that is."

"When did you first meet her?"

"Look, Mr. Reed—"

"All right," he said, interrupting me, "I'll tell you. Nancy was so eager to rub shoulders with one of her golfing heroes that she got to know the Fullards. Deliberately. Let's face it. Charming as they are, Peter and Denise Fullard are not the kind of people she'd ordinarily choose as friends. She used them blatantly."

"I realized that."

"Did it never occur to you to ask why?"

"You've already given the answer. She was keen to meet Alan Saxon."

"Then why didn't she wait until *we* introduced her to you? Nancy is much closer to my wife than she could ever be to Denise Fullard. It was only a matter of time before we invited you and Nancy Wykoff to dine with us. Why the rush?"

"She's impulsive," I said. "Didn't want to waste any time."

Reed was frank. "I've never met anyone less impulsive than her. Don't get me wrong," he pleaded, holding up both hands. "I like the woman. Melinda adores her. But we both take her for what she is."

"And what's that?" I asked, feeling my hackles rise.

"Put it this way. Nancy Wykoff has been married twice. On both occasions, she chose a millionaire as her husband. Women don't do that on impulse. There's an element of calculation involved."

"There's an element of calculation involved here as well, Mr. Reed," I retorted, "and I can't say that I appreciate it. Everything you've said so far about Mrs. Wykoff is calculated to make me very annoyed. What's behind it all?"

"Let me get straight to the point."

"I thought you already had."

"Oh, no. It's still to come, believe me." He sat forward. "Do you remember that argument we had about the battle to secure this site?"

"All I remember is that you refused to argue."

"My hands are tied, Alan," he said reasonably. "I told you that. This is a dog-eat-dog world. Nobody pretends that business deals are sacred rituals conducted between holy men. It's war by checkbook and casualties can be high. Now, with regard to the Blue Dolphin, there are certain things that I'm unable to discuss with you—or with anyone else, for that matter. But that doesn't mean I don't want to help," he stressed. "And it hasn't stopped me making my own inquiries."

"Into what?"

"Circumstances surrounding the acquisition of this site."

"Go on."

"I'm desperate to see Lynette and Jessica released," he claimed. "When I told you I was helping the police all I could, I was being perfectly honest. But there's one thing I haven't told them because it may steer them in completely the wrong direction."

"Then why tell me?"

"Because I think you have a right to know."

I watched him carefully. "I'm listening, Mr. Reed."

"Have you ever heard of Fleary Intercontinental?"

"Yes," I said. "It was one of the main contenders for the purchase of this site."

"How do you know?"

"Nancy Wykoff mentioned the name to me."

"And how did she get hold of it?"

"From your wife, surely." He shook his head. "She must have done."

"No, Alan," said Reed. "I'm very touchy about the Blue Dolphin, as you found out. I don't like it when people try to probe too deeply into its brief history. That's why I was so upset when I discovered that Nancy had been pumping my wife for information at your behest. And she did it very skillfully, it seems," he conceded. "Melinda is not easily duped but Nancy Wykoff managed to do it."

"Go back to Fleary Intercontinental."

"They're global players in the hotels and leisure industry."

"So?"

"My wife didn't say a word about them."

"How can you be so certain?"

"Because Melinda has a good memory," he said. "I made her tell me everything that Nancy had winkled out of her, down to the last full stop. At no stage did Fleary Intercontinental come into the discussion."

"Then why did Nancy mention the name to me?"

"I may have the answer to that."

"How?"

"Because I've been doing some detective work on my own account."

"And?"

"Do you know who the president of Fleary Intercontinental is?"

"Someone called Mr. Fleary, I suppose?"

"James Julius Clark Fleary, to be exact. That's why I asked you how close you were to Nancy Wykoff," he explained. "Do you know what her maiden name is?"

"No," I said, bracing myself.

"Fleary. The president of Fleary Intercontinental is her elder brother."

I was astounded. Nancy Wykoff was the one person whom I'd trusted enough to confide in. I not only felt as if I'd just been knocked down by that car I met on the road. It had reversed at speed to run over me again.

Almost as soon as Calvin Reed left, the telephone rang. It was Rosemary to say that she'd woken up from her nap and was coming to have lunch with me. I resented the intrusion. It gave me no time to recover from the impact of what the manager had told me. I was still stunned at the revelation about Nancy Wykoff. Could *she* somehow have been involved in the crimes that had plagued the Blue Dolphin? It was a terrifying thought. Had I, in effect, slept with the enemy? I tried to replay all the conversations I'd had with her since our first meeting, weighing her words, searching for clues and dreading that our intimate moments might have been part of some elaborate confidence trick. The most telling strike against her was the fact that she'd used the Fullards as a stepping-stone to me so that she could win me over at the earliest opportunity. Before I even had time to settle in at the Blue Dolphin, she moved in. I recalled the ease with which she'd rattled off the information garnered from Melinda Reed. If her own brother's company had been in contention for the purchase of the site, it was no wonder that she had a command of such details. I felt shocked, betrayed and humiliated to the same degree.

Was I really the victim of a grand deception? I tried hard to find excuses for Nancy's behavior, some explanation that would absolve her of all charges. It was significant that Calvin Reed had brought me the information. Why had he come to me instead of going to the police? Was he using the link between Nancy and Fleary Intercontinental as a smokescreen behind which he could hide? Because suspicion had now shifted to her, it didn't put him in the clear. It was Reed who was so keen to find out where I'd been when I visited Ella Dobbs, and it was he who deliberately chose to send her husband to pick me up at the airport. I was confused. There were no fixed points in my world any more. My lover might be exploiting me on her brother's behalf, my employer might have ordered an attack on my life, my daughter had been kidnapped, the golf course on which I'd lavished so much time and devotion was under siege, and my partner was in despair. I was adrift in a sea of uncertainty.

Rosemary's arrival did nothing to allay my innate sense of panic.

"What's happened?" she said, as I opened the door to admit her.

"Nothing."

"You look terrible, Alan."

"I had a bad night."

She swept past me. "I asked for that."

"How was your nap?" I asked, closing the door. "Feel any better?"

"No, I only dozed off for a short while. I keep thinking about Lynette."

"Me, too, Rosemary."

"How are she and Jessica coping?"

"They're a resilient pair."

"You need more than resilience in a situation like this."

She sat on the sofa and I found myself sinking down at the other end of it. Her antennae were twitching. She glanced around the room.

"Has *she* been here again?" said Rosemary.

"Who?"

"That so-called friend of yours."

"No," I replied, stung by the reference to Nancy Wykoff.

"I could see her waiting to pounce on you in the restaurant."

"She wasn't waiting for anything, Rosemary. If you remember rightly, Nancy was there before we even got to the restaurant. She was having coffee with Melinda Reed."

"And keeping one eye on you."

"I have that effect on some women."

She reined in her scorn. "We mustn't start bickering again," she said. "That's not going to bring Lynette back to us again. Any word from Mr. Hadlow?"

"Not to me," I said. "He's saving his firepower for Calvin Reed."

"Why is Jessica's father so disagreeable?"

"He thinks he's just being assertive."

"Why haul the manager up there simply to complain about room service?"

"There's more to it than that," I explained. "There are wheels within wheels, Rosemary. When this site was up for grabs, Redfurst Leisure, part of the Hadlow business empire, put in a bid for it."

"And failed, presumably."

"I don't think he'll ever forgive the consortium that pipped him at the post."

"Why?"

"Because they beat him at his own game. Naked skullduggery. Mr. Reed is a symbol of his rival's success. That's why Hadlow is lashing out at him. He's using the kidnap of his daughter as a stick with which to beat the Blue Dolphin."

"I don't see that the hotel is at fault," she said.

"Neither do I, Rosemary. But, then, we don't have a score to settle with it."

"Is Mr. Hadlow really so vindictive?"

"Cross him and you'll find out."

"Oh dear! I hadn't realized that he had a connection with the Blue Dolphin. That rather complicates matters, doesn't it? No wonder he was so edgy."

"In fairness, he was very calm on the telephone."

"Yes," she agreed. "He made them let both girls speak on the line. I nearly fainted when I heard Lynette's voice," she said, taking out a handkerchief to dab at her eyes. "She sounded so beaten down. What have they been *doing* to her, Alan?"

"Try not to dwell on that."

"I can't help it."

"I know," I said, moving close enough to touch her hand. "It's hard."

She nodded. "Will Mr. Hadlow be able to raise the money in time?"

"We'll have to wait and see."

"I'm not happy about the idea of your being involved in the exchange."

"I am," I said. "Lynette needs me there. And I want to be on hand to calm Hadlow down if he tries to argue with the kidnapper. That could be fatal. I don't want him to blow the whole operation."

"Be careful, Alan."

"I will, I promise."

She looked at me so tenderly that I thought she was going to kiss me, but the moment soon passed. The telephone rang and I got up to answer it. The call was brief but encouraging. I was actually smiling as I went back to the sofa.

"That was Inspector Morley," I said. "Progress at last."

Hope flared up in her eyes. "They know where the girls are?"

"No, Rosemary. I'm afraid not. This concerns the man who tried to run over me earlier today. He flew out of Bermuda this morning. The police have just arrested him at Kennedy Airport in New York."

"Oh, I see," she sighed. "It's nothing to do with the kidnap."

"It could be. The inspector believes that the crimes are connected."

"Does he think this man was involved in the abduction?"

"No, but he's certainly implicated in the murder. What the police haven't worked out yet is how it's linked to the kidnap. Someone must be implicated in both."

"Who?"

The names of Nancy Wykoff and Calvin Reed came into my mind as possible suspects. Both would have been in the right position at the right time, though their motives were unclear. Would a genuine golfer like Nancy want to cause damage to a golf course? Would a manager really want to inflict such dreadful problems on his own hotel? Yet my doubts about both of them remained. Rosemary picked up on my agitation.

"You know, don't you?" she asked.

"No, I don't. Honestly."

"But you have some idea."

"It's only a long shot, Rosemary."

"Tell me," she insisted. "If you have even the vaguest notion of who might be behind Lynette's kidnap, I want to know who it is. *Please*, Alan. Out with it."

"I can't name any names."

"But?" she prompted.

"There was a bloodbath when this site came onto the market. The consortium that won the day, GGM, created some powerful enemies. I don't think they simply went away to lick their wounds. One of them wanted revenge."

"Against the hotel, yes. I see that. But why pick on Mr. Hadlow as well?"

"Redfurst Leisure, a Hadlow company, was involved."

"On the losing side."

"That time, perhaps. But he's been the victor in most of the battles he's fought in Bermuda. It hasn't gained him any popularity awards, I can tell you that."

Rosemary was despondent. "Is this what our daughter's caught up in?" she said, shaking her head in dismay. "Some squalid row between rival businessmen?"

"One of those businessmen is about to get her a job."

"What?"

"Hasn't Lynette told you? She wants to go into publishing."

"Yes, she mentioned that."

"Apparently, Hadlow is going to use his contacts to shoehorn her in."

"I know, Alan. I was rather pleased when Lynette told me that, but I'm very dubious about it now. In fact," she admitted, "I'm deeply worried about her friendship with Jessica. Look where it's got her."

"Jessica is not to blame for that."

"Her father is. Indirectly."

"I was the one who brought his daughter to Bermuda."

Rosemary winced. Her own part in the sequence of events was pricking her conscience. She looked tired and dispirited. I tried to rally her.

"What about some lunch?" I suggested. "Bernard Hadlow may not rate the room service here but I do. Would you like to see the menu?"

\|l|l\l\l\\l\\l\\\l\\\l\\l\l\l\l\l\l\l\l\

The meal was a godsend. Though we only ate a light salad apiece, it somehow gave us the strength to go on. It also allowed a more detailed discussion of events. Lynette dominated our thoughts. We talked about the mistakes we'd made with her in the past and the effect our divorce must have had on her at such an impressionable age. I came perilously close to telling Rosemary about the cannabis but drew back at the last moment out of consideration for her feelings. Both of us were ready to shoulder our share of the blame for past errors. We ended the meal in a flurry of promises to do things for our daughter that we'd always meant to do and to look after her more zealously in the future. If, indeed, Lynette had a future. Rosemary stayed for a couple of hours then went back to her room. We'd arranged to meet later so I suddenly had some precious free time. I decided to put it to good use. I called on Frank Colouris.

When I tracked him down, he was leafing through a document in his office. He gave me a cordial welcome and offered me coffee from the percolator. I accepted. It helped to make my fact-finding visit seem more like a casual chat.

"Mr. Reed was hauled over the coals by our mutual friend," I said.

"So I understand, sir."

"Do you think he'll live?"

"Oh, yes," said Colouris with a grin. "Hotel management toughens you up. It'll take more than a barrage of abuse from Mr. Hadlow to upset Mr. Reed. The two have met before, apparently. When Mr. Reed was working in Barbados."

"Which hotel was that?"

"I can't tell you, sir."

"But part of the same chain as this?"

"Presumably."

"I really came to ask you about Maurice Dobbs," I said.

"There's not much I can tell you, sir."

"Were you aware that he had a criminal record?"

"Of course," replied Colouris. "It's in his file, but so is the fact that he's kept his nose clean for the last five years. Or so it appeared. That's why our transport manager took him on. According to him, Mo was a good driver."

"What let him down were his people skills."

"There were no problems at first or he wouldn't have held the job down. At least, that's what the transport manager told me. As it happens, I wasn't here when Mo was first appointed," he said. "When I arrived at the Blue Dolphin, I didn't know the guy from Adam. He was just one of hundreds on our staff."

"But you know a little more about him now, Mr. Colouris."

"Too much!"

"Is that girlfriend of his going to come back to work?"

"Yes," he replied. "But not for some time. I gather that the funeral is tomorrow. Angela Pike still has to get through that. Things could be a bit strained. Mo's wife *and* his girlfriend will be there. No love lost between those two."

"Oh, I think they'll put any differences aside."

"What makes you say that?"

"I spoke to Mrs. Dobbs this morning," I told him. "It seems that Angela Pike called on her. They didn't come to blows. They had too much in common to do that. To my amazement, Angela—Angie, to her friends—spoke up on my behalf. That's why Mrs. Dobbs wanted to see me."

"How did you find her?"

"Struggling to make sense of it all. Just like us."

"What did she say about her husband?"

"Very little," I replied, not wishing to confide too much in him. "She just wanted to hear a firsthand account of the discovery of Mo's body." I drank some coffee. "I don't suppose that you have his file here, do you?"

"Yes, sir." He indicated the filing cabinet. "Right there."

"Could I possibly take a peep at it?"

"I'm afraid not, Mr. Saxon. It's confidential."

"But I only want to establish one simple fact. It would take two seconds."

He shook his head. "Sorry. Strict company policy."

"Nobody need ever know."

"You're putting me in a very awkward position, sir."

"I'd hate to do that, Mr. Colouris," I said, changing my tack. "Maybe there's another way round this. Instead of showing me the file, could you simply look up something for me yourself?"

"That's tantamount to the same thing."

I tried a last possibility. "Answer me this, then. It's a general inquiry. It won't compromise you. When an employee of yours has two addresses—a home he's just left and one he's just bought—which would be in the file?"

"Both, I guess."

"Thank you."

"Why do you ask?"

"I was curious, that's all."

"There's more to it than that, I reckon."

"Not really."

Colouris had confirmed what I'd expected. Mo's original address would be on file and therefore available for inspection by Calvin Reed. When he'd been told where I'd been by my taxi driver, Reed knew that I must have seen Ella Dobbs. If her address was on file then so was her telephone number. Colouris looked puzzled. I tried to distract him with a compliment.

"You've done a terrific job with your staff," I said.

"Have we?"

"Yes, Mr. Colouris. The murder investigation has left the hotel under a dark cloud but you'd never guess it. When I walked through the lobby just now, your employees were carrying on as if everything was under control."

"Business as usual. That's our motto."

"Doesn't *anything* rock the Blue Dolphin?"

"The kidnap hit us pretty hard," he confessed." Coming on top of the murder, it was a dreadful blow. Luckily, the details haven't been released to the general public or there'd be a lot more unrest among the guests. Even our well-trained clerks and porters might show signs of strain then."

"Mr. Reed doesn't, and he knows about both crimes."

"He's a very exceptional man, sir."

I remembered the conversation I'd had with the manager earlier on.

"That's what I'm beginning to find out," I said.

I was crossing the lobby when I spotted Melinda Reed. She was waiting outside on the patio. Wearing a T-shirt and a pair of white shorts, she was holding a tennis bag. I was surprised. She looked too much like a bird of paradise to do anything as energetic as playing tennis. I went through the front door and hurried across to her.

"Alan!" she said, exuding sympathy. "I'm so sorry you're going through all this."

"So am I."

"It must be agony."

"It is," I agreed. "But if all goes well, it should resolve itself this evening."

"I'll keep my fingers crossed."

"Thanks."

"Calvin tells me that your ex-wife is holding up remarkably well."

"Rosemary is indomitable."

"It's that English stiff upper lip," she said with envy. "In her place, I'd be a wreck. I don't know how the two of you can remain so calm on the surface."

"You should see what it's like underneath!" She gave a brittle laugh. "I didn't know you were a tennis player. After your experience with that boyfriend of yours, I thought you'd have been turned off the game for life."

"No, I like a gentle hour on court. Keeps me in trim."

"Who are you playing?"

"Nancy Wykoff."

I blenched slightly. From the easy way she announced the name, I decided that Melinda Reed knew nothing about Nancy's connection with a rival hotel chain. Her husband had yet to confide that information in her. My first instinct was to vanish before Nancy turned up, but I didn't want to waste an opportunity to find out a little more about her. I glanced around to make sure that she was not coming.

"How long has she been at the hotel?" I asked.

"Best part of a week."

"Have you played tennis with her before?"

"No, this is the first time I've managed to lure her onto the court."

"Be careful," I warned. "If her tennis is anywhere near as good as her golf, you could be in for a torrid time."

"No," she replied, "I don't think so. Nancy only took up the game properly when she turned fifty." She laughed at my obvious astonishment. "Hey, have I let the cat out of the bag?" she asked. "She looks years younger, I know. It's a great advert."

"For what?"

"Cosmetic surgery, of course." I frowned in disappointment. "Don't be like that, Alan. It'll come to us all in time. Nancy makes no secret of the fact."

I disagreed. She looked and acted like a woman fifteen years younger than her real age. Even in bed, the deception was completely convincing. I'd never have guessed she was that much older than me. I was torn between shock and admiration. Then I remembered Calvin Reed's cautionary words about her.

"What's her background?" I asked.

"Why?" she teased. "You planning on getting acquainted with her family?"

"I know she was a sportswriter at one time. What came after that?"

"Ask her."

"I don't like to pry."

"Well, don't get me to do it for you," she said reproachfully. "I know you prefer to work that way, Alan, but I can't say that I approve."

"I'm sorry about that," I mumbled.

"So you should be. I was mad at Nancy when I found out, and even madder at you. I'm still not sure if I forgive you. I hate being used like that." She looked over my shoulder. "Ah, here's my tennis partner!"

I turned to see Nancy Wykoff bearing down on us. She wore a light blue T-shirt and a pair of red shorts. A baseball cap kept the sun's glare at bay. When she saw me, she waved a hand in greeting.

"Hi, Alan!" she said cheerily. "I didn't expect to find you here."

"I thought golf was your game," I remarked.

"Oh, it is. I'm hopeless at tennis. I only took it up four or five years ago."

That put her in her mid-fifties at least. Even older, possibly. I was amazed. When you looked at Nancy Wykoff, what you saw was certainly not what you got. She truly defied the passage of time. But, if Calvin Reed was to be believed, it was not entirely the work of a plastic surgeon. She had a natural talent for keeping certain things extremely well hidden. Her smile was as bright as ever.

"It's crazy, isn't it?" she said. "I was a tennis correspondent once, yet I never enjoyed playing the game myself. Until now, that is."

"Why not come and watch us, Alan?" invited Melinda.

"No, don't!" exclaimed Nancy. "It would be embarrassing."

"I have other things to do," I said. "You'll have to excuse me."

"Of course."

I paused. "Why did you come to the Blue Dolphin?" I asked her.

"I told you," said Nancy. "Melinda and Cal are old friends."

"Yes, but why did you choose this month? It's not the best time to visit Bermuda. You could have come when you could see the island at its best."

"It *is* at its best, Alan."

"Is it?"

"You're here. I knew you would be. That's why I came."

Where he'd been standing, I don't know, but Troy Morley had obviously been watching me. As I went back into the lobby, he materialized out of thin air to take me aside.

"Have you made any headway with Mr. Hadlow?" he asked.

"Only a Sherman tank could do that, Inspector."

"He still won't play ball?"

"Not with the police," I said. "He wants to keep it simple. Just me, him and a bag full of money. And before you ask me," I continued, "I don't want to be wired up either. If things get hot, you might hear me saying some very rude words."

"Do you know what you're letting yourself in for, Mr. Saxon?"

"Not really."

"We've handled situations like this before."

"Do you always catch the villains?"

"Most of the time."

"What about the ones who get away?"

"They usually renege on their promises," he said. "They grab the money but give nothing in exchange. Be sure you *see* the girls before you hand anything over."

"Where will you be?"

"Standing by. You only have to call."

"Thanks."

"As I told you, Vincent Rodriguez is now in custody. We know that he had an accomplice but he's refusing to say who it was. In fact, he's refusing to say anything."

"Will he be extradited?"

"Yes, but these things take time. We've arranged with the NYPD to send two of our officers to interview Rodriguez over there."

"Meanwhile, his accomplice is still in Bermuda?"

"So we believe."

"What makes you think the murder and the kidnap are related?"

"Their close proximity, to start with. One day, you find a dead body on the golf course. Soon after that, your daughter and her friend are abducted."

"But not because of *me*," I reminded him. "Bernard Hadlow was the target."

"You were the one they tried to kill, sir. Not him."

"Do you think this Vincent Rodriguez was involved in the kidnap as well?"

"We have to consider the possibility."

"But you're certain that the crimes are linked?"

"Fairly certain, Mr. Saxon."

"On what evidence?"

"Call it a policeman's instinct."

"My father always claims he has that," I said, wincing at the memory. "Only I called it something else. I don't think you'd like to hear what."

"How is Mrs. Saxon coping with the pressure?" he asked.

"A lot better than me, Inspector."

"If she needs help—trauma counseling—we have trained officers you can call on."

"Thank you," I said, "but Rosemary wouldn't even consider it."

"Someone ought to be with her when you go off to make the exchange. Mrs. Saxon will be under the most intense strain. If she doesn't want a police officer, at least advise her to have some moral support. What about your partner, sir?"

"Peter Fullard? He couldn't support a broken matchstick."

"His wife, then?"

"Denise has flown home."

"I'm sure that Mr. Reed would volunteer."

"Oh, no!" I said firmly, still unable to trust the manager. "Let me put it to Rosemary. If she feels the need for company, she'll find it somehow."

"Very well, sir."

I was touched by his patent concern. Troy Morley had been placed in an unenviable position. The kidnapper had warned the police to keep their distance and Bernard Hadlow had flatly refused to cooperate with them. All that the inspector and his men could do was to watch from the sidelines. Morley knew what Rosemary would be going through and offered to provide help. I was certain that she would spurn it. Harrowed and terrified, Rosemary would nevertheless put on a bold front. To admit that she couldn't cope alone would be a sign of failure and she would never admit that. I felt proud of her. She had a perverse sort of courage.

"How can they expect to get away with it, Inspector?" I wondered.

"They've managed so far," he conceded.

"I hoped you might have located the girls by now."

"It's not for want of trying, sir."

"There can't be all that many places where they could be."

"Remember the old Turkish proverb."

"Proverb?"

"Yes, sir," he explained. "'He who steals a minaret, knows where to hide it.'"

"I'm not with you, Inspector."

"Preparation is everything, sir. Before they snatched your daughter and her friend, they knew exactly where they'd take them."

"Do you think so?"

"Oh, yes. And two young women are a lot easier to hide than a minaret."

It was late afternoon and time was running out. I wanted to be in Hadlow's room well before the promised call from the kidnapper so that he and I could discuss strategy. My visit to Frank Colouris had yielded one nugget of information and my encounter with Melinda Reed had given me a further insight into the mysterious Nancy Wykoff. Both she and Calvin Reed remained high on my personal list of suspects, but I'd raised neither name with Troy Morley. If either of them was involved in the kidnap, I was in the best place to find out. Besides, I wanted to get at them first. The deep rage that had been building inside me since Lynette's abduction would burst into flame eventually. It remained to be seen whether Nancy or the manager was caught in the inferno.

Curiosity took me out to the tennis courts. All were occupied. Making sure that I wasn't seen, I found a vantage point from which I could watch the match that interested me. Melinda Reed was serving with a confidence and power that belied her sedentary lifestyle. Her movement about the court was fluent. It was her partner, however, who fascinated me. Nancy Wykoff's long legs got her to the ball without difficulty and she played some cultured strokes. Yet whenever she seemed to be getting on top, she either netted the ball or hit it out, apologizing each time and chiding herself aloud. Melinda was too involved in the match to realize that she was being allowed to win by a superior player. Nancy was no beginner. A sportswriter who covers the tennis circuit doesn't pick up her first racket at the age of fifty. She was a good player, pretending to be a novice. Once again, she was engaged in a deception. Was it simply out of force of habit?

I saw enough for my suspicions about her to harden. The fact that I'd spent the night with her was no longer a pleasant memory. It filled me with remorse. There was one more call that I needed to make. After watching Nancy hit another ball into the net, I slipped away.

"Can I help you, sir?"

"I hope so," I said.

"Where do you want to go?"

"Nowhere."

"You don't want transport?"

"Not at the moment."

"Then why come to me?"

The transport manager was a short, stubby man with the face of a garden gnome. Dressed in a smart uniform, he occupied a tiny office at the rear of the hotel. A cheroot was stuck in the corner of his mouth but it didn't impede his speech in any way. He looked so much like my idea of Rumpelstiltskin that I half-expected him to stamp his foot in fury. Instead, he was very amiable.

"I wanted to speak to you about Maurice Dobbs," I said.

His expression darkened. "Poor old Mo! What a way to die!"

"How did you get on with him?"

"Very well," he replied. "After all, I was the one who gave him the job. Mo had been a naughty boy in his time. Went to prison. It wasn't easy for him to find work. I took a chance and it paid off. He couldn't thank me enough." He squinted at me through a cloud of smoke. "Hey, I know you, don't I? Alan Saxon. Your picture was in the paper. You were the one who found Mo hanging from that tree."

"He picked me up from the airport when I first arrived."

"When was that?"

"The day he got the sack."

"Yes," he sighed. "Pity about that. Mo came to me for help."

"What did you do?"

"I spoke to Mr. Colouris but it was no use. Mo had to go. Mr. Colouris had no choice. Mo changed over the last couple of weeks. Don't ask me why. Before then, he was one of the most cheerful drivers I had."

"Why did you send him to pick me up at the airport?"

"But I didn't, sir."

"I thought that Mr. Reed specifically asked for Mo."

"Oh no, Mr. Saxon," he said, rolling the cheroot from one side of his mouth to the other. "Mr. Reed told me to send Joel. He's the best driver we have."

"Yes, I've met Joel. So why didn't he come to the airport?"

"There was a change of plan at the last moment, sir."

"What do you mean?"

"The bell captain rang me. Said that the manager wanted Mo to meet you instead." He gave a shrug. "I did what I'm told. I stood Joel down and went in search of Mo. But that was the funny thing."

"What was?"

"He'd already gone. Mo knew he was being sent to fetch you before I did."

Rosemary insisted on being there. I'd have preferred to go to Bernard Hadlow's room on my own but she was determined to come. On the way there, I mentioned Troy Morley's kind offer, but it was predictably turned down. Rosemary wanted nobody else near her. She was eager to hear the instructions from the kidnapper in case we were permitted another snatch of Lynette's voice. When he let us into the room, Hadlow was grim-faced.

"Problems?" I asked.

"Not with the ransom," he said. "That's finally tied up. It's this waiting."

"I know, Mr. Hadlow. It's torture."

"No more contact from them?" wondered Rosemary.

Hadlow scowled. "None, Mrs. Saxon. They want us to squirm."

"As long as they haven't harmed the girls."

He said something under his breath before inviting us to sit down. Hadlow had been drinking. A glass of whiskey stood on the table with a half-empty bottle beside it. I hoped that it wouldn't dull his brain or slow his reactions. We were about to enter a situation that was fraught with danger and needed to be alert. When he offered us a drink, Rosemary asked for tonic water and I settled for bitter lemon with ice.

Standing beside the coffee table was a large black briefcase. I guessed that it must contain the ransom and stared at it with a mixture of hope and envy. How much was in there? Where had it all come from? Would he ever see his money again?

Hadlow was a poor host. Resenting our presence, he made little effort to put us at our ease. Conversation was intermittent. Long pauses separated the brief exchanges. He refused even to discuss tactics with me. While the kidnapper was in charge, he insisted, we should simply obey orders. Only when the girls were released could we go after those who'd held them. He swept aside all my attempts at advice. I was making one more suggestion about how we should behave during the hand-over when the telephone rang. We'd been tricked. Having told us to be there at seven, the kidnapper made contact exactly half an hour earlier to catch us off guard. When Hadlow snatched up the receiver, the voice seemed to fill the whole room.

"Mr. Hadlow?" said the man.

"Yes."

"Is Mr. Saxon with you?"

"Yes."

"I thought he would be. Do you have the money?"

"Yes."

"The full amount?"

"Down to the last dollar," said Hadlow.

"Good. We can start."

"Can we speak to the girls?"

"Later, Mr. Hadlow. If all goes according to plan. Now, listen."

Our instructions were short but explicit. We followed them to the letter. Hadlow carried the briefcase and I went after him. Descending to the ground floor by means of the service elevator, we left the hotel by a rear exit. A Ford Mondeo was waiting for us, its key in the ignition. While Hadlow started the motor, I retrieved the mobile phone that we were told would be in the glove compartment. It rang immediately.

"Yes?" I said.

"Tell Mr. Hadlow to drive in the direction of South Road."

"Then what?"

"That depends on whether you're followed by the cops."

I passed on the message and we set off. My role was now clear. Hadlow was the driver and I was his navigator. The police might not be tailing us, but someone had us under observation. It was an eerie sensation. We were within fifty yards of South Road when the kidnapper came on the line again.

"Tell Hadlow to turn left," he said.

"Turn left," I ordered.

"Keep going until you reach Harvey Road on your right."

It was a tense journey. Bernard Hadlow wouldn't have been my ideal traveling companion at the best of times. Under those circumstances, he was insufferable. To begin with, he was a poor driver, crashing the gears with the regularity of a man who spends his time in chauffeur-driven limousines. I wondered if he'd ever been behind the wheel of a car with manual transmission. He was also going too fast. I urged him to slow down but he ignored me. When we reached Harvey Road, we turned right and carried on until we came to Ord Road. Instructed to bear left, we went a short distance before we were told to turn down a side-road. Then came the first shock.

"Stop the car behind the shed on your left," said the voice.

I passed on the command and we ground to a halt.

"Get into the pick-up truck and put on the caps."

A dust-covered truck was standing behind the hut. Taking the briefcase with us, we did as we were told. When I glanced in the rear-view mirror, I saw what a change to our appearance the caps made. We might have been quarry workers on our way home.

Navigation became more complicated. The kidnapper guided us across open country before making us join a lane that snaked its way down to the coast road. After following that for a couple of miles, we went through a network of side-roads until we found ourselves on Middle Road. If the police had been foolish enough to try to shadow us, they'd surely have been shaken off by now. Light was starting to fade. I knew enough geography to realize that we were now in Southampton Parish, but the kidnapper's knowledge of the island was far more detailed than my own. He took us down lanes that I didn't even know existed until we eventually came out on a deserted stretch of road near Turtle Bay.

"Can you see an abandoned house ahead of you?" asked the voice.

"Yes," I said.

"Pull in behind it and stay in the lorry."

I gave Hadlow the order and we swung off the road to park out of sight behind the ruins of what had once been a quaint old cottage. There was nobody in sight at first. Then a motorcyclist in black leather and crash helmet stepped out in front of us and beckoned us out of the lorry. As we got out, a second motorcyclist came up behind us. When he spoke, we recognized the voice that had been giving us the commands.

"Put the briefcase down," he said.

Hadlow obeyed and we turned to see a tall, slim figure in leathers. Like his companion, he was wearing dark glasses. The strap on his crash helmet hung loose, showing that he'd had to remove it to make the calls on his mobile. Whatever heroics I'd planned were put on hold. The tall figure had a gun.

"Count the dough!" he snapped.

The other motorcyclist picked up the briefcase and ran to his companion's side before opening it. I caught a glimpse of bundles of notes, neatly stacked inside. Aided by a torch, the count was swift and accurate. The man with the gun was pleased.

"Well done, Mr. Hadlow!" he sneered. "For the first time in your life, you actually managed to keep your word."

"Where's my daughter?" demanded Hadlow.

"Don't rush me. You'll get her back."

"What about Lynette?" I said.

"Both girls are being held in a safe place," he explained. "They won't be released until we've got well away from here with the ransom and are able make contact with our colleague. Once he's got clear himself, I'll ring you to tell you exactly where to find your daughters. Lovely girls," he said with a chuckle. "I enjoyed their company."

Hadlow started. "If you've laid a finger on my daughter…"

The words trailed away as the gun was held close to his head. Hadlow was trembling with rage but didn't dare to move. Having made his point, the man backed away again. He handed the gun to his companion.

"Keep them covered," he said. "I'll tell him everything went perfectly."

He turned his back to us and removed his helmet so that he could make the call on his mobile. My eyes went to his companion, slighter of build and less aggressive in manner. The hands that had counted the money were slender and manicured. I was certain that they belonged to a woman. It might be my only chance. The man would not scruple to shoot the pair of us in cold blood but I doubted if his companion would. I put my theory to the test. Putting on his helmet, the man swung round to face us as he did up the strap. I was on him in a flash, darting forward and diving headlong at him, knocking him to the ground. Grappling hard, we rolled over and over.

"Stop it!" yelled the woman. "Stop it or I'll shoot."

But she'd given herself away. Hearing her voice and emboldened by my move, Hadlow sprang into action. I heard a scream of protest from the woman as he attacked her but I was too preoccupied to pay any attention to what was going on. My adversary was not only strong, he was wearing protective clothing that took the sting out of my punches. At the same time, the leathers made him cumbersome. Leaping up, I kicked him hard in the stomach and took the wind out of him. Before he could recover, I pinned him to the ground, undid the strap of his helmet and wrenched it off to use it as a weapon. When I'd clubbed him hard with it a few times, his resistance slowly faded. Hadlow, meanwhile, was still struggling with the woman. Then the gun went off and he let out a yell of pain. I turned to see him dancing on one foot. Abandoning any rules of gentlemanly behavior, he swung an arm with such vicious force that he sent her flying. As she hit the ground, the impact knocked the gun from her grasp. I was on it like lightning and covered both of the motorcyclists with it.

"Are you all right, Mr. Hadlow?" I asked.

"It's my foot!" he cried, sitting cross-legged on the ground. "The cow shot me in the foot." He pulled off his shoe to reveal a blood-soaked sock. "Look what she did!"

"Can you hold the gun?"

"I think so."

"If either of them so much as moves," I said, handing the weapon over, "shoot!"

"Don't worry, I will."

I inched off his sock to examine the wound. He'd been lucky. The bullet had grazed the outside of his foot, causing more pain than permanent damage. I tore off my T-shirt to bind the wound tightly then took the gun from him. The two of them were still cowering on the ground. Grabbing the briefcase, I gave it back to Hadlow so that he had something to comfort him. Money was by far his best medicine. The anger that I'd banked down for so long now burst forth. As the man tried to get up, I kicked him under the chin to send him sprawling back, then I sat astride him. This was the kidnapper who'd put two innocent girls through the most terrifying ordeal. He deserved no quarter. I thrust the barrel of the revolver so hard against his forehead that he squealed in protest.

"Now, then," I said, "where do I find Lynette and Jessica?"

The boat was exactly where he'd said it would be. It was anchored in a cove a couple of hundred yards from the shore. I'd reached the place by motorbike, borrowed from the kidnapper and his accomplice. They'd have no need of it now. They were tied up back to back with a long rubber hose I'd found in the rear of the pick-up truck. Nursing his wounded foot, Bernard Hadlow was covering them with a gun. He'd left them in no doubt about his readiness to use it. I couldn't wait for police back-up. Hadlow could summon that. The girls had been locked up long enough. I wanted them free.

I must have looked a curious sight, standing on the beach with a bare chest and a crash helmet. But there was nobody about to see me. The cove had been selected with care. It was too rocky for water sports. Its beach was small and steep. The boat was riding gently on the waves. It looked like any of the other countless hundreds of craft dotted around the island. Because they were in a floating prison, Lynette and Jessica could be moved at will. The only means of getting to the vessel was to swim. I stripped down to my jockey shorts then took the plunge. The sea was cold and my teeth began to chatter. But I swam on, powered by the desire to save the girls and end their torment. I knew that there was only one man aboard. I just had to hope that he was not armed as well. I also prayed that he didn't come out on deck in time to see my head bobbing in the water. It took me longer than I'd anticipated reach the boat. The swim had tired me and I held on to the anchor chain until I began to recover. Lights were on inside the vessel. It was over thirty feet in length and could probably sleep six or more. Only two of its passengers concerned me.

Hauling myself aboard was a tricky exercise. My hands were wet and I lost my grip more than once on the slippery wood. Eventually, however, I got sufficient purchase to drag myself over the bulwark. When I stood up on deck, I was colder than ever. My hair was plastered to my head, my jockey shorts were sodden and water dripped off me in rivulets. I made my way to the door that led down to the cabin. Without even taking the elementary precaution of looking for a weapon, I pressed on. Anger was my best armor. It made me heedless of danger. When I opened the door, I heard a man's voice from down below. There was a teasing menace in his voice.

"It's such a waste of two gorgeous bodies," he said. "We've had you all this time without making the most of it, but I think I should do so now, don't you? By way of farewell. Who shall I have first?" he asked with a sly chuckle. "You, Jessica? Are you up for it? I bet you fuck like a dream. Or what about you, Lynette? You're just my type. Why don't we see what's under that T-shirt of yours?"

The ripping sound put fresh urgency into me. I went swiftly down the steps, on past the galley and through the door ahead of me. Bound and gagged, the girls could do nothing to resist. They watched in amazement as I burst in. Seeing the man about to molest Lynette, I went berserk. I hooked an arm around his neck, dragged him back, then swung him round so that I could dash his head against the edge of the open door. Blood spurted everywhere. He howled in pain then tried to fight back, elbowing me hard in the ribs. I turned him to face me and hit him with a relay of punches until my knuckles were raw. He flailed and kicked and even tried to gouge at my eyes but the advantage of surprise told. Weakened by my initial attack, his resistance gradually disappeared. I didn't stop punching until he lay unconscious in a pool of blood at my feet.

When I turned to the girls, I saw tears of relief streaming down their faces.

"It's all over now," I said, gasping for breath. "You're safe."

Chapter Eleven

Wrapped in blankets, we were taken off the boat by a police launch. Jessica Hadlow was soon reunited ashore with her father. Both were then taken to hospital, Hadlow to have his injury treated and his daughter to be given a medical examination. Jessica was in a far worse state than Lynette, weeping continuously from the moment I released them. Her awesome self-confidence had evaporated completely. The three kidnappers were all in police custody. Summoned by a call from Hadlow, Inspector Troy Morley had brought Rosemary with him so that she could comfort our daughter. Not even realizing that her mother was on the island, Lynette was overjoyed to see her and collapsed in tears. As a car took us back to the hotel, I had my arms around both of them. It was a closeness I hadn't felt for years. When we reached our destination, we took Lynette straight back to the suite from which they'd been abducted. A policewoman accompanied us in order to take a statement from her and the hotel doctor arrived in case medication was needed. The inspector stopped me outside my door with a word of complaint.

"Why didn't you wait for police back-up?" he asked.

"It was too slow, Inspector."

"You might have got yourself killed."

"That was my daughter on the boat. Nobody was going to stop me getting to her."

"Well," he said with a grudging smile, "I admire your bravery but I deplore your commonsense. Get yourself cleaned up, then we'll talk."

I went into my suite and through the connecting door. Under Rosemary's watchful gaze, Lynette was being examined by the doctor. The policewoman waited patiently for a chance to speak to her. The girls were safe at last. They'd suffered little physical damage but the psychological scars were deep. Only time would heal those. There was little that I could do for a while beyond adding my sympathy. Some unfinished business beckoned. Going back into my own suite, I had a shower and put on some warm clothes. Three people might have been arrested, but a crucial figure in the kidnap was still at liberty. I was convinced that it was either Nancy Wykoff or Calvin Reed. Spurred on by her brother, Nancy might have a motive, but the evidence was weighted more strongly against the manager. He was in a position of control and knew exactly where I'd be at any given moment. In advance of our arrival, he also knew that I'd be bringing Jessica Hadlow, a name he recognized at once. Had he tipped someone off about her presence on the island, perhaps even supplied the master key that let the kidnappers in? Nancy could never have done that. And what was his connection with Maurice Dobbs' murder? Why had he been on duty so late on the night in question?

I dialed the operator and asked to be put through to the bell captain. A cheery voice soon came on the line. I recalled seeing the man in his little eyrie. He was a black Bermudan in his fifties with an infectious smile.

"Bell captain," he said deferentially. "How can I help you?"

"My name is Alan Saxon," I told him.

He became even more respectful. "Oh, yes, sir. I know who you are. I made sure that I took your luggage up myself."

"That's what I want to ask you about."

"The luggage?"

"No, my friend. The day I arrived. Mo picked us up at the airport."

"That's right, sir."

"You passed on a message to the transport manager, I believe."

"I did, Mr. Saxon. I told him to stand Joel Arnott down and to send Maurice Dobbs in his place. Those were the manager's orders. And that's what happened."

"Why didn't Mr. Reed ring the transport manager himself?"

"I've no idea, sir."

"Is it usual for him to go through you?"

"But he didn't."

"The message was that the manager had changed his mind."

"Yes, sir, but I didn't speak to Mr. Reed himself."

I was puzzled. "Who did you speak to, then?"

"His deputy," he said cheerily. "Mr. Colouris."

When I got to his chalet, Frank Colouris was putting the last few items into a travel bag. I could see him through the window. I tapped on the glass and he looked up in surprise. He relaxed immediately when he saw who it was. Opening the door to admit me, he had his helpful grin back in place.

"What are *you* doing here, Mr. Saxon?" he asked.

"I called at your office but you weren't there. The duty manager told me that you were taking some time off."

"Yes, that's right. I'm due a week's vacation and there are problems back home."

"Home?"

"In New York. A close friend, in a critical condition."

"His name wouldn't be Vincent Rodriguez, would it?" I said pointedly. His eyelids flickered but there were no other telltale signs. "Or perhaps you knew him as Raymond Ziegel when he was here. You're right, Mr. Colouris. Your friend is in a critical condition. He's in police custody."

"I've never heard either of those names before, sir."

"No? What about the names of Lynette Saxon and Jessica Hadlow?"

"What exactly are you getting at?"

"Let's make it easier, shall we?" I said sarcastically. "We'll start with a name you do know. Maurice Dobbs. Why did you send him to pick me up at the airport?"

"But I didn't. Mr. Reed took care of the arrangements."

"You rescinded his choice of driver. The bell captain confirms it."

"I was speaking on behalf of Mr. Reed."

"No, Mr. Colouris, I think you were speaking on behalf of a company, not of an individual. My guess is that it was either Fleary Intercontinental or Iliffe Temperley Holdings. One of them is your paymaster."

This time, there was a more visible reaction. He pursed his lips and stared hard at me. Colouris had obviously heard about the arrest in New York and the successful resolution of the kidnap. Accomplices, who were in a position to link him to the crimes, were now being questioned by the police. One of them would eventually name Frank Colouris. It was time for him to make his escape. He retrieved his grin but it was far less confident now.

"You're making one hell of a mistake, sir," he said.

"You were the one who did that when you sent Rodriguez to kill me. That was the second lousy driver I got from you," I protested. "First, I had Mo in a bad mood. Then, I have someone who tries to flatten me. Now I know why. You were scared of what Ella Dobbs might tell me and you had good reason. She knew that Mo had been paid to sabotage the Blue Dolphin golf course. That little piece of information explained a lot."

"I'm sorry," he said, "but you've lost me."

"You decided that Mo had to be killed," I said, pointing an accusing finger. "You may even have had a hand in the murder yourself. Rodriguez certainly did. The police will want you on that account. But there's a second charge against you, Mr. Colouris, and it's one that I have a very personal interest in. Thanks to you, my daughter and her friend were kidnapped and put through an appalling ordeal."

"But I did all I could to help, Mr. Saxon."

"To give a pretence of helping, maybe."

"You've got me wrong."

"Have I?"

"This is crazy!" he argued. "You have absolutely no evidence."

"It's called elimination of alternatives," I told him. "It has to be you, Mr. Colouris. As a trusted insider, you were in the ideal position to call the shots. Someone wanted the golf course sabotaged so that it wouldn't be ready for its opening next year. Who better to supervise it than the person nominally in charge of security? Everything went well until Mo started to fall apart. That's when you sacked him—and no doubt warned him what would happen if he opened his mouth too wide."

"This is very entertaining," he said, moving away, "but you'll have to excuse me."

"No chance," I said.

"I have to be on my way."

I blocked the door. "You're going nowhere, Mr. Colouris."

Without warning, he opened a drawer in the desk and pulled out a gun. It was done so swiftly that I had no chance to stop him. The odds suddenly turned in his favor. His expression hardened.

"I should have killed you myself," he said, advancing on me, "then the job would have been done properly. And just for the record, Mo was murdered because he tried to blackmail me. When I sent him to the airport, it was his last chance. He was supposed to keep you under observation. That was all. You were an unknown quantity, Mr. Saxon. I knew that I could put the fear of death into Peter Fullard, because I'd met him, but I wasn't so sure about you. So I made certain that Mo picked you up."

"So that he could moan at us the way he did?"

"No," he replied. "So that he could record every word that you and Jessica Hadlow said during the journey. I was just as interested in her as I was in you. Both of you were targets. Mo was wired up, you see. Did you know he was into electronics?"

"He talked about little else."

"He'd made the equipment himself and had it strapped under his shirt. People are always off guard in a taxi, Mr. Saxon. They speak freely. It's the ideal time to eavesdrop. I wanted to hear what sort of a guy you were, and listen to what Jessica Hadlow had to say for herself."

"Far too much!"

"So I gather," he said. "Just like her father. Unfortunately, Mo disobeyed orders. He was my spy. But, instead of letting his passengers do all the talking, he worked himself up into a rage. I heard it clearly on the tape."

"Don't remind me."

"He had to go. I couldn't trust him after that. When I sacked him," he continued, "Mo lost both a job here and a lucrative sideline. He'd been so reliable until the last couple of weeks. Discreet and efficient. Mo got around. He was my eyes and ears at the Blue Dolphin. And he had no scruples about sabotaging the golf course. He earned his corn, no question of that. Until the day *you* arrived," he said bitterly. "I couldn't keep a guy who fouled up like that. It was too dangerous."

"You really upset him when you gave him the push."

"I paid him off and told him to keep quiet but—oh, no— he couldn't do that, could he? Mo drank till he had enough courage, then he rang and threatened to go to the cops, if I didn't come through with some real dough. I agreed to meet him that night." He gave a grim chuckle. "You saw the result at the end of a rope on the golf course."

"Did you string him up?"

"I made sure I did," he confessed. "I wanted the pleasure. When you got into the clearing, you passed within a few yards of me. While you were gaping at Mo, I doubled back here so that it looked as if I'd been in bed."

"What about the kidnap?"

"That was a bonus."

"Try telling that to my daughter."

"She wasn't the intended victim. Lynette happened to get in the way."

"That's why I'm here, Mr. Colouris."

"We wanted Jessica Hadlow so that we could get at her monster of a father. Do you know what that bastard did?" he asked, curling his lip. "He drove a dear friend of mine to an early grave. Grant Iliffe was one of the sweetest guys you could meet. One in a million. He got me started in this business. Then a certain Bernard Hadlow tried to steal his company from under him."

"Iliffe Temperley Holdings."

"Grant had spent a lifetime building it up. He wasn't going to hand it on a plate to someone like Hadlow. So he fought him off. Hadlow didn't like that. He launched a smear campaign against Grant. I couldn't begin to tell you how disgusting it was," he said, grimacing at the memory. "He threw so much shit at him that some of it was bound to stick. Then the attacks got more personal. How would you like it if you got hate mail about your wife and daughter, Mr. Saxon? Or if you were afraid to pick up your telephone because of the filth you'd hear? What would you feel if someone dug up your past and fed the bits you'd rather forget to the media? It was revolting. Hadlow's men were mercenaries," he asserted. "By making his life an absolute misery, they killed Grant Iliffe just as effectively as if they'd stuck a dagger through his heart. That's why I couldn't resist the chance to strike back at Bernard Hadlow. He deserved it."

"He might have, but his daughter didn't. Neither did mine."

"Too bad," he said callously. "Anyway, I've got to go. Out of my way."

I stood firm. "No, Mr. Colouris."

"Don't do anything stupid," he warned, holding the gun on me. "Death by lethal injection is a much easier way to go than being shot. Mo didn't feel a thing. He was far too drunk. You'll feel every bullet." He waved the barrel. "Move aside. Go on."

Watching him carefully, I edged away from the door. He zipped up his bag with his free hand then slung it over his shoulder.

"Turn round," he ordered.

I paused. When I turned my back on him, I was certain that he'd club me from behind. He'd smash my skull in so that I was in no position to raise the alarm after he'd gone. Frank Colouris had already killed Mo. He'd have no compunction about battering me to death. Turn my back and I was his next victim. I sought to distract him.

"You sent Rodriguez after me in that car, didn't you?"

"Yes," he admitted. "That's another job I should have done myself."

"How did you know where I'd been?"

"I watched the direction your taxi went. I guessed you were going to see Ella Dobbs, so I checked with the hotel switchboard. You took a call from her earlier. I rang her later on to confirm it. When she told me you'd left on foot, I had to act fast. Mrs. Dobbs might have told you something vital," he explained. "I know that Mo had been to see her before he rang me that night. If he'd spill the beans to anyone, it would be to his wife. I couldn't take any chances."

"So you ordered Rodriguez to run me down."

He grinned. "Let's call it killing two birds with one stone. I'd not only be eliminating someone with incriminating evidence against me, I'd be causing irreparable damage to the golf course. Peter Fullard wouldn't have gone on without you."

"Peter's tougher than he looks, especially when his wife isn't around. He wouldn't have abandoned the project that easily." I scratched my head. "What puzzles me is why you wanted to sabotage your own hotel."

"It would take too long to explain. Suffice it to say that GGM—the consortium that owns the Blue Dolphin—had it coming. The way they disposed of Grant Iliffe's bid for this site was brutal. He never lived to exact revenge—but I did. It took me nine months to get a job here, but I managed it in the end. Payback time could begin."

"So you delayed work on the golf course?"

"Oh, that was just the start, Mr. Saxon, believe me. If Mo hadn't cracked up on me, I'd have made sure that course would never be in a fit state to open next year. And once I'd finished on the course, I'd have begun on the hotel itself. There's no limit to the havoc you can create when you have a master key."

"Yes, you can let kidnappers into my daughter's suite."

"I told you. They weren't after her."

"Just tell me why you didn't let my daughter go," I said.

"Turn round—*now!*"

"Jessica was the one you wanted, not Lynette."

"Turn round! I won't ask you again."

"No," I said defiantly, hands on hips. "I'm not going to be clubbed to death so that you can get away scot free. By the time they find my body, you'll be off the island. Go ahead and shoot, Mr. Colouris," I challenged. "I can stand the pain. Because I'll have the consolation of knowing that the sound of gunfire will bring people running. I may be dead, but you'll spend the rest of your life in a prison cell. No room service in there."

"Do as you're told!" he yelled.

"Make me."

Raising the gun, he came at me with a howl of anger. I was ready for him. As he tried to strike, I caught him by the wrist and twisted hard. There was a loud report as the gun went off and the bullet lodged in the ceiling, sending a sprinkling of plaster down like so much confetti. The alarm had been raised. It was only a matter of time before someone came. I didn't wait to be rescued. Bringing a knee up into his groin, I made Colouris gasp in pain. He dropped the bag to the floor. Slamming his other hand against the door, I made him drop the gun. As it hit the carpet, I kicked it well out of reach. He came back at me like an animal, grabbing me by the throat and trying to throttle me. Fury gave me a surge of strength. Here was the man behind all the problems that had afflicted us on the island. I was ready to kill him. After pulling his arms away with sheer force, I got a leg behind him and threw him down, hurling myself on top of him to rain punches to his face and body. He fought back hard and I had to absorb a lot of punishment myself. Raised voices were soon heard outside but I paid no attention. All I could think about was pounding Frank Colouris to a pulp.

They must have heard the sound of a struggle and peered through the window. Someone put a shoulder to the door. When it burst open, Troy Morley entered with two uniformed police officers. Calvin Reed brought up the rear. I was still hitting Colouris with all the power I could muster. They had to pull me off him. Covered in blood, he was still cursing me as the two policemen dragged him upright. Reed was thunderstruck.

"Alan—what the hell are you doing?" he demanded.

"Saving the Blue Dolphin," I gasped. "This is the man who organized the sabotage and set up the kidnap of Lynette and Jessica."

"This can't be true." He turned to his deputy. "Is it, Frank?"

"I almost got away with it," boasted Colouris. "And nobody would have been any the wiser. I'd have destroyed that golf course and brought this hotel to its knees."

"But *why?*"

"We'll sort that out, sir," said Morley, taking charge. He nodded to the two policemen. "Get him cleaned up. I'll be out directly to question him."

Colouris was taken out unceremoniously. The inspector retrieved the gun from the floor. My nose was bleeding and my throat was still hurting from the attempt to strangle me. I was panting and disheveled. Morley clicked his tongue.

"You never learn, do you, sir?" he said without sympathy. "Stop trying to take the law into your own hands. Your luck may run out next time."

"There won't *be* a next time," I promised, using a handkerchief to stem the blood from my nose. "Thanks for coming when you did. Your timing was exemplary."

"We heard the gunshot. You should have waited till we arrived."

"When he was trying to strangle me?" I replied. "That's not something I take lightly, Inspector. Besides, I wanted a piece of that bastard myself."

"I'm so sorry about this, Alan," said Reed, clearly anguished. "Frank Colouris, of all people! Until we came in here, just now, it never occurred to me that Frank was involved in this. He was above suspicion."

I nodded ruefully. "He took full advantage of the fact."

"If I'd been more vigilant, none of this would have happened."

"You did say he was the kind of man who got things done."

"And what terrible things they were!"

"Don't blame yourself too much, Mr. Reed," said Morley. "He fooled all of us. Who was he working for?"

"Iliffe Temperley Holdings," I said.

"Who are they?"

"One of the companies that tried to buy this site. Colouris wanted revenge."

"What's his connection with them?"

"Ask him, Inspector. I'm sure he'll tell you the full story— including the bit about how he strung Maurice Dobbs up on the golf course." Reed was aghast. "Yes, I'm afraid so. Your deputy manager was the mystery hangman."

"It looks like being a very long interview," said Morley. "You'll have to excuse me so that Sergeant Woodford and I can unravel this whole business. Will you be all right now, Mr. Saxon?" He grinned broadly. "Or do you intend to make any more suicide bids against armed assailants?"

"I just want to be with my daughter."

"Of course, sir. Will you be staying in Bermuda?"

"Definitely," I said. "We've got a golf course to finish."

"Good luck with it!"

Troy Morley went out and left me alone with Calvin Reed. He was writhing apologetically. His mask of imperturbability had gone. He was human, after all.

"I can't tell you how stupid I feel," he said. "Being taken in by Frank like that."

"We were all easy victims."

"What must you think of me, Alan?"

"Well, to be honest," I said, "I have a much higher opinion of you now than I did earlier. There was a time when I thought that you were the evil genius behind the crimes."

"*Me?*"

"That's how it looked."

"I don't know whether to be insulted or flattered."

"I boobed," I confessed. "I fancy that I owe you an apology as well."

"Mine is the far greater lapse. Can you ever forgive me?"

"I'm sure I can."

"Thanks, Alan."

"That's okay—Calvin."

He gave me an impromptu hug of gratitude. We'd broken through the barrier at last. "Mr. Reed" had gone forever. I had someone much better in his place.

I spent some time in Colouris' bathroom to clean myself up, but the face in the mirror was not a pretty sight. Three separate fights had left me with an array of cuts and bruises. My nose had finally stopped bleeding but a swollen eye and a dark blotch on one temple gave me a hideous appearance. I went swiftly back to the hotel, keeping my head down. While I was waiting beside the elevators, Nancy Wykoff came scurrying over. She'd changed out of her tennis gear and wore an emerald green dress.

"Dear God!" she said in alarm. "Look at your face!"

"I'd prefer not to, Nancy."

"What happened?"

"Somebody wasn't too keen to hand over my daughter."

"Yes, I've just heard from Melinda. They caught the kidnappers. It's all over."

"Not quite," I replied. "I still have to find out the full details."

"But your daughter is safe and sound."

"Safe, yes. I'm not sure how sound Lynette is. Her friend came off worse. Jessica is still in hospital. Lynette is very jangled."

"It must be a tremendous relief to have her back."

"It is," I said, forcing a smile. "It's wonderful. A huge weight off my mind." I remembered something. "By the way, how did the tennis match go?"

"What? Oh, Melinda beat me hollow."

"Did she?"

"Three sets to love."

"How did that happen?"

"She was just too good for me."

"Not from where I was standing," I recalled. "I popped out to watch you playing, Nancy. You tricked her. You're no beginner. You're an experienced tennis player who let someone else beat you on purpose."

"No, I'm not."

"You didn't fool me. I played golf with you, remember. You've got talent. Your hand-to-eye coordination is exceptional. Far better than that of your tennis partner."

"I was rusty, that's all."

"You're a true competitor," I said, "but you only pretended to compete."

She was shamefaced. "Was it that obvious?"

"To me, it was. You could have wiped her off the court."

"Melinda's a friend."

"Does that mean you have to pull your punches?"

"I didn't want to show her up, Alan," she explained. "Hell, you don't work as a sportswriter for as long as I did without being proficient at some sports. I play lots. Golf and tennis are only two of them. But Melinda Reed only plays tennis. She makes light of it but it's a kind of obsession. Honestly, it means so much to her. She has coaching twice a week and takes the game very seriously."

"So you didn't want to hurt her feelings?"

"Exactly."

"You'd need a stronger reason than that. You like winning, yet you deliberately lost out there today. Why? It wasn't only to protect Melinda's fragile ego."

"Maybe not," she conceded.

"So why not come out with the truth?" I asked. "You let her beat you because Melinda is very important to you. She needs buttering up. You have to keep in with her, and you couldn't do that if you slaughtered her on the tennis court, as you could so easily have done. Melinda is a vain woman. Her pride would be injured. She'd bear a grudge. Am I right, Nancy?"

"You're right about her being a special friend."

"I thought that *I* was a special friend as well, Nancy."

"You are, Alan. You know that."

"Not any more."

"Have you forgotten the other night?"

"That was before I discovered what your maiden name was." Her face clouded. "Oh dear!"

"Why didn't you mention your connection with Fleary Intercontinental?" I asked. "You didn't hear about that company from Melinda Reed, did you? You didn't need to. Your brother just happens to be the president of it."

She licked her lips. "I can explain."

"It's too late for that, Nancy."

"Don't get sore at me."

"What do you expect—a round of applause?"

"Alan—"

"You deceived me," I protested. "You pretended to get that information from Melinda but you knew most of it already. That's why you came to the Blue Dolphin in the first place. You used your friendship with Melinda to dig out the details of what went on behind the scenes when this site came up for grabs. Your brother's company was one of the bidders. Only you somehow forgot to mention it to me."

"It's not the way it looks."

"What's that—the family motto?"

"OK," she said in exasperation. "I admit I kept it back from you, but there was no reason for you to know about my connection with my brother's company. It didn't concern you. This is how it happened," she went on. "When Jim heard I was coming to Bermuda, he asked me to check out the Blue Dolphin. Purely as a matter of interest."

"Pull the other leg—it's got bells on!"

"I swear that my brother had no designs on the place," she retorted. "Jim is not that kind of guy. While I was here—to meet you, principally—I agreed to take a look round on his behalf and report back. To do that, I had to keep Melinda sweet."

I was rueful. "Yes, you're good at keeping people sweet."

"When she realized I'd been snooping on your behalf, she got riled up. Our friendship tottered for a moment. I worked hard to repair it. Playing tennis with her was part of the repair work. And, yes," she confessed, "I could have won every game without breaking sweat, but that would have estranged her even more. There are several other things I need to find out for my brother. Melinda is my only channel for doing so. I'm not a saboteur, Alan," she argued. "I'm only a loving sister, trying to help her brother. In essence, it's nothing more sinister than nosiness."

"Calvin Reed may disagree. He was the one who tipped me off."

"Shit!" she exclaimed. "Does Cal know as well?"

"So will Melinda, in time. I think you'll have to find another tennis partner."

"But it's all a silly misunderstanding."

"Like the other night."

"Don't let this come between us, Alan," she pleaded.

"Oh, I won't," I said coldly. "But while you're at it, you might find yourself another golfing partner as well, Nancy. I prefer people who play to the rules. You know where you stand, then."

"I thought we had something special."

I was scornful. "So did I until I realized what was going on. You didn't want me for myself, Nancy. You just wanted one more scalp for your collection. Why does a woman with your money and position bother with someone like me? There's only one explanation, isn't there?" I asserted. "You wanted Alan Saxon's name in your scrapbook, along with all the others who've doubtless fallen for your bogus charm.

Do you know what I think, Nancy? You're just a superannu-
ated groupie."

Our eyes locked for a full minute, then she capitulated.
Whatever there had been between us had now vanished. I
was livid at the way she'd kept back such a vital personal
detail when she was telling me about the battle to secure the
site. She was hurt at having been found out. Alan Saxon,
the affable golfer, had turned into a fiercely protective father
and that brought our relationship to a decisive end. I'd lost
Nancy Wykoff as a friend but gained Calvin Reed in her
place. It was a good bargain.

Nancy contrived a philosophical smile.

"You have to admit that it was nice while it lasted," she said.

"Tell that to your brother," I suggested.

Ⅶ╢┌╲┘╷╲╱╲Ⅶ╢╲Ⅶ╱╲╱╲Ⅶ╲╷┌╲╱Ⅶ╷╷╷╱

When I got back upstairs, Peter Fullard was pacing up and
down the corridor like a tiger in a cage. He rushed across to
embrace me but paused when he saw my facial injuries.

"You look dreadful, Alan!" he exclaimed.

"I think I'll live."

"They said you'd be back soon. That's why I waited. You're
the hero of the hour. You rescued the girls from the
kidnappers."

"My need was greater than theirs, Peter. Talking of
which," I said, "I really must get back to Lynette. I still
haven't heard what went on while she and Jessica were held."

"Before you go, I've got some good news."

"Denise is on her way back?"

"No, no," he said with a nervous laugh. "Denise is safely
back home now. And the first thing she did was to dispatch
a supply of grass seed from my nursery. It'll be here in no
time. But what happened was this," he went on. "As soon as
Denise left, I stopped feeling so embattled. I haven't been
cowering in fear in my room. Far from it. I was energized.

I've been working on the plans with renewed enthusiasm and—believe it or not—I think I've found ways that will improve our course."

"Good."

"When I don't have to worry about Denise, I can work like a demon."

"There may be a lesson in that, Peter." I used my card key to open the door of my suite. "You'll have to excuse me now. Let's meet later on."

"But I haven't told you the other thing yet," he said with an apologetic gesture. "I didn't mean to do it, Alan, I promise you."

"Tell me another time."

"But I need to warn you. It concerns Clive Phelps."

"Then it's well down my list of priorities," I said, stepping through the door. "Let me spend some time with my daughter, then I'll take a look at your improvements to the golf course. I knew you wouldn't be twiddling your thumbs. Well done, Peter!"

Before he could say anything else, I closed the door gently behind me. Rosemary came through the connecting door from the adjoining suite. She flung her arms around me and hugged me tightly. There were tears in her eyes.

"Lynette told me what you did," she said. "You were so brave."

"I did what any father would have done, Rosemary."

"It's not what Mr. Hadlow did."

"Give him his due," I said. "He tried. And it *was* his money."

"I'm so glad it's all over, Alan. It's been intolerable."

"How is Lynette?"

"Holding up," she explained. "She's in the bath at the moment. That's all she wanted to do when she'd given her statement to the police. Take a bath."

"What did she say in the statement?"

"I'll let her tell you herself. The main thing is that there was no physical abuse."

There might have been, I thought, but I said nothing about the situation that I'd found when I clambered aboard the boat. It was a time when Rosemary needed nothing but good news. I told her about the arrest of Frank Colouris and of his link with one of the companies that had failed to buy the site on which the hotel now stood. She was pleased that the murder had now been solved but more relieved by the release of the girls.

"Any word about Jessica?" I asked.

"Yes, Alan. Her father rang. They're keeping her in overnight. She was still in a state of hysteria so they've had to sedate her. Jessica's not as resilient as we thought."

"What does Mr. Hadlow intend to do?"

"He'll stay with her. Technically, he's a patient as well."

"And what about you, Rosemary?"

"Me?"

"Yes, how do you feel? You've had so much pressure to cope with."

"I got through it somehow."

"Thanks for being here," I said. "It made all the difference."

"That's what Lynette said." There was a pause. "Alan."

"Yes?"

"About the other night…"

"Why don't we just forget that?" I suggested.

"But I wanted you to know the truth," she said. "I *did* come into your bed. I felt the need to be close to you, that's all. Do you mind?"

"No," I replied, after thinking about it. "Not at all."

She kissed me on the cheek, more out of gratitude than passion. Lynette walked through the connecting door. Her face was pale and drawn but her eyes sparkled. Wrapped in a white bathrobe, she came tripping across the room to hug me.

"Daddy!" she said. "Where've you been?"

"I had to call on someone, Lynette, but I'm back now."

"Don't go away again, will you?"

"No, darling. How do you feel?"

"Exhausted."

"You really ought to be in bed," suggested Rosemary, holding her arm.

"Let me apologize to Daddy first."

"There's no need," I said.

"But there is," insisted Lynette. "I was the one who brought Jessica. I was desperate to have her on holiday with me. Bermuda sounded so exotic. Jessica kept talking about all the treats she'd get her father to give me. I thought I had a chance to give *her* a treat as well."

"You weren't to know that this would happen."

"I feel as if I've caused so much trouble."

"That's rubbish!" I said. "It's not your fault at all, Lynette. All you have to concentrate on is getting over it. That goes for Jessica as well. The pair of you will have lots to talk about when you get back to Oxford."

She lowered her head. "I doubt it."

"What do you mean, darling?" asked Rosemary.

"Well, I'm not sure that I want to be friends with Jessica any more."

"Why not?" I asked. "I thought you liked her."

"I did until we came here. She was so positive about everything. The trouble was that she wanted to make all the decisions. You should have seen the way she pushed Rick and Conrad around." Her memory was jogged. "What's happened to them, by the way?"

"They told the police all they knew and went on their way."

Lynette gulped. "They told the police *everything*?"

"Apart from what happened on the beach," I said quietly. "Conrad confided in me but he didn't think those particular details were relevant to police inquiries."

"What are you talking about?" asked Rosemary.

"Nothing," I replied, catching Lynette's eye. "It's dead and buried now."

"Yes, it is," added Lynette. "Completely."

It was all the reassurance I needed. The subject of cannabis would not even need to be raised now. Lynette knew the effect it had had on them, lulling them into a state of uncomplicated pleasure, rendering both girls more vulnerable to attack. The horror of the kidnap had led her to make a sensible decision. She'd learned her lesson.

"If only she hadn't been so stupid," she went on.

"Who?"

"Jessica. She provoked them, Daddy. They had us in their power and she talked to them as if they were dirt. That's why they gave her a far worse time than me," she said. "I told her to cooperate but she wouldn't listen. I mean, the woman was nice to me on the boat. She told the others that I ought to be released. It wasn't me they were after."

"Why didn't they let you go?" I wondered.

"Because Jessica began to scream and shout. She said it would be cruel of me to desert her. They were really annoyed by the way she yelled at them so they gagged her to shut her up." She began to whimper. "I had no chance of release after that."

"You need sleep, darling," said Rosemary. "Doesn't she, Alan?"

"Yes," I agreed. "We can talk about it in the morning."

Holding her between us, we led her back to her bedroom and helped her into bed. Rosemary promised to sit beside her until she fell asleep. Before I could volunteer to do the same, I heard the telephone ringing in my room. I went off to answer it, leaving them alone. When I got to the receiver, I paused. The telephone had caused me so much distress that I was reluctant to pick it up again. Yet it couldn't be ignored. With an effort, I lifted the receiver and put it to my ear.

"Yes?" I said.

"Alan, it's me!" he announced. "Clive."

I was taken aback. "What are you ringing me for, Clive?"

"The story, of course."

"What story?"

"Oh, come off it, Alan," he said jocularly. "You don't ring me up for information about some fat-cat businessman without a very good reason. I'm a journalist. I might only write for the sports pages but I can sniff a juicy story when I come across it."

"You're quite wrong, Clive."

"That's not what Peter Fullard says."

I was shocked. "You've rung him as well?"

"Three times. I finally prized it out of him."

"So that's what he was trying to tell me," I said to myself, recalling Peter's attempt to warn me earlier on. "You got at him, Clive."

"He says there's been murder and mayhem at the Blue Dolphin golf course, though he refused to give me details. What he did say, however," he asserted, "was that Alan Saxon was up to his neck in it. Correct?"

"I'll tell you when I see you, Clive."

"That's too late. The story will have gone cold by then. Come on, Alan. Give a friend a break. If I take an exclusive to the news desk, it'll do wonders for my profile at the paper. After all, I did help."

"That's true," I said.

"I rang Barbara, shared a few delicious memories with her, then asked her to send you that fax. Out of interest, I got her to send me a copy as well, so don't try to bluff me, you old fox. Spit it out. Why did you want the low-down on Bernard Hadlow?"

"It's a long story, Clive."

"Give it to me in vivid detail."

It was no more than he deserved. Once they'd questioned the four people in custody, the police would issue a news bulletin about the kidnap. Bernard Hadlow's name would guarantee that the story would command worldwide attention and I flattered myself that my name might arouse more local interest. Clive Phelps wanted to be first in line. Without his assistance, I'd never have gained so much information about Hadlow and his business empire. A reward was in order. Knowing that he'd get nothing from me on the phone, Clive had worked on Peter Fullard instead. The strategy was a success. My partner had eventually blurted out the truth.

"Are you still there, Alan!" shouted Clive into my ear.

"Yes, I am."

"Then give me the bloody story."

"I will," I said. "It all started with the theft of some Bermuda grass…"

About the Author

Keith Miles, aka Edward Marston, Conrad Allen, and Martin Inigo, came from Wales to read Modern History at Oxford. He has been a university lecturer and radio, television, and theatre dramatist, and in addition to writing has worked as an actor and theatre director. He is the author of several mystery series, one Elizabethan in background, another revolving around the Domesday census of 1086 A.D., another set in the Restoration era, another brought forward to the early 20th century under the name Conrad Allen, and yet another focusing on Frank Lloyd Wright under the name Keith Miles. As Miles and Inigo, he has also written mysteries with golf and sports backgrounds. His Elizabethan novel *The Roaring Boy* was a 1996 Edgar Allan Poe Award nominee for Best Novel.

The author is a well known host and raconteur at mystery events and served as the 1997 Chairman of the Crime Writers Association. When not travelling or fulfilling speaking engagements, he lives in rural isolation in Kent.